THE
LOVING
HUSBAND

Christobel Kent

D0109104

sphere

SPHERE

First published in by Sphere in 2016
This paperback edition published by Sphere in 2016

1 3 5 7 9 10 8 6 4 2

A CIP catalogue record for this book is available from the British Library.

ISBN 978-0-7515-6241-5

Typeset in Bembo by Palimpsest Book Production Ltd, Falkirk, Stirlingshire
Printed and bound in Great Britain by Clays Ltd, St Ives plc

Papers used by Sphere are from well-managed forests
and other responsible sources.

MIX
Paper from
responsible sources
FSC
www.fsc.org   FSC® C104740

Sphere
An imprint of
Little, Brown Book Group
Carmelite House
50 Victoria Embankment
London EC4Y 0DZ

An Hachette UK Company
www.hachette.co.uk

www.littlebrown.co.uk

Praise for Christobel Kent

'A gripping thriller, beautifully unfolded, with gorgeous, evocative writing. It builds to a shattering climax and there's an eerie sense of place that cleverly captures the particular claustrophobia that wide open spaces can provoke'

Erin Kelly

'*The Crooked House* is a brilliant read, dark and vivid and almost unbearably suspenseful with an atmospheric setting in the wild estuary village and a sense of menace and claustrophobia as the local community clings to its secrets'

Cath Staincliffe

'*The Crooked House* is a psychological page-turner imbued with depth and humanity. *Broadchurch* meets *Rebecca*. I simply loved it'

Allison Pearson

'*The Crooked House* hooks the reader through the gut from the first dark page, driving you on in a lather of fear and excitement until the great reveal. The author's bleak estuary flatlands are every bit as menacing as the Cornish crags of Daphne du Maurier: this is geography as psychodrama, calling the survivors home for a day of reckoning'

Rowan Pelling

'*The Crooked House* is a terrific, powerful and unsettling novel, beautifully written; I read it with my heart in my mouth'

Jill Dawson

'Oh my goodness – what a book! Such evocative writing; such a brilliantly visual book, and so beautifully tense . . . just glorious'

Clare Mackintosh

Also by Christobel Kent

The Crooked House

For my mother

Acknowledgements

I'd like to thank the amazing team at Sphere: my brilliant editor Jade Chandler and the very patient Katherine Armstrong who took the reins while Jade was otherwise engaged with motherhood, Cath Burke for presiding over the transition and supporting me during it, Sphere's tireless and perpetually enthusiastic publicity geniuses and the unflappable, ever-reassuring Thalia Proctor who always seems to go the extra mile. Without Richard Beswick of Little, Brown, I'd never have written at all, and my agent, Victoria Hobbs, deserves a medal for her cool head, insight and constancy. My own (living) husband Donald Robertson, doesn't need me to say that none of it could happen if I didn't have him.

He was in the room. She didn't know how long she'd been asleep, but she'd been dreaming.

In the dark something padded between the furniture, and loose change clinked softly. The mattress gave beside her.

In the dream there'd been a wide littered beach and a man looking down at her, standing very close, the sun high behind him so she couldn't see his face. The man reached into her breast pocket, she felt his fingers nosing, and he drew something out that glittered. Then the beach had gone and the space beyond the bed was all muffled blackness, no light came in from the landing. She might have been underground.

Cold crept under the duvet. She felt the furred brush of his leg against hers and obediently she turned away but his hand slid under her T-shirt; it rested on her hip and held her there on her side with her back to him. His hand was heavy.

Something blinked red off to the side, she couldn't tell

1

if it was inside her head or if she'd opened her eyes: the partial numerals of the radio alarm on his side of the bed. She knew if she turned her head they'd tell her the time but she didn't move, her eyes closed, wanting the wide beach again, she wanted to know what it was the man had pulled from her pocket, but he was gone.

Behind her something else shifted, his body – heavy like his hand or was she dreaming that – bulky and hot, was pressed close and she heard his quick breath. He wasn't going to sleep. And then his hand moved downwards, his palm was rough on the smooth of her backside. His fingers were between her legs and as they moved inside her she held her breath. It had been so long, for a second she didn't know if she could still do it, but all the more reason. She knew if she stopped, if he stopped, after all this time, it would be the end of them, it would be disaster. And then he said something into the hair at the back of her neck, something unrecognisable.

She didn't turn her head on the pillow and ask what he'd said so the words stayed mumbled, strange. But she let her breath go, and then his hands were on her shoulders, and he was inside her.

The cry woke her. If she hadn't learned with Emme that however deeply unconscious and dreaming she was, that sound would reach through the layers of sleep and drag her out, her second child would have taught her, once and for all. *You wanted him*: how many mothers had had to tell themselves that? She had wanted him. Fran jumped up, to get to him before he woke them. Woke Nathan in bed beside her, Emme, in the next room. Silence.

She felt a thump in her chest as she remembered, a pulse of nervous triumph. Nathan, who by all rights should sleep till winter dawn, the sleep of the just and the satisfied. She could still feel a heavy warmth in the core muscles, a weight that wanted her pinned to the bed still.

Silence.

Had the baby cried out in a dream, and gone back to sleep? She listened, wondering how it could still be so dark. And quiet. Her hand wandered over the duvet as she looked for the red-lit numerals of the alarm clock on his side. Except . . . she leaned low, following her searching hand. The duvet was flat and smooth, as tidily straight against the pillow as a hotel bed. Empty.

Nathan wasn't there. And then she was rigid, alert.

The clock said 02:07.

Chapter One

The sunlit room existed in another world, where the air smelled of coffee and flowers, where the traffic hummed outside and each house down the street had a tree on the pavement, as far as the eye could see. Fran came out of the bathroom with the tiny plastic baton held out in both hands and for a second the sun was full in her eyes and dazzling her, until Nathan moved into the light, in front of her.

'Are you all right?'

Her heart was beating so hard she thought it might jump right up her throat and out of her mouth before she got a chance to say the words. Gently he took the little piece of plastic from her; she didn't know why she was so astonished, that it should have happened to *her*, but she was. Nathan didn't look at the little plastic window, it was her face he studied, as if he was memorising it just as it was then, in that miraculous moment wiped smooth and new.

She hardly dared look back because it was all too quick, he couldn't possibly be ready for this – but then she saw he was smiling. More than that: she saw everything she was feeling mirrored there in his face – the panic, the amazement, the thrill – as if he had absorbed it all.

'Yes?' he said, eager.

'I . . .' she said. 'We . . .' And then his arms were around her, holding her tight against him, so tight, so warm. So safe.

Sunday night, Monday morning
02:07

He might be beside Ben's cot, he might have woken before she did, her sleep might after all have been even deeper than usual, all things considered, and for a second a little happy world bloomed in the dark, the loving husband who'd looked down at her head on the pillow and thought, let her sleep.

Fran stood on stiff legs, the lazy warmth all gone to tension. It was so dark she felt unbalanced and she put out her hand to steady herself, moving hesitantly barefoot on the rug until she made the door and felt for the switch outside it. Light flooded the landing, lit the wide boards that tilted crazily the length of the old house, it exposed the rug worn thin, the dust in the corners. Silence.

Ben was asleep in the cot, an arm thrown back, chest rising and falling in the light from the door; she turned slowly in the dark room, checking its corners as if he might be standing there watching her, monitoring her panic. There was no one there.

Moving on down the corridor she set her face against the door jamb to Emme's room. She saw the pictures on the wall above the bed, silver in the landing light, saw her daughter sleeping. Turning away, Fran whispered, 'Nathan.'

But the labyrinth of rooms around her all sat quiet under the eaves, the twisting staircases, the odd angles, the low secret doors that had made him turn to her in front of the estate agent with his face all lit and say, *Don't you love it*, as she tried to hide her discomfort.

'Nathan?' Her voice was high and thin, but not a whisper any more. More firmly. 'Nathan.' The children didn't stir. She was on the stairs, quick, holding her breath, down.

The kitchen looked untidy under the bad lighting: they still hadn't done anything to it; a year in, they'd done nothing. *Why not?* Jo would say if she saw it. *Isn't that Nathan's area of expertise?* Someone else's grimy farmhouse kitchen: she hadn't expected to find Nathan here, boiling a kettle, unable to sleep, it wasn't that kind of a room, not the heart of the home. It hadn't been that for the farmer, anyway, a man with oddly dyed hair and greasy clothes stiff with dirt. He might have been fifty, or seventy, Fran hadn't been able to tell. *No wife*, he'd said from under a lowered brow, as if to explain the kitchen, *women don't like the farming life*, although to Fran that had seemed the least of it.

There was a front door set at the centre of the house's handsome façade, with a wide hall behind it and an ancient cavernous fireplace but they still hadn't managed to get the door open in its Adam-pillared surround. Damp had

7

swollen it: even the agent had muttered agreement. So they came in and out of the kitchen door instead, a mean little door that opened onto a yard with bolts top and bottom and a big rusty key.

She was standing behind it. She put a hand to the door's high frosted pane, feeling how cold it was, the glass, and the kitchen itself. The room had no warm range to keep it cosy. Nathan had said *Maybe we can get one put in*, to convince her, *maybe, when we've got the cash*. His clouded eyes, making the calculation.

Nathan.

Under its ugly lighting the room seemed to crystallise around her. She tried to keep it neat, but things appeared. The mugs on their hooks, the tidy pile of newspapers and bills on the table and Emme's drawings pinned to the dresser, *roses are red, violets are blue* because she hadn't been able to wait till next Sunday, the day itself. Valentine's. The dirty doormat under her bare feet. She looked down and saw the mat was rucked and askew; she saw bootprints, she registered wet mud on her skin. Leaning on the door she contemplated the dirty sole of her foot.

The bolts had not been shot. She put a hand to the key but she knew before she turned it that the door was unlocked. She didn't want to open it, to step out into the wide dark that carried all the way to the horizon. Nathan's mud-crusted boots stood beside the mat and she slid her feet into them, took a coat from the hooks at random, that was Nathan's too, scratchy wool. She didn't want to do the next thing.

Why hadn't she looked at the clock's numerals when he came in, to know now, how much time had passed?

8

Had she even opened her eyes? She remembered the red light of the alarm, she remembered how deep the dark in the room had been otherwise. She remembered holding herself under as she came, burrowed still in sleep as she lay on her side with Nathan's weight still behind her and pushing. She remembered thinking, this is the trick, the trick is just to stay quiet, to stay inside, eyes closed, and then she came, with an exhalation. She'd let go, drifting into sleep. She remembered the exact weight of his hand on her.

Fran stood thinking a moment as the act's ripples spread, the consequences, *had they, had he, what about* . . . and then she opened the door.

Even in daylight stepping out here took a conscious effort to keep the spirits from dipping: the sheer emptiness of it made her head ache, the uninterrupted flatness. At night it was different, it seemed less empty, it harboured pockets of deeper dark, the outbuildings, a line of poplars, a distant grain silo. Landmarks that by day were dwarfed by the wide, bleached, lovely sky, invisible in the night they still seemed to cluster, they offered places of concealment.

Emme had come out to look for an abandoned doll one evening and had run back in whimpering about funny noises and Nathan had looked up from the sofa. Fran hadn't been able to see his eyes that time, the light reflecting off his reading glasses, she couldn't have said if he was being accusatory because he had said nothing. And then there'd been a noise from upstairs, Ben in his cot stirring, and she'd run out of the room.

The cold was clammy, coating her face in the dark, and she pulled the coat round her. It smelled of him, of Nathan.

She stepped carefully, still uncertain, in the dark; her balance felt off. One hand holding the coat together, the other one reached out into the darkness, her hand flapping stupidly, to stabilise her. She should have brought a torch.

The yard was cluttered, she had to step carefully or she'd trip. She moved past the shed. There was a faint orange glow far off to the side that revealed the line of the horizon, but it wasn't sunrise. A February sunrise would be more than five hours off, it was the lights of the town, miles away but low-lying, and the light it shed went a long way on the endless flat windswept plain.

The barn loomed. The farmer had kept chickens in it, a battery shed. You could smell it from the back door then, and even Nathan's face had turned stony. The estate agent had stood with his back to it as if to bar their way. In the car on the way home Nathan had said, his eyes on the road, *It's prefabricated, there are people who take them down for you, take them away and put them up somewhere else.* Fran had sat stiffly in silence in the passenger seat, trying not to see it, even though she'd been the one that had insisted. A single bulb swinging and the chickens' eyes red, a thousand of them and more. The smell had been indescribable.

No one had come to take it away yet but Nathan had taken down the walls, to let air blow through it, trying to get rid of the smell. Now it loomed, a roof on girders – she walked inside. What was she afraid of? She didn't know. Something.

The air was still contaminated with decades of chicken shit and entrails and she held her arm across her face, the rough wool against her mouth. She looked up in the dark, her eyes must have made some small adjustment to it because she could make out the structure's concrete rafters. She'd stood here next to Nathan as he contemplated them, that time when she told him she was pregnant again although she'd felt he must know. Wondering what he was thinking, his face pale, upturned. A builder contemplating a structure, estimating concrete's stress levels. Now, she realised she was holding her breath. She made herself scan the roof space, straining her eyes and seeing nothing. She walked on across the powdery dirt floor, out of the back of the barn.

This was what she was afraid of. The yawning space, the black distance: it stopped her. It upset Nathan to see her panic, she had to control it. His face tense, fourteen weeks into the first pregnancy, to see her eyes wide outside the room where they'd scan her, to see her arms stiff by her sides on the high hospital bed. And after Emme was born, when she ran breathless to her cot in the middle of the night to make sure she was alive, she'd heard Nathan make a sound under his breath. And now they were both on their own in the house behind her, a four-year-old and a three-month-old, in that house that should feel like home but still made her heart clench in her chest as the light faded around it every night. She'd left the door unlocked, anything could happen, anything. She turned round but the barn obscured her view of the house and quickly she turned back to the horizon.

There was something there.

Something like a snake, something darker than the dark, it was just in front of her. She couldn't see it, she couldn't hear it, didn't know if it was under her feet or it was about to flap in her face but something was there. She couldn't move.

Far off, a car's headlights swept the plain, a lone bush was illuminated, the black furrows of a ploughed field fanned out, grasses on the edge of a drainage ditch – a something else. She saw herself, or a mirror image of herself, across the fields, a figure silhouetted like a scarecrow in an old coat on their edge. Then the car's lights moved on, casting long low shadows away to the horizon and gone, only not before she'd seen what was at her feet.

There was something in the ditch. In one sweep of the light she took in a shoe. Then the length of him, head down, and she dropped to her knees.

He was in the ditch.

12

Chapter Two

With his knuckles bandaged and a bright graze to his forehead, that first time Nathan had walked into Jo's crowded kitchen and looked straight at Fran it was as if he already knew her.

Jo's kitchen had also been her front room, and the door that Nathan pushed through opened straight off the street, the flat being one floor of a London cottage barely big enough for Jo, let alone eight of them elbow to elbow round a fold-out dining table, but Jo was nothing if not ingenious, and London was London. Magazine publishing at the level Jo and Fran inhabited didn't support anything but cramped, unless you went out beyond the furthest reaches of the tube.

Straight away Jo was on her feet, explaining to them around the table (a cousin of Jo's; one of her exes and his wife; a girl from a different magazine; a foreign guy; none of them Fran'd seen before or since) how she knew Nathan.

Or how she'd met him at least, as it turned out Jo barely knew him at all, he'd been hauled in to make up the numbers after a terrible speed-dating evening he'd been to for a bet and Jo for a joke (or so she said). Then she was exclaiming over his injuries, and as he explained them (he'd come off his moped, it was new and he wasn't used to it, 'I'm a menace,' he apologised, 'but no one else got hurt') all the time he kept looking at Fran, ducking his head in that shy way she somehow already recognised and without thinking she had shifted at the table to make space for him beside her.

It had been a month since Fran had broken up with Nick and it had still been raw, heading over to Jo's that night in the wet London dark, negotiating streets and buses alone. Lugubriously, someone (Carine on the problem page, with her poker-straight hair and obsessive-compulsive shoe collection) had said to her, you have to give it a year, even if you're the one who ended it, until he's not the first thing you think of when you wake up. And as Nathan held her gaze from Jo's front door Nick was abruptly shifted from the centre of her imagination, the place he'd occupied for nearly two years, out to the periphery. Tough.

So sidelined was Nick, so suddenly, that she'd forgotten about the roses, twenty a day since she had turned to him at the door of his newest place, a cavernous ware-house club space in east London and said, *I've had enough of this*, and walked away. Pale roses – nothing as obvious as red for Nick with all the hours he'd put in on the design of the clubs – but there they were when, coming back from Jo's that first night with Nathan behind her she pushed her front door open, in vases and buckets and jars, on the sink and the breakfast bar and even up on the sleeping ledge.

Nathan had taken her home on the moped, a spare helmet in his box, shrugging, sheepish. 'Someone always needs a lift,' he said, and she had marvelled at his organisation. And she'd asked him up, stone cold sober. She didn't want to say goodbye to him, it was as simple as that. He'd made her smile, he'd loved a book she'd loved, she'd seen him watching her mouth move as she spoke, making her breathless. 'Are you sure?' he said, smiling as she put her key in the lock and asked him. 'I mean, yes, please.'

At her shoulder in the doorway she'd heard Nathan make a sound, almost a laugh, and the first thing she'd done – before she got time to get nervous or to wonder, was it too quick, she hardly knew the guy – was to lift them one bunch after another from their water and dump them, dripping, in the bin.

'You're not a ballerina in your spare time, are you?' was all he'd said, holding open the plastic sack for her to drop another bunch in. 'They throw these on the stage.' She had laughed, being not at all the ballerina type, not tall or wiry but compact, with inconvenient breasts – and with one hand on the place where her hip flared from her waist, he had ducked and kissed her, quick and dry and shocking.

'He's a change for you, isn't he?' said Jo, eyeing her over a cup of coffee the next day in the newest café in the streets below the office block, a crowded place with wooden benches outside. The rain from the night before had cleared and the day was sparkling. Jo had nudged her out from in

15

front of her screen at midday, wanting the news. 'He's certainly not a Nick, is he?'

'You mean, he's not flash,' she said, and it warmed inside her, her new secret. 'No. Nathan's not flash.'

She had felt the beginnings of a blush, then, pushing the thought of Nick back where it belonged in the past. Nathan came from the real world, where you got up and went to work every morning, and he wasn't flash. In the dark, he had been different too. In her bed. He was quiet, he was methodical, he was determined. It seemed to her he had a plan that involved working her out, what she liked. 'This?' he said on that first night, stopping, lifting his head, waiting for her to respond. She was used to something wilder, more headlong, something that knocked the breath out of her: Nick had even left bruises, sometimes. She liked this, being made to wait as he circled her, keeping his distance. She sipped her coffee in the sunshine, under the rinsed blue sky, hugging her secret.

'Is that maybe just as well, though?' said Jo, still eyeing her tentatively. 'At this point. I mean, it's not like you've ever had it easy. Give yourself a break. Someone decent.'

'Huh,' said Fran, still thinking of him, then looking up. Registering, almost with a sigh, what Jo was talking about. 'Yes. Maybe.'

Because Jo came from a background as settled as they came, one brother, one sister, her mother a nurse, her father a solicitor, mortgage long since paid off, the lawn cropped to velvet and tomatoes in the greenhouse. They still came to London to take Jo, thirty-four, out to a restaurant on her birthday, and although she grumbled, Jo seemed to like it. But Fran had never known her father, although her mother had told her they met at art school and he'd ended up – she'd said vaguely, when Fran had asked, aged twelve – *In India, or somewhere*. Gentle and sweet and hopeless, Fran's mother had died of pneumonia (self-neglect, the doctor who came to sign the certificate had said angrily) in a rented bedsit in Brighton when Fran was twenty-one.

What Jo meant, sitting on the hewn wooden bench in new London sunshine, was perhaps it was time for a safe pair of hands. 'He said he was a builder?' Jo had relaxed into sharpness now, grilling her.

'Something like that. Project manager. He runs building sites.' He had talked to her about his job, lying back on her pillow, watching her get up, walk into the kitchen. 'All over the place, but he's based in London. He seems very . . . practical.' Her thoughts wandered to his long-fingered hands, the safe pair of hands.

She'd cut herself, halfway through chopping an apple. He'd been there even before she'd known she made a noise, a gasp caught in her throat. He'd been out of bed and behind her, and he'd reached round and taken the knife out of her hand. 'Where's your first aid kit?' Smiling at her blank expression, never having had a first aid kit, taking her hand between his to examine it. 'Sit down,' he'd said. 'Let me.'

Of course it didn't stay like that, not exactly. She wasn't stupid, she knew relationships had to change, had to develop. Babies changed things.

Five years, and they had rushed past Fran in a blur while she tried to grapple with it. Opening the door to a new flat, a different house, Nathan working, working, working – away for days then home too tired to talk. A baby, slick and red in a midwife's hands and Fran watching Nathan's head turn to her in the delivery room, watching for his reaction.

She knelt in the mud, in the dark and tried to pull him up but she already knew, from the cold unyielding weight of him, that Nathan wasn't coming back. In her chest panic contracted to a shrieking certainty, made of terror. He was gone.

Chapter Three

'Is there someone in the house? Fran?' The voice on the line was steady but urgent.

'Not in the house,' she said, and her breath ran out.

Where was her mobile? Crashing into the too-bright blur of the kitchen, there'd been no time to look so Fran was standing with her back against the bolted door holding the wall-mounted handset that had been there when they arrived. They had almost not renewed the landline contract, was the thought that banged about in her head as she tried to form sensible answers. *What is your address?*

'Try to keep calm, Mrs Hall.' The emergency services operator was patient. 'Your postcode?'

She couldn't remember. She should know her own postcode.

And her responses were delayed, out of sync: she didn't know what she knew. What if he *is* in the house? What if he doubled back? How long was I out there?

She held her breath, listening. Nothing.

'Mrs Hall?'

'I saw someone outside,' she said. Clarified. Her tongue felt thick.

Across the wet field, her feet sliding in the boots as she had run, there had been a moment when she almost blacked out from not breathing and she had had to steady herself. On through the high ghostly space of the barn, but it wasn't until she was back on the doormat in a welter of mud and cold sweat did she remember what she'd seen. The brief outline of a man against the headlights. A man or a scarecrow, there one minute, one fraction of a second, then swallowed up by the dark.

She'd knelt beside Nathan, trying to arrest her own slide into the ditch, smelling the cold mineral sludge down there below their bodies, tasting bile in her throat. Last night's wine now rose sourly back inside her. What was he doing out here?

'Nathan.' Half lying against his utterly unresponsive weight she pleaded, breathless. Desperate. 'Nathan.' She reached her hand down to his face that must be turned away from her in the dark because all she could feel was his hair. Stiff, dead hair. Wet. A sticky soft place under the matted strands. 'What the hell . . . Were you . . . What the hell . . .' She couldn't finish the sentence but it didn't matter, because no one was listening. She lowered her head to him, searching for the smell of him in the dark, the smell of his skin. Blood was in the air like iron, and the muddy smell of waterlogged land, but she couldn't smell him. She found his hand and lifted it to her lips, and it rose inside her, a choking sob. Nathan.

In the kitchen the hair rose on her scalp in terror as she clutched the receiver. 'He was so cold.'

There were so many things she wanted to ask the operator, but the woman was on her set course and would not be diverted, however many times she had to repeat herself. Telling Fran to remain calm. Someone was on their way. They would be there soon.

Don't hang up.

She went on holding the handset, facing the wall, and then she heard a sound, behind her, tiny but distinct: the sharp crack of something hitting a window.

At a crouch Fran was across the room in seconds, the receiver of the phone dangling behind her, she was at the door, her hands shaking as she felt for the key she had already turned, the bolts she had slid. Locked; locked. She fumbled for the switch and turned off the light and held herself there, against the door, trying to listen over the pounding of her heart and the blood roaring in her ears: *Stop*, she told herself. Upstairs they were asleep in their beds, Emme and Ben. If she were to fall, or faint, or scream, they would be unprotected. *Stop*. Listen. Fran listened.

In the dark now there was only quiet. No footsteps on the gravel under the window, no whispering at the door behind her. He wasn't coming. He wasn't coming.

It took a while for her to register that the sound of the sirens came from outside her head, that it wasn't just a version of the ringing that had been in her ears since she knelt beside him. She saw the blue light first, revolving at the corner of the kitchen window. She heard the slam of a vehicle's door and the murmur of voices but numbly she waited. She didn't move when she saw the knuckles rapping on the window, heard the 'Hello there?' Then the voice said, 'This is the police, Mrs Hall. We have an ambulance. Mrs Hall?'

Then there was the sound of another vehicle, the heavier wheeze of a diesel engine, and the light changed, yellow beyond the blue. She stayed put as the strangers muttered on the other side of the back door: *Nathan*, she pleaded, silently, *Nathan, Nathan*, and a sob rose in her throat, my Nathan, my warm Nathan.

Cold.

A fluorescent jacket appeared in the window, where the stone had struck. 'Is it your husband, Mrs Hall?' came a man's voice. 'Mrs Hall? ' and she knew she had to answer them.

Police. Police. She wasn't ready for that. As she came outside a man stepped forward beside the policeman and she looked at him instead. A man in a tabard with his backpack full of medical equipment, he was older, almost sixty, a face pouchy and kind, and hope flared inside her, desperate and dreadful. There was a female paramedic too, with dreadlocks tied back, weary. Fran stared from one face to the other. 'Please help him,' she said, taking hold of the man's sleeve. 'He's called Nathan. I'll . . . he's out there.'

They had torches and at the sight of the beams swinging ahead of her, lighting the wet grass, the fear jumped and sprang like electricity. 'He was still here,' Fran told them, 'I thought he'd been waiting for me to come,' but they kept walking so perhaps she only thought she'd said it. Turning to look for corroboration somewhere she saw the policemen motionless at her kitchen door. Sanity, she under-stood, wasn't something she could take for granted at the moment, and with that thought the future rose ahead of her, black and busy. A whole different life was waiting and as they walked towards the barn it was already being recon-figured.

From where he knelt on his haunches the middle-aged paramedic looked up at her – she could see the sag of his chin in the light from his torch – and said, 'Is there a relative you can call? Anyone?'

There was no one.

Just the two of them, she and Nathan, each of them alone, although strictly speaking Nathan did have a family, they just weren't the kind that kept in touch. Nathan's father was up north, a long way up and old. Nathan's mother was in a home with a version of dementia that wasn't Alzheimer's: Nathan had explained that to Fran care-fully. There was a sister but she was working abroad. Miranda.

'You like him, right?' She and Jo were standing on the roof of the magazine's offices. Head down over the cigarette she was lighting, Jo didn't answer straight away.

It was a clear day, cool. Up till then she'd told Jo it all, progress reports. Nathan was a good cook, he had taken her to Brighton for a weekend, they'd gone to the cinema, she'd met his best friend from home, Rob. Two months in Nathan had asked her to move in and Jo had just shrugged. 'Good for you.' He had a nice airy maisonette, handier for work than her bedsit on the end of the Victoria line, so why not? She had been sheepish about telling Jo it was more than that. Not just practical. He was so assured, so clever. Watching a news item on television he'd always know the back story, and yet his hand always went out to make sure she was there, on the sofa beside him.

But this news was different, it was bigger. Fran was nervous. On the cool rooftop she eyed Jo's cigarette with envy. Actually smoking it would make her throw up, though: even the smell made her take a step back.

There'd been one night, maybe five years earlier, and both of them heading for thirty when Fran had gone with Jo to a baby shower, a new phenomenon, that had ended with the two of them getting hammered and a bit hysterical with it. At two a.m. from behind the cubicle door of some club's toilets she had heard Jo say, with drunken solemnity, 'If I'm not knocked up by the end of the year I'm going to top myself.' When she emerged she just walked to the mirrors to reapply her eyeliner as if nothing had happened, but it wasn't the kind of thing you forgot.

'So?' Fran was waiting for an answer. They weren't strictly allowed on the roof, health and safety, but everyone did it. The question was obviously leading somewhere and Jo eyed her, warily.

'Why?' She held out the pack to Fran, who shook her head, and Jo's eyes had narrowed even though she already knew Fran had been trying to stop for months. It wasn't Nathan who wanted her to give up, Nathan had said nothing.

'Sure,' said Jo, shrugging. 'I like him.' She turned and leaned with her back to the rail, examining Fran. 'He's clever, I'll give you that. Ambitious. Early days though, right?'

Fran looked out over the gleaming slate roofs then, not

24

answering. You could see as far as Sydenham Hill to the south on a day like this, the Crystal Palace radio mast, close-packed terraces curving away and up, warm red-brick in the sun; to the north Highgate and the big gleaming white sentinels of blocks once modern, housing for the masses. 'I'm pregnant,' she said.

'You what?' Jo went still, the smoke curling from the cigarette in her hands. She let it fall on to the felt, ground it out. 'Fran? Tell me you're joking.'

Smiling, sheepish, Fran held Jo's gaze, buoyed up by the euphoria that had still not subsided, after a week, more, even if it had an edge to it now, fear of the unknown.

'Fran,' said Jo, and a note of alarm came into her voice, 'it's . . . how long have you been together? Three months?' Fran felt her face examined, Jo frowning into it. 'Christ alive,' she said. 'Are you going to . . . did you . . .' a warning note creeping in, 'was this *planned*?'

At that Fran had pushed herself off the rail so abruptly that Jo stepped back. 'Not planned,' she said, giddy with recklessness. 'You can't plan everything, though, can you?' Unable to stop herself, defiant, angry, even as she saw some little shutter go down in Jo's face, she went on. 'I mean, I'm thirty-four.' An intake of breath. 'I want a baby.' Jo's face stiff now. 'And I love Nathan.' Just the tiniest sound escaped Jo then, of impatience that summoned up all those times they'd rolled their eyes together at the word *love*, before she grabbed Fran's hand, her shoulder, in a hug. 'He's been amazing,' said Fran. 'Really.'

He had, too. Kneeling on the bathroom floor beside her as she vomited those first six weeks, not just mornings but coming in queasy from the tube ride home, murmuring to her, 'It's OK,' holding her hair back. 'It means your body's working.' Unperturbed, he had a knack of generating calm. He was patient as they sat together waiting for the first scan.

'It must be so hard,' he said, turning to her as they sat side by side on the plastic chairs under the pinned flyers about healthy eating and chlamydia. 'Without your mum,' and she'd found herself suddenly, stupidly speechless, with tears coming into her eyes.

'You're the one who introduced us, anyway,' Fran said there on the rooftop, arms folded, trying to laugh, 'I hold you responsible for my happiness.' But Jo's face was stubbornly serious. 'It's just – it's just so soon,' she said, beginning to shake her head. 'You hardly know him.'

'It's what I want,' said Fran, but Jo still wouldn't smile.

Had she felt sorry for Jo, who had so little faith? And her thinking she did know. Thinking her future was safe, at last.

The policemen had to stoop to come through the back door. There were two of them, an older and a younger. They told Fran their names but she couldn't keep the information in her head.

Lights moved beyond the kitchen door, refracted through the thick bottle glass. They asked her questions, and she mumbled answers. Yes, he came home. She tried to remember times, to construct sentences, but all she could hear was her own voice saying, over and over, 'I don't know.'

They'd told her. They'd told her, and even though she already knew, even though she had knelt in the mud and felt his cold skin, however many times they patiently repeated their phrases, the words just wouldn't go in. 'I'm sorry, Mrs Hall. It was too late. We were too late to save him.'

Her mind jumped and raced, there was a hum in her ears; only at moments did the room come into focus, plates on the dresser, unwashed dishes on the draining board. The policemen talking to each other, one mumbled the strange word, 'Weapon,' as they both turned their backs on her and she saw a head shake from behind. Then 'His mobile?' Muttered in reply, 'Nothing on the body.' And they turned to face her.

He spoke to her. 'We can't find your husband's mobile, have you any idea . . .' but all she heard was *on the body*.

On the body. And she found herself rising to her feet, the room swam, the two faces looking back at her, men she didn't know in her kitchen. Looking down at her, the older one about her age, about Nathan's age. The younger one was just a kid, he looked like he might be slouching out through the school gates. Go away, go away, where's Nathan? I want Nathan.

'I'm sorry, Mrs Hall. Your husband's—'

'He's dead,' she said, blank, trembling as it sank in, all over again, worse this time, new layers to it. She suddenly remembered Nathan coming through Jo's front door and smiling, Nathan with his hands on her hair as she knelt in front of him in the dark, Nathan late, then pacing and unable to look as Emme was born, stalking out of the delivery room. 'Oh, God, oh God. Nathan.'

From upstairs she heard Ben start to cry and as she moved, breaking for the door she heard the older policeman say behind her, sharply, 'Bring him down.'

The nightdress had buttons down the front, for feeding. She'd bought it at random, she hadn't thought till now that it was too short, it had too much cheap lace. She sat at the kitchen table and pulled up the sweater and man-oeuvred Ben across her exposed breast, her eyes down as she heard something tapping: the younger man's foot, his knee jiggling nervous below the table. Under the layers, invisible, Ben latched on and with that tiny trigger some-thing loosened, oxytocin or whatever hormone it was, and she felt exhaustion lapping at the edges. Her shoulders dropped and she heard one of them clear his throat. There was a silence that grew, and she kept her head down for as long as she could. When she looked up the younger policeman was looking at Ben across her body, openly curious. It was the older man that spoke.

'You're going to need a bit of sleep, an hour or two at least,' he said, averting his eyes. 'There'll be someone outside. The examiner will need at least twelve hours with the body.' Patiently, but in a second of clarity she saw something else in the man's eyes. That cool look, that judging look, that was there then it was gone. 'There's evidence, you see,' he told her, 'physical evidence that won't be there in the morning. This time has to be used to collect it.'

'There was a man out there,' she said, sitting up straight. 'When I was with Nathan, there was a man, on the other side of the field. I saw him, just for a second. Where there's a road, on the far side, there are some trees. The only trees for a long way. That's where I saw him.' She saw a glance exchanged between them, excitement.

'That's very important information,' said the older man carefully. Was it that he didn't believe her?

'I'll show you,' she said, wildly, and on her lap Ben made a noise of protest. 'He came after me, he was at the window.'

'Did you see his face?' said the younger man, eager, in a nasal accent.

She shook her head, she tried to explain. 'It wasn't him, it was a stone, I heard it, he threw something at the window.'

His superior was sitting back in his chair. 'Why didn't you tell us this before?'

She stared at him. 'I didn't . . . I . . .'

He sighed. 'Look, Mrs Hall,' he said, and she heard something in his voice, no more than a trace, something not friendly, 'we're going to have to talk to you some more, when you're . . . You're clearly in shock. Are you going to be able to get some sleep, now?'

She stared, trying to make sense of what he was saying and with the word *sleep* she felt a rush of longing like hunger, she wanted a clean pillow, she wanted darkness. She wanted to wake up and this wasn't real. 'I . . . yes,' she said obediently, and heard her voice shake.

He nodded, approving. 'In the morning we can sort out alternative accommodation for you,' he went on but before she knew what she was saying it was out, too sharp, too sudden, 'No,' she said. Alternative accommodation: social services.

His eyebrows went up. 'Well,' he said, and they were on their feet. 'We'll talk about it again. In the morning.'

She could hear them moving about outside as she set

Ben in his cot and walked, almost catatonic, from room to room, pulling curtains closed, checking bolts, going back to do it again. She went in to the bathroom.

His razor sat on the basin, in a small puddle of soap not yet dry. He must have shaved before he went out and the sight did something to her. Because not knowing how she got there, suddenly she was on her knees, she was crouched under the basin, shaking and retching and it was there, folded into a foetal crouch, that she finally let go and slept. She woke some time later to creep on stiff, cramped legs into their bed and as she drifted back her last thought was that everything was changed, even the air in their bedroom, even the sheets, he was gone.

Chapter Four

Monday, still

Pregnant with Emme she'd had bad nights, long, long nights with strange dreams. One morning when she rolled out of bed tetchy and spoiling for a fight, as big as a cow or so she felt, as swollen and shapeless as a field animal, Fran had heard a cool warning note in his voice, his back turned to her as he made her tea.

'Are you OK?' Patiently.

If she opened her eyes Nathan would be there now. He was standing with his back to her in the corner of the room.

It was light, and Emme was tugging at her shoulder. Groggily she surfaced, she tried to smile into Emme's anxious face, then suddenly she was wide awake, and bolt upright, she was at the window. The day had come.

Just visible through the skeleton of the barn was a tented structure, gleaming blue-white in the thin grey morning. 'Mummy, is it late?' she heard from behind her, and her hand to her head she turned.

'Ben,' she said. The red lights on the clock said 8.20. 'What's happened to Ben? He should—'

Her face still crumpled from sleep, Emme looked confused, 'Mummy?' she said, head on one side. Then frowning, 'You covered him all up, you silly.' Fran turned to look to where Emme pointed, to the bed, and for a heartbeat she didn't understand, then she did.

Under the quilt Ben was flushed, but with the cool air he stirred. He was breathing. Her throat constricted, Fran stopped herself snatching him up and shaking him awake. 'Silly,' she said, trying to smile, calm, but in her head it whirred, calculated, recalculated. *How, when.* She must have woken in the night, gone and got him more or less in her sleep and brought him back to bed with her. She remembered standing at the window, but she couldn't remember getting Ben – had she already got him? She tried to recover a single detail but she couldn't: the thought was frightening. And if she'd been that oblivious she could have smothered him. He stirred on the pillow and she whispered to Emme, 'Go and find your school clothes, baby, go on.'

She saw Emme, as she retreated to the doorway, small as she was, taking in all the altered detail of their life without knowing it until she paused, solemn, and settled on her question.

'Where's Daddy?'

From outside there was the sound of footsteps on the gravel; it gave Fran the smallest opportunity to look away, anywhere but at the small frown line between Emme's pale, wide-set eyes. She got up from the bed and knelt close to her, putting her cheek against Emme's. 'He hurt himself, darling. He fell over and hurt himself and he had to go in the ambulance. He was very poorly.'

She felt Emme pulling away, and released her.

'Can we go and see him?' said Emme, her mouth stubborn, and as for a long moment they looked at each other, Fran realised she was hoping, waiting for her to work it out for herself. She thought of Nathan and Emme, side by side on the sofa, staring up at her.

'Not at the moment,' she said. Fran didn't want control of this moment, this pivotal moment in Emme's small life, but she had no choice. 'We'd be in the way. And you have to get to school, don't you, sweetheart?'

For a long moment Emme just looked at her, and then she turned and padded towards her room, and suddenly Fran could remember the feel of Nathan's shirt, sticky and matted, the horrible softness under it and, wobbly, she rose to her feet. A sweat broke on her forehead. She got to the bathroom in time, holding the door closed behind her with her bare foot as she vomited, trying to do it silently and failing, yanking at the flush to cover the sound.

Unsteadily she came back into the room. On the pillow Ben was breathing evenly, pale now, his eyelids just fluttered as she watched him and she thought of all the new chemicals in her system, the panic, the adrenalin. The nausea churned, but there was nothing left in her stomach. She picked Ben up, and still he didn't wake. Carefully she took him along the corridor, past Emme wide-eyed in her door. She set him down in his cot and then heard a little shuddering sigh as he shifted, and he was back to sleep.

Walking back along the dim angled corridor in the sudden quiet Fran wondered for one moment of surreal, horrible hope, was it all a dream? But then she was in her bedroom and the flat white light of the new morning was flooding in from across the broad watery plain.

The policeman would be coming back to talk to her, and with that thought the panic rose inside her, those men in her kitchen. Staring. She wasn't supposed to be frightened of the police. They just felt like two men she didn't know, in her kitchen. She felt sweaty, suddenly.

The bed: still now, on Nathan's side, the quilt was smooth and flat. She sat, abruptly, where she'd slept, she felt her body threaten to fold and collapse and she leaned forward, her face in her hands. In this room, just hours ago.

He'd picked up his phone, he'd got dressed. They hadn't been able to find his phone.

It occurred to her that she didn't know where she'd left her own phone. It was as if a flashbulb had gone off on what happened last night, blinding her. Some of it stood out, stark: the policemen in her kitchen, Nathan's body head-down in the ditch, blood all over him. But all the small things had gone. Had she put her phone away? The drawer on her side of the bed was open, just a crack. But she couldn't remember the last time she'd looked inside.

'Mummy?' It was Emme, hovering in the door, watchful. She was half dressed, a vest and mismatched socks. 'Clever girl,' said Fran. 'Now skirt. I'll be there in a minute.' Emme stood there a minute before turning, dragging her feet along the corridor. Fran leaned down and opened the drawer.

No phone. But there was something.

It was an envelope, not stuck down, a card inside. A heart, a thorned rose, old-fashioned lettering. *Baby, It's You*, it said. She opened it, but it was blank. Not quite blank: the faintest trace, where a ballpoint had rested, as if he'd

34

taken out the pen to write and not known what to say, when it came to it.

Nathan, Nathan, Nathan. She hadn't thought he would. Why was it on her side, not on his, waiting to be sent, when had it been put there? Her head ached. She closed the drawer, she didn't even want to touch it. She would leave it there, where he'd left it. They were words from a song, weren't they? *Baby, It's You.*

Her phone must be downstairs. She'd taken to putting it out of sight, on a shelf, under a pile of magazines, because Nathan always seemed to turn his head to examine her when she picked it up.

She could hear Emme in her room, talking to her dolls in a busy monotone. Don't, she told herself. Don't cry. She got up and went to the window, feeling like she was made of stone.

Below her a man was standing quite still as if he'd been there for some time, a dark stocky man. He was looking straight up at her.

He stood in the kitchen as she boiled the kettle; he could have been an ordinary guy, weatherproof jacket, a dark fleece, scuffed shoes. Aftershave. But policemen had power, they weren't ordinary.

'DS Doug Gerard,' he said, holding out a hand, and Fran's gaze flicked to Emme sitting head down over her cereal, in her school uniform. 'I did introduce myself last night.' An apologetic cough. 'I don't think you were in a state to take it all in.' Understanding: he sounded understanding. Gerard had shadows under his eyes as he looked at her and, with him back in the kitchen, last night loomed,

35

terrible. The smell of the standing water and the mud was in her nostrils.

At the table Emme carefully lay down her spoon.

'Emme, Mr Gerard needs to talk to me,' said Fran. 'Will you just run upstairs and make sure your room is all tidy?' Fran saw Gerard's eyes settle on the smear of blood at the sink, another one on the wall beside the phone. 'And could you have a peep at Ben? Make sure he's still asleep?' Emme gazed at her unblinking, opened her mouth to protest and seemed to change her mind. She slid off her seat and ran to the door.

There was no sign of the younger man.

'Ed's outside,' the policeman said. 'Detective Constable Ed Carswell.' She just stared. 'May I?' Touching a chair. She nodded and Gerard sat. No milk, no sugar: she set the mug in front of him. 'Your husband's body has been taken to the police mortuary,' he said. 'We'll assign an FLO to you.' His voice was steady, calm.

'FLO?' Fran felt herself stiffen at the initials, at the thought of the ranked police officers with their grades and insignia, waiting on her doorstep.

'Family Liaison Officer,' Gerard said as he slipped his arms out of the waterproof jacket and took a sip of the tea. What would Nathan have thought, this man at her table? 'She's there to keep you informed on the progress of the investigation, to help out however she can, she works for both sides. The family and the police.' It sounded like he'd said all this before, the professional reassurance. There was an edge of something else, an itch to be out of there, leaving her to someone else. 'She's very experienced.'

'A woman,' she said, grasping at the fact, and he nodded.

36

'I'd have liked to have had a female officer along last night but . . .' He smiled. 'It's not like visiting your GP. We can't guarantee . . . in an emergency situation.' He hesitated, eyeing her over the mug and then Fran felt a tremble, as if her body was getting away from her.

'I told you there was a man there,' she said. 'I did tell you, didn't I?' The tremor grew, her hand on the table shook. 'Let me show you, now, I can show you where.' She pushed her chair back, wanting to get up, but he held up a warning hand. 'He wasn't afraid,' she said, urgent. 'He was just watching me. He came after me to the window.'

'Yes.' Gerard didn't move. 'You said you didn't see his face.' She subsided.

'Did you find anything? The man. There was a man.' She tried a different tack because he didn't seem to be registering. 'Do you have any . . . he was at the pub. He came back from the pub. The Queen's Head.'

'We'll talk to them.'

'What about . . . criminals?' She didn't know what she was imagining, someone recently released from prison. The world was full of violent people, and she hadn't known it, until she found herself in the field. Ghosts roaming the dark. 'Is there anyone known to you?'

Gerard's gaze was steady. 'Well, we're considering a number of possibilities. That's part of the job, yes. There are hardly any itinerants this time of year, though, there's a spike in crimes associated – seasonal workers, that kind of thing, although we can't, we don't draw any automatic conclusions—'

'That's not what I meant,' said Fran, desperate. 'Are you

37

talking about . . . traveller communities? Or . . . or . . . migrants? I'm not racist, I'm not suggesting—'

His expression was flinty, and she stopped.

'I'm sorry.'

He nodded. 'We look at burglaries in the area, we'll find a trail that way often, a spate of them, they go from house to house but in this case . . .'

She looked around, wildly. 'Were we burgled?' *Someone in the house.* 'I don't . . . I don't . . . nothing has gone, that I can see . . .'

DS Gerard lifted a hand. 'As I was about to say,' he said, mildly, 'there was only one report of a break-in last night and that was the other side of Oakenham, likely enough only kids anyway, by the sound of it.'

Fran stared at the table, head down. 'Right,' she said, almost a whisper. 'So you haven't caught anyone.'

'The first few hours are crucial, for gathering evidence,' he told her and she felt him examining her face. 'You'll have heard that.'

She barely shook her head. 'I don't know anything. This . . . nothing like this has ever happened to me before.'

There'd been a police raid on one of Nick's clubs a couple of months after they'd started going out. He'd been called out at three in the morning to deal with it and had come in again pale and tight-lipped as she was getting out of bed, making coffee. 'Bastards,' was all he'd say. She'd been at that club with him the night before: it was a classy place, restored to the original Edwardian fittings, tiny tables round a polished dance floor, each one with a little lamp and an old-fashioned phone.

Little booths upstairs: she could remember it as if it

was yesterday suddenly, though she hadn't thought of the place in years. They'd sat in the gallery looking down on the dancers, with champagne in a bucket, and he'd told her about his plans. He'd gone to talk business with someone in the office and she'd gone down to the dance floor. An hour or so later she hadn't stopped, flooded with the feeling and forgetful of where she was or why she looked up and there he was. Watching her from above the carved wooden balustrade, and when she looked up he had smiled.

Nick wouldn't let her near the club while the police were there – it was closed for eight days. He'd gone voluntarily to the police station to talk to them but he wouldn't let her come and collect him when they'd finished. She'd never even talked to a policeman, but was that a brush with the police? She'd forgotten all about it, until now. They'd dropped the charges eventually, whatever they were.

They'd walked past that club one day, she and Nathan, with a newborn Emme in the buggy. It had closed down and he watched her, as she paused to examine the fly-posters that plastered the boarded doors. She had never talked to Nathan about Nick, or about how it had ended, but he had put an arm out, around her shoulders as she stood there. 'You don't mind,' he said, ironical, 'your boring married life?' She'd leaned her head against him. He had known, without her having to tell him. It seemed so comforting.

Gerard was looking at her, as if he could see the thoughts in her head. Nathan's arm around her. Their boring married life, far off as if through the wrong end of a telescope.

'Of course,' Gerard said, 'we'll also need to talk to you

39

about your husband's own contacts, social life, work . . . his movements last night . . .'

There was a tap at the door and Carswell's head appeared round it. He looked like a teenager. Gerard nodded to him and he slipped inside. 'Detective Constable Carswell,' he said, bobbing his head to her.

Fran made as if to get to her feet but Gerard put a hand on her arm in a second. 'He can make his own.'

'Little one asleep?' said Carswell, his back to them at the kettle. 'My sister's got one tharr'age.' He didn't seem to expect an answer.

'Did your husband have friends out here?' Gerard asked. 'Old friends? Lads he went to the pub with?'

She shrugged, helpless, yes, of course. Nathan must know people, he at least left the house every day, he visited sites, worked on estimates. Overhead came the sound of Emme's footsteps, and she set up a tuneless singing. 'He went to the pub for a bit of peace and quiet,' she told them, and DS Gerard nodded.

'New baby and all that,' he said, sympathetic. 'It's a difficult time, isn't it?'

'We're . . . we were . . .' She started again. 'This was what we wanted. Kids. Getting away from London. We were happy.'

'But no friends yet?'

'There's Rob, Rob Webster. An old friend of my husband's, he lives out here. The other side of Oakenham.' Gerard nodded to Carswell, who wrote in a notebook, painstakingly. 'He works at the hospital, in some lab or other. His number's on my phone, only I don't know . . .' She looked around, wildly. 'I think Nathan put it up there by the landline when we moved.' She'd insisted, remembering her mother's scrawled list when she was a child. What parents did: doctor, dentist. Gerard nodded and Carswell got to his feet and was behind her at the phone. She didn't turn to look.

Rob was tall and awkward, his skin almost blue-white for an outdoors type, his knuckles raw from mountainbiking. Still a boy, he seemed to her. 'This . . . all this . . .' She had her hand to her mouth suddenly. 'He's Nathan's . . . he was our best man.' And all she could remember was Nathan's hand falling on Rob's shoulder, introducing him. *I've known this guy for ever.* His best friend.

'I'd better call him,' she said.

'We can do that,' said Gerard. 'Don't worry. It might be better, coming from us. He might know something.' He tilted his head. 'What about any other friends? Of your husband's?'

She shook her head, uncertain. Rob, Nathan's only friend. Was that unusual? For a man to have just one? At the wedding, along with a handful of girls from the magazine, she'd dredged up three or four from school, they'd turned up dutifully. She hadn't seen any of them since, maybe she'd never see any of them again but she'd been glad to have them there. When she'd been going out with Nick, he seemed to have dozens of people he called his mates. Nathan had had Rob, and a couple of people he worked with. Julian Napier, he was one of them. Her brain wasn't working.

Watching her, Gerard hesitated, the mug between his hands. 'Tell me something,' he said, his voice level, calculating, to the sound of Emme's footsteps coming back down the stairs. 'I'm interested.' He was almost a head taller than her, and stood between her and the door. 'You've been married how long, four, five years?' She nodded. 'Why did you come here, you and your husband?'

'Why?' she said stupidly, hearing in his cool tone, *Go back where you came from*.

He smiled then, as if to reassure her.

'I mean,' he said patiently, 'why here?' Tilted his head. 'Why now?' He left it a long moment before saying, 'More space, was it?'

She just stared. 'For the kids?' he said, prompting her.

'My husband's from round here. He grew up not far away.'

They'd visited the bleak little village with its boarded-up shop only once since they moved, at Emme's insistence, to see the house he'd grown up in. It was a small cottage with moulting thatch almost down to the ground, tiny windows and low ceilings, and Nathan had stood a moment with his hands in his pockets, frowning at it before saying, 'That's it. Nothing to see really.' And marched them back to the car.

'And we love it here,' she said. 'The house, and everything.'

Gerard was watching her.

'So that explains why your husband wanted to come here. What about you?'

Chapter Five

They hadn't come here for more space: they'd only had Emme when they moved. And she didn't think they'd have another child.

'Everything all right, otherwise?' said her GP at the six week check. 'You and your husband?' The health visitor had asked the same question after going through a questionnaire with her when Emme had been a week old. 'What are your feelings about the way the birth went?' A neat blonde woman with a bouncy stride, she read the questions from a clipboard, intended to check for post-natal depression, though she never said so, and Fran had answered everything with determined cheerfulness. 'Yes, yes. Fine.'

And unless they meant, are you having sex again yet, it *was* fine, wasn't it? She couldn't imagine having the conversation with anyone but Jo, but Jo didn't come, she sent an expensive dress with a card tucked into the tissue paper: *Congratulations!!* Two exclamation marks, which was so not

Jo it was as if she'd been made to write it at gunpoint and was sending a covert message. *Love, Jo. X.*

Her mind wandered, late at night, on the brink of sleep, or sometimes if they were watching some movie or other, it didn't even have to be a sex scene though the first time it happened that was what it was. A man kneeling in front of a woman was all it took, her hands on his shoulders, stroking his neck, his face turning up to look into hers and Fran had to close her eyes a second, so vivid was it, so sudden. A hotel bedroom with a long window open, rain outside on a dark lake and the exact feel of Nick's hair between her fingers. Hearing the pleasure sound, some explicit gasp from the box, Nathan had glanced up at the television screen from his laptop then back down while Fran had just kept still, the heat rising at her neck.

Then there'd been a night when she reached for him in the dark where he lay with his back turned to her; sliding an arm across she felt the muscle of his belly go taut. His hand had come up quickly and taken hers, holding it still. He had murmured something like a warning and when she understood she had pulled the hand back and lain flat, her heart thumping.

'Let's go shopping,' she said to Jo on the phone, trying for cheerful. 'Nothing fits at the moment.'

She'd thought, when they were alone together, squeezed into a changing room on Jo's lunchbreak and laughing at some terrible outfit, it would come naturally. It would be like old times. But with Emme parked in the corner gazing at the bright lights and Fran frowning down at her little soft roll of belly and at the buttons on a pale, soft, perfect, beautiful silk shirt that, besides being dry-clean only,

44

wouldn't do up over her chest, she couldn't quite come up with the right words, somehow.

Jo caught her looking down at herself, and cleared her throat. 'Fran,' she said, wary.

Fran hadn't been bothered by the belly, those first weeks and months, it was part of the deal. Then one evening she'd been reaching up for something in the kitchen and her shirt had come untethered from her jeans and there'd been something behind her, a sound, from Nathan, and she'd had to sit back down, tugging at herself. Although when she looked up he was only smiling. Loving.

'Fran,' said Jo. 'Look. Is everything all right?' And at the reluctance in her voice Fran had to look away, grabbing her trousers from the floor. She was going to be asked something she didn't want to answer, or told something she didn't want to hear.

'All right?' she said, dressed and decent again. 'Oh yes,' and then, stupidly bright, 'It's been so lovely, doing this, even if . . . well, the weight'll come off, I just have to relax. It's been just like old times.'

She geared herself up to talk about it. But he watched her so closely, he knew her inside out, and hanging up his jacket when he came in from work he seemed to know what she was going to say even before she finished the sentence. 'We need to . . .' she began. And suddenly he was there, right up against her, Emme between them, her small downy head turning, eyes looking unblinking from one of them to the other. He stroked Fran's hair.

'I'm sorry,' he said. 'I know, I know. I'm not sleeping.

And it's work.' And he sighed and subsided on to the sofa, patting the space beside him.

'What about work?' said Fran, leaning against him. He rested his chin on her head.

'Oh,' his voice had a grim edge, 'just . . . well.'

'What?' she said, keeping still.

He sighed. 'A project I've been after for . . . oh, years now. Lots of bureaucracy, you know, all the permissions. I've put a lot of work into it. Putting together a tender, and someone's thrown a spanner in the works.' He took his chin away from her head and tilted her face up to him, looking into it, frowning. 'Some jobsworth in the planning department. These people.' And he got up quickly and got a bottle of wine that had been in the fridge for months. They hardly ever drank, these days. 'So,' he said when he came back, handing her a glass, taking a big gulp from his, 'how was the baby clinic?'

He did seem interested, to give him credit, or at least he sat and listened while she talked, gaining in confidence, although she could hear herself, talking on. Moving from Emme's weight and the health visitor's approval to her own childhood, bedsits and head lice and moving schools. 'Mum specialised in evading the authorities,' she said at one point, and he let out a laugh, surprised.

'She did love me,' Fran said. 'It was mostly the money, and having to manage everything on our own.' Carefully she set her empty glass down. 'It makes you think, though,' she said, not nostalgic exactly but softened towards her exasperating mother by Emme. 'Having her. Don't you find yourself remembering stuff? Things you thought you'd forgotten.'

46

He poured himself another glass of wine, and before he'd taken a sip was ready with how dull it had been, his parents were so quiet, his father so strait-laced, his mother uptight. Fishing trips along the fen, a wistful story about squatting in a derelict house with mates, a long, last summer, swimming in an icy flooded quarry. Leaning back on the sofa. 'It seemed to last for ever,' smiling. And then an offer, college or something like it. 'As soon as I could get away, I was out of there. I didn't need to be asked twice. I never really went back home after that.'

After so long without it the wine sent them both off to sleep unresisting – she even heard him snore as she dropped off, woozily content that something had been said, at least. It was only when she woke, before dawn and with a little knot of hangover forming behind her eyes, that she felt obscurely wrong-footed. It took her longer to realise that nothing had changed, except that the conversation couldn't be had again. When he turned over to her a week later she held her breath but he just said, reasonable but no kinder than that, no sweeter, 'Can't you sleep?' and then 'Should I get you something?'

DS Doug Gerard was watching Fran across the table. He was watching her mouth. Her eyes.

He's out there. It drummed in her head. He's still out there. The man I saw. She wanted to tell them. He's going to come back. But Gerard spoke first.

'Look,' he said, firm but reasonable, as if it was the most

straightforward thing in the world, 'I think it would be useful to get you down to the station. Interview you and get this all down on paper, cover all the bases, put you in touch with the team.' Behind them Carswell shifted, but Gerard went on, smoothly, 'And while we're at it, talk about sorting out somewhere for you to be while all this is going on. You're naturally feeling highly vulnerable . . .' But his eyes said something different, they roamed the room, inquisitive. He smiled. 'Alternative accommodation, if you remember, last night—'

But he stopped, an eyebrow lifted, because Fran was shaking her head. She wanted to shove them to the door and slam it and bolt it. If she told this man, this DS Gerard, *The man I saw is coming back*, what would he say? Would he look at her and ask, so gently, so reasonably, *Why would you think that?* As if she was crazy. As if she was suspect. In her head she saw something that was growing, pushing its way through a rotten window frame. *Because he was still here. Because I saw him. Because* . . .

And if she did what the policeman wanted, if she left? If she gathered the children and went to hide in some safe house, some miserable bedsit? He'd still be out there, and instead the police would be in this house, with this man, this Doug Gerard opening her cupboards. And then she was on her feet, still shaking her head, stubborn.

'We're not leaving here. This is our home.'

Gerard looked at her a long moment, severe. Carswell had moved around from behind her and was next to him now.

'All right,' Gerard said carefully, and he was standing, zipping his fleece. 'So why don't you show me where you think you saw this man?'

And there was something in the way Gerard was looking at her that brought a sweat out under her arms, as if he knew what kind of woman she was, what she'd done, what had brought them here. As if he already knew the exact chain of events and he was just waiting to see if she'd tell him.

Chapter Six

We love it here.
That had been a lie, too.

On the drive up, she had felt a sinking as she registered the landscape flattening, emptying and London was left behind. They had passed the grey spires and towers of Cambridge, a smudge on the horizon, then a famous cathedral rising like an island, some old flint churches hiding among trees and, increasingly, nothing. The road had dwindled to an arrow-straight single carriageway with fields butting dead-level up against it: not even a hedge, barely a tree to soften it, and landmarks turned into outlandish things, nothing natural or old or familiar. A single wind generator, vast up close, like something from space; a concrete silo as big as a tower block sitting alone in a field ringed with wire fencing; a stretch of shiny solar panels all tilted towards the flat grey sky.

A truck had passed them going the other way at speed and it hadn't slowed or conceded room on the narrow carriageway, roaring by so close the car shook and as Nathan at the wheel wrestled them back off the verge they could see the mud crusted on its big tyres.

When they had got out of the car, finally, the first thing that had struck Fran was the noise: it was empty but it wasn't quiet, and walking into the lee of the big house, the agent walking towards them, she could still hear it. A distant roar that must have been traffic on some far-off invisible motorway but felt like something stranger, diffusing uninterrupted across the plain like smoke.

Beside her Nathan spread his arms like a king, looking up. 'All this space,' he said, and she had seen the wide pale sky reflected in his eyes, a great barrelling mass of cloud building along the horizon.

Emme was in her room. With Gerard standing behind her Fran called up the stairs, sharp and urgent, and Emme appeared at the top. Her small face was pale.

'I need you to wait up there for a bit, sweetheart,' Fran told her. 'I've just got to show the man something.' She felt abruptly breathless, her heart speeding in her chest just at the thought of stepping back outside, as if he was still standing among the poplars, waiting. *Someone killed your daddy.*

Who? Who? Who would kill him? Nathan, steady Nathan, husband and father, always in control, Nathan who never lost his temper. Did people die for barely any reason, on no provocation? She knew they did: a botched burglary, an idle beet-picker high on GHB, road rage. Spill the wrong man's pint in a pub and he follows you home. But Nathan got back, he parked the car, he came inside our house and wiped his boots on the mat and hung up his coat. He came to bed. That was the part that made it her fault, she couldn't get rid of that thought. If she'd done something different in bed, if she'd said the right thing, if she'd turned and held on to him, in the dark.

She swallowed. 'Emme?'

'Is it about Daddy?' said Emme, solemn, not moving, and Fran took a deep breath.

'Yes,' she said, then quickly, thinking, Don't tell her any more, mustn't frighten her, 'Just stay up there. Please. I won't be long.'

She walked past Gerard in the kitchen, quickly; she didn't want him to see how afraid she was. She was at the door and turning the handle, dizzy with panic but still moving, and then DS Gerard was behind her in the yard. She kept on, one foot behind the other, and then they were past the shed and the horizon yawned. The huge sky was streaked across with the remains of rain cloud, tinged pink towards the east: this was what Nathan had wanted. The big skies, his kingdom. The pale tent gleamed at its centre; a man in a white hooded boiler suit straightened from what looked like a toolbox to look at them. Another suited figure emerged from the tent to stand beside him.

She must have staggered because the horizon tipped and

then Gerard was next to her, with his hand tight on her arm. 'Are you all right?' he said. She wanted to shake him off but the pressure on her arm steadied her, and she stood stiffly. She couldn't look at the white tent but wherever she looked it sat at the edge of her vision. 'This can wait,' Gerard said. 'We can come back with the FLO later, the weather's going to hold.'

Fran stared at him. 'No,' she said, clenched. She looked towards the poplars and for a second she thought he was there, standing motionless between the leafless trees. She froze.

'See something?' asked Gerard, quickly. The row of bare trees. No one there.

'No,' she said, with a gasp, 'no, I . . . nothing.' She began to walk stiffly across the yellow grass, soaked with last night's rain. The sound of run-off trickling in the ditches in her ears, under the distant hum of traffic they couldn't see. The chicken barn's roof had a dull sheen, and the field under its stubble was wet, sticky: she heard Gerard make a sound of disgust, lifting a shoe clogged with mud.

'The pub.' She stopped abruptly. 'He'd been to the pub, he came home. The Queen's Head. Maybe someone there . . . maybe something happened. Maybe someone followed him home.'

'You did tell us,' said Gerard, and she thought his eyes slid away from her. 'We'll go through it again at the station.' He gestured ahead. 'One thing at a time.'

Her heart pounding, she worked her way round, walking away from the men along the ditch to the place where there was a plank set over it. The road was beyond them, perhaps half a mile away, the row of trees – she fixed her eyes on them as she walked, watching. The same road that other car had been travelling on, the car whose headlights had swept the flat land at some time after two in the morning. That morning: it seemed to her not just longer ago but in a different life.

One foot then the other and there, where it was dark behind her eyes, the figures moved in the landscape, two a.m. Nathan walked out across the field to the ditch, someone followed him – or waited for him. She thought of the blood, the front of his body soaked, blood congealing sticky on her hands as she pulled at his deadweight.

She stopped, trying to subdue the shivering that rose inside her and failing, looked from the tent to the road, gauging angles, distance.

'There.' She pointed and Gerard was kneeling in the mud, he was looking.

'Right,' he said, interested at last. 'Yes.'

When they got back to the kitchen DS Gerard had asked her if she'd be all right to take Emme to school on her own. 'Ed can come with you,' he said, shifting as she fed Emme's arms into the sleeves of her coat at the table.

Out in the black field, standing beside him, she had heard his breath catch and accelerate as he peered down between his knees into the clogged stubble. 'Well,' he said, a hand up to shade his eyes, 'you're sure this would be where you saw him?' A pause, the hand shifting a little so she caught a glimpse of his face, wary. 'And definitely a man, right? A male?'

How could she be sure? The whole night ballooned in her head like a nightmare: none of it seemed real. 'I think so,' was all she had managed, as she had knelt beside him to see.

Emme had been waiting for them, solemn, in the kitchen.

Gerard seemed uneasy around Emme: she was quiet. 'I'll be OK,' Fran told him. 'I'll be quick.' And she had almost run round the side of the house pulling Emme, to give her no chance to stop and turn and look.

They hurried, out of the village and along the wet road under the big sky, towards the school. It was on the edge of the next village, no more than a low-lying cluster of buildings and a copse. Leaning into the wet wind Fran held Emme's hand tight, tugging her onwards, past puddles, past roadkill, a bird no more than a smear of feathers. In the buggy Ben was too startled by their jolting pace to protest.

Fran kept up breathless conversation with Emme as they went, so as not to think, answering questions she'd usually let drift: *Yes, no, cows could sleep standing up, it would be fish fingers for supper, babies learned to walk when they were one.*

Where's the hospital? stopped her in her tracks. 'In town. Not far.' Holding her breath for the next question, the question she would have to give a real answer to: *What's in that tent? What were you looking at, what was that man picking up?* But Emme went quiet then, and then they were in the playground, and Fran was pushing the wooden gate open, scanning the women milling at the school door, the children perched on the climbing frame.

Beyond the school building the line of the horizon was visible and the stretch of an unkempt field, its grass yellow from wintering. High in the sky over it a speck vibrated against the white sky, a lone sparrowhawk hovering on the lookout. She watched it, tense for when it would dive; she felt Emme lean close against her.

It had been Nathan who had first pointed a bird of prey out to her, and once she knew, they seemed on his radar all the time. She'd seen his head turn in the car to register them sitting on fence poles as they passed, the distinctive curve of the beaked head, the low-folded tail feathers, the perfect poised balance. Emme tugged, reaching to point now as out in the field it swooped, plummeting straight down into the shaggy grass. Fran put an arm across her shoulders because she knew too, Nathan had taught her the names. Birds of prey. Sparrowhawk, red kite, marsh harrier.

Searching the faces, Fran didn't know if it was her imagination but as the other mothers filed in it seemed to her there were more whispers, more glances than usual. It wasn't until Karen shoved the gate open ahead of her with a bang, though, and shouted, that Fran knew who she'd been waiting for. 'Harry! Just wait a bit, Jesus,' Karen yelled. Her son, a small, scruffy boy with a sharp little red nose, had run in ahead of her and was already talking busily into Emme's face, interrogating her about some character from a cartoon or computer game.

'He's all right,' said Fran, as Karen arrived behind him. She could see straight away that she knew.

When they'd asked, is there anyone you can call, the thought of Karen had fluttered briefly, a spark of hope. But it had been three in the morning, and they hardly knew each other, not really.

At the end of Emme's first week at school Fran had lost track of her in the playground and it had been Karen who'd spotted her wandering and brought her back, unasked. 'Always worst-case scenario, isn't it?' she'd said, and Fran could have hugged her. 'Tell me about it. Under a car or abducted. Funny that.'

She came to a stop in front of Fran now, standing between her and the others, like a guard. Karen was a big woman and slightly dishevelled but she always put on her face, lip gloss, blue eyeliner to go with dark blue eyes, mascara meticulously applied, starry in the grey playground. It was why the other mothers whispered about her, not with her, making a show of herself and not caring either.

Karen was a single mother, Fran thought. She'd heard Harry asking, wheedling for a visit to his dad. *Dad always takes me to Kentucky*. Fried Chicken, she guessed. Not the racetrack. This morning in the cold Karen had her son's sharp red nose.

'Are you all right?' she said quickly, regarding Fran with level kindness, and with that look she felt it bubbling up inside her.

'No,' Fran said, keeping it together, just. 'I . . .' She felt herself staring hard, straight ahead so as not to lose it. 'No. Not really.'

'It was you found him?' said Karen in an undertone, and Fran stared.

'How did you know?' she whispered. And Karen just turned her head a fraction, towards the others. 'Do they all know?'

Karen shrugged. 'Or think they do.'

'How?' Fran said, her voice strained.

'Oh, love,' said Karen, sorrowful. 'Human nature, isn't it? You're in the sticks, now. Nothing better to do out here

57

than poke about in other people's misery.' She pulled her coat tighter around herself, frowning hard at something.

'She doesn't,' said Fran, nodding towards Emme. 'She doesn't know, I mean. I haven't . . . I haven't . . .' And as her voice cracked Karen was there right next to her, her round warm shoulder pressed against Fran's.

'All right,' she said, firm. 'It's all right, darling.'

A bell rang and she could see the tall teacher who held it seeking someone out among them.

Eyes in the back of her head, Karen said, 'Ignore her,' and she bent to zip Harry's fleece. She gave him a little push and he headed for the queues forming at the school door.

Emme hesitated, looking up from one of them to the other.

'You want me to have her, after school?' said Karen, putting out a hand to pat Emme's shoulder, and obediently Emme fixed on her, listening. 'You fancy that, Emme? Pizza for tea.' Emme turned to Fran, pleading, wide-eyed and silent.

And Fran found herself nodding, just to see her smile. Watching her run, schoolbag flying, to catch Harry at the door she told herself, It'll come soon enough.

'I'll let them know in the school office if you like,' said Karen.

'Really?' She felt stupidly grateful, not to have to go in there. 'Thank you.' Karen flapped a gloved hand. 'You'll tell me? If there's anything, if she's . . .'

Karen nodded. 'Come for her whenever.'

At the gate Fran turned, and Karen was still standing there, watching her, and for just a second she caught a look, sharp and thoughtful, a wondering look. Then Karen was moving off, towards the school door, and in the buggy Ben twisted to look up at her, straining. As Fran set her hand on the gate and the empty road home beckoned, she could feel it, still there somewhere under her ribs, a hard tight knot of fear.

As she knelt beside him in the field Gerard had fished a pen from a breast pocket and flipped the sodden scrap on to it from out of the wet stubble. With his other hand he had pulled a clear plastic bag from his jacket's side pocket.

She had still not even been sure what it was they were looking at, she had been able to hear her own breath, raw in her throat as she leaned in. 'What?' she said.

He had his forearms on his knees and the bag held up between them, a finger and thumb at each corner. 'God knows,' he said, guarded, keeping her at bay. 'It could be just random.'

She couldn't make it out at first. Something knotted, brownish. Tan-coloured, familiar and not familiar. A colour she never wore: a pair of women's tights.

Chapter Seven

The police car was still there when she got back from school, but there was no one inside it. A van was parked next to it and out in the field beyond the barn she could see them taking down the pale nylon tent. She pushed Ben inside, asleep in the buggy. The kitchen was empty.

A horrible feeling sat in her belly, made of the knowledge that she was on her own. That she'd never wake up next to him again, the sight of her cold kitchen, the house that needed work, the children who needed to understand where he'd gone. Disbelief. *How?*

The blood on the wall jumped at her: a man in a white boiler suit had come in last night and photographed it, hadn't he? Did that mean she could clean it off? Looking at it Fran remembered something. She left Ben in the buggy and lifted the receiver, she dialled her mobile number, and listened. It would be on silent because that's how she kept it but if it was in the room she would hear it vibrate.

She heard nothing. She pushed the door into the corridor open a crack and listened. She thought she heard it, that tiny buzz, she strained to narrow it down, hall, sitting room, upstairs . . . but then the answerphone cut in and the sound was gone.

It was there. She'd find it, then she'd call people. Then.

She set her back against the wall and dialled again, Nathan's number. She closed her eyes, waiting for his voice, steeling herself. But that wasn't what came: *The number you have dialled is not available.* She hung up. Try again. The list was there on the wall beside her: *Doctor, Dad* – Nathan's dad – *Nathan, School, Dentist, Rob Work, Rob.*

Was it only last night? Only hours ago but time seemed to have stretched: it felt as though she'd travelled miles in her sleep. How far could he have got, the man in the field? He could have got to the next county, he could have got to Scotland. But he'd waited, and watched. He didn't want to go anywhere.

She dialled. It rang and rang and rang. She imagined Rob in the lab, stooped over his slides, with his red teenager's knuckles. She almost hung up then he answered, out of breath. And suddenly she couldn't speak.

'Nathan?' he said. 'Nathan?'

Their number would be in his phone, under Nathan. Of course. So the police couldn't have spoken to him yet.

She found her voice. 'No, Rob. It's me.'

'Fran? Sorry, I was . . . the phone was in some zip compartment in my backpack, I couldn't get to it. I thought he . . . I thought you were going to ring off.'

'Backpack?' she said, momentarily derailed. 'Where are you?'

'Outward bound course,' he said, shyly, and dimly she remembered something, he'd wanted Nathan to go. 'In Wales. Well, not so much of a course, just me walking. You can tell Nathan he's not missing anything. There's cloud cover down to the ground.'

'No . . .' She couldn't even start to say it. 'Nathan . . . He's . . . Nathan's . . .'

'Fran,' he said, his voice rising, 'Fran, what is it? What's wrong?'

Then she could only hear his breathing on the other end of the line, growing ragged, as she told him. She stopped talking, she squeezed her eyes shut, she didn't want to hear, or see.

'Nathan's dead? He's dead?' He sounded lost, bewildered. 'He was supposed to be here. I asked him to come months ago, he said he was too busy.' His voice rose.

'The police want to talk to you,' said Fran, feeling a creeping anxiety, that this was going to make someone angry, but suddenly it seemed important that she be the one to break the news, whatever DS Gerard said. This was Rob: this was his best friend. 'They'll try and call. They keep asking. Who he knew. Did anyone . . . Who would want to do this to him, outside our house, in the middle of the night? Rob?' She heard only dull silence. 'But Nathan? Did Nathan have . . .' She searched for the word, but it didn't seem right. 'Was there anyone . . . did he have *enemies*? People . . . back here, was there anyone . . .' She heard a kind of gasp, as if he'd sat down abruptly.

'*No,*' he said, then, desperate. 'I don't know. I don't know. He said – the last time I saw him – work seemed to be getting him down, that was all.' Pleading. 'But that couldn't . . . work couldn't—' He broke off. 'He's dead.'

'It's all right,' Fran told him. 'No, I shouldn't . . . I should have let the police talk to you first, I just didn't want it to be . . .' and she heard her voice break. 'Oh, Rob. I'm so sorry.'

'I'm coming back down. This fucking mountain.' It was the first time she'd heard Rob swear. 'Why didn't he come? I've got to walk out of here, I'm on my own. I'll see if I can get a lift off, I've got some battery left on the phone but the signal's not good. Are you all right, Fran? Are they making sure you're all right? You're on your own with the kids.'

'I'm all right,' said Fran, stupid tears coming to her eyes. 'They might call you. I'm sorry. The police might call.'

'That's all right,' said Rob. 'Just tell them – I'm coming back. I'll be there—' He broke off. 'Shit, shit. I'll be there as soon as I can.'

And the line went dead.

Slowly, she hung up. Ben lay sleeping in the buggy, pale and still, and she leaned her head back against the wall.

The thin light was coming through the window over the sink, showing up the dirt. Fran walked towards it, thinking. She dipped a cloth in the washing up bowl and wiped one pane, then the next. Reached for a tea towel to dry them off but on the second one she stopped and leaned closer. There was something, not on the inside. She put the tea towel down and went to the door, outside into the yard. *Where, where.* She looked, searched. There.

A nick in the thick glass. Fran put her finger to it and felt the sides of it. She leaned up closer and saw it quite

63

clearly, tiny and almost perfectly round, as though something small and round had struck the thick glass from outside, and felt triumph, *yes*, only then as quickly the white flash of terror, like a flare illuminating the scene, the yard, the dark yard.

He'd waited for her to find Nathan but he hadn't gone, not then. He'd waited until she was inside and then he'd come, softly across the field, right up to the house. As she had stood there under the kitchen striplighting, holding on to the phone with her back to the window he'd been watching her.

Fran was stiff and cold; she rubbed both arms fiercely. All this from a tiny fleck in the window pane, a blemish. She looked around for the pebble he'd have thrown but the yard was littered with them, it was half gravel. She looked across at the men beyond the barn, in the field: they'd been in the yard, too, peering inside the dilapidated shed. Could she have shown them handfuls of dirt and stones, to fingerprint or whatever they did? They'd have thought she was nuts. She turned and went inside.

Ben was stirring in his sheepskin cocoon so she lifted him out quickly and still in her coat she sat to feed him at the kitchen table. She looked back at the door, the mat askew, the floor heavily marked with bootprints, and something began to tick, her wet feet at the door, mud on them as she had slid them into Nathan's boots. Nathan had been out in the field, not wearing boots, just the shoes he'd gone out to the pub in. Wet mud on the floor last night. She tried to make sense of that, but just the image of Nathan taking off his shoes at the door defeated her, the way he knelt, untied a knot, methodical, fastidious. Fran looked at the table where the two-day-old newspaper lay. She could remember Nathan opening the paper, saying something. A stack of books she'd ordered for herself, one cardboard parcel not even opened yet though it had arrived weeks ago. A plastic carrier bag with something flat and square in it.

The evidence bag containing the sodden tights had been removed.

There was something else, distinct from misery. It sat at the base of her skull where fight or flight lived, waiting.

What was in the carrier bag? What did it matter? This was just distraction. But she leaned over Ben to turn it towards her, tilted her head to look inside, her breathing constricted. She heard a sound from upstairs and everything stopped. Someone called down, 'Mrs Hall?' DS Gerard.

He was in her bedroom, standing at the far side of the bed and looking down.

'What are you doing up here?' Fran said from the doorway, trying to sound reasonable. The room was full of pale clean light, flooding across the landscape. She remembered, as if from far away, how much she had loved it, their first morning here. Gerard stood between her and the windows. 'Don't you have to have a warrant or something?' Trying, too late, to make it sound like a joke. DS Gerard looked up, gave her a stiff smile. 'Just trying to save time,' he said. 'I'm sorry if I startled you.'

'I got Rob on the phone,' said Fran.

'So I gathered.' Gerard let out a sigh. 'It's a difficult conversation to have. It must have been a nasty shock for him.'

'I just . . . I wanted to be the one to tell him,' she said, stubborn. Gerard nodded, non-committal.

'He's up a mountain in Wales. He's coming down. He's got to walk out though, it's some kind of course—'

Gerard cut her off, gently. 'It's fine. We'll make contact with him. It's fine.' His voice was so calm and level, she found herself wondering, does he care? Does he even care? He frowned, and she could feel her heart thudding as she came up to the bed on the opposite side.

'What is it?' she asked.

'Do you think now might be a good time,' he said, quiet, reasonable, 'to get down to the station?'

Ali Compton was late by seven minutes, but it didn't matter, it turned out. 'Not here yet,' said Derek, looking up from the front desk. Sergeant Derek Butt, in weary receipt of more stupid jokes than Ali could remember. Sometimes she wondered if he'd stuck at desk sergeant, evading promotion, just because of his name. She didn't even have that as an excuse, compassionate grounds not counting for much as an excuse for career stasis, with them that mattered.

'Thanks, Derek.'

'He's requested interview room four,' he told her, watching for her reaction, and Ali raised an eyebrow.

'Oh yes,' she said. 'That's interesting. Pressed for space are we today?'

Interview room four was no one's favourite place. The station — state-of-the-art, three years old — had a nice new airy set of rooms specially designed for the bereaved. It doubled up as an interview suite for children but as far as she knew — and Ali, like most of them, had a grim radar for incoming cases involving minors — it wasn't in use.

'Nope,' said Derek. 'Not exactly.'

66

'Ah well,' Ali said, 'I'm sure he has his reasons. As sure as I am that, being Doug Gerard, and a believer in full disclosure and gender equality, he will bring me right up to date.' She sighed. 'Anything else I should know?'

'I believe the wife was the one that found the body.' Derek averted his eyes, expressionless. 'And there was a call from DI Craddock, asking when DS Gerard was expected back.'

Doug Gerard had given her the impression Craddock was letting him have his head with this one. Maybe that had just been wishful thinking, or maybe this wasn't just a domestic, after all. She saw Derek frown at her shirtfront and she pulled the cardigan closed over a blob of something that must have landed on her shirt between buttoning it at the top of the stairs and saying goodbye at Mum's kitchen door. Mum looking up at her, lip quivering. 'I'll be back to make you a sandwich,' Ali had said, already dreading the grief she'd get over that at the nick. 'That's sorted with work. Half one at the latest. I've put it in a note.' Two weeks off was a long time.

'Oh, shit,' she said, looking down.

'More like porridge, if you ask me,' said Derek mildly. 'Long time no see, Detective Constable Compton. How was your leave? Barbados, was it?'

'Yeah, right,' Ali said, smiling in spite of herself. She liked Derek. 'Can't you tell by the tan?' And then from behind her she heard the pneumatic hiss of the automatic doors.

Ali saw the baby first, because the woman's head was bent, looking down at him in the car seat. Asleep, pale cheeks, she could even see eyelashes. Stubborn little mouth.

Detective Sergeant Doug Gerard was coming through the door beside the woman, smooth-chinned for once and it looked like he'd scrubbed under his fingernails too. Aftershave. That walk he had, there was a word for it, lord of all he surveyed though he was no more than a DS. Not for much longer if ambition counted for anything, and it did.

Carswell bringing up the rear, surreptitiously picking his nose. Ali was already resigned to the possibility that before she knew it Ed Carswell, who had nothing going for him but low cunning and a panting desire to impress Doug Gerard, would be telling her what to do, too.

Then the woman looked up from the baby and Ali had to keep a lid on it because she knew who the aftershave was for. A woman, not quite any woman, but a vulnerable one, halfway decent would do, and Fran Hall was more than that. Even knackered, even terrified, she had one of those faces. DS Gerard had scrubbed up for that face; the swagger he took with him everywhere, whether the victim was good-looking or not.

'This way, Mrs Hall,' Gerard said, all reassuring, heading for the stairs behind reception, and Ali saw her take it in, the gloomy stairwell, the wall already scuffed, three years in, from surly lads scraping their boots along it as they were led down.

'Sorry, we're under a lot of pressure for space,' Ali heard him lie, 'we'll be down in our basement interview rooms.' Then, almost as an afterthought, as Ali came after them, 'This is Ali Compton,' and he glanced back at her. 'Your FLO. The best we've got.' Maybe the victim's wife would pick up the sneer attached to that, maybe she wouldn't.

'Mrs Hall,' Ali said. And the woman stopped then and although Gerard made an impatient noise she didn't move, stubborn. 'Fran,' she said, and Ali thought, Not just stubborn. She's in shock.

In shock or not Fran Hall turned to Doug Gerard then and said, 'I want her in there too.' Nodding at Ali, unblinking. Behind Ali, Carswell let out a nervous snigger.

'I had thought,' he kept his voice reasonable, but Ali could see Doug Gerard was annoyed, 'for the preliminaries I thought it might be as well if Ali − Detective Constable Compton − took charge of . . . of the, of your . . .'

'Ben's asleep, though,' said Fran Hall, holding herself very stiff. 'And I'd like her in there. Please.'

Even Derek Butt was looking over, curious, Carswell gawking excitedly and that flat, dead look on Gerard's face that said, *She's not a fucking nurse, you know, a* chaperone, *you're not* entitled, but all he said − smooth as you like, as if he was humouring her and it was all the same to him, anyway − was, 'I don't see why not.'

Cramped and windowless, reserved for toerags, there was barely room for a solicitor and his briefcase in interview room four, let alone three police officers and a woman with a baby seat. If the baby in it began to cry . . . well. That'd be Ali out of the picture.

'Just a minute,' said Gerard on the threshold, jerking his head to Ali to follow him out. 'Let's track down another chair, shall we?' Closing the door on Carswell and Fran Hall, he stood under the corridor's striplighting, legs braced as if he was about to go in for a tackle.

'Right,' he said in a level undertone, pissed off and not bothering much to disguise it now.

'What's the story?' Ali said, holding her ground. 'They've been here a year, he's from round here. She found him, I know that, three a.m. call. Someone with a grudge? He got into something?' She frowned. 'Is the wife a suspect?'

Gerard made as if to pick something out of his teeth. 'Look,' he said, examining his fingertip, looking up at her as an afterthought. 'Obviously there's no time to bring you up to date on progress, on our thinking so far.'

Ali folded her arms across her chest, getting the message straight off: as far as Gerard was concerned she was a glorified nanny. 'Right,' she said.

'So for the moment,' droning, 'I'd like you to act as . . . a fresh pair of eyes, let's say. I'm interested in your impressions, unencumbered.' My arse you are, thought Ali. 'And of course . . .' leaning close so she got a whiff of sweat under the aftershave, 'I don't want you getting under my feet in the incident room, your place is in the field.'

'No desk for me, then?' said Ali, mildly. Surprise surprise.

He ignored her. 'But you'll remember you're part of the investigative team. Everything you get out of her comes straight to me.' Then Doug Gerard grabbed the plastic chair parked at the door, and put it into her hands.

Back inside she set the chair at Fran Hall's side of the table, and taking advantage of the minute or two Gerard stood there muttering to Carswell above their heads, she leaned towards Fran Hall. The victim's wife was perched frozen on her chair, her hand still on the handle of her baby's car seat, ready to grab him up and run.

'Sorry about the room,' said Ali and she saw Fran Hall look round, dazed, as if she hadn't noticed where she was.

Ali had seen that particular look before, her head followed

70

Fran Hall's trying to work it out, but then Carswell and Gerard were sitting down opposite them and Gerard was explaining that this was just a chat, she wasn't under caution. They would be recording it, was that all right with her? Fran Hall just nodded, still dazed. No idea, thought Ali, but then again if Gerard's got anything to do with it he'll keep us both in the dark for the duration. Carswell, his mouth open in concentration, pressed buttons on the recorder, and the woman flinched at the sound.

Battered wife? There was a bit of that about her, and Ali'd seen enough of those to know. Was that the theory they weren't bothering to update her on? Ali had a look at her but the woman's eyes slid away, dodging. Battered wives often lost sympathy all round on account of that look; she'd seen jurors turn stony at the sight of them: how could they let it happen? Easy, is the answer to that. But the baby looked healthy and there was nothing visible on Fran Hall, no bruises, no hair yanked out, no burns or scarring.

'A couple of things,' said Doug Gerard, leaning back. 'First. He was at the pub, you said?'

Fran Hall nodded. 'The Queen's Head.'

'In the village, right? He was a regular?' Gerard knew something, Ali could hear it in his voice.

'Once or twice a week,' Fran Hall said, very quiet.

'You didn't go with him?'

She hesitated, shook her head.

'He'd walk there, I suppose?'

She shook her head again. 'He took the car. He . . . it was quite a long walk, right at the other end of the village. He wasn't much of a drinker.'

71

Ali looked at Gerard, then Carswell. Who took the car to the local pub? Idle locals who knew they wouldn't be caught? Fat, lazy, habitual drunk drivers? Was that who Fran Hall had been married to? Gerard didn't look back at Ali.

'Well, forensics will tell us that. If he'd been drinking.' He tapped his pen on the table, turning it. 'Another thing, though,' he added, casual. 'His clothing was disturbed and we wondered . . .' Ali looked up, from him to Carswell.

'What?' Fran Hall said, interrupting. 'Disturbed, what do you mean by that? Disturbed?'

Gerard sounded patient. 'Was he in the habit, maybe, of going outside to urinate? Last thing at night, coming home from the pub?' When Hall just stared at him, he said, 'Going out for a—'

'I know what urinate means,' she told him.

'It's a territorial thing,' said Ali, thinking, He won't like that. 'Like dogs. Some men do it.'

'Maybe round here they do,' said Fran Hall, white-faced, and Gerard shifted in his chair. If he was in any doubt as to whether to dislike her, thought Ali, it's gone. Hates a smart mouth on a woman. Ali didn't think it had even been meant that way.

'Are you saying he might have been . . . there might have been . . .'

'No evidence of anything sexual,' said Doug Gerard, with that smile he probably practised in the mirror, full of himself. 'No other evidence, I should say. At present we're looking at it as an explanation as to why he was out there, in the middle of the night.'

Fran Hall sat very still, and he put on his soft voice.

Showing that he cared. It did work with plenty of suspects, give him that, as well as in a chat-up situation.

'Timing. I need to go over that again with you.'

'Timing?' Fran Hall pressed herself back into the seat, arms straight, hands under her thighs. On the other side of the table Gerard crossed his legs, easy, one ankle resting on a knee, black socks, a bit of ankle. Ali reached into her pocket for her notebook and there was a flicker in Gerard's face, of irritation. She took out a pen from the other pocket.

'You said,' Gerard pulled out his own notebook to consult it, 'your husband came in at around midnight, maybe after midnight. You woke up around two hours later and he was gone.'

'Two oh seven,' said Fran Hall, so quiet you almost couldn't hear it.

'But you couldn't put an exact time on when your husband first came in?' The room was silent: number four always felt to Ali like a padded cell. There'd be psychology in them building in an interview room this much like a dungeon, but she didn't fancy looking too closely at it.

'I didn't look at the clock,' Fran said, and Ali saw her swallow. 'I heard him, the change in his pockets. He'd turned the light off in the corridor, I don't know why.' She sounded choked. 'I looked at the clock, I was . . . I didn't know if I was awake or asleep, really, it was just red lights, I didn't register . . .' As Ali watched she turned her head, as if she was looking round her own bedroom in the dark.

'It couldn't have been earlier? Around, ten, say?'

Fran Hall shook her head, pale. 'I'd have only just gone

to bed by ten. I read for a bit. I got up, I went . . . to the bathroom.' Her eyes slid sideways to Ali, then back. 'Anyway. I didn't go to sleep till close to eleven. When he came in I'd say I'd been asleep for at least an hour. Deep sleep, whenever that comes.'

'So you feel it was after midnight.' Ali bent her head over her notebook, writing it all down, there might not be time to listen to the tapes. They might not make it easy. 'He woke you.'

'Yes. He did. Well. Not fully.' Ali raised her head, shot a glance at the men. They didn't seem to have heard what she had heard.

'Did he say anything?'

Fran Hall shook her head, still looking at him like she was half hypnotised. 'No,' she said slowly, blinking. 'Why?'

Gerard going all poker face. 'We're working out timing. Time of death.' She stared. 'It's to do with the forensic people, input from you goes into the equation.'

Ali scented bullshit – plus he wouldn't catch her eye. They went over the timing again, and then another time. She didn't write it down after a bit, just watching, trying to work it out. Fran Hall's hand was back on the handle of her child's baby seat; the wedding ring was loose on it, nails cut short but kept nice. The trainers, muddy but not the kind you bought round here, not the kind you wore. Gold chain round her neck, good highlights but grown down almost to the end, months, maybe a year since Fran Hall had had her hair done.

Ali put a hand to her own hair and grimaced: she couldn't even remember when she'd washed it last and their eyes met, just for a second.

74

Then it seemed to be winding down, though Ali couldn't see what they'd got that was new. Gerard yawned, uncrossed his legs, leaned forward and folded his notebook and as he turned to Ed Carswell, started on about the weather and some five-a-side match at the weekend that might have to be cancelled, Ali leaned forwards.

'Do you work, Mrs Hall? I mean, did you, before – work outside the home?'

'Yes,' said Fran Hall slowly, eyes wide, glancing from Doug Gerard, who had stopped mid-conversation to frown at Ali. 'Yes, I worked on a magazine. In London.'

'Magazine,' said Ali, nodding, offering her respect. 'Nice job, that. Glamorous. You gave up work, all that, to come out here?' Gerard was looking tetchy. He didn't like the idea of Fran Hall up in London, Ali could tell, up in London dressed up smart, chippy little Doug Gerard from, where was it? Up to Hull or somewhere. Nowhere. She ignored him. 'Must have been a hard choice, coming out here,' she said, quiet. 'Must have been a sacrifice.'

'Not as glamorous as people think,' said Fran Hall, and her lips were pale. 'A lot of travel, and it was the children. I wanted to be home with the children.'

'Just one though, right, when you moved out here?' Fran Hall's eyes were wide, and Ali went on, 'Just the one child. Or were you expecting him already?'

'No, I, no—' But before Fran could finish her answer, Doug Gerard had pushed back his chair with an impatient scrape and was nudging Carswell to switch off the recorder. He was on his feet and Fran Hall got up too, only looking sideways at Ali a second, a flash of something there then gone, but Ali had seen it all right.

75

She looked frightened. That look that would turn a jury against her. She looked guilty.

'Let's get you home,' said Doug Gerard, and leaning to lift the baby seat Fran Hall looked at him as if the word meant nothing.

Chapter Eight

'We'll take her back,' Gerard had said to the female officer outside the police station. The FLO. Then he'd turned back to Fran. 'This is DC Compton's first day back off leave, a half-day by prior arrangement, there's a certain *domestic* situation needs some sorting, I believe.'

Bewildered, Fran said, 'But she . . . I . . .' Then she caught the look Ali Compton gave him and in that flash she recognised the situation: she had heard it enough times when she'd had a job of her own to go to, like *domestic* meant sitting by the fire with your feet up.

'If you need me,' said Ali Compton, quickly, so close Fran could see her roots showing, the mesh of fine lines at her eyes, 'I'll be right over. That's all you need to know.' She looked strained and tense.

'All right,' said Fran, reluctant to surrender her.

'You try to get some kip this afternoon,' said Ali, holding

on to her at the elbows. 'When the baby sleeps, you sleep. All right?'

Gerard had made an impatient noise but Ali Compton ignored him. 'If I hear nothing from you I'll be there in the morning.' A glance at Gerard, then back at Fran. 'Is that all right? We can have a bit of a talk then. Go over things.'

Ben was stirring in the car seat. It had seemed to Fran that she had no choice, so she'd said, 'Yes. That'd be good.'

It occurred to her in the back seat of the police car, looking at the back of Gerard's square head, the rash on Carswell's neck where he'd gone too close with the clippers, that if Ali Compton had been the first to arrive on the scene last night it would have been very different. She felt as though she was tangled tight in what she'd already said, she'd left out things she couldn't begin to explain.

Sacrifice, that was the word Ali Compton had used, looking at her that way. But they said that was what it was all about, having a baby. You had to give things up. Feeling like a woman a man might look at in the street, for starters. Feeling like someone wanted you.

It wasn't like she needed it, that's what Fran had told herself. There was plenty to tire her out, lugging big cheerful Emme in and out of the buggy, to the swings, to toddler group, in a sling to the supermarket, Fran seemed to be running a sweat from the moment she got up anyway. She would climb out of bed to give Emme a feed in the dead hours of the pre-dawn, letting the baby fog drift over her, enveloping them while Nathan moved to and fro out there in the real world. In a sweat and forever wiping stuff, the rim of the bath, smears of mush from the baby's chin and her own tired body.

And then Emme stopped breastfeeding. She turned her face away one day and reached instead for the bowl of yellow mush sitting on the table, and that was it. No more than a day later it felt different, things looked sharper, less forgiving. Her sore, unused breasts were just the start; in bed her nerve endings seemed to prick and she would shift, restlessly, feeling the quilt like a weight.

She had gone back to work, part-time.

Nathan had seemed keen: it had been his idea. 'Get your life back,' he had said. His arms were gently around her when he said it, he had been stroking her back like a father. She'd been on her knees rooting stuff out from the sofa one evening, Emme finally asleep after an hour of patient grizzling. She wasn't a difficult baby, Fran had come to realise, this was just how it was. Anyway, kneeling there with her backside in the air and her unwashed hair falling in her face she had felt his hand on her hipbone from behind and she had twisted away from him.

'This isn't working, is it?' he said, mild, and she felt her heart race, eager in expectation of what came next. But she'd been wrong. He took her hand in his. 'You need to get back out there. To work.' The West End a bus ride away, all this time.

She sat back on her heels. 'Seriously?'

It made sense: she needed something else to think

79

about. Not just them. She knew he wanted the flat back to himself now and again, too; he'd been used to working there during the day when he had no office or site to be occupying and it wasn't the same with her and Emme crashing in and out, the baby talk and clatter in the kitchen.

Fran found a nineteen-year-old Lithuanian girl to do twenty hours a week minding Emme. Katrina was pale and stolid, but her face at least softened when she picked the baby up, and she lived with her mother round the corner, in local authority accommodation, she could have Emme there if Nathan needed the flat. She could do evenings too, she said hopefully but Fran told her that wasn't really necessary, they didn't go out much.

Except then there was a do, and Nathan was going to be away, a conference on new methods in concrete, he said. Manchester. She supposed she had thought, when she went back to work, their evenings and weekends would be more precious, but instead Nathan seemed to feel easier about spending time away. 'It's obvious,' he said, reasonable, when she asked. 'You've got help now. There's Katrina.' Head cocked. 'What is it, anyway? The do.'

Fran didn't know why she played it down, answering him, why she said, 'Oh, just a thing, work thing. It'll be full of advertisers, men in suits.'

When in fact it was the magazine's ten-year anniversary party, and champagne till midnight in a club. Fran had been surprised even to be on the list and since the email had dropped into her inbox she had been fretting. Whether she could even remember how to put make-up on, never mind who she'd talk to.

She could have declined; Jo had. She would be on holiday, she said dismissively when Fran had asked her if they could go together, and Fran had faltered. It had been Carine from work who'd chivvied her back on board, full of problem-page wisdom about not losing touch with yourself as a woman, the benefits of social interaction, about dopamine release on the dance floor.

'You are so elegant,' Katrina told her with a bewildered expression Fran couldn't quite figure out, when she came out ready to leave – she could only hope it was because the girl had only ever seen her unkempt in jeans.

'I wish,' she said, but they smiled at each other. Emme on the floor beside her looked up, wide-eyed, then tipped forward to stroke a shoe, which was dark red suede, a high heel, too impractical for anything but a party. The dress – it was silk, a long-ago present from Nick and she'd never worn it with Nathan out of anxiety that somehow he'd know – was looser than before but as far as she could tell not shapeless, a deep slit in the back.

The magazine had done a deal with the management of the vast art-deco hotel off Piccadilly Circus with a newly refurbished club in its basement, cavernous and gleaming with gold tile and mirrors, dark polished rails, mahogany and velvet. It had been so long since she'd walked into a scene like this, the glitter of jewellery swinging from women's ears, in their hair, the tight little groups, the trays of tall shining glasses skimming the crowd, but even as she stepped into the soft dark at the bottom of the stairs it came to greet her, folded itself around her, warm and familiar as if she'd never been away.

She took a passing glass and a man in a suit turned

to look at her. 'Do I know you from somewhere?' he said, serious, and tipping the drink to her lips Fran had laughed.

'No, really,' he said, turning away from the man he'd been talking to. 'I've seen you. Not for a while, though.' His eyes wandered, from the earrings that dangled by her collarbone, up to her face, looking for something.

'Oh, I've been very busy,' she said, letting her life blur behind her, nappies and washing up. Fun, she thought, I remember that, and she tipped the glass again.

It was almost three when she roused Katrina on the sofa and told her to go home, the girl's moon-face rising up from the cushions pale and shocked in the dark sitting room. 'Go,' said Fran, pushing money into her hand, scrabbling in her purse for more to stop the girl looking at her.

She had slept no more than an hour before it woke her, shame as cold as the slap of seawater, and she was scrambling out of the bed to get to the bathroom.

By the time Nathan got back thirty-six hours later with a stack of brochures about concrete and cheerful anecdotes about wine bars and dodgy hotel rooms, the dress had been put out with the rubbish and she'd cleaned her teeth so many times her gums were bleeding. He didn't ask her about the party so she didn't remind him, and if he noticed the way Katrina avoided her eye on the Monday morning, he didn't say anything.

Fran should have let the girl sleep, shouldn't have put her out into the street, but she hadn't been able to stop herself.

The office was full of aftermath stories: she told herself hers wouldn't even have registered if she'd tried to join in.

Besides, it had been dark enough for no one to have noticed one more of them steadying herself against the wall in heels too high, teetering into a taxi, flushed and glittering. Jo got back from her holiday a week later and only said, 'You're looking skinny,' impatient still, with an undertone of anxiety. 'Are you OK?'

To which the answer was, no. 'Fine,' she'd said, brightly unconvincing. 'Running around, you know.'

'If you say so,' said Jo, and as she turned away Fran had the sense of watching something she wanted slipping out of her grasp.

She began to have panic attacks, obscurely triggered: the way Nathan looked at her or a rising querulous note in Emme's babble in the highchair. At night she would lie in bed while the trembling rose from her legs, assailed by thoughts that Emme was ill, that she was ill, that she would hear Emme calling in the night and she wouldn't be able to go to her. She went to the doctor – a harassed woman who had little time for the worried well in the inner city – and was given a brochure on relaxation techniques. 'We don't prescribe tranquillisers any more. Have you tried swimming?'

So when, four months later, Nathan came back from another course (Lincolnshire this time, and eco-building methods) and announced, looking at her warily – because he knew how she felt about the countryside, she'd always said that living there must be like being buried alive – that he thought they should move out of London, she had gone up to him and buried her face in his chest as if he had offered her salvation.

And with one word she had let it all go: the bus to

work and the heads turning in the office, Katrina's face, Jo's face. Her own thin, sleepless face in the mirror and the doctor looking up from her notes and seeing her still there, saying, 'Was there anything else?'

'Yes,' she had said to Nathan, her face still muffled in his shirt, and she had felt his arms tighten around her.

She should be grateful to have them there, shouldn't she? The two policemen. If there'd been anyone there when they drove slowly through the village and turned in at the house, anyone watching from across the field among the poplars, a police car and two men climbing out of it would have sent the message, she was protected, wouldn't it? Stay away.

Lunchtime was long gone. They'd offered her a sandwich in the police station as they climbed the stairs from the interview room: egg and salad cream that she could hardly get down. It must be past two, though the white sky offered no clue, it could be five, a day that already seemed like it had lasted a lifetime.

As they climbed out of the police car, there was a break in the cloud and the pale, low sun came through it, slanting down and flooding the wide plain beyond the barn, sending a silver gleam off the standing water. 'You should see the skies,' Nathan had said, dreamily, thinking of some time far off. 'The sunsets, sunrise. Seems like the edge of the world.' He'd wanted to bring her to the edge of the world.

The advantage, she thought as she stood there scanning

the horizon, holding the fear down there somewhere in the pit of her stomach, was that she'd be able to see him coming. *Just leave, just leave, just gather the kids up and leave, don't wait for him to come back, are you nuts?* Just as soon as she worked out where to go. For now, she had to watch.

Gerard turned to look too, his hands in the pockets of his jacket, shoulders hunched. 'Snow. They say, anyway. Snow by Saturday.' He looked at her. 'Hope your boiler's been serviced lately.' He locked the car. 'I'll see you inside.'

They all crowded into the kitchen, and she was lifting Ben out of his seat, damp and straining himself to a fury. Hungry. 'Sorry about that,' Gerard said easily. 'I know it must have seemed like we were just going over the same thing, again and again.' He laughed, reassuring. 'It's not like we're trying to catch you out.' Carswell was at the door, peering through the glass into the yard, his narrow shoulders hunched, and his head turned a fraction at that.

'It's the timing, we can't seem to work it out. Your husband said nothing when he came to bed, you said.'

He had murmured into the hair at the back of her neck, but she hadn't heard. She wanted to tell the truth, she wanted to be on the right side, she wanted to give this man what he wanted. She couldn't see how he would need to know, that her husband came into bed and put his hand between her legs from behind, even though she could remember in that moment precisely how that had felt, where he'd positioned his index finger, his forefinger, his thumb. Her mouth opening, yes.

'I was fast asleep when he came in,' and she wondered then, when would this stop? 'I told you. I'd been dreaming.'

His head turned slowly at that and for a moment as she wondered if he was going to ask her about her dream she felt a rush of heat, of shame, what if she had volunteered that information? *He hadn't fucked me in a year and then he did and then he died and I had been dreaming, I had been dreaming of—*

Why would that be of interest? *Shut up.*

'I've got to change him,' she said, turning to Ben, and quickly she was across the room and at the door.

'All right,' said Gerard staying where he was, mild. 'Well, how about we take a look in his study while you're up there, how would that do? Would you be happy with us doing that?'

All she wanted was to be out of the room. 'Yes,' she said, and she was climbing the stairs. She could hear a murmur behind her in the kitchen but she kept going.

Ben's backside was red from sitting too long in the nappy and she was careful with him as he arched his back, sore and angry. She leaned to kiss his little round stomach, the popped belly button. A bit of kip, Ali Compton had said: it seemed a long way off.

She was on the edge of the bed feeding when there was a soft knock at the door, and she pulled her sweatshirt down so nothing was visible. It was Gerard. 'Ed's made a cup of tea,' he said, frowning.

'I'll be down in a minute,' she said wearily, but he didn't move.

'There's something we'd like you to have a look at,' he told her. 'In your husband's study.' Spreading his hands in a gesture of helplessness that didn't convince her. 'Technology not my strong point, I've got to say. Ed's on the case, though, new generation. You got a computer yourself?'

'No. Well, yes, but—' and then from somewhere outside she heard the door open and there was a rattle, an exclamation.

'Jesus,' he said, and called, 'Carswell!' then, under his breath, 'Christ, that kid . . .' But then it came back to her, with the distinct sound, the sound of bins disturbed, the acoustic of the yard's enclosed space.

'I did hear something outside,' Fran said. 'As I was going to sleep, so I suppose around ten thirty, eleven. I thought it was some animal, you know. After the wheelie bins.'

Arms folded, legs apart, it felt like he was towering over her. 'Did you see anything? An animal?' She shook her head. 'I didn't look. It was just one sound, a sort of scuffle, then I didn't hear anything else.' He pursed his lips, examining her.

'Right. But you hadn't heard anything else, a car, say?'

'I was in bed. We're at the back of the house here, you can't really hear . . . Why?'

'Just working on timing,' said Gerard, reassuring, but she wasn't reassured, it wasn't an answer. 'That's all, trying to work out who was where.' He turned to look at the stairs. 'Well, when you're ready?' And when she didn't move, 'Your husband's computer?' he said, and then she was on her feet, Ben over her shoulder.

When she came into the kitchen Carswell was on the back doorstep, righting the bin in the yard; he gave her a sheepish look.

Gerard looked at her, his head on one side, and when he spoke his voice was soft, though the words jumped at her. 'I know we'd ruled out a break-in,' he said, stepping out of the kitchen and into the dim hall, where the door to Nathan's study was open. She followed him, Carswell bringing up the rear. 'And it's not the usual sort of thing a burglar goes for, but . . .' She stopped in the door. Gerard was squatting at the side of Nathan's desk, where his computer sat.

'Hard drive's gone,' said Carswell, at her ear. She could heard his breathing, coming and going excitedly as he bounced on the balls of his feet.

'What?' She felt stupid.

'Someone's cleaned it out.' Gerard's head on one side, examining her. 'The computer. There's a big hole where the data used to live.'

'Cleaned out. You mean someone, the man who . . . you mean it was taken last night?' Silence. *Inside? He came inside?* 'Is that what you're saying?'

Gerard glanced at Carswell. 'We'll get the machine dusted for prints,' then 'Listen,' looking back at Fran, 'I know your feeling so far has been that whatever has gone on here, this is your home, I can understand that.' And it sounded like something rehearsed, to entice her, and she began shaking her head, even though the warning patter had set up inside her, the fear.

'You're not keen on alternative accommodation,' Gerard said, and before she even said it he spread his hands again, as if absolving himself, a look across at Carswell again that said, *I tried*.

'No,' she said, and swallowed. 'This is our home.' She looked from door to window, gauging what it would take. To make it safe.

He nodded. There was a pause. 'We can give you a panic button, if that would make you feel more secure. Staying here.'

And she saw it reflected in Carswell's face, the flicker of excitement at her fear, the black gleam in his eyes of the outside, trying to get in.

Chapter Nine

Coming here had been a joint decision, of course it had. They'd talked about it.

Mostly Fran had listened while he talked, with Emme under his arm on the sofa under the high vaulted space of their flat's one lovely but impractical room, Emme playing with something but listening too, Fran could tell by the way she went still when he mentioned certain things. What they might do with the space, a playroom, a nursery, the attic space. He talked about Emme exploring in the fields, learning to swim in an old flooded quarry; he talked about the place as though he knew every inch of it. He talked about creeping out of the dismal cottage before dawn to go and lie in reed beds waiting for the ducks to rise, whispering to his little sister to keep quiet as she begged to come too.

'You shot them?' Emme's voice uncertain. He just squeezed her against him absently, his eyes focused somewhere else. 'The ducks, Daddy.'

He smiled down, vaguely. 'And then we went and lived in a magic house. We slept on the floor and we never washed and we cooked in the garden on a fire.' Emme had settled back then, nodding, as if she knew exactly the place. 'It was called Black Barn,' he said. She'd shivered at the name and he'd smiled. 'After a big barn there'd been behind the farmhouse, though it had burned down long since.'

Had Fran said anything? She couldn't remember now, she'd concentrated hard on seeing things through his eyes. That's right: at one point she'd asked, *Where's the nearest station? For work?* He'd stopped abruptly, impatient, she had watched him controlling it. *Twenty minutes to the nearest station, but everything's online, isn't it? And if you go back to work, you might be travelling, London's not the be-all, these days.*

The station was in fact more like forty minutes away but she didn't find that out until they'd been there two months. Never mind the school, Nathan's trump card, the village school that made her nostalgic for the place on the dangerous corner of their London street, with its screaming hordes and harassed teachers.

It had happened more quickly than she had expected, that was all. One minute they were driving back to London and she was going over it all in her head, cloud-cities scudding in white light and the emptiness, the ghost-roar across the plain. And the next he was in the kitchen on his mobile phone, making an offer. Two days after they'd viewed it. She had been on her feet in the doorway open-mouthed when she heard, 'So you'll put it to the vendor?'

Hanging up he had just smiled at her. 'Come on,' he said, easy.

'It's not set in stone, is it? We can pull out at any time.'

Shrugging. 'But the way the market is…' She'd hesitated, then Emme, almost on cue, had tripped over a box of toys because they'd run out of space to store the stuff and begun to wail.

'Sure,' she said. 'Right.'

To judge by the number of For Sale boards in Oakenham and the villages, it turned out, the market wasn't going anywhere fast, but by then they'd jumped, their boats had burned. And it meant they'd got the place cheap and just as well, now she wasn't earning.

She tried calling Jo the night before they left, a hot night in the almost empty flat and Emme perched on the bed watching a DVD because Nathan was out somewhere, farewell darts in a pub in Tufnell Park with a builder. 'You've got to keep them on-side,' he said in the doorway, a quick cool glance round the empty space. 'It's all about the contacts book.' He'd had an energy about him since they'd come back from the viewing, heightened when contracts had been exchanged, a restlessness. The door had swung closed behind him even as she was saying, 'Fine.'

She'd told Jo, when the offer was accepted, over a stiff drink in a park somewhere, Emme in tow because she had been nervous and with good reason. Jo's stare had been blank with incomprehension that looked like hostility. 'I don't know what makes you think that's a good idea,' she'd said. 'I mean, where does that leave you? In the middle of nowhere. If it all goes tits up?' And Fran had shrunk into herself at that because her only answer was, 'It won't.'

Sitting among the boxes, the walls and shelves all bare, she listened to Jo's number ring, on and on. There'd been no answer, and she'd hung up.

The weather broke as the removal van's rear door rattled down and they – Nathan and Fran with Emme under her arm – were forced abruptly inside, under sudden sheets of rain so heavy it blurred the horizon, the poplars, even the outline of the chicken barn. It was as though they had stepped through a waterfall and found themselves standing in a dank cave, among cardboard boxes.

From the door Fran watched the driver run for his soaked seat, hunched under the downpour with his jacket pulled up at the neck and then the door banged behind him and he was off without a wave, the faded lettering on the shutter disappearing into the grey, and they were on their own. The kitchen smelled, of mildew, mouse and cooker grease. Overhead thunder cracked, astoundingly loud, and Emme, already shivering in the sudden chill, began to whimper. Fran had had to galvanise them then and there, to avert anything worse.

'Your room first,' she said to Emme, identifying a box of toys and clothing, pushing Emme ahead of her on the narrow back stairs. Below them Nathan stood, stock-still. She didn't turn to ask him why, not now, not yet.

She'd told him about Jo, late the night before, lying in bed under a crumpled sheet with all the noise outside still going on, just loosened up, blearier, drunker. Nathan, though, she could have sworn hadn't drunk a drop despite having been out three hours, he came home jumpy with the same energy he'd gone with. He just made an impatient sound at the mention of Jo's name, '*Her*,' he said, contemptuous. 'Well, to be honest, good riddance. If you ask me it's people like her's why we're going.' And he'd turned on his side.

Unpacking Emme's things, shaking the duvet out on the

93

little bed under the big handsome sash window, she observed the rain gusting across the wide grey fields. And then, in a brief hiatus in the relentless rolling, cracking thunder, she'd heard an ominous trickle that rose to more like a running sound somewhere at the far end of the house, somewhere overhead. She went out of the room, along the corridor that tilted as if a big hand had just taken it and put a twist in it, at the top of the stairs she had to put her hands to the wall, disoriented by the slope of the boards. He was still standing there, where she'd left him.

'Nathan?' At the alarm in her voice he had turned, and smiled, and she felt the house settle, and stabilise, for the moment. She realised that she was thinking of it as floating, not rooted – or was it that the land wasn't land? The rain would have to stop soon. 'Can you hear that?' she said, and he tilted to listen. 'The roof,' she said, and then he moved.

He'd been hyper after that, moving from one end of the house to the other, turning out boxes in search of stuff, a particular pair of pliers, a stepladder, a torch. Emme had trailed in his wake for a while before retreating to her bed, pressed against the wall and rubbing the ragged ear of her yellow rabbit against her upper lip. As she stood in the doorway watching her Fran saw something move, down along the skirting, and she felt her breathing stutter. Emme's eyes were on her. A spider? It was there, and then it was gone, under the bed on the dusty boards. Bigger than a spider should be but it scuttled, leggy.

When she'd been a child spiders had made Fran hysterical, she could never have borne even to analyse what it was about them that terrified her, although that swift motion, the many legs tapping up and down like hairy levers, was

94

a lot of it. She had managed to switch the panic off but still it lurked, far back somewhere. Emme's fear was, if anything, worse. There would be spiders in a place like this, of course there would.

'You hungry?' she said to Emme, so she would not look down. Emme shook her head just once, settling on the pillow, and the rabbit's ear flopped, across the thumb in her mouth. Fran made herself cross the room, back to the bed, pulled her legs up under herself beside Emme and stroked her cheek. 'Hot milk?'

But even as Emme nodded *yes* her eyes were drooping closed and by the time Fran got back upstairs with the milk she'd been asleep, toppled on the pillow. As Fran eased the duvet out and over her she heard Nathan talking in a low voice downstairs.

He was at the back door, blocking someone's entry, but the visitor must have heard her come into the room because he moved to look over Nathan's shoulder. Nathan stepped back, reluctantly, and the man took a step inside, ducking to pass under the lintel; his head gleamed bald, dark as a conker. His eyes were light-coloured in a creased brown face, he might have been forty or sixty, she couldn't tell.

'Mr Dearborn wants to put his pigs on our field,' said Nathan, expressionless.

Outside, the rain had stopped, but everything seemed to be dripping. The farmer stomped on the mat.

'Alfred,' he said, holding out a hand. 'They call me Fred.' He smiled round the kitchen, benign. 'Been a while since I was in here.'

She could feel calluses on his palm, and his hand was warm. A farmer, then, but nothing like John Martin, who'd been in such a hurry to sell them the place; Martin who smelled of unwashed clothes, Martin with his weird dyed hair and his eyes that seemed to move independently of each other. If Dearborn smelled of anything it was the outside, chaff and hedges and diesel, he had a broad, lined friendly face.

'Did you know Mr Martin, then?' she asked, curious.

'Ah, Johnny,' said Dearborn, ruminative, looking into her face. 'Not a man you get to know,' and he laughed abruptly. 'I been in his kitchen once or twice. He wasn't keen on having me on his field, though. Anyway.' He took a step back. 'Didn't know you was just arrived, you'll need a day or two. Settle in.'

'Pigs,' said Nathan, sitting at the kitchen table after he'd gone, leaving that scent of fields behind him. The bottle of wine was nearly finished. 'I told him I'd think about it. It's money, I suppose.' But he spoke lightly, not gloomy, looking up at her with a sudden smile. 'Up in a minute.'

And she needed sleep, anyway, she felt it descend abruptly, weighing her down. As she left the room he was lifting a box on to the table.

Some time later, Nathan asleep beside her, Fran was woken by a sound that propelled her instantly out of bed. Her heart was going like a hammer. The sound came from along the corridor, a strained, high-pitched stream of breathless terrified nonsense. Fran knew immediately that it was Emme. *Who else could it be?* As she came through the door Fran could see her sitting bolt upright on the bed, moonlight on her face through the uncurtained window. The sky must have cleared: it was extraordinarily bright. Emme babbled on, unconscious, her eyes wide open, and Fran

96

took her shoulders gently, set her face in front of Emme's and then as she felt Fran's hands, as her eyes settled black on Fran's face, she screamed.

No no, thought Fran. 'Don't, shhh.' You'll wake him, no.

She put her arms around Emme on instinct – the room suddenly seemed to contract and narrow around the two of them on the little bed and on the periphery of her vision out to the side through the cool glass Fran felt more than saw the horizon, rippling away from them under the brilliant moon. Then as suddenly as it had come, whatever it was evaporated, and she felt Emme go limp in her arms. Gently Fran laid her back down on the pillow, but her round pale face was smoothed out, untroubled. She didn't make a sound or a movement, not even when the boards creaked as Fran crept backwards to the door.

When she got back to the bed she could see Nathan's mounded back, he had turned on his side, away from her and the door, but his breathing was shallow and even, as if he hadn't surfaced. For some time, though, Fran could feel her heart pattering on, agitated, asking itself questions: Is it here, is it this house, is it somewhere in the dark flat fields surrounding them, is there something wrong with this place?

And answering. Nathan brought them here, her and his child, he wouldn't have done that if it was a bad place.

Would he?

The next day she measured up every window and ordered curtains and blinds online in a plain heavy fabric, blackout-lined. They arrived ten days later and she hung them herself. Nathan was out when she put them up, he hadn't told her where; he hadn't been happy with the cost of the curtains, so she was relieved to be on her own doing it. And Emme had followed her from room to room, handing up the little plastic hooks and rings, gazing, nodding her approval.

She had asked Emme that first morning if she remembered a bad dream and Emme had at first looked quite perfectly blank, but then she turned and ran silently away, up the stairs. When Fran caught up with her she was on her knees, looking under the bed. Fran had knelt beside her, but there was only dust under there, and Emme's face beside hers, tilted down with tumbled hair, had looked perplexed, then tearful. 'Dreams aren't real,' Fran had told her, pulling her on to her knee.

'I don't like it here,' Emme had said.

That first week before the curtains arrived, Fran had moved through the house with determination, sweeping and hoovering and putting stuff away while Nathan hummed and whistled, coming in and out, jumping in the car on mysterious errands.

'Where is it this time?' she said, trying to sound cheerful about it when he got up from the breakfast table for the third morning in a row, putting on his good jacket and reaching for his briefcase. 'Appointment with an architectural practice in Chatteris,' he said promptly. 'Shouldn't be more than a couple of hours. Though I might stop in at Homebase on the way back. Anything you want?'

She couldn't find a reason to complain, or at least not without sounding as if she was nagging: he would even call in at the supermarket for her, without asking, bringing home cardboard boxes full of dried goods, beans and pasta, canned tomatoes, as if the end of the world was approaching, as if they were stocking a bunker.

'I don't mind doing the supermarket shop, actually,' she said to him after a week or so, itching to get out. 'I'd quite like the change.'

He had raised his eyebrows. 'Didn't have you down as a Stepford wife,' he said, indulgent. 'Sure. Sure.' But they only had one car, and he did seem to need it most days, taking it upon himself now to tell her why – setting up contacts or visiting premises, a drink with Rob in Oakenham – so not much changed, in the end. And when she did find herself in the supermarket with Emme she only felt slightly hysterical and slightly foolish at having made the fuss.

Home alone, she moved through the rooms, trying to get to grips with the farmer's DIY, flimsy boarded up corners and disconcerting plywood cupboards jammed in, painted orange. Prising one open beside a fireplace in the room she had decided would have to be the guest room (a big one opposite theirs, looking out over the road with a long sash window and panelled shutters painted shut), she found a figurine on its side, made of painted china, a shepherdess with a crook. It might have been one of those things old ladies have on their mantelpiece only the shepherdess had big breasts, she leaned forward provocatively and one hand was on an exposed nipple. Fran had dropped it quickly into the black refuse sack she'd brought upstairs. At the end of the day with Emme asleep and supper laid, Nathan at the table and in a good mood she went and got the bag, thinking it would make him laugh, or something.

Even as she got it out, seeing the leery tackiness of it she thought, no, actually maybe not, a prickle at the back of her neck but it was too late by then. He set down his knife and fork, and grunted. 'Nice,' he said, cold.

She had stuffed it back inside, hot with shame. He thought it was some kind of come-on. Hauled it all the way out to the wheelie bin in the yard before coming to sit back down, cheeks burning. Nathan was eating again, as if nothing had happened.

Finding himself some office space put Nathan in a good mood. 'It's on a new development,' he said, jubilant, arm on the dusty mantelpiece like a lord of the manor. Emme had gazed up at him, mute, waiting for him to praise the work they'd done all day (just as Fran was waiting for him to find fault). 'Nice and compact, just room for me, maybe a secretary if things take off.'

'I could do that,' she'd offered quickly, and he'd looked at her, thoughtful.

'Really?' he said, lightly, dubious. 'I mean, sure. Once Emme's settled, maybe. I thought you might want to work from home.' She had been taken aback that he had made assumptions, had formed plans he hadn't talked to her about.

After that he was out of the house more or less every day – *I'm paying for the office, after all* – climbing cheerfully into the car, home again at five thirty, smelling of handwash and new carpets where Fran could only detect mildew and bleach on herself.

She'd been pondering her options when Nathan had said to her one evening, 'Oakenham's nice, actually.' Giving her a sidelong glance and she realised, to her shame, that she'd almost been waiting for his permission. It wasn't as if he wanted to keep her at home, was it? 'Emme'd like it. Feed the ducks, there's swings, all new, not the lethal old stuff we played on, and there's a good butcher. Some great old houses.'

Something about the way he said it prompted her. 'Is that where it was? You told me. A house by the river, the summer. That summer, when you squatted.'

He'd cleared his throat. 'Did I tell you about that?' he said. 'Yes, that was Oakenham.'

She'd wanted one of those bicycles with a kind of frontcar arrangement, the thought of that, jumping on the bike and heading off with Emme seemed to her a brilliant solution. Nathan frowned, though, and told her they were dangerous. She thought, rebellious, she might put money by and buy one anyway, but when it came to getting the growing pile of cash out and spending it she always chickened out. Something about the thought of Nathan's face darkening when he saw it.

There were buses to Oakenham, it turned out, and she'd gone partly out of curiosity about what he'd told her, his last summer at home. There were some old houses, crumbling red brick, backing on to the river, willows and boathouses. There was a baker's with shelves in the window, a good butcher's with a queue out into the street some days. To her surprise after three or four visits they called her by her name, there. Jo would have laughed. She was going to have to stop referring her life to Jo for inspection, Fran realised. Jo wasn't there any more.

It hit her with a sickening thump every time her mind returned to it, that hole in her life where once there'd been

Jo, there'd been friendship, someone to talk to. Someone to ask, is this normal? To laugh the horrible stuff off with, the weariness, the guilt when she snapped at Emme, when she felt trapped even though she was out here with people who loved her, even though she had it all. To tell Ben was on the way. She woke early, again and again, trying to work out what it was that had got between her and Jo, she lay there, trying not to panic, until one morning Nathan had turned over and made a sound in his throat, of irritation. Fran trained herself to lie very still after that, however early it was, however sure she was he was asleep.

He hadn't mentioned getting a secretary again, and then she had other things to think about. Then she was pregnant with Ben.

It had taken her by surprise: she'd more or less stopped thinking about sex, and why they weren't having it. But then one warm evening at the end of their first summer out there in the sticks, he got home after a trip to London to see Julian Napier about a project, full of beans about something, energetic and cheerful and talking on and on, about the traffic, the weather, Julian had taken him up the Shard for their meeting. 'The *view*,' he said, throwing out his arm to sweep an invisible horizon, triumphant. 'On a day like this.'

It had been hot that day even out in the fen, a warm ripe smell coming off the fields and a heat haze as she and Emme had walked back from the shop in the next village, a shimmer rising from the straight road. There had been cut golden stubble on one side and black earth on the other, the hedges dark. As the farmhouse came back into view for a moment the chicken barn disappeared behind it, the nearest bungalow fell away and all she could see was the house's tall handsome outline and the long grass of their field bleached pale and soft behind it, rippling as far as the poplars. She'd felt Emme's hot hand in hers, and looking down at the neat parting, the patient set of her small shoulders, she'd thought, Well. People have it worse than this, people a century ago lived like this.

So when Nathan came home happy, too, it just seemed to fit, with the day: she didn't want to look at it too hard. She'd made supper and his hand had been on hers every time she laid down her knife. Then when she got up to load the dishwasher he'd been behind her, his hands light on her hips. In fact, for a moment she *had* hesitated – thinking, Hold on. Hold on. After all this time? – but she hadn't quite dared to say it. Sod it, she'd thought, why not? Why not? And when it turned out to be a one-off, well, she was too busy throwing up to start on rehearsing those conversations, again.

She didn't know if Ben had been part of the plan, but it wasn't like Nathan was a man who rolled over and touched her out of habit, or need, and if she knew nothing else about him, she knew he always had a plan.

So soon enough she was taking the bus in to Oakenham with a growing belly, she couldn't have ridden a bike if she'd wanted to. And one warm afternoon, sitting beside the buggy on a bench by the river, Emme asleep in it, her shopping in its knotted bags hanging from the handles, Fran had closed her eyes in the sun, had told herself, it was all right. It was all suspended, while Emme slept. Then she opened her eyes and there was a man on the bridge standing there, looking at her, and time started again.

103

Fran did think sometimes, almost with a start, of the Nathan who had walked into Jo's front room, scraped and battered like a teenager from the scooter accident, because he hadn't left London with them, he wasn't the man she lived with now, the man who watched her, frowning, who lay beside her sleeping as still and separate as a statue. Sometimes she wondered who that Nathan had been, and where he'd gone. It was almost as if she'd dreamed him, and now she'd woken up to find he'd never really been there at all.

Chapter Ten

Something woke her in the chilly thin light of early afternoon, and she jerked upright, disorientated. She was fully dressed on top of the bed, Ben beside her in his sleepsuit, and when Fran saw him, it all came rushing back, a tidal wave.

Not even a day had passed, not even another night. She still had that to come.

She swivelled on the bed in search of the radio alarm clock: four thirty-two. Her stomach growled, hollow, but she felt sick. They'd left less than an hour before, going for the panic button.

'We'll be back,' Gerard had said, his hand on her elbow, warm and heavy. 'Don't worry.'

She'd lain beside Ben on the bed as he wriggled, suddenly overcome with the need for sleep: he must have dropped off beside her, mercifully. They'd have gone back to the police station for other reasons, too, wouldn't they? They'd be talking about her, about what she'd said, they'd be adding things up.

'Ed'll have another word at the pub,' Gerard had said as they climbed into the car. 'Someone will have seen something. We'll get him, Fran.' A reassuring smile, a direct look, into her eyes: she wanted to believe him. She wanted to trust them. On the bed with her eyes closed she had repeated it, a mantra. We'll get him.

What had woken her? In her chest her heart had gone straight from sleep to panic, hammering. Her legs felt heavy, her arms weighed down but she made herself go to the front window to look, standing off to one side, in case. Nothing. No one.

She came down slowly, she could feel the fear in the roots of her hair. Out through the kitchen in a daze, unbolt the door and then stand there, on the doorstep, holding her breath. Thinking, Foxes, broad daylight, looking round her cluttered yard as if she'd never seen it before. The row of wheelie bins, the uneven slates on the shed roof, the broken guttering. The gravel. Then she turned again, to look at the kitchen window, fearful, not wanting to see that tiny nick again, looking anywhere but at the glass.

On the window sill Emme's treasures: an oyster shell she had unearthed somewhere, miles from the sea; a miniature watering can Fran had given her for her birthday. The watering can was on its side — somewhere in Fran's head a tiny alarm set up, she felt her heart pick up speed. There was the long rectangular terracotta pot they'd planted up with hyacinth bulbs, back in their old life, months back before Christmas. The green tips had just started showing, last week? The week before? A lifetime ago. Fran stopped. She stopped breathing.

Where were they? The tips. She could see only earth, nothing green. As if the world had gone into reverse, as if all around her things had stopped living, growing.

And then her hands were in the wide pot, scrabbling, unearthing one bulb after another topsy-turvy in the soil, unable to make sense of why, who . . . until it came into her hand, as if meant to be there. The black handle of a knife.

She could hear them talking outside in the yard. They had been on their way over with the panic button anyway, Gerard said, when the car pulled up outside less than ten minutes after she called. They'd found her there, in the middle of the kitchen with her back to the window, dirt under her fingernails, trying to stop the trembling.

The forensics guys took longer to arrive, but they were there now, and when she saw the white suits out there beyond the glass it was as if it was starting all over again.

'She found it,' Gerard was saying. Standing at the door she could hear him, the voice he used for other men, dry, sceptical. 'At first she said she didn't recognise it. Never seen it before.'

How was she to know? A knife covered in blood and soil? How could that be anything to do with her? How could it be the same knife that lived, blade-tip down for safety, in the jar of kitchen implements beside the sink? Only when Gerard had asked again, had insisted, had she looked. Only then had she seen it was not there, and she'd heard a sound come out of her own throat that she didn't recognise, a sound so hysterical she had to put her hands over her mouth to shut herself up.

She heard footsteps. When Gerard came back in she was sitting back down at the table in front of the mug of tea they'd made her.

'It's going off for analysis,' said Gerard, pulling the chair out beside her. 'It's all right, Fran.' As if she was a child. 'It's all right.' It wasn't. It wasn't all right.

Carswell came in, breezy. 'All right if I set this up now?' he said, prising at the box they'd brought with them. Panic button. The thing he took out looked cheap, a black plastic box with two buttons, one red, one black.

'Nathan must have heard something outside,' she said slowly. Her brain felt like a swamp, things stirring, surfacing. 'Don't you think? He must have grabbed the knife, maybe he heard something . . .' She stopped, and then her head was in her hands, just to stop them looking at her, Carswell curious, Gerard's smile set to compassion but something else behind it.

'We're hoping the forensic analysis will give us some leads, there,' said Gerard, reassuring, his hand hovering over her shoulder. 'It's good you hardly touched it. Finding the murder weapon's a big step forward.' He glanced sideways at Carswell, then back. 'Really, a big step.' He cleared his throat. 'You going to show her how it works?'

She had had to get out: her cue was the white-suited forensics officer sticking his head round the kitchen door to say they were off. Gerard had followed her outside, beyond the shed, looking through the chicken barn. She wanted him to go away.

They'd stood either side of her, Carswell showing her how the gadget set and reset; Gerard had been giving her the rundown, earnest, absolutely intent on her. Because they hadn't just been coming over to show her the panic button.

Gerard had waited till she stepped away from Carswell: it was just a button and another one to reset it, he only had to show her twice. 'We've been to your husband's office, Fran,' he said, and when she turned quickly she saw him watching her for a reaction.

'There are officers working round the clock.' Gerard's eyes following her face. 'We're looking at everything we can think of. Who might have seen him at the pub: the landlady's on her way back from the cash and carry now, we're going there straight after this. Your husband's friends, this Robert Webster, who he's caught up with since he got back, his exact movements last night. There's CCTV we're examining on a couple of junctions.' A pause. 'His business dealings.'

Then Gerard had stepped closer to her, taking his voice down a notch and Carswell had turned away, fiddling with his gadget still. 'I know you're still in a state of . . . shock, and finding the weapon must have been very traumatic. But . . .' and he let out a weary sigh, 'Mrs Hall. Fran. I'm finding it frustrating, how little you feel able to tell us. It's as if you've been sitting at home with your fingers in your ears and a blindfold on.' The picture was so vivid she felt panic rise inside her, and she'd blundered past him to the door, needing air. He'd followed her out into the yard, she felt like flailing him away from her.

He'd walked patiently behind her as she set off blindly

away from the house, catching up with her at the barn. 'His office,' he repeated now. 'You're seriously telling me you never went there?' It sounded like an accusation.

The sky was low and leaden and the wind had moved round, coming from the north. Direct from Siberia: it was relentless. At the back of her brain panic ticked: he brought the knife with him. Right up to the house. He buried it there.

'He didn't . . . we didn't . . .' She took a breath, swallowed. 'I knew where it was. The Sandpiper.'

'He'd been there, how long?' A note of impatience had crept into Gerard's voice.

'Almost a year.' Did she need to go through it all, her offering to be Nathan's secretary, the subject just getting dropped, all that? 'He's a project manager, he wouldn't be there half the time. I didn't go and see him for the same reason I didn't go into his study. He liked to keep work and home separate.'

Suddenly Fran wished she'd asked the FLO to come over, she should have insisted. The woman. Ali Compton.

'Does your wife come and bring you lunch then?' she said, then wished she hadn't, felt anger rise. 'And what about those tights? The pair of tights.'

'If I had a wife,' said Gerard, and he studied her. 'I've put the tights in for analysis but you know . . .' He exhaled impatiently. 'This is the country. You find all sorts, in ditches, fields, lay-bys. Lads.'

Lay-bys. Fran remembered a news story, from a few months after they moved, the early autumn and the half-burned body of a woman had been found in a lay-by off the motorway – the same road you could hear if you stepped out beyond the barn. She'd pointed to the picture in the paper when – finally, about ten at night – Nathan had come in, pale, tired-looking, from the terraced houses that had turned into a nightmare, he said, something to do with listed building consent.

She wasn't sure where the houses he'd been working on were. The first time she'd asked she thought he'd said Oakenham, but she must have got it wrong because he said the motorway had been stationary on the way home and Oakenham was nowhere near the motorway.

'Drugs,' was all he'd said, then turned away.

Fran had felt a small shock at the coldness in his voice, as if it was directed at her. 'How do you know?'

I've never done drugs, she wanted to say, indignant, and although that was in a way misleading, given the life she'd had with Nick, it was also true, not her thing, plus her mother had been there, done that, sitting on the Indian throw over the collapsing sofa, ash from an untidy joint dusting her cardigan.

Nathan shrugged, his back to her. 'Isn't it all down to drugs, these days?' but he only sounded non-committal now and she wondered if she'd imagined it. That he was reproaching her for her former life, or was it something else, some old bitterness, something she didn't know about? Someone else? He'd never talked about previous girlfriends. But when he turned round again he had been smiling and offering her tea.

Now it was Gerard with his back to her, as if he had stopped listening. He was looking at a battered little car moving beyond the barn, beyond the field; he raised a hand to his eyes.

The car was heading for the village, and they both turned back towards the house, as if it might be coming there. It went out of sight and there was Carswell at the back door, waving.

'Kid's awake,' he called. 'Upstairs.'

Fran ran. She was on the landing with Ben, red-faced and thrashing in her arms, when she heard the car pulling up outside and she froze. 'Could be Ali,' she heard muttered from the kitchen and she started down the stairs, her heart suddenly lifting at the thought of Ali Compton.

But it was Karen. At the foot of the stairs Fran saw her big frame in the doorway to the yard, bundled in a big coat with purple fur at the collar. Wellies with flowers on them, and Emme and Harry behind her. Fran got up, marvelling that her brain had hidden Emme away, protecting her. Then feeling the dangerous rush, love didn't seem enough of a word for it as Emme looked up, the careful guarded look, the neat fringe. Then she and Harry barrelled past and into the room, not looking at the two men stationed one at the cooker, the other at the sink, and they were pounding upstairs.

'All right?' said Karen, looking only at Fran.

And Fran felt something ease inside her, at the sound of her reedy insistent voice. Four months in that school playground, the little windswept huddles of mothers with their backs turned to her, like a punishment, and Karen the only other outsider.

'The knife,' she said. 'We . . . they . . . I found a knife. They think it's the . . . weapon.'

Karen paled, visibly. She put out a hand to Fran's wrist. 'Where was it?' Fran just shook her head. 'You look knackered,' said Karen.

'How's Emme been?' Fran looked at the clock. It was almost six.

'Fine,' said Karen, and she pushed her way inside in a gust of perfumed fur. 'She's been fine. I think . . .' Shifting a bit so her back was to both the men. 'She knows something's going on. Of course.' She was almost as tall as the men, and the metallic blue eyeliner glittered under the lights. Her eyes swept over them, and she reached for the kettle. 'I think she doesn't want to be told, not yet. I think you want to give her space.'

Fran looked up at the ceiling: there were small muffled sounds, where they were playing. 'I'm not going to tell her before bed. It has to be right. It has to be the right time.' She doesn't need to know about the knife, out there among her treasures. Never.

'Ali'll have some input on that,' said Gerard. 'She's got a lot of experience. Put you in touch with child bereavement experts.'

'My dad was a policeman,' Karen said as if he hadn't spoken, her back still to the two policeman as she stood at the sink. She leaned to turn on the tap and went on, frowning, 'He left us years back, I was only a scrap.' It was hard to imagine Karen a scrap. 'Died of drink and diabetes before he got to sixty.' Her mouth set in a tidy line. 'Now Mum's doing the internet dating, new hair, new life, happy as Larry.' She set the kettle down and clicked it on. When they turned back into the room, DS Gerard was in the doorway and Carswell, his face pale in the low grey light, was already outside.

'We'll leave you to it for the moment, then,' said Gerard, looking at Karen, expressionless. 'But we'll be back before you know it.' It sounded like a warning. 'If you wouldn't mind just leaving things as they are, for the moment? The study.' He smiled, courteous. Karen was watching him levelly, but their eyes didn't meet. 'Don't touch anything,' said Gerard. 'Is what I mean.'

'Can't stand them,' said Karen, not bothering to wait till the door closed.

'I'm sure they didn't guess.'

Karen suppressed a smile, looking round the room. 'Whyn't you go and sit next door?' she said. 'I'll bring us some tea. You have got a next door, haven't you? Place this size?' Fran got up, Ben asleep and heavy as a sandbag against her shoulder.

The sitting room was cold. Carefully she put Ben down on the sofa. It was days since she'd been in here. The ceiling was low, but when the fire was lit it was snug. She could hear Karen clattering in the kitchen, opening drawers, and she knelt to lay the fire. There was a neat stack of kindling: Nathan liked cutting it, and there as she bent over in the dark fireplace with Nathan in front of her, all around her, Nathan's voice in her head, it crept in. The unanswered question, *What if*.

What if someone had been in the house? Not just the man in the field, waiting, not just in the yard. If he'd already been in, below her as she slept, moving through the house.

The two men had been talking in low voices as she came down the stairs with Ben. Something had changed, it had been there in their tone, what did they know? If Nathan hadn't taken the knife out with him, then someone had been in to get it.

114

She could ask them when they got back: she could ask Ali Compton. That was what an FLO was for, wasn't it? To tell her what the hell was going on.

Numbly she set a match to the kindling, she sat back, she found herself brushing at herself, her front, her sleeves, as if there was something stuck there, clinging to her.

The logs were dry, and by the time Karen came in the fire had taken.

She'd found a tray, laid it with a clean tea towel, a jug of milk, two mugs. One of them had the name of a flooring company on it, another one of Nathan's freebies.

Karen sat beside Ben on the sofa: he stirred. Carefully Fran picked him up and settled him back on her knee on the armchair by the fire.

'Harry's dad used to hit me,' said Karen, lifting the mug to her mouth. She was almost talking to herself, it seemed. Startled, Fran kept silent. 'Well, I say used to, he did it the twice. Should've gone after the once, well, yeah.' Her eyes settled on Fran, flat. 'I took it all the way to court, baby under my arm, Mum in the gallery. He got a two-year suspended sentence.'

'Nathan never . . .' began Fran. 'That's not . . .' but Karen was shaking her head.

'All I mean is.' She sipped the tea warily, even though she'd made it herself. 'God almighty, I don't know what I mean. There's things you have to just . . . get sorted. You can do it, with or without. Maybe that's what I mean. With or without the man.' She was frowning. 'And don't take any rubbish from them.' Karen jerked her head back towards the road, the policemen's departing car. 'Those men. Big kids.' She was showing Fran the future: *On your guard*, she

115

was saying. *Don't trust anyone*, she was saying. She seemed to know what she was talking about.

'Christ, though,' she went on, setting the mug down so abruptly it spilled. 'So. You found him? Went out there and . . . what? Middle of the bloody night and you're out in the fen?'

Did they think it was her? Took the knife from her own kitchen? Buried it, pretended to find it?

Upstairs there was a rush of small feet, along the corridor, breathless chatter, then back again and a door closed, softly.

Fran didn't quite trust the relief she felt then, of having someone there to talk to. Someone who wasn't a police officer. 'Well, I woke up and he was gone.' She found herself telling Karen only what she'd told the police, after all. *I was asleep, he came in.* Karen sat back in the chair, hands around the mug, and nodded but Fran could see, at a certain point, a certain flatness to her expression that Karen knew, this wasn't all of it.

As Fran skirted them, though, the facts – if they were facts, was a dream a fact? – stood their ground. The dream of another man standing close to her, the feel of his fingers through the fabric. Then the sex. She had to clear her throat mid-sentence at the memory, what she was saying was something like, *All I know is I'd been asleep at least an hour* but what she remembered was his hand on her waist from behind, just where it met the hip bone, the cold as he pushed the fabric up to expose her. His erection, pressing into her.

She held the mug tight, kept talking. When she'd finished – *I don't know how long it took for the ambulance to arrive, it seemed a long time* – Karen waited a moment or two as if

116

there must be more, then set her mug on the tray, leaning forward with both elbows on her knees.

'So he never hit you or nothing?' Fran was stunned. She felt Karen searching her face, unafraid. Was that what she thought? 'Because I could've killed Danny, when he smacked me that time,' and Karen's head moved sideways just a fraction at the memory, as if in recoil. 'Harry was in his car seat and he woke up with the noise. I could've just, if I'd had something in my hand, a knife, anything, I could've. Done it. No problem.' She sat back again.

Fran could barely form the words. 'No, never,' she said, stiff with shame. 'He never hit me.'

Other things, though: it came to her like a revelation. There had been times when a particular expression came over his face, saying no to something she suggested, or when he turned away from her in bed, when he simply failed to answer, when she had felt, How do I get out of this? If I wanted to get away, how would I even do it? *I could have killed him.* It was just something women said, wasn't it?

Was that what the police thought? 'Nathan wasn't that kind of bloke. He wasn't violent.' She hesitated. 'Not with me, not with the kids, no sign of it, ever. Never angry.'

Fran moved away from the thought of Nathan angry. 'He was dead when I found him. There was a lot of blood.' She swallowed, remembering how it had felt sticky, her hand under the kitchen tap as she waited. Blood on the telephone handset. *The knife.* 'He was very cold.'

Karen nodded. 'You told me he was from around here,' she said. 'First conversation we had, you told me, months back.'

117

Had she? She didn't remember.

'Had he been back in touch, like with mates? I mean, that can be trouble. Place like this, bloke like him, buys a nice big house, wife and kids, he's got it all.' She fumbled in her bag, taking out a pack of cigarettes then putting it away again. 'Comes back lording it, that's how some of them will see it.'

Fran did remember, then. Early days, Emme's term had just begun. Karen had been leaning in over the wrong side of the school fence and puffing on a Silk Cut, she had pink tips to her hair then. Leaves had been blowing around the playground in eddies. 'You come from London?' Karen had said to her, incredulous. 'To a dump like this? What d'you do that for?' And Fran had given her the story. Nostalgia, swimming in the river, feeding the ducks.

Karen had tilted her head and was eyeing her. 'Things aren't always how you left 'em, that's all. People.' She rolled her eyes towards the door. 'So has he picked up again with anyone?'

'I know Rob. No one else. And Rob's not . . . he's . . . a sweetheart.' She went on. 'They'd kept in touch, all this time.' Karen barely nodded. 'He was Nathan's best man.'

She remembered a blur of suits and pastel dresses at their wedding, a bobbing feather in a hat. Rob had been staring at her and she had looked down and seen a button come undone on her shirt, which had been par for the course. Who else had been there? Who would she have to tell?

'Look,' she said stiffly. 'I'm sorry, I've got to, got to, I think I need to get some sleep now.' As she stood she saw something, down the side of the armchair. No wonder she hadn't been able to hear it: her mobile. No more Nathan to frown at her when she typed a message, or read one. Both hands full, she left it there. How long since she'd looked at it? A day.

Karen was already on her feet, not needing to be told twice, her face closed. 'Harry?' she shouted up the stairs, and there they were instantly, clattering down together, Emme peeping around from behind Harry when they got to the bottom.

It was bitterly cold on the doorstep. Karen looked up at the blue-grey cloud and said, 'Snow, I heard, Sunday, to cap it all. Wouldn't be surprised.' She pulled the big coat tighter round her, her sharp red nose buried in the fur. 'God almighty, that's all we need.'

'Thanks,' she said quickly, and before she could stop herself she had Karen in an awkward half-hug, Ben briefly crushed between them, before she let go again almost instantly.

'You get some sleep,' said Karen, raising her eyebrows. 'You and Emme both. And with a sharp tug on Harry's hand she was round the corner and gone, before she could soften.

Upstairs Fran laid Ben down, still swaddled, his small dark face was set in a frown. He looked like Nathan. Emme had followed her up and stood there beside her with her hands on the cot's bars, obediently silent.

As Fran straightened from the cot she hardly recognised her own smell: sweat and stress and twenty-four hours of weirdness and strangers in her house. When had she last washed? A bath before going to bed last night, it felt like days ago. She found herself wondering, would the police

119

even allow her to shower? What if . . . *Don't be stupid*. If they wanted evidence off her they would have asked by now.

Emme yawned. Fran stroked her small face, tucking a strand of hair behind her ear and Emme looked back up at her. A smudge of pizza on her chin, her school sweatshirt needed a wash. 'Bath time,' she said.

With Emme in her room having closed the door carefully on Fran to hide from her some mysterious project she and Harry had begun, Fran went into the bedroom, a tangle of dirty clothes in her arms.

It was this room that had sold the house to her: high-ceilinged, flooded with pale north light, she could remember walking into it with Nathan and stopping to look. The two long sash windows were set in alcoves with panelled shutters, although – she had soon found out – they were thick with layers of ancient paint and wouldn't budge. Layers of wallpaper, faded pink, yellow garlands. The glass was thick and wavy with age, and if you stood at the right angle you could see the line of poplars, that had been in full leaf when they'd bought the place, the fields had been green and you could imagine, whoever this house had been built for two, three hundred years back, standing looking out to the horizon.

If you stood in the wrong place all you could see was the chicken barn. Nathan had turned vague whenever she asked about getting it taken down; first vague, then irritable. And so it stood there, a black silhouette in the darkening field, and Fran thought, that pig farmer will know someone to take it down. She wanted it gone.

The bed was unmade still. She didn't even need to think

when she'd last changed the sheets because it was always Saturday morning, two days ago. They looked grey, from where she stood.

Kneeling on the edge of the mattress Fran leaned across it, she put her face down on the sheets to breathe him in, the last of him, sooner or later all those microscopic traces of them, him and her together, would be gone, because that was what happened, you couldn't slow it down. Like her own body though, it smelled strange, alien. And then before she could stop herself she was half across the bed, and tearing at it. In less than a minute it was all in a heap on the floor, sheets, pillowcases, duvet cover, the lot.

Marching the heap downstairs Fran stuffed it all into the washing machine, ninety degrees, pre-wash, leave nothing to chance. She made it again swiftly, so as not to think about what she was doing, the smell of clean sheets, that was all she wanted. This was her home.

She was in the shower when the police came back.

Emme was still behind the closed door of her room as she came out on the landing, Fran could hear her in there, talking in her version of a teacher's voice to someone imagined or a stuffed toy, perched on the bed.

It had been when she turned from the door that she heard their voices in the kitchen, and within minutes she was dressed. At the bottom of the stairs she looked into the kitchen, nodded and went calmly into the sitting room. It was still there, her phone down the side of the armchair. The battery was completely dead. She pocketed it and then walked back into the kitchen. She felt clean, at last.

Gerard had said, don't touch anything: had that included showering? Tracking down her own phone? He'd meant

121

Nathan's study, and obediently she hadn't even opened the door. Now she wished she had.

The neck of her sweatshirt was damp, her hair twisted up but still wet. Doug Gerard examined her. He was good-looking, she found herself thinking with a shock. His eyes were grey. 'Hey, Mrs Hall,' said Carswell, giving her his best eager smile. Gerard looked impatient, just at the sound of Carswell's voice. She wondered how long they'd worked together, how they got on, outside work.

'Did you talk to the landlady?' she said, breathless, and saw them exchange glances.

'Yes,' said Gerard, slowly. 'I think we need to go over that with you.'

'Who was he with?' she said, folding her arms across herself stubbornly. 'Have you got any names?'

'It's . . . it looks a bit more complicated than that.' Gerard frowned. 'Mind if we have another look in that study, if that's all right with you?'

She didn't move. 'Fine,' she said, and they wandered off together, closing the door into the study behind them.

She had hardly started on the washing up when they were back, Gerard first through the door and frowning.

'Where did you say *your* computer was then?' he said, casual, and she shifted on her feet.

'It's being fixed,' she said, alarm bells going off, why was he asking? 'You want it? Nathan took it in months ago, he took it to that place in Oakenham . . .'

Something had got spilled on the keyboard, though she didn't remember doing it. Fran had used to keep it on a table in the bedroom and one morning she'd sat down on it to check her emails and found the keys sticky, then it wouldn't turn on. 'I'll take it in,' Nathan had said, then, 'Yeah, I'll pick it up next time I'm over that way,' then, 'Guy says he's still working on it.' She'd mentioned getting a new one but he'd turned away, clearing his throat. 'Maybe when the work starts coming in. And there's data.' Frowning. 'On kids' exposure to computers at home. All sorts. No harm in keeping them away from keyboards as long as possible, hey?' And he'd smiled, that brilliant smile that changed everything.

She shook her head. 'I can use my phone for most of it.'

Though that was less and less, under Nathan's gaze. 'What are you doing?' he'd ask, sharply. 'Who's that?' Plus she hardly got emails any more except from marketing companies, catalogues, the occasional bright round robin from Carine or someone who didn't matter. Jo's replies to any enquiry had got sporadic and dispiritingly brief, Fran had given up. Before the laptop gave up the ghost, she had had a guilty, painful habit of trawling back down through the inbox for old correspondence with Jo, when emails had run to pages, filled with exclamation marks, pictures and links attached. In some ways it had been a relief not to be able to do that.

'It's nice not to depend on the internet,' she said, dully. Spouting Nathan.

Gerard turned to look at her and she shrugged under his gaze, uncomfortable as she felt the past five years lapping up against her. 'You must have used his now and again?' Gerard said, and she stared at him, as if he should have known how that would have gone down with Nathan. 'Did you not even go into his study? Poke around, just natural curiosity?'

'He was . . . he liked things like he'd left them,' she said, and Gerard chewed his lip.

'Fussy, was he? But still. Check his pockets now and again? Wives generally like to keep tabs.' There was sourness in the look he gave Carswell, before he turned back to look at her and pulled out a chair.

'Tell us about your husband's friends, for example,' he said, and she stared.

'I told you about Rob,' she said.

'The others, though,' he said and she began to explain, 'He wasn't that sort of—' but the policeman interrupted her, leaning forward on the table, looking earnestly into her face. 'I mean, when he went to the pub. You said he went a couple of times a week.' He sat back. 'He must have mentioned someone?'

'There must have been others from way back, but I got the impression they'd all moved on,' she said, desperate. Thinking. 'There was this summer they all lived together. Squatted.'

'Summer? Who lived together?' said Gerard quickly, leaning forward.

'Just lads. I don't know. Their last summer before they all went their separate ways. Rob would know. There was someone – he said he'd heard he was still around, he said he might look him up. Something . . . did something in the trade, building trade.' She put her face in her hands. 'I'm sure I can remember if I just . . .'

'All right,' said Gerard, soothing again. 'All right, yes. It'll come to you. If it comes to you.' And in that moment his manner grated on her, she wasn't a child. She wanted to shake it off.

124

'It's the pub, you see,' said Gerard.

'You said it was complicated,' she said, scenting something.

Behind him Carswell had been making tea and now he came around and set the mugs down in front of them before pulling out a chair on the other side of Fran. She looked from one of them to the other and for a second she had a mad impulse to stand up and shout and scream. *This is my kitchen. I want my life back.*

'It's just, y'know,' said Carswell conversationally, 'she says he wasn't in that night at all. The landlady says. In fact,' and he turned the mug on the table in front of him, tilting his head to examine the logo on it, 'she said he isn't a regular, like. Seen him maybe a handful of times since you moved in?'

'Do you think I'm lying?' The words came out before she could stop them. Gerard's eyes narrowed. 'He went out a couple of times a week,' she said, stiffly. 'Thursdays and Sundays, usually. He said he was going to the Queen's Head.'

Gerard's face invited the thought. *So if you're not lying, he was.*

But what he said was, 'And he'd usually come in, what sort of time?'

'I told you. Not late. Around closing time, eleven, that sort of time.'

It was unreal, she had to stop it. She felt if she stood her head would hit the ceiling, things would go flying.

Gerard didn't move, sitting back in his chair relaxed, contemplating the room, the sink, the stove, the row of mugs. 'But this time it was later,' he said, nodding thoughtfully. 'Just trying, you know. To get the story straight, in my own mind.'

'It's not a story.'

'You know what I mean,' said Gerard, easily. She saw his gaze settle, and looked where he was looking.

She gestured with her free hand, Ben's head asleep on her other forearm. 'What's that?' she said, and he got to his feet, crossed the room and brought a bag across.

He pushed it towards her but she shook her head and peering inside he slid out a flat square box of expensive chocolates. 'Huh,' he said, surprised. Fran recognised the packaging, the French name on the box because she'd buy them for herself once in a while, way back when. In another life, in London. It was a small box, modest, but thirty quid's worth of chocolate. Nathan.

Fran felt sick. 'I don't know where they came from,' she said, and she could hear the edge of hysteria in her voice. 'Has someone come round? Has someone been here? I don't know.'

Carswell gaped.

'Take them away,' she said. 'Please. I don't want chocolates.'

Gerard stood up and handed the box to Carswell, who made to hide it behind his back and said, 'Nice one, boss. You shouldn't have.' They were watching her. She felt their eyes unpicking her reaction.

She held herself very steady. 'I need to call his family now,' she said. Then, feeling their hostility like a wall, 'If you don't mind.'

They stood aside.

Chapter Eleven

His family.

From the beginning Nathan had been . . . not evasive exactly, more, impatient; more, dismissive.

'My dad's . . . well,' he had said abruptly, one evening, Fran five months pregnant and suddenly looking it, and they'd been talking about getting stuff, laughing on the sofa about whether he could put a cot together. 'You get to a point, don't you, when you see what they're like. Really like.' Warily Fran had nodded, because she did know, because she'd got to that point fairly early, with her mother. Her dreamy mother, who would rather have been a sister than a parent.

Nathan's mother was in institutional care: she'd been bedridden for more than two years, unable to feed herself for five. He went there to see her three or four times a year, he said. Thinking of her own mother Fran had asked if she could come with him but he had been categorical.

'They say she's losing the ability to swallow,' he had said, coming back the last time. So there was only really his father.

'A miserable bastard, is what he is,' Nathan had said, and she remembered him getting up, then pacing, sitting down again. And when eventually Nathan took Fran up there, at her insistence, she saw that a miserable bastard was exactly what he was, now at least. John Hall lived in sheltered housing in a village near where he'd been born on the north-eastern coastline, near somewhere called Alnwick. It was high and blowy but beautiful, and the one-bedroom bungalow was comfortable, but he grumbled about it. Staring in disgusted disbelief at the handrails, elbowing Nathan out of the way with silent hostility when he tried to wash up.

'Told you,' said Nathan, climbing cheerfully behind the wheel for the long journey back. And when they told him they were getting married and he announced he couldn't come, not with his hip, he was waiting for the op, she hadn't protested.

She had, though, supposed that Nathan's sister would come: Miranda. Because that was what this was for. Having no family of her own, unless you counted cousins she hadn't seen since she was a toddler (after her mother took her to Greenham Common in a sling and was arrested they had been more or less disowned as an embarrassment). There needed to be someone beyond the two of them, beyond the half-dozen friends. Nathan, though, had just shrugged. 'She's on secondment to the office in Seoul for a month. She can't get leave, she's in the office at six every morning, weekends. It's that kind of job.' She was something in finance, selling emerging markets, whatever that meant.

'Couldn't she . . . They fly round the world all the time, don't they? In that kind of job?' And when he just shrugged, 'I'd just like to meet her,' she said, and had heard herself, plaintive, needy.

'No,' he said, and his voice had been hard for a second, before he softened it. 'I've tried.'

So it had been just the handful of them, the sharp-suited developer trying to pick Carine up on the registry office steps and Rob, shifting to get out of Julian Napier's booming orbit.

This man, said Nathan in the Italian restaurant after, as he settled an arm on Rob's narrow shoulders, *has known me for ever*. Rob had blushed at that, but whenever Fran thought back to that afternoon, Rob was always blushing.

At one point – the table by then a litter of coffee cups and the dregs of crazy drinks – Nathan had got up to go to the bathroom and Jo, whom Fran thought had gone home, had slipped into the seat beside her. 'Seems like a nice guy,' she said, nodding towards Rob. 'Not that I could get more than a couple of words out of him. Kind of a sweetheart, though?'

'Sure,' said Fran, watching him as he fiddled with his phone, shy, anxious. Nathan protected him: she liked that. That was the place Rob had. 'To be honest, I probably know about as much about him as you do. But yes.'

The edge rubbed comfortably off her elegance after the hours at the table, Jo had sighed. 'This is what you want, though,' she said, frowning. 'That's all I care about.'

She'd felt grateful for the concern she heard in Jo's voice. But she hadn't thought, Why is she so worried? At the bar Nathan was smiling, talking to the developer, he'd taken

129

off his tie and looked young. Exhilarated. 'Yes,' said Fran, because in that moment, Emme in her arms and Jo sitting next to her, it was true. Who could tell the future, anyway? Sometimes you just had to jump.

Back in the flat, half out of her uncomfortable dress, Fran had sat with Emme on the sofa, settling her. Nathan was in the bedroom moving around for a bit and soon there was silence, although she heard the ping of his phone once or twice. When finally she pushed the bedroom door open, at close to eleven, he was asleep on the bed, his face turned to the wall. His clothes were folded neatly on the chair, his phone was on the bedside table by his head, its screen face down.

With relief Fran stripped off the dress and stuffed it into the washing basket, although she never wanted to see it again. Her flesh was marked where it had dug in at the waist. Motionless as a log, Nathan let out a snore and then before she could think about what she was doing Fran was padding around to his side of the bed. Picking up his phone.

She looked at the messages. There was one from Julian, the construction bloke. **Nice do. See you Thursday.** She had thought he was in Leeds on Thursday. And the other one was from Miranda.

There was no message thread attached to either. But Miranda's was a response to something. **I don't believe you,** it read. Indignant. **A bit of warning might have been nice. Address? So I can at least send a present?**

'I tried,' he'd said. But he hadn't.

Absently she rubbed the screen to clean it, she could see her fingerprints, then realising what she was doing she

130

set it down in a hurry. Had he even read the messages? If he hadn't, he'd know someone had. That she had.

But when he looked up at her from his cereal the next morning, dressed and neat and shaven with the phone on the table beside him as she wandered in dishevelled with Emme in her arms, he didn't say anything about it.

She opened her mouth to ask, any word from Miranda? But then he'd have known she'd looked at his phone. And besides, maybe there were reasons, maybe she just needed to be patient and he'd tell her why he hadn't wanted his sister at their wedding, why she didn't know where they lived. She didn't want to get up from the breakfast table and challenge him.

To stand up with Emme in her arms and say, you lied.

'Who?' The old voice was suspicious, and hoarse with underuse.

The mobile had taken its time recharging. The message box told her she had four unread messages but she didn't open any of them. Nathan hadn't gone to the pub. Hadn't been going to the pub. All those times he left the house in the evening when she could have done with him there, on the sofa, going up to Emme when she panicked, when she cried. Where had he been going?

She went straight to the address book, not even sure if she had his number but she did.

'Fran,' she said. 'Nathan's . . . wife.' She had not spoken to him since their visit, although she'd sent carefully

131

composed cards, with photographs of the children – his grandchildren. She was in the bedroom. Ben, who'd woken again, his routine all out of whack, as she waited for the mobile to charge, was staring up at her from the bouncer at her feet, then frowning down at a row of plastic elephants strung across it.

She could hear Carswell and Gerard in Nathan's study – they'd put on blue latex gloves. Carswell had snapped his at the wrist, grinning at her behind Gerard's back.

Shit, she thought, the mobile sweaty in her hand, shit, shit, I can't do this.

'Mr Hall, something's happened to Nathan. I'm so sorry. I'm . . .'

Ben went still in the bouncer, looking for the source of alarm.

Family. They'd swabbed her for DNA, they'd taken her fingerprints. She wasn't family.

'Spit it out,' he said, sharply, and for a moment it was as though a different man was speaking, a man used to being in charge. She told him.

There was a long silence when she'd finished, and when he spoke the authority was all gone. 'It was an accident?' He asked that several times.

'We don't know,' was all she could say. 'I don't think so.'

But he didn't seem to process that. 'He was always reckless,' he said, gravelly voiced though Fran couldn't tell if it was due to emotion. He seemed paralysed: if she didn't ask a question he fell silent. 'I thought I should tell Miranda,' she said tentatively. Silence. She tried again. 'Should I tell Miranda?'

'Miranda?' He repeated the name as if she was a stranger.

Below her Ben was frowning with concentration at the elephants, dark-browed. She persevered. Eventually Nathan's father agreed, he'd call Miranda. 'She's very busy, you know,' he said, sounding aggrieved.

She asked him how he was. If he was all right, if they were looking after him in the sheltered housing, but he didn't seem to be listening. 'I won't come down,' he said, although she hadn't asked. 'I'm too old.' Then, 'What about his mother?'

'She won't understand, will she?' said Fran, as gently as she could. 'Perhaps it's better not.' He grunted, which she took as agreement. She told him she'd tell him how things progressed, but he was dismissive, as though it was of no further interest to him.

'I'm tired now,' he snapped, eventually, and then hung up before she could say anything.

She lifted Ben from the bouncer and pressed her face against his temple, breathing in the smell of his warm skin.

She looked at the messages on her phone. One from Karen from yesterday, asking if she was all right. One from the headmistress of the primary school, this morning, asking if Emme was all right. A reminder about a dental appointment. A missed call, from a number the phone didn't recognise. Fran stared at it a moment, then carefully she set the mobile back down on the bedside table to continue charging.

She thought about opening the drawer in the little table but told herself not to: she didn't want to go down there crying, or worse.

They were waiting for her in the kitchen, leaning against the side. There was no sign of the latex gloves.

'All right?' said Gerard. 'You spoke to the father?' She nodded, Ben across her shoulder. She didn't sit down.

'What do you think's happened to his hard drive?' she asked but he just made a dismissive gesture with his hand.

'I'll get to that,' he said.

'It matters to me, if someone came into my house. If someone was in my house.' The thought hammered. While she was upstairs.

'I understand,' he said, and his voice took on that soothing note. It made her angry. 'It's why we've given you the panic button, we've done the print sweep, it's troubling, you're right. It's a vital line of inquiry. But if I'm honest . . .' and he fixed her, making her look at him, his pale eyes, the bit of stubble on his chin, 'it's confusing. We don't know when the hard drive went. It's not something a burglar takes.' A glance up at Carswell. 'He could have removed it himself.'

'Why would he do that?' She felt her mouth set, stubbornly enraged at his patient tone. 'All those times he said he was at the pub. Where was he going?'

Gerard looked at her a long moment, then he sighed. 'There are reasons for men disappearing of an evening, some of them are innocent, some of them not so innocent.' Carswell made a schoolboy sound under his breath and Gerard gave him a sharp look. 'Are you sure you had no idea, no inkling, that . . . something was going on?'

'Something?' she spoke sharply. 'What was going on?' And his face went bland, smooth.

'Oh, we don't know that yet, do we,' he said, and it came home to her that although Doug Gerard was a policeman, that didn't mean he felt obliged to tell her the

134

truth; what was it they said, *the whole truth, nothing but the truth.* 'We'll find out, though,' he told her. 'Don't worry, Fran, we'll find out.'

And when he set his head to one side, looking at her mildly, she thought, with a shock, He looks like Nathan when he does that.

'You didn't seem to want to know much about your husband, if you don't mind my saying so, Fran.' Gently. 'Am I right?'

She took a deep breath. 'I need to get the children to bed now,' she said, surprised by how firmly she spoke. Something to do with that look that made her think of Nathan and something to do with Nathan's father: knowing she never had to talk to him again. 'I need to get things straight, in here.'

There was a silence then, that grew, and then Fran took the three, four steps to the door, her hand on the latch. 'Thanks,' she said. 'You've been . . . it's been . . .'

'A long day,' said Gerard, soothing. 'Yes, sure. Of course.'

But for a long moment he just stood there – and then she had to step aside because suddenly they were on the move, they were going, first Gerard – the faint lingering smell of his aftershave, his solid bulk, taking his time – then Carswell, hunching his narrow shoulders, touching his hand to his forehead in a salute, zipping his bomber against the cold.

She closed the door behind them and set her back against it.

Upstairs Emme had fallen asleep on the floor of her room, curled around like a dormouse in pillows and cushions she'd pulled down off the bed, at the centre of the mysterious project she had been working on with Harry. Teetering, fantastical, it was a cross between an igloo and a fortress and a beaver's dam, bits of different construction kits, plastic and wood, turrets and drawbridges, more wall than interior as if the two of them had sat inside and built it around them, layer on layer.

Twenty-four hours earlier, Nathan had been alive. They had survived twenty-four hours.

The ridge ahead as she trudged in the darkness wasn't a hill, more like a wall, it was some kind of old earthwork, Saxon or whatever. Ali had learned about it in primary school, forty years ago. There weren't any hills here. She walked steadily, her hands in the pockets of the waxed jacket that had been her dad's.

There was someone up ahead, in the undergrowth that ran along the top of the hill, a rustling. Ali kept walking. The rustle was low down, and when the dog heard her coming it began to bark. She followed the sound, making her way up, she could hear her own laboured breathing. Not as fit as she'd once been, hundred-metre sprinter when she was sixteen, a brief couple of years of beating all-comers. That clean feeling. A walk was better than nothing, every night she could she slipped out of the back door. Fresh air. Jesus, it was cold though.

'Derek,' she said. 'Bit late for you, isn't it?' Derek Butt whistled and the dog was there, panting somewhere at their feet in the dark, pushing warm against her leg. She'd get a dog too, given a free choice.

Out of uniform Derek Butt always seemed smaller, the colour washed out of him. Just a little gingery bloke.

A decent little gingery bloke. Ali could smell the fags, it was why he was always the one took the dog out, his wife wouldn't let him smoke in the house. 'All right?' he said.

She sighed. 'You know. A bit uphill just now.'

'Your mum, is it?' She didn't know how Derek knew, except that they all knew, Mum lost by the railway line, Mum at the bus stop in her slippers.

'It's always Mum,' she said, stuffing her hands further down in her pockets. 'And the rest.'

'Doug Gerard sympathetic, is he?' said Derek Butt.

She snorted. 'Doug Gerard wouldn't know sympathy if it gave him a lap dance,' she said. 'It's fine.'

Doug Gerard had appeared at her back door with a box of chocolates. 'For your mum,' he said, grinning, and she didn't know what he was playing at. Something. He'd watched her from the kitchen door, putting the box away carefully. 'We like to keep you sweet,' he said. 'Take more than that,' she told him, moving to close the door, but there was his hand high up on the door jamb, fancied himself as Steve McQueen, standing like that in her doorway like no one could resist him. 'We'll get her,' he'd said softly, then. 'With or without you, DC Compton.'

The dog ran off again and Derek sighed. 'He thinks she did it,' he said.

'Yes,' said Ali. No other reason for taking her down to interview room four and they both knew it. With a kid. A babe in arms. She'd watched Gerard opening the rear door of the vehicle for Fran Hall, acting like her knight in shining bloody armour. 'He seems to think it being her knife clinches it.' She set her lips in a line. 'I don't know

137

if the DI's letting him have his head with that. Craddock. Have you heard? '

'Doug Gerard's ambitious,' he said. 'That goes a long way, as things stand. You push hard enough, you get what you want.'

'That where we went wrong, then, Derek?' Doug Gerard with his modern flat overlooking the river, she'd seen him showing the pictures on his mobile. Balcony. Loft-style. Master bedroom, all that, just waiting for the next bird to fall for his serious look. And there was Derek smoking in the back garden of his semi, and her listening for Mum in the night.

'You think she did it?' asked Derek, jamming his hands down in his pockets and she could hear him feeling for the fag packet, deciding against it.

'No,' she said, before she knew what was going to come out of her mouth. 'There's something though. In her eyes, that look they get. Scared.'

'Her husband's just been offed.'

Could you expect a bloke to understand it? Some did: Derek probably would, if he'd spend any time with Fran Hall, he was a kind man. He tried. 'Yes,' she said, patiently. 'I get that, yeah, she's scared shitless, though I don't think Gerard cares, he tells himself she's just scared shitless of being put away. It's something underneath it. She's waiting to be told she's done something wrong. A dog that's been hit too many times.'

'He hit her?'

She shrugged. 'Not necessarily. Doesn't have to be, does it? Just control. Let's say, I'd like to talk to someone about what that marriage was really like.'

138

'He's got Sadie on to it,' Derek told her, and he turned looking for the dog, restless. 'See what she got up to. He reckons that's a woman's job, you know. Gossip, friends. Someone's got to have seen her, if she was up to something.'

DC Sadie Watts, little Sadie just out of college and itching with dissatisfaction every time Gerard chose Carswell over her. Ali had walked past her at her desk, sitting there mutinous at the computer, a fleece zipped up to her ears so Gerard couldn't look at her boobs. Been there, done that.

'Up to what, exactly?' she said, as if she didn't know, they thought they were all at it, didn't they? Shagging around. Derek shifted, uneasy. 'I want to know about him,' Ali said. 'Before I want to know about her. I want to know about Nathan Hall.'

'You'll have to fight Gerard for that one,' said Derek, and he whistled into the darkness for the dog. 'You know that, don't you? He wants the glory.' The dog was there, jumping up, and Derek lowered his face towards the animal, eyes shut as it tried to lick him, smiling in spite of himself.

Sadie Watts wanted the glory too, come to that, sticking her nose in, stamping her foot at being left out.

Ali stood there on the ridge a long time after he'd gone, in the cold. The big black fields laid out in front of her, lights here and there. There was a kitchen waiting for her, a dishwasher to be unloaded. There was Mum upstairs, spark out on her medication. She turned, measuring distances, looking for landmarks. The red eyes of the wind generators, Oakenham, the straight gleam off the big ditch that was Cold Fen, that would lead all the way to Fran Hall's house, five miles off and out of sight.

Somewhere out there a couple more kids without a father, and Fran Hall all there was between them and chaos. And they want glory, she thought.

It rang, somewhere far off in the dark house.

The sound wove through the corridors, it ran up the stairs, it pulled her through an awful tangle of dreams: a face at a window, bony hands reaching in. And she was upright, in the bed, she was turning to look for the red numerals on the alarm clock, and all the time in the dark the pattering question, *Was it happening all over again?*

Fran stumbled out of bed and to the door, groping in the dark, a hand to either side on the stairwell, following the sound down through the house to the telephone that hung on the wall just inside the kitchen door. She grabbed for the receiver.

'Hello?' Her own voice echoed down the line, her own blood pounding in her ears.

In her head she saw blood smeared on the wall, the black glass of a window and she swung back, out of the kitchen and into the hall, she pressed herself against the wall. All around them, around the house that sat up too tall, too visible in the vast flat plain, she felt the dark thicken and gather itself, not empty, not empty at all, it was whispering to her, down the line. And then there was a tiny gentle sound, a soft click, and the line was dead.

Chapter Twelve

Tuesday

Two days. Less: thirty-six hours.

'I want to know what's going on,' she said into her mobile phone, standing stiff-legged in front of the pub with Ben strapped to her. The bitter cold hurt her head, it froze her feet in her boots. 'With the investigation. What did they find on the . . . murder weapon?'

'DS Gerard is out on a call, I'm afraid, Mrs Hall,' said DC Sadie Watts stiffly. 'I believe he's on his way to you. With DC Carswell.' Disgruntled.

Young, thought Fran. What did she know about the world? What did she know about what this was like? 'I want to talk to my Family Liaison Officer,' she said. 'To Ali. No one seems to want to tell me anything. That's what she's for, isn't it?'

'Part of it, yes,' said DC Watts. 'I think DS Gerard, as far as I know he's . . . he's instructed Ali to meet him there.'

Fran hung up.

The pub might once have been pretty but it wasn't any longer. A cramped building with a low roof dwarfed by a

141

stockade of dark Leyland cypresses. There was a big car park, untidy, a pile of something under stained tarpaulin and crates stacked against the pub's back wall, and Fran stood at one end of it, with Ben strapped to her in the sling that brought her out in a sweat. It was just past nine, and the pub was closed. Fran was watching the back door.

Emme had come into her bedroom at seven as she was changing Ben. Although Fran hadn't heard a sound from her room she was fully dressed in her uniform.

Is it time yet?' she said. 'I want to be early. I want to see Harry.' There had been an urgency in her voice that had made Fran take hold of her hands.

'Emme,' she had said. 'Emme. What is it? Did Harry . . . did you have a nice time with Harry last night?'

'Yes,' Emme had said, frowning, pulling a little against Fran's hold on her and Fran let go. 'I want to go to school. Miss Bates is teaching us football today. It's numeracy first lesson.' Her hair had been brushed but the parting was wonky. Fran pressed her lips against it, waiting for Emme to ask about Nathan, but she didn't: she pulled away, instead.

The puddles had frozen overnight as they walked to school, Ben in the sling for warmth, Emme stamping on the ice, over and over, to hear the sound, to see every puddle crazed. The police hadn't said when they'd be back, but they had her mobile number.

The head teacher, June Rayner, had frowned, disapproving, as Fran stood across the desk from her, under the literacy posters, and a collage. 'Your daughter should be at home,' she stated.

Fran had held her ground. All she knew was, she had to keep things steady. 'School is a safe place for her at the moment,' she said, and there was a stand-off, the teacher compressing her lips. Then Rayner had sighed.

'I'll do my best, but I'm going to call you. If there's anything—'

'That's what I want. I want you to call me. Emme's safety is what matters.'

A light went on in one of the pub's lower windows. *Lounge bar*, it said on the door.

So where did Nathan go on those evenings when she heard him whistling under his breath, when he left the bathroom smelling of aftershave and called cheerily to her from the back door, if not here?

She'd left London to atone for something, it was why she'd agreed to come here. For messing it up. For making a mistake. She hadn't admitted it, certainly not when she was saying her goodbyes at the office.

But Nathan? He'd come because it was his childhood home, he wanted to recreate something here. That was how she'd understood it at least, when he'd talked about the frosted fields in the mornings, the wide glassy river, lads swimming in the reservoir. Until she saw the mangy thatch of the cottage he'd grown up in, and put it together with the angry text from Miranda and understood that there had been no happy childhood.

A woman came out of the door carrying a crate and set it down. She was middle-aged and heavily made-up for the early morning and the flat Fen light. The landlady, who knew her husband was a liar. What else had he lied about?

Gerard had said, the name will come back to you, and she'd wanted to slap him. Who was it? Someone connected

143

to construction and who might be useful. She closed her eyes.

Scaffolding, Nathan had said, pouring her a glass of wine in the kitchen one evening, months back, both children finally asleep. *Of course, they're a rough lot, scaffolders.* Nostalgic. *He never was that presentable, either.*

She couldn't remember the name. Fran stood there with Ben's small hands in hers where they hung to either side of the sling and tried to remember, but she couldn't. If she had a name to tell the police, anything, perhaps things would be different. Would they trust her, then?

She'd only gone to the pub with Nathan once, early on. They'd sat outside with Emme, and she'd been pregnant and drinking tomato juice.

Fran turned and headed away from the pub and the woman's stare, towards the edge of the village.

She had been drunk, that night that had led to this, all this. Drunk on an empty stomach, cheap cocktails and the sight of herself in flattering lighting and art deco mirrors. Was that her excuse?

Against her in the sling Ben was hot and heavy. She began walking past the houses strung out along the high street, one after the other curtained and silent.

Karen's house was a straggler on the extreme edge of the village, a bungalow down a lane that led nowhere. Neglected hedging on either side of the lane had turned into overgrown spindly trees, and it was dripping and dark. Karen's was the only house. As she approached it she realised it wasn't even a house, it was a mobile home that had been bricked in but there were window boxes.

She hadn't really mentioned Karen to Nathan, had she?

She'd been in the house once or twice but Fran had made sure Nathan wasn't around, because she knew he wouldn't like her, she could admit that now. And a small shock came with that realisation, that now he wouldn't know, Nathan wouldn't ever be able to frown at Karen's purple fur collar, at the music she played in her car, country ballads and show-tunes. Now there was no Nathan.

The little car was in the driveway, and a light was on in a net-curtained window. It was ten but the sun was still low on the horizon, a pale disc coming up over the line of cloud that stretched like a mountain range. She knocked, feeling her breathing, quick and shallow, as she waited and then the door opened. For a second Fran thought, she doesn't want me here but then Karen's face relaxed, and she started to say something, half a joke, half a question.

But Fran was already unstrapping Ben, not knowing this was what she'd come for until she was on the doorstep, and Karen stopped talking and held out her arms to take him, instead.

'Could you just take him for a bit?' she managed finally. 'Just have him for me, could you? Not long. I won't be long, I just need to . . .'

And Fran had a problem with the words because it all rushed up inside her, the same reel of images. Her knees in the mud, her hands feeling for Nathan's face in the dark, a man silhouetted against headlights with his arms down by his sides.

Karen took the baby from her.

There was a car Fran didn't recognise at the house when she came around the bend back from Karen's and she

145

slowed her step, but it was a woman climbing out, stamping her feet, a woman in a parka. Thick bottle-blonde hair, and as she turned, as Fran came up close she saw the faded blue eyes, crow's feet. Ali Compton.

Karen had said it, on the doorstep, with Ben tucked effortlessly into the crook of one arm and sound asleep. 'Don't look so flaming guilty. Don't let them make you feel like that. Bloody coppers, act like they're God. They're just men.' Not this one: a woman was different. This woman.

'Where's the baby?' said Ali, and for a second Fran felt a surge of resentment: what she wanted to say was, *Mind your own business.* 'I left him with a friend, I was going to . . .' She hesitated. Would Ali Compton understand? 'I wanted to get out for a bit. Clear my head.'

Nathan had never liked her running. In London he'd told her it was dangerous, on the roads there were cars; in the parks and on the towpaths there were muggers and addicts. She had always had the sense, too, that he wanted her in sight, somehow, even if he wasn't there he wanted her in the house. He wanted to know where she was. Just like this woman, like the police. They'd try to stop her, they'd judge her. At a time like this. But she had to do something.

'Shame,' said Ali, 'I'd have liked a cuddle. Not that I'd say that in front of DS Gerard, of course.' She pushed her hands down in her pockets. 'You'll find people step up to the mark, situations like this. They're not all bad, out here.' Then blowing her breath out in a cloud, 'I hope the council's got the gritters out.'

'Come in,' said Fran, resigned. 'Not that it's much warmer inside.'

'These old houses,' said Ali Compton once they were in, standing at the foot of the stairs and looking around. 'Draughty.' She gave a quick shiver. 'Nice place, though.' Curious.

'You want to have a look?' said Fran, hesitant.

'Sure,' Ali said, straight away.

Fran walked ahead of her stiffly, past the stairs, although she had seen Ali Compton pause and peer up. Gerard hadn't needed an excuse, had he, to go up her stairs. Into her bedroom. She pushed open the door to the study, the little clean, cold room, the curtains he always kept drawn. They went along the passage. Ali Compton stood looking, up at the high ceilings Nathan had marvelled at, the carved plasterwork, the black and red tiles and the big empty fireplace.

'Handsome, my old dad would have called it,' she said. 'Funny, I was born twelve miles away but I don't really know this place at all. Cold Fen. Which is a good thing, isn't it?' Chatty. Friendly. 'And to my knowledge we haven't had a call-out here in years so it must be . . . well. Must have been a safe enough place.' She hadn't taken off her coat. 'All this space, it must have felt like you were rattling around in it for a bit,' then, quickly, 'Let's have a coffee, shall we?'

Ali Compton took her coffee strong, milk and two sugars. Fran stirred, handed it to her. 'You've got to call me Ali,' and Fran nodded.

'Thanks,' she said, 'Ali.'

'We had a briefing this morning,' Ali went on. 'They'll be along shortly. DS Gerard and DC Carswell.' Her mouth set; she didn't like them, that came as a revelation. 'This is our time to talk. We need to make the most of it.' She cupped her hands round the mug.

147

'I don't like having them in my house,' blurted Fran. 'Nathan wouldn't have . . . he'd have . . .'

'It's our job,' said Ali, wearily. 'It's murder, love,' and Fran found herself moving off round the room just at the sound of the word, the sickening sound, found herself moving stuff, setting books in a pile, that plastic bag, wiping down the draining board, putting plates away, cups, but the clatter didn't drown it out. She stopped, and Ali laid a hand on the table. 'Sit down,' she said, and Fran sat.

'I shouldn't have said it,' she said. 'About men round here being like dogs. In the interview.'

Ali Compton gave her a smile. A real one. 'Don't worry about it,' she said. 'Gerard's a big boy. Sometimes I think he needs a bit more barracking, to be honest. Just between you and me.'

'Nathan did go outside, sometimes, in the evenings. Just stood in the yard looking – that's what I thought, anyway. He liked having a big place, a field.' She spoke haltingly. 'What did they find on the knife?'

Ali Compton looked at her, a long moment. 'It looks like it was certainly the murder weapon,' she said. 'It was his blood. The handle had been wiped.' A pause. 'Was your husband a violent man, Fran?' she said, and Fran froze. 'Did he hurt you?'

'Why are you asking me that?' And something flickered, at the corner of her vision, at the back of her brain. 'Do you think I . . . because it was my knife, I'd used it a hundred times. Do you think I—'

'Look, this is just you and me, DS Gerard isn't here. I haven't got my notebook out, I'm not recording anything.

148

You and me, talking. I'm asking because . . . well. Call it an instinct.' Very quietly. 'Did he hurt you?'

'No,' she said, and there it was in the corner of her eye, still flickering. *But.* 'He . . .' and she stopped.

'All right, if you tell me he didn't, he didn't.' She leaned a little towards Fran, and staring down at the table Fran saw her bitten nails, her roughened hands. 'It's our job to consider everyone a suspect, you know that, don't you?' she said, looking into Fran's face. 'And if things don't add up, if people don't tell you everything, then you have to keep pushing until they do.'

'What doesn't add up?' said Fran, quickly.

'Time of death,' Ali said, unhesitating. 'For example. By the time we got to your husband – by the time *you* got to him – you said he was cold? Very cold?' Fran nodded. 'The pathology report points to him having already been dead some time. Hours.' Ali examined her. 'Could you have been wrong? About him coming in at midnight?' and when she didn't answer Ali leaned in, even closer.

'Maybe I shouldn't say this.' Her pale blue eyes looked into Fran's, her mouth turned down, troubled. 'Your knife or not, I don't think you had anything to do with your husband's death. All right? That's my instinct. That doesn't mean I think you're telling me everything about your marriage, either, though.'

Fran couldn't look away. My marriage, she thought. That secret thing. 'That might be because there's stuff you don't know about it yourself,' continued Ali and then Fran pushed back, hands against the edge of the table. 'Or maybe there are details that never seemed important, where he got to, who he spoke to. His work, his friends here, all that.'

149

'I . . . I just . . . It wasn't always like this,' Fran said, and how lame it sounded. 'We did use to do stuff together, till the, till the kids . . .'

'But they came along almost straight away,' said Ali softly. 'And then you were . . . then there was no going back. Was that how it felt?'

Fran blinked, unable to say it. But Ali went on, as if she knew anyway. 'And then you came out here. He brought you out here.'

A silence.

'He grew up here,' said Fran, defensive. 'He told me about that. What that was like.'

'Such as?'

'Just, just . . . hanging out. His last summer here, with his friends. They all shacked up in some squat, some farm-house, he talked about it like it was paradise, only . . .' She paused, because it didn't ring true any more, in this land-scape, the frozen plain, the poky cottage where he'd grown up. How much, in fact, had he told her?

And as if she could read her mind Ali said, 'Where was it exactly? The squat. When would this have been?'

And all Fran could do was shake her head. 'His father might know more,' she began, quailing at the thought, at the memory of something his father had said, the word *reckless*, then, 'Rob. Rob can tell you. His friend Rob.'

'Yes, yes. He's been in touch, Doug said. DS Gerard said.' Frowning, she went quiet. 'But you,' she said, at last. 'What about your friends? Where you worked? What did they think about you and Nathan, about you coming out here?' A pause. 'Do they know what's happened?'

Jo, thought Fran, *Jo*, and she held Ali's gaze a moment,

feeling something swell in her throat, threatening to choke her. 'What happened at your briefing, this morning?' she said, hoarse, stubborn. 'Aren't you supposed to be telling me that? What about suspects?'

'It's not even thirty-six hours,' Ali began and as that hit home the future loomed, terrifying.

'Have you got a single suspect apart from me?' said Fran, standing up, wanting to shake something off, the fear, Ali's dogged pursuit. 'Because you're right, I had nothing to do with my husband's death, someone's out there still, someone's . . .'

Then Fran sat back down, the shock of it, remembering it. Had she dreamed it? Had she dreamed that, too?

'Last night,' she said, wondering, feeling Ali's eyes on her, 'someone phoned the landline last night, about midnight.' Zero zero thirteen, by the clock as she walked back into the bedroom, unbalanced in the dark. 00:13. Not a dream. 'When I answered . . . he . . . they . . . hung up.'

Ali was on her feet, and in the same moment there came the sound of a car pulling up on her gravel.

Chapter Thirteen

The trainers were old and pulverised, the sports bra too tight, but the feeling was the same. The sensation of things falling away, as Fran concentrated on the breathing. No babies, no house, no police. No Nathan.

There was something in the air, sleet driving sideways.

'You go,' Ali had said, flicking a look at the two men. 'You need some space.'

How long did she have?

Karen had said she would get Emme from school again. Turning to go back into the house she had flicked on the light switch and Fran had seen a row of framed photographs at all heights along the hall, family portraits. Karen had murmured down into Ben's hair. 'When he wants his mum back.'

It was the police who would ask questions, if she stayed out too long. Ben would be fine, he'd be happy in Karen's neat safe house.

The knot inside Fran tightened, but she kept on running. She was out in the open now, on the flat. Up ahead was the row of poplars, then the remains of an ancient bus shelter.

The grey sky seemed to flatten everything. It looked like there was nowhere to hide in a landscape like this but there were places. In a ditch, standing motionless behind the trunk of a poplar, around a corner, below the line of sight. She was in the trees now, leafless but thicker than they looked from the back of the house.

Why are you out here? It was inside her head. *What the hell do you think you're doing out here?* Out here where anyone – *anyone* – could see her. Leaving them there, inside her house. When she got back, they'd have gone where they wanted, opened every cupboard, every drawer.

Ali had told them about the phone call straight away. Doug Gerard had looked flatly uninterested and she'd seen Ali harden. 'I've said it before,' he said. 'We can find you accommodation, Fran. You and your kids. If you don't feel safe here.' And he'd crossed to the phone, dialled. Four digits, to find out who the last caller had been.

'I did that already,' Fran had said from the table. 'It said, the caller withheld their number.'

'Look,' he said patiently, 'plenty of people do that, with-hold the number, it doesn't mean anything. It will have been a friend, just heard the news.'

'After midnight?'

'His sister? Perhaps she'd have miscalculated the time difference, if she's in the Far East?' Brushing it aside. 'There's something we need to go over again,' he said. 'One last time.' The same question, drilling deeper into her head

153

though, each time. 'Look,' Gerard said, 'I want you to think. What would you say is the earliest it could have been, when your husband came in?' He spoke softly.

'Eleven thirty?' she swallowed. 'But I'm sure it was later.'

'And you couldn't have, say, dreamed it? Imagined it? You did say, you were sound asleep.'

She began to shake her head then, knowing what was coming next. Cautious, she said, 'I don't know.'

They were looking at her. 'I don't know,' she said again. Then, at a desperate tangent, 'I left the baby because I wanted to go for a run.' To forestall it, whatever was coming next. 'I left him, Ben. I need to get out. I think it'd help.' But she didn't move: there was a pitying look on Gerard's face.

And there was something in the sigh he let out then that told her, before he said it, and Fran felt herself go very still. 'Only the results we've got so far indicate beyond doubt that your husband died some time between ten thirty and eleven, so around the time you were going to bed. Around the time,' he paused meditatively, 'that you said you heard a noise outside.'

She felt heat prickle, up the back of her neck, across her forehead. *Beyond doubt.* 'Right,' she said, her voice strained. 'Well I must, unless . . . I must have . . . I don't know.' Her throat closed up.

'We'll conduct a fingerprint search, anyway,' said Gerard, his tone reassuring, gentle. 'Of your bedroom. You know, to be sure.'

She just nodded, dumbly. 'I . . . I . . .' Ali Compton was close to her suddenly, her hand was on Fran's arm.

'You go for your run,' she said, quietly. 'Clear your head.

154

We'll sort the fingerprinting for tomorrow, you won't know we've been in there.'

Ahead, the bus shelter was bigger than she'd thought, a brick box with a dark doorway and something spray-painted on it. Her chest burning, as she ran Fran looked back through the trees, searching, and what she could see now was a tractor with long mechanical arms spread wide for sowing moving slowly, almost invisibly, across the far end of the field.

Fran turned away so quickly, swerving for the other side of the road, looking for an opening in the poplars, that she almost tripped – there were deep ruts on that side of the road where someone had parked when the mud was soft, now frozen hard. The opening in the bus shelter was an empty black rectangle: no one there.

She scanned the low hedge for an exit point: there. She could loop back. Thought she could. Keep going, her steps pounded, it was the only message she had. Keep on. The tractor turned, lumbering slowly, and she saw that the field was nearly sown. The sun was low in the sky now, almost to the top of the hedge.

It had been Jo that had started her running. They'd go so slowly through the streets of red-brick houses and cherry trees, just talking, grumbling, gossiping. She thought of Jo's face, defeated, in the café. *What do you even know about him? You don't know anything about him.*

The tractor was almost at the end of the row. She glanced up at the cab and saw that it was the man who'd come about the pigs, Dearborn, and he was lifting a hand, he was waving. Fran lifted her hand in response and in that moment she felt dizzy. She tried to think when she'd last eaten but all she could remember was that box of chocolates Gerard had put in Carswell's hairy-knuckled hands. She was in the rutted lane between the hedges.

The sound came after her, a roar magnified in the narrow space. She was slower, her legs like lead. The tractor must be gaining on her, she could sense the noise blocking the space behind her but she didn't want to stop, she couldn't afford to slow enough to turn and look back. And then the last shot of whatever her body had been holding in reserve kicked in, for just long enough, her legs found the rhythm.

At the end of the lane Fran swerved out of the way, grabbing a post to steady herself and feeling the prickle of the hedge at her back, the sweat sticking her T-shirt to her ribs. The tractor was going more slowly than she'd thought: she'd had plenty of time all along. It was huge this close up, its thick clogged tyres taller than her. In a thundering rush it swung out past her, scattering clods of black earth, into the road. She leaned on the post, feeling the pounding of her heart, and then she saw the red lights blink on: no more than twenty yards past her, the tractor had stopped. She saw the man's silhouette in the cab, his hat, she took a step back and something in the hedge dug into her painfully.

He was climbing down.

In the end it wasn't until she got round the side of the house, past the empty police car and to the bins behind their screen in the yard that Fran stopped. The light was ebbing, it was almost dark: she estimated four o'clock. Four thirty. She set her back against the wall, leaning down with her hands on her knees, getting her breath back.

156

He had walked slowly, lopsided with a dodgy hip or a bad leg. She just watched him come: she could out-run him if she had to. Dearborn.

She straightened, feeling the sweat cool on her. 'I heard,' he said. 'I heard what happened.'

'Yes.' Her throat felt clogged, she coughed.

He took a step nearer. 'You all right? With them kiddies.' He began to shake his head, almost bewildered. 'I never knew. Never knew it were him.'

'Him?'

'Your husband. Went to school with him, I did, well he were a good couple years younger and it were just the prim'ry but . . .' His head was still shaking slowly, side to side. 'Never recognised him, and then he . . . well, he called hisself something else in those days.' For a second she froze, she thought, this is it . . . but he was still talking. 'He were Alan Hall, them days,' and she understood, she nodded with relief.

'Yes,' she said, remembering the registry office, *Alan Nathan Hall*. 'He didn't like it, he . . . well . . .' and for some reason she felt that she needed to apologise, to explain. 'People do that, don't they, when they start again, new life, new town.'

'Do they?' said Dearborn slowly, pulling off a glove and rubbing his forehead with the back of his hand, leaving a streak. 'You staying put, then?' Frowning. He looked around a moment as if trying to understand. 'They got any ideas, who it was?'

'I . . . they're following things up.'

'Pikeys,' said Dearborn, but he didn't seem convinced. 'Or them foreigners. They'll round someone up.'

157

'I'm staying,' she said, not knowing where it came from. 'It's . . . our place.' *And we've got nowhere else to go*, but she didn't say that, she could sense the offer already, on his lips.

'I'll talk to the wife,' he said, on cue. 'You'll need something. For the kiddies, casserole, she does a casserole.' She began to shake her head. 'Dog,' he said, and the thought cheered him, 'That's what you need.' And he straightened, thinking. 'I'll look out for one for you. Lab'd be nice for the kiddies, not much of a guard dog but . . .'

Nathan doesn't like dogs, she thought. 'That's kind.'

'I did wonder . . .' Dearborn began, then broke off.

'What?' she said.

'I thought you didn't like the place,' he said. 'Just got that feeling. Old Martin . . . well.'

John Martin, with his dyed hair. 'What about him?'

'Nothing. Places get a reputation, just kids scaring thesselves talking about ghosts and graves, all that. Men what end up on their own, he did let the place go. Is why you got the place so cheap, I suppose, silver lining for you, in't it?' She stared. 'Nothing,' he said, uneasy.

'Silver lining, not really.' But he was backing away from her now, turning in that lopsided way.

'Dog,' he said, pausing, 'that'll do it.' And he was hurrying away.

He swung himself up into the cab with a surprising strong-armed grace, she saw how his upper body compensated, and realised she was cross-checking against her memory, the silhouette in the field. Too top-heavy, too short, shoulders too broad. The tractor roared into life. She waited until he was round the bend before setting off again, fast this time, to clean it out of her, to shake it up. Ghost stories. Graves. Still moving fast she swerved in past the house, into the yard and down. Head down between her knees, thinking.

Opposite her the tall plastic bins with their coloured lids – green, blue, black – were ranged against the wooden screen. You could tell when a fox had got into them but none had been overturned, nothing had been disturbed. So close to the house. With the knife in his hand, pushing it under the soil in the pot.

Her head felt miraculously clear. The red lights on the radio alarm clock blinked at her from that darkness, two nights ago, crystallising into a shape. The first digit had been a zero. After midnight: it had been after midnight when he came in. After midnight.

Fran closed her eyes: she was a blank, no children, no husband. This was easy. Don't think about the implications: concentrate on the facts.

She couldn't prove it. She could have dreamed it all, or imagined it. But she was sure. Her cheeks were burning with the exertion and the cold felt good. From beyond the screen she heard footsteps, someone clearing his throat. Then voices but she stayed where she was, eyes closed, relaxed but listening.

'No doubt about it,' Gerard was saying. 'Latest would be eleven, really.'

'Why would she make it up?' Ali Compton was insisting. Fran heard Gerard sigh.

'You know the drill,' he said. 'And you know what we know, about her. This isn't your straightforward happy family now, is it?'

Compton snorted. 'When are they ever, DS Gerard? I'd

159

be more interested in what he'd been up to, wouldn't you? I'd like a look at that Sandpiper place.'

Fran heard him make a surly sound, and he said something she didn't catch. Then, 'I want to be back here in half an hour.'

She heard a car door slam, the ignition fire, wheels beginning to reverse over the gravel. Her own car was sitting on the drive, no longer blocked in, she could climb in and drive. Half an hour, to escape. But there was Emme, there was Ben, they were hers, she was theirs, two days in a row she'd given them to Karen and she needed to get them back. She squinted at the sky to gauge the time: the sun was dipping again. Time to start again, dealing with it.

Inside the house the landline began to ring.

Fran straightened, her legs already starting to stiffen. She came out from behind the fence in a hurry but before she got to the door she could hear that the phone had stopped ringing. As she tried the door, registering that it was still unlocked, there was DC Ed Carswell standing by the phone she'd used to call the ambulance, with the smear of blood still on the wall beside his head.

She saw him take her in, his eyes moving up and down, checking her out in the running gear, the tight leggings – and with her anger the world rearranged itself around her, it parted for her. She walked straight up to him and held out her hand for the phone. Carswell gave it to her.

'Nice legs,' he said, smiling. He didn't bother to lower his voice. There was no one to hear, after all.

Chapter Fourteen

Gerard screeched up on the forecourt of one of the light industrial units of the Sandpiper estate, coming to a halt so suddenly Ali was thrown forward in the seat. He turned to look at her, lairy, hoping for her to have a go. 'I'm too old, DS Gerard,' she said, 'to be impressed by a boy racer.'

'You're too old for all sorts of things,' he said, and shouldered his door open. 'Not my idea of a hot date, this.'

Ali remembered the Sandpiper being built. It had been nothing more than a collection of ramshackle sheds and lock-ups for years, dodgy as you like but almost part of the landscape, tucked in the lee of a field and a lay-by. Then the land-grab craziness drifted out from Cambridge and it was all retail units and get rich quick, a mish-mash of cut-and-shut cowboys, storage and office units.

On the other side of the road a mechanic eyed them from over the bonnet of a truck, the unit next to him had a long shutter with a big silver sign saying *Club Sound*

161

Logistics. 'Come on, if you're coming,' said Gerard behind her.

He let them in through an anonymous door with frosted glass, not even a nameplate, she didn't know how he had the key but it was probably by chucking his weight around. He went in ahead of her, pushed open a flimsy internal door.

Ali looked around. A cheap veneer table in a corner with a telephone on it, two of the usual padded office chairs, a bookcase with a couple of handbooks on building and design regulations and a well-thumbed paperback, some lads' airport book about black ops, embossed lettering.

'He was actually paying rent on it?' Gerard shrugged, nodding, working up to something. 'There's nothing here,' she said. Gerard's grin told her he was pleased that Nathan Hall had got one over on the wife, lying to her, keeping her in the dark. 'So it's a . . . what?' she said. 'A front?'

He was looking at her. 'You're the smart one, DC Compton, you tell me.'

'Drugs?' said Ali, and he turned away from her and went to the window, one of those that only opened a crack, with dusty vertical blinds across it. He put a finger to one of the slats, pulling it open.

'So your theory is?' She was talking to his back. Silence, hands in pockets: it almost sounded like he was whistling.

'Well,' said Doug Gerard, eyeing her over his shoulder, half a smile on his face. 'Working from home's no life for a bloke, is it? He could have just wanted to get away from her and those snotty kids.' Trying to wind her up; Ali just stared back. 'Or there might be something out here he was interested in,' he said then, the smile going cold. 'Or someone.'

162

'You think he was shagging the nice lady who runs the softplay centre?' she said. She came up to the window, putting a foot at least between them, and looked through the slats, where he was looking. The mechanic was wiping his hands on a rag, staring across the road. 'Or was he the kind that likes a bit of rough trade on the side? I thought it was her you had fingered for playing away.'

'Getting warmer, DC Compton,' he said, sarcastic.

Gets him going, she thought, the thought of other people shitting on each other. Is that because of the job? You see too much of it.

'So what exactly did DC Watts find out?' was all she said. 'Sadie. I heard you had her on Fran Hall's case, who she's been seen with, what she's been getting up to.' He grinned, knowing. 'If she's been getting up to anything, that is,' she said stiffly.

'Ah, Sadie. Little Sadie. I'm looking forward to that debrief.' She resisted the urge to knee him in the nuts. Undignified, that would be, but worth it. One day. She waited.

'Seen with a man,' he said, pursing his lips. 'I told you.'

'It's not a crime to talk to a man in the street. It's not like Sadie Watts has found hotel records or saw them up against a wall. She got nothing. *Nothing.*'

'Come on,' said Doug Gerard, 'it's written all over her, you know that as well as I do. We done here, then, DC Compton?'

She folded her arms. 'After you,' she said as he went for the door.

'Shagging someone else,' he said, turning around again just as she came after him. 'I told you. You get a feel for that kind of thing.'

163

'If I catch you feeling any kind of thing,' Ali said, staring back at him, 'between you and me, I'll have you at a tribunal before you can check your bollocks are still where you left them.'

He was still laughing as he stood at the passenger door and held it open for her. She yanked it out of his hand. 'Let's just get back to protecting the public, shall we?' he said, giving her that face.

'If you can remember how to do that,' she said, and slammed the door, missing his fingers by millimetres. At least she saw him jump.

'Hello?' Fran said into the phone, looking at Ed Carswell stonily until he turned, unabashed, and away. She watched him wander down the hall into their sitting room and she closed the door.

'Mrs Hall? This is Julian Napier.'

The voice was immediately familiar, rich and gravelly, upper-class.

'Julian,' she said, and all at once implications were dumped back in her life: she was going to have to tell people. Tell this man.

'Is, ah, is Nathan there?' His cheeriness slightly forced. 'Been trying to get him on the mobile phone.'

She had to tell Emme.

The bedside clock had said four when Fran left the bedroom to come downstairs, and outside the light was almost gone. Tuesday: a future stretched ahead, weekends alone with the children in the cold rooms. Sunday would be Valentine's Day.

After hanging up she'd marched into the sitting room. Carswell had been loitering there in the gloom, flicking through a book on the side. 'If you don't mind staying in the kitchen,' Fran heard herself say. He'd put his hands in his pockets and nodded, like a schoolboy.

'You can wipe that, now,' Carswell said as they stepped into the kitchen, pointing at the smear on the wall by the phone. 'We've got a shot of it.' She closed the door on him.

She'd stood in the shower for ten minutes, scrubbing at herself. She'd heard voices downstairs but stayed put.

The only time Fran was in this house without the children was when Nathan took them out, on Saturday and Sunday afternoons, an hour, maybe two at some park or other. It seemed bigger up here, without them. She was aware of the small noises, birds, mice, spiders, aware of the big dark roof space above her head.

She'd give it half an hour then she'd call Karen.

All three of the police officers were in the kitchen, the men standing, Ali Compton at the table. Carswell avoided Fran's eye when she came through the door.

She was wearing a big jumper of Nathan's, old jeans, trainers. She'd stood in front of the wardrobe for a long time: grey, black, white, stuff stretched out of shape and faded. In the back, out of sight, was a new dress. She never wore dresses any more. She'd bought it a month ago.

She reached over to Nathan's side and pulled things at random towards her face: the sleeve of a suit jacket, but all it smelled of was the dry cleaner's. Out of the corner of her eye the dress appeared, in plain sight. Nathan must have spotted it, but he had said nothing.

165

Ali was sitting at the table: it had been cleared, a stack of papers neat on the dresser. There was another pot of tea. Fran didn't sit down.

'I didn't dream it,' she said. 'I didn't imagine it, I didn't get the time wrong. It was after midnight when someone came in here, into the house, and if Nathan was killed at eleven at the latest . . .' and she paused, to let them know she didn't care if they knew she'd overheard them, 'then it wasn't Nathan.'

There was a long silence, and then Gerard spoke into it, and she heard triumph.

'Right, now we're getting somewhere.'

She'd thought the sex would get better. But it was too late by then. By then, Fran fancied him, and her judgement was skewed. And what had drawn her was that lightness in him, the refusal to be pinned down. Hard to get.

A week after that first time, they went to see a film together and Nathan invited Fran up to his place. Methodically he took off her clothes and led her into his bedroom. He didn't get hard straight away, and she didn't know why, it felt like a reproach straight off, even when he smiled, sat back on the pillows, when he said, 'Why don't you see what you can do,' looking down at her, cool as you like. He had lain there, the light still on, and she had put her hand between his legs and touched him, she felt the soft weight of him. She leaned down and put his heavy cock in her mouth and then she knew it would

166

work, at least, it did work, she had been obedient, and was rewarded. Of course, she couldn't stop herself wondering, then, and later, what if it hadn't, what then? Try harder.

She made sure she never went near the club, anywhere she might see Nick, or think about him. And then she was pregnant.

Chapter Fifteen

Why don't you see what you can do. She'd forgotten that, forgotten crouching on the bed between his legs and his hand guiding her head down. The light staying on, when she wanted it off. When she had resisted for just a second and looked up she had caught a look on his face that she'd forgotten too: a remote, curious look as if she was a game, an experiment. When he smiled that look was gone, as if it had never been, but it had been.

You work it out, don't you? What marriage is all about.

Fran waited for them to ask — how would they phrase it? Did you *have relations?* — but they didn't. The possibility sat in her head, it hummed like a great sinister engine hidden away, in a cellar, in a basement. She told them he'd come to bed, that was all — then backtracking, helpless, *But I might have dreamed it, after all* — she told them she'd gone back to sleep.

Gerard told her they'd send the team back in, in the

morning, to check the bedroom. She didn't tell them that the sheets she'd slept in were dry and folded and put away: it seemed too late to tell them that. She felt dog-tired, as if the adrenalin had drained her.

'Ed said someone called,' said Gerard, pacing now in the kitchen, like an animal. 'Asking after your husband?' It looked to her like he hadn't shaved, his chin was dark with stubble.

'That's right,' she said wearily, not even surprised that he already knew. 'A business contact. Julian Napier, Napier Construction. He said he'd been trying Nathan's mobile.'

The name stopped Gerard's pacing. 'Napier Construction,' he repeated, interested. 'Upmarket. Is that . . . you've met him?'

'He was at our wedding,' she said, shortly. 'Look—'

'It wasn't Mr Webster, then?' Probing. 'On the phone.'

'You mean Rob?' There was an insinuation in his voice that she didn't quite understand. Then she did.

'Rob's Nathan's friend, not mine,' she said, sharply, angry on his behalf, Rob. Rob, with a sob in his voice, mourning. 'Have you spoken to him? You don't know Rob.'

'No,' said Gerard, reasonably. 'That's true. In answer to your question, we did get him on the phone, yes.' Dubious. 'He's updated us, too. A puncture in the Black Mountains that necessitated an overnight stay.' She closed her eyes, picturing Rob's worn-out little car, neglected because he cycled everywhere, and wishing suddenly that he would get here, nervous, stuttering, brave Rob. 'Very . . . punctilious,' Gerard said. 'If that's the word.'

'Rob will be here,' she said, and suddenly she felt sick

169

with tiredness, with that nameless insistent throb at the back of her head, that there was someone. Someone. Someone in your bed. She wanted her children. 'Look,' she said, 'I know you're here to help, but . . .'

Gerard was on his feet, palms out. 'Yes, of course, message received. But if you like, Ali can stick around. I mean, she can stay the night, all part of the service.' Compton at the table nodded agreement.

'No. I mean, thank you. But at the moment . . . not now. No thanks.' There was a silence.

A door slammed somewhere in the road and she turned towards the sound with such a rush of relief she thought they'd all see it in her face, the sound of Emme's voice, high-pitched, chattering. Then Ben, howling.

In her purple fur collar Karen pushed through the door with him in her arms, his face red with the exertion, eyes squeezed shut, cheeks wet, and suddenly all three of the police officers were on their feet and at the door behind her. Emme edged out of their way, standing at the side.

'It'll be around eight thirty,' Gerard told her. Carswell was already outside, Fran could see his shoulders hunched against the cold.

'Fine,' she said and Gerard was out too, their heads together. Carswell was stamping his feet.

Fran took Ben from Karen and sat down with him at the table, pulling up her sweater. Hiccupping with sobs and grappling for the breast, abruptly he settled and was silent. Emme came up beside Fran, standing very quiet at her shoulder. A hand crept out and settled on the fine hair on Ben's head.

'Look, said Ali, lingering in the doorway, 'are you sure

– it's part of the job, you know. If you're not happy being on your own.'

Karen looked from one of them to the other, taking in the situation, and pulled out a chair. 'She's not on her own, is she,' she said, plonking herself down, and reluctantly Ali Compton gave in. She reached into her breast pocket for a card and set it on the table in front of Fran.

'Call if you need me,' she said. And just like that, they were gone.

'Had he been crying long?' said Fran to Karen, in the sudden silence. She could feel Emme's small hand tight on her upper arm, and turned her head slightly towards her. 'You all right, lovely? Nice tea? ' she said and Emme whispered yes, but held on tighter.

'Just started up when we got here, I swear,' said Karen. 'It was Emme wanted to come home. I'll just get Harry out the car and—'

'No,' said Fran, sharper than she'd meant to sound. 'I mean . . . thanks, Karen. This was a lifesaver.' She leaned her cheek towards Emme's. 'Run upstairs a minute, Emme,' she said quietly. 'And turn the light on in Ben's room for me? I don't want to trip over.'

Fran waited till Emme was out of the room. 'You know what they're saying,' she said. 'Nathan told me he was going to the pub, once, twice a week, but the landlady never saw him. You hear that? Has she been talking about me?'

Karen was on her feet, the starry-lashed eyes fierce in her set, pale face. 'Do you think I'm that kind of bitch? Pretend to be your friend so I can talk about you behind your back?'

Fran just shook her head, too weary for a fight, and

171

Karen's anger deflated abruptly. 'I haven't heard anything,' she said. 'And for the record, I am a cow, but I'm not that kind of cow. But they haven't got him, have they? Useless sods.' Nodding towards the door. 'But you said it yourself, there's someone still out there. It's not safe for you to be on your own.'

'You're on your own too, aren't you? At least I've got a panic button.' Karen just stared, taken aback, and Fran said, 'I don't know what I'd have done without you, Karen, honest. But I can't live like this.'

And she flipped a hand up from where she held Ben, gesturing to the neat pile of papers on the dresser, the mugs, the footprints tracking in from the door. 'People in and out of my house. I can't think straight.'

Karen eyed her narrowly, then she nodded, just once, and stood up. 'You know where I am. If you need me.'

And then they were on their own.

Fran knelt beside the bath, Emme sitting solemnly among the bubbles meticulously working at the rigging of a little wooden boat, and Fran soaped her small bowed shoulders. Ben had fed himself into such a stupor that he didn't stir when she laid him down. Once he was asleep she had walked from room to room, Emme following her, quiet. She mopped the bootprints from the floor, and wiped the phone, quickly, although Emme didn't seem to have seen the blood. She checked the window fastenings, the bolts on the kitchen door, the lights on the boiler. 'It's going to snow,' she said to Emme. 'Maybe at the weekend,' and Emme nodded, unblinking.

In the bath Emme had got the rigging untangled: bent

over it in concentration, her firm little chin not Fran's. 'Mummy,' she said, not looking up, 'Harry said sometimes daddies don't come back.'

Fran thought about the long night ahead of them. 'Your daddy and Harry's aren't the same,' she said, eventually. Emme looked up then, holding the boat out. 'He wouldn't leave you on purpose,' Fran told her, taking it from her and reaching for a towel. 'Bedtime.'

She sat a long time beside Emme, waiting for her to sleep. She hadn't even got up to go, only shifted herself in preparation, when Emme sat straight up in the bed, and babbled, her voice steady but rising. 'The bad man came, bad man. In the roof. In the cupboard. Don't.' A nightmare, Fran told herself, her own heart racing though, for what would come out of Emme's mouth next, scrabbling for where she'd heard that before, *the bad man* – and then as quickly as she had sat up Emme fell back on the pillow.

He wouldn't leave you.

They'd been in the delivery room hours, it seemed, with nothing happening but the pain, when suddenly alarms started sounding, and lights went off, voices raised in the corridor and they poured in. Two midwives, a student nurse, a tanned consultant with a foreign accent, South Africa or maybe Zimbabwe, and then Fran couldn't see Nathan from where she lay pinned on the bed, her knees raised and spread, at the centre of all the commotion.

173

Then she did: he was at the wall, pale and blank, staring at the door.

At ten pounds and facing the wrong way, back to back, the baby had got stuck and something was happening to her heartbeat. Fran tried to understand but it was too technical, the consultant leaning down to her talking about recovery time didn't make sense and she was distracted by his aftershave, the heavy gold link bracelet on his wrist. She tried to see over his shoulder to Nathan but he wasn't there any more.

They cut her: she heard the sound and hoped Nathan was in the corridor. Emme was born in a hot gush of blood and the last Fran heard was someone talking about transfusions before she lost consciousness, or they sedated her, she didn't ever know which. When she woke up she was on her own in a white room magically, blissfully quiet, a private room, and wondering who'd arranged it, or paid for it. Not exactly on her own, because there was Emme, bound in white by some expert hand, her crimped and folded red face visible through the Perspex cradle they'd put her in. Nathan didn't appear until the evening. After they'd given her some lunch she had reached for her mobile to call him but didn't, instead she let it fall back on the hospital cabinet out of lassitude, blood loss or hormones. He would come when he came. She remembered his white expressionless face turned away from her behind a student nurse's shoulder in the delivery room, and then abruptly she was in no hurry.

He came through the door with flowers and magazines and chocolates that lay undisturbed on the end of the bed until the nurse moved them. He stayed less than an hour, nervous the whole time. 'They said you'd need to sleep,' was how he excused himself, and he hadn't looked at Emme in her cot until right at the end and only then despite himself, stealing a glance, as if he was afraid of her.

Patient in the dark, at the far end of that long tunnel that had led them from that brightly lit hospital bed to here and now, Fran sat on Emme's bed until her daughter's breaths lengthened and grew even at last and only then, stiff with waiting, did she stand and leave the quiet room.

Some time long before dawn Fran woke, and she struggled up out of heavy sleep on some command she couldn't remember, only really knowing she was awake when she knocked into something as she moved across the room. Then she was at the window, the cold coming through the glass.

The sky had cleared and although she couldn't see the moon the landscape was illuminated by it. A man was standing on the edge of the field, legs apart, hands folded in front of him. As if mesmerised she watched him, numb to danger. Then she saw the police car, parked under the row of bare poplars, the stripe down its side showing black in the moonlight. She went on watching, but the man didn't move, and slowly she went back to bed, and slept.

She dreamed of DC Carswell, his narrow little face close to hers in a confined space. The policewoman was there too, Ali Compton, standing in the shadows by a door, but she had her back to them. Carswell put his hand on her breast, he cupped it, he tilted his head to examine her reaction and Fran felt her mouth open, but not to protest. She closed her eyes and saw the other face, a different face, familiar, and she waited for him to kiss her. The police-woman in the corner hummed something, so as not to hear.

Chapter Sixteen

Wednesday

Fran woke as the pale sun was coming over the horizon and immediately she was out of bed, still groggy with sleep but on full alert. A number of things were wrong: she staggered a little and reached for the wall, trying to work out what they were.

Her breasts were hard as rocks, her nightdress was damp where they'd leaked. Ben hadn't woken her in the night. That never happened. She steadied herself and leaned down to switch on the bedside light and saw something on the floor, dislodged from under the bed by her bare foot, but she didn't have time for it. Hoover. Later. A scrap of something blue.

Ben.

He was sleeping, soundly, noiselessly, his face was calm and rosy and the blanket was so neat it looked like he hadn't even stirred all night. Fran straightened from the cot.

She had to tell Emme. She walked into Emme's room and sat down carefully on the edge of the bed. Emme was curled around herself tight, her duvet was askew. The soft

177

golden hair was matted at the back of her head from her restlessness on the pillow. The knowledge of what she had to do, to say, sat in Fran's chest like a stone. Should she have Ali Compton give her advice?

She remembered the dream. Ah, shit, she thought. Shit, shit, shit. For a second her skin crept all over, for shame. Just a dream. It wasn't a policeman she'd wanted to kiss, though. It wasn't Nathan, father of her children, either.

Leaning down to Emme's cheek, pressed sideways into the pillow, Fran set hers against it. Emme's breath had that sleep smell, baby-sour. She stirred, turned, her eyes opened and ranged, away and back, across the ceiling above Fran's head, blank. The bad man, in the roof, in the cupboard, thought Fran. 'I've got to tell you something, Emme.'

My baby, she thought.

'It's about Daddy.'

Emme sat up, wriggling into place, then her shoulders dropped, attentive. She watched Fran's mouth as she spoke. 'Daddy hit his head,' Fran said, keeping her voice. 'They tried to make him better but it didn't work.' She stroked Emme's hand. 'He died, Emme. Daddy died. He didn't want to, but sometimes we can't stop it.'

She stopped talking and slowly Emme's eyes travelled up, and met hers. 'Where is he?' she asked. Her gaze was steady.

'They have to keep him in the hospital.' She swallowed. 'Emme, we won't see him again. You can think about him as much as you like, he'll still be your daddy. But he won't be here.'

'Harry said he wouldn't come back,' said Emme and she stared down, frowning, her arms squeezed against her body.

'Harry doesn't really know what happened.' Fran leaned down to look into her face. 'You can stay at home with me, today, if you like. With me and Ben.'

Quiet, blank, Emme looked past her, to the door, back to her face. 'No, thank you,' she said, obedient but firm. 'I don't want to, thank you.' And she was wriggling past Fran, she made for the door. Fran heard her feet on the stairs, careful.

They left early for school. There was no sign of the police as they came out of the kitchen door, Ben buttoned under Fran's coat in the sling, Emme muffled and silent in scarf and gloves. The puddles in the yard were frozen hard.

The fields stretched out flat and white with frost to either side of the road. The long straight line of a drainage ditch stretched away from them at an angle, unwavering and black in the frost, and the sky was pale and hard and bright overhead. A high-pitched whine took them by surprise, coming from behind them as they came out of a corner and then a scooter almost skidded on the ice as it swerved to avoid them. A kid, a skinny teenager helmeted but not dressed for the cold and hunched against it, he righted himself just in time and kept going.

When she had first slept with him, Nathan had still had the bruises on him from coming off his scooter. It was the next morning, as he rolled to get out of the bed, there had been a big greenish-yellow one on his torso, another on his back weirdly shaped, like a footprint – he had laughed them off. He'd sold the scooter soon after: he said he'd lost his nerve on it. She'd thought then, they'd been lucky, it could have been a write-off considering the damage

179

done to Nathan, but there wasn't a scratch on it. Nathan had been lucky to escape serious injury; now Nathan was dead.

She stopped in the road so abruptly that on the verge Emme turned in surprise, only her eyes visible between the layers of bundling, staring.

So Nathan hadn't come off his scooter. But if he'd been mugged why wouldn't he have said? He hadn't seemed like a man traumatised by something like that, walking through Jo's front door, smiling at her. She thought about that bruise shaped like the imprint of a boot and with Emme's eyes on her she set off again, fast.

As the playground filled up they stayed against the fence, Emme obedient for once, holding her hand. The bell rang and the small queues began to form at the door. Fran knelt. 'Are you sure about this, Emme?' she said, and Emme nodded, pulling her school bag up and hugging it against her. Then her eyes flickered away.

'I can't be late, Mummy,' she said, and she tugged her hand suddenly out of Fran's. 'Look after Ben, Mummy,' she said, and she ran.

Standing to watch as Emme's queue disappeared inside the school, Fran became aware of faces turned towards her in the small milling group of mothers she knew only by sight still, one of them detaching herself to head towards her. As she approached, Fran had the firm impression that the woman – pale, pudding-faced – had been deputed to come over. She planted herself in front of Fran, a grimy shopping bag hanging from her arm, and looked at her with dull curiosity.

'Sorry to hear,' the woman said. She didn't sound sorry.

Fran nodded, wary. "F there's anything we can do,' she went on. 'Kids an' that.' There was a pause. 'I'm Sue,' she offered, as an afterthought.

'Thanks,' said Fran, thinking with sudden unmanageable emotion that she wouldn't even let this woman hold Emme's hand, *not even her hand*, but the woman – Sue – went on. 'Whass'it like, then, that old house? Martin's place.'

Fran opened her mouth but didn't trust herself to say anything. She had to restrain an impulse to step back. There was no sign of Karen. "Cause I heard that there were shit all over it,' Sue went on, darting a look back over her shoulder at the knot of women that had discharged her. 'I heard, you had to get professional cleaning in, it was that bad.'

She sniffed, waiting. Fran stared at her. 'No,' she said, slowly. 'The house was clean enough when we came.' She thought of the statuette in the spare bedroom's cupboard.

'Kept his business in bags, all over the house,' Sue went on with relish. 'Martin were a headcase, 's'all I'm saying.' As if she might not have understood. The little huddle seemed to have lost interest, their backs were turned now. 'I bet he never wanted rid of that place neither. Police thought of that? Headcase, even before his wife left. Where's he gone then?'

'He didn't leave an address,' said Fran, unwilling, but there was something in what Sue was saying that held her there. 'I think he said he was going to somewhere by the sea. Up to the Wash.' Then it registered, what she'd said. 'He wasn't married.'

'He tell you that?' said Sue with satisfaction. 'He were married, all right. She upped and gone, didn't she? Soon

181

after she went, the newspaper gone up at the windows, he tell the postman she took the nets with her.'

Fran just stared, the thought of John Martin living in the dark behind battened windows silenced her.

'Anyhow,' Sue said, hoisting her shopping bag against her, 'anything we can do, like I say, kids an' that.' And she was walking away.

The police car passed Fran on the way home, slowing. She would have liked to keep on walking, past the house and on, but Ben was stirring against her in the sling and they were waiting in the car in her drive. Carswell was getting a silver toolbox out of the car when she turned in.

Ali Compton came inside with Fran, leaving the men outside. She closed the door behind them and put on the kettle without saying anything then turned, resting against the side.

Fran felt the heat rise, between her and Ben's warm heavy body, as he began to struggle a little in the sling. Methodically she began to unstrap him.

'Fran,' said Ali, and there was a warning in her voice. 'Fran. There's something we're not talking about.' A pause. 'The man that came into your bedroom that night.'

'I could have dreamed it,' Fran muttered stubbornly, head down. She extracted Ben's arms from the straps as he stared up at her, with Nathan's dark eyes.

She hadn't, though. All the tiny things that told her the man in her bedroom had been real buzzed and flickered in her head but they were like fireflies, she couldn't catch them. She hoisted Ben against her, set her cheek against his, but she knew Ali Compton was watching her.

'But if you didn't,' said the policewoman. 'You said he came upstairs. He came to bed. So we'll get the bedroom dusted too, right? Like we said.'

Fran stared at her, hypnotised. Once she said it, once she released it, it couldn't be put away again, it would never be caught. Could a man have killed her husband then come softly up the stairs to find her, and she hadn't protested, she hadn't known the difference, or hadn't cared?

'I . . . yes, of course.' Fran stepped back, away from Ali Compton. 'Sure. I'll leave you to it.' She took a breath. 'I want to make some calls, anyway.' Jo.

Ali looked at her, calculating something. Fran made for the door. But she wasn't quick enough.

'He got into bed with you,' said Ali, looking at her, earnest. 'Didn't he? The man you thought was your husband.' And what she said next didn't follow but somehow Fran had known it was coming. 'Something had gone wrong,' Ali continued softly. 'Hadn't it? In your marriage.'

Fran stared.

'You need to be completely honest with us. You know that, don't you? It's the only way we can help you.'

Chapter Seventeen

His flat had been on a main road at least, not some suburban side street, not nice houses with trees where Fran would never have got a cab, not at two in the morning. She'd lain wide awake, head aching from the booze, nausea rising inside her, naked beside a man whose name she didn't know.

She had no idea where it was, she didn't want to know, she even kept her eyes closed to block it out until her head began to spin and she had to open them again. It had been quick, though, ten minutes, maybe fifteen, in the wet deserted streets. She wanted it to be further away, she wanted it to be the other side of the world.

For weeks Fran had felt physically sick with terror that Katrina must have known, must have understood, that sooner or later she would give it away. She never did, she never said anything, but Fran's life was gone. Sometimes she felt as though she'd never get it back.

She had had to tell someone. She thought she was going mad.

'Look,' Jo had said, relenting enough to meet her eye. 'You know what? It's better than that surrendered-wife crap. Nathan this, Nathan that.'

'Hold on,' Fran had said, protesting, 'is that how I've been?' She tried to remember the few conversations she and Jo had had, since Emme, since the wedding, and her heart sank. Maybe she did mention Nathan too much. Maybe it had sounded like that. She couldn't after all have expected Jo to hear the things she never did actually say, like, *I wish it was like old times, you and me. I wish, sometimes I wish I had my old life back.*

Didn't everyone think that, now and then? But Jo was frowning, she was still talking. 'Baby baby baby. Look, it's your body. I'm not saying it's healthy exactly, for you and him, but Christ. It happens. Get over it.'

They'd talked about something else, then: Jo had a boyfriend, she said. 'Not a boy, exactly,' she'd said, wry. 'He's nearly fifty, been married once already, teenage kids. I like him, though.' A pause. 'He's a builder, too. Seems like a grown-up.' Then they walked back in through the big revolving doors to the magazine, and up separate staircases without a word.

Fran made herself think, There's been no rift, things just evolve, but Jo's angry face when she said, *Baby, baby, baby* took too long to disappear. She'd just have to get on with it.

They moved out of London.

She didn't ask herself why he wanted to do this, suddenly. She told herself, this isn't surrendered-wife crap, I'm making it work. She cleaned the house, made the curtains, she took the bus to Oakenham with Emme in her buggy, walking her around and around until she slept, to the butcher's and the baker's and the swings. She sat by the river with her bare legs stretched out in the sun and her eyes closed repeating to herself, *I'm happy, we're happy.* What else could she say?

Then one day she'd opened her eyes and there on the bridge was a man watching her, and with the way he looked at her it all came back. He had waved and she had sat up, her hand to her mouth.

Was this, she wondered as she walked home that day, a different, secret energy humming inside her, so much that Emme turned in the buggy to look up at her as they jolted along the towpath, how life worked? You settled into a groove, a family like other families, life as flat and endless as the wide, rich, dark-earthed fields, you assumed this was it and then you hit a stone in the road, someone turned and smiled at you in the sunshine as if they knew what you were thinking and everything was different.

It was nothing but a tiny grain of difference, that old chemical in the bloodstream; it was just daydreaming. She had bought the dress, after going into Oakenham's only decent clothes shop five, ten times and pretending to consider things, inventing occasions for the benefit of the increasingly wary middle-aged proprietor. A party, a weekend away. But they never went out to dinner or to hotels. No one invited them to parties.

Sometimes it brought her up short, breathless with anxiety, what would Nathan say? *Who are you buying pretty dresses for then?* But all he ever said was, 'How was your day?'

No harm in dreaming. And then she would smile back. 'The usual. You know.'

And sometimes she even wondered if he did know, and he was happy for her.

Carswell and Gerard filed into the kitchen, carrying a silver box, and Fran went quiet. 'We'll give downstairs a quick once-over first,' said Gerard. 'If you need anything from upstairs before we get started.' She bobbed, yes, and they moved inside the house. Carefully Carswell closed the door behind them.

Fran turned back to Ali. 'Things were OK, honestly. I don't know what I can say. Whose marriage is perfect? He was away from home a lot, that's the only thing that upset me, conferences and all that. But . . .'

It pattered in her head, freezing her under Ali Compton's kind look. She's asking about my marriage because she thinks I must have known, all along. She thinks I asked the man into my bed, they're sure even if I'm not, he wasn't Nathan, he wasn't a dream, they think I had a lover, they know . . .

'We were fine,' she said, lowering her voice, getting to her feet. 'Look, I've just got to . . . I'll be quick.'

Fran took the stairs two at a time.

In the bedroom she set Ben on the carpet on his back, and put a little hooped contraption of dangling plastic animals over him. She could hear them moving around downstairs. Ben quieted, reaching over his head for a red elephant, his small foot setting itself with determination flat against the floor to lever himself towards them.

187

She put her finger to the mobile on the bedside table and the screen sprang to life: 10.18 a.m., Wednesday 10 February. Sunday was Valentine's.

Nathan. She sat back on her heels. Nathan.

They never did Valentine's, it hadn't ever figured, nothing to look forward to except possibly some scoffing, from Nathan. But this year he'd bought a card.

She reached for the drawer in the bedside table, but as she hesitated a message sprang up on the mobile's screen. **Are you OK? I saw it in the paper, is that Nathan? Nathan's dead?** She stared at it for no more than a second, her thumb trembling over the delete button. Gone.

Fran could feel her heart beating, fast, then she heard a man laugh, downstairs, and she jumped up. She put the mobile in her pocket.

They were in her sitting room: Gerard and Carswell, the box already packed back up again and they were standing looking at their bookshelves, Gerard with his hands in his pockets. 'All right if we go on up now?' he said. Then, 'These yours?' He nodded at the shelves, awkward. Novels, books on design, architecture.

'Some of them,' she said.

From upstairs she heard Ben make a small delighted growling.

Carswell selected a book, tipping it out: a big glossy book of Helmut Newton nudes. Someone had given it to them, it wasn't their style, though she liked some of them. If she ever left it out on the coffee table it was designed for, Nathan would put it away, carefully. Carswell opened it and she saw Gerard turn his head away from the sight of the long gleaming legs, breasts. Carswell turned a page or two then Gerard cleared his throat and hurriedly Carswell put it back in its place.

'Where's . . .' She couldn't remember Ali Compton's rank, she realised. 'Where's Ali?'

'She had to take a call. She'll be outside. You want her? We can wait.'

Fran shook her head, though she did want her. 'It's in the newspaper. I didn't know.'

'We had to give out some information,' said Gerard, apologetic. 'It helps. People come forward.'

'*Has* anyone come forward? What's happening? Have you found anything out?' She was angry, suddenly. 'I don't know what's going on. You don't tell me anything, you just follow me round like . . . like . . .' She stopped. She took a deep breath. 'The results of the post–mortem, for example. All I know is, he was dead by eleven. How did he die? I'm his wife. His wife.' She had to stop again. Carswell was watching her with curiosity, a kid prodding some insect. 'I'm his wife. I want to know.'

'He bled to death,' said Gerard, levelly. 'The wound to the abdomen hit an artery. As Ali will have told you . . .' he fixed her with a look that was almost a reproof, 'the knife you found, the knife from your kitchen, seems certain to have been the murder weapon. The handle had been wiped, there were traces of your DNA on it but then it was your knife. As you did eventually confirm.' The under-current of hostility was unmistakable.

'What about the tights?' She heard herself, stubborn, to conceal panic. 'Don't you think they . . . might mean something? He might have left them there? Meant to use them for . . . I don't know.'

189

Gerard raised an eyebrow and she saw Nathan in him again.

'Fran,' he began, and she wanted to shout, *Don't you 'Fran' me*, 'I know you must feel helpless—' and she began to shake her head.

'No,' she said but he went on, telling her.

'Like there's nothing you can do. You have to trust us.'

She said nothing then. Gerard pursed his lips, disapproving. 'Yes,' he said, 'well, we've had some joy there.' He smiled stiffly. 'There was DNA on them we've got on the database, as a matter of fact. A female we've got on record.'

'On record for what?'

Carswell fidgeted. 'Not murder, if that's what you're asking,' said Gerard, gently. 'No history of violence.'

'What, then?'

He looked at her, weighing something up, then sighed. 'A caution for shoplifting, two convictions for soliciting, a public disorder offence.' He held his hands out, palms up. 'Gillian Archer. We're trying to trace her, the last address was Cromer, ten years back.' He watched her. 'Norfolk,' he clarified.

'Yes, I know,' she said.

'Why don't you sit down a minute?' he said. 'I'd like to go over it again.'

'I've left the baby upstairs.'

'He sounds fine. Do you want to go and get him?'

She shook her head and sat down, quickly. 'What do you want to know?'

'He came to bed,' said Gerard and she held her breath; she nodded quickly.

'It wasn't . . . I'd have known if it was a . . . an intruder, in my room. Wouldn't I?'

190

He sat down beside her on the sofa, she felt the cushions give. 'You'd be surprised,' Gerard said, gently. 'People tend to assume things they hear and see are normal. They look for a normal explanation first.'

She felt tears prick her eyes at the kindness in his voice. 'I heard the change in his pockets,' she said. 'He got into bed.' She shook her head, unable to speak.

'Did he . . . ah . . . did he . . .' Gerard hesitated. They were both looking at her, Carswell from the bookcase, restive, and instead of saying *Yes, yes, he did*, she shook her head, fiercely. Shame burned her. How could she have not known. 'I'm sorry,' said Gerard, 'but I have to ask. So he got into bed and you went back to sleep. There was no . . . sexual contact?'

From upstairs there was a small thud, and a wail.

She stood up, stiff and hurried. 'No, I'm sorry, I've . . .' and he moved back on the sofa to let her pass.

Ben had rolled on to his front, was all. He strained to look up at her in panic, stranded, red in the face. She knelt to pick him up and found herself looking under the bed. She'd seen something, hadn't she? For no reason she could fathom the thought that something, anything, some tiny scrap of packaging or nothing had been there and was now gone, filled her with panic, too. Fran scooped Ben up against her and leaning down she felt with her free hand, patting under the bed: nothing.

She sat back on her heels, flushed, and there was Ali Compton in the doorway. 'All right?' said Ali, anxious.

'Fine,' said Fran, restraining herself from looking again. It had been blue, metallic on the inside, like, like . . . all she could think of was the packaging on a pregnancy test,

191

but it wasn't that. Stiffly she got to her feet, looking for her mobile, then remembered it was in her pocket.

'They haven't found his phone yet, have they?' she asked.

'Not yet.' Ali looked into the room, the long windows with the line of the horizon visible through them, the walnut chest of drawers that was all Fran had got from her mother, the big old bed they'd bought at an auction, Nathan looking exasperated as she bid on it. 'No phone yet, it's one of our priorities.' The policewoman hesitated. 'He just had the one? Phone.'

Fran stared. 'Why would he need more than one?'

Ali Compton grimaced, just barely. 'Some men do,' she said. 'If there's stuff going on they don't want their wife knowing about, for instance.'

Fran shifted Ben around, stood up and set him on her hip.

'I'd guess the wife usually doesn't know about a second phone, either,' she said, tough. 'I never saw one.' She could see the study door, closing behind Nathan, before he'd leave for work sometimes, at night. She'd hear him in there after she'd gone to bed. 'Someone removed his hard drive,' she said. 'Someone took his phone.'

Ben gurgled, reaching for Ali Compton, and she smiled, she held out a finger to him. 'There's things they can do to track a phone, if it's active, but if it's been destroyed . . .'

Ben took hold of the finger she held out, grasping it with determination, tugging it to his mouth. Half laughing, Ali Compton let him take it. 'You got children?' Fran asked, because the broad, kind face looked like a mother's to her, but the policewoman shook her head tightly.

'Just didn't happen.'

Fran heard Carswell and Gerard at the foot of the stairs, waiting to come up, and suddenly she wanted out. She swung Ben round so quickly the finger was yanked out of his grasp, but she had the advantage of surprise. He didn't start crying till they were past the men and she was picking up the car keys from the hook inside the kitchen door.

Out.

The trolley rolled out of her grasp in the supermarket car park and she had to catch it before it bumped into the car's tailgate. She stopped, staring at the word written in the streaked dust.

Fran had no idea how long it had been there; she hadn't looked at the car in days. Climbing in an hour earlier she hadn't gone round to the rear, she'd just strapped Ben in, flung herself into the driver seat, and off.

It could have been there days. Would the police have told her if they'd seen it? It was innocuous enough.

YOU

Fran had told them in the kitchen, blunt, almost as an afterthought as she got to the door, that she had to get food. 'I hope you'll be done when I'm back,' she'd said, before she could stop herself.

DS Doug Gerard had said, courteously, that he totally understood, that they'd do their best and she'd felt guilty then, turning away quickly to the car before she could say, *Whatever, never mind.*

She looked around herself at the sea of cars, the wide flat landscape beyond. There were people moving between the cars, couples, mothers wrestling with toddlers, men on their own with a single carrier bag, but no one turned to see her.

YOU

All around her the dull gleam of cars under the huge low sky.

It hadn't really been food she'd come for. Standing in the frozen food section, where she found a mobile signal, Fran had dialled the number of the magazine. She still knew it by heart. The sound of the receptionist's greeting, 'Bartle Pawson Publications, can I help you?' with that rise to the voice at the end, brought tears to her eyes, instantly, a whole other lost life springing up in the desert of glass-fronted cabinets and frozen chicken thighs, a world of packed streets and cafés and desks and work. Work.

'Joanna Sinclair, please.'

'Who's speaking?'

Did she think, when she'd hung up, that there'd been an intake of breath when she gave her name? 'I'll try the number for you.'

In the event the assistant didn't miss a beat. 'No, sorry, she's out of the office until tomorrow morning, that's why you've been put through to me. Can I leave a message?'

Anger fired inside her, so sudden that she had to fight to make her reply civilised. It could be true. Give her the benefit of the doubt. Fran asked the woman's name. Camilla. *If you don't mind just saying I called, Camilla? Fran Hall. That's great. Thank you, Camilla.* Seething. She hadn't known this was inside her, all along: rage.

Then it was rage that powered her through the aisles, shovelling stuff into the trolley – milk, bread, meat, fruit – and it was when she found herself beside the bananas

194

(she hated bananas, Nathan lived on them, *had* lived on them) that she came to a halt. She had taken a breath and gone back, more slowly, replacing things on the shelves. She had no appetite, none. Nathan was gone. Coffee, she needed coffee. One bottle of wine, then she even put that back. Smile at the woman on the checkout. Keep moving, get back to the car, then you're on home ground, then you're safe. Except she wasn't.

In the trolley Ben had caught on to something in her sudden silence and he was straining to sit up out of the straps. In a quick movement she leaned down and with her sweatshirted forearm wiped the word out. She didn't give a fuck if it was evidence. She had the right.

Emme? Emme wouldn't have written *You*.

Strapping Ben into his seat she slowed, aware of his eyes following her. He looked so like Nathan: the dark hair, the eyebrows, a certain severe, disapproving look, but she felt her heart lurch, because he was hers now, only hers. She leaned down and kissed him beside his ear. She felt his hand come up, inquisitive, to tug at her hair and she kept her face there patiently, breathing in his smell. Had Nathan wanted them, either of them?

Uneasy, Fran straightened, disentangling Ben's hand. The morning after his conception Nathan had gone down to make her a cup of tea while she lay there in unexpected sunshine with her eyes closed, just basking in it, not quite able to believe it. And of course she shouldn't have believed it, because it didn't happen again – but then Ben was on the way. Not quite a miracle. Luck, chance, unimpeded biology: he had been planned. Something stirred, a suspicion.

And there in the cramped car, that was his car, that still harboured his smell where her bed no longer did, she tried to see Nathan's face. Tried to imagine it, there were bits of it, but it wouldn't come and before she could stop it the outlandish idea ballooned in her head, making her heart beat faster, faster, the crazy idea that it wasn't the man in her bed who'd been a stranger, it was Nathan she didn't know.

Beside her on the passenger seat the phone rang. 'Mrs Hall?' That disapproving voice, June Rayner. Emme's school. 'She's talking about a bad man,' said Rayner.

'I'm coming, I'm coming to get her now.'

Chapter Eighteen

The bad man.

Emme at three, almost four, dancing around the kitchen with the kite's tails getting tangled in the chair legs. 'Come on, Daddy, come *on*.'

Their Saturday mornings had been a routine from quite early on. That September had been bright and warm and the wide flat fields had some colour at last, golden stubble and dark low hedges, the strip of poplars turning yellow and fluttering, thrilling gold and silver in the low constant wind. Every Saturday Nathan would take Emme off after breakfast. *Exploring*, Emme would say, gleefully secretive.

Left behind in the echoing empty house, Fran would walk through the rooms, shifting things, wondering when it would feel like home. There was a hatch into the loft at both ends of the long corridor upstairs and she'd stand and stare up at it, estimating the great length of the space above them in the steep pitched roof, and what could be done with it.

'Once you get rid of the rats,' Nathan had said, with that curt laugh, and then he had frowned at her dismay, because she hadn't known that's what the sound was, the skittering and clicking over their heads. 'All old houses have them,' he said, dismissive. The next day he came back with poison for them, delighted at what the countryside had to offer: unlicensed chemicals and old-fashioned hardware stores. The scratchings and scuttlings did stop, for a while.

In November it got sharply cold, fresh turning to bitter, and with the hardening of the weather at night the sounds in the attic returned, the clicking and scuttling. Fran, pregnant by then, had to wind the two of them round and round with scarves and coats before she'd let them go. She'd felt reluctant that day, she was heavy and slow on her feet. The Saturday they stayed out late.

The sunlight had been thin and brief and the house was cold, a chill hung in the corridors. When they weren't back by two Fran went upstairs in a sulk, lay down and slept. She woke three hours later to find it almost dark, and them still gone. Sitting up on the bed for a moment she didn't even know where she was, the grey half-light made everything unfamiliar, furniture mounded under heaped clothes, the outline of the curtains furred and dim, and there was a strange smell coming from somewhere.

Sweetish, almost rich, for a moment she thought she must have left something cooking and as she stood to get off the bed it cloyed in her throat, her stomach heaved. She padded downstairs and the smell was there too, warm and diffuse, it evaded her. She had to try not to imagine carcases boiled down, bones stripped for dog food. As her insides rebelled Fran held still, gripping the banister till it all settled. It could be something to do with being pregnant, she told herself, phantom scents, hypersensitivity. Or – as the smell seeped in cold under the kitchen door and seemed to metamorphose from animal to chemical – it could be something spread on the fields. Where were they? Sliding her feet into boots, feeling the grit in them, Fran pushed at the door.

The wind had dropped, the sound of the far-off motorway was no more than a whisper for once and the light was low and eerie. At first Fran thought the smell was gone but then in the same moment she thought that the inverse was true, in fact it was everywhere, now, it hung in the air all around her and there was a sound, a kind of hum that went with it. She walked away from the house, across the cramped yard, around the low shed with its sagging roof and towards the big hollow barn.

It must be some trick of thermals or eddies, she told herself, the wind thrumming in the barn's girders or the running water that lay invisible in the land, below the sight-line, it couldn't be in her head, like the smell. Fran walked towards it. The floor was clumped black here and there with couch grass and thistles growing through the concrete, all four sides of the barn were gone but the roof rose dark and cavernous – if she took another step she would be underneath it. She stopped. Beyond the barn, through its girders, as her eyes adjusted to the grey dark Fran could see the short line of leafless poplars, unmistakable in their symmetry, only at their base was a patch of denser shadow. A car was parked there.

Fran felt the hair lift from her scalp, but she couldn't

move. Inside her something came to life and turned, a quick blind panicked squirming. The baby.

Then from behind her came the solid thunk of a door slamming, a gasp, footsteps and a high-pitched cry that carried across the muddy grass. *Mamamamama.*

It was Emme. With the sound of her voice the rigor abruptly dissolved and Fran had turned and run, lumbering in the boots like an awkward animal, towards the house. Emme slammed into her as she reached the yard, the small head against her big tight belly, the arms flung round her, shoulders hunched up to her ears.

'Nathan?' called Fran over her, blindly. And then he was there, coming out of the darkness towards her. For a moment his pale face was a blank and then something shifted and let go and he looked human again, and weary.

'What happened? You were *hours.*' She couldn't disguise the accusation in her voice.

'It was the bad man,' said Emme, breaking free just as Nathan turned away from them both and headed for the back door, one stride and he was inside, leaving the door open behind him.

'Bad man?' said Fran, reaching for her hand, and Emme hung her head, her lip protruding.

'Daddy said don't tell. Daddy had to make him go away. Daddy said he would call the police.'

When Emme pushed the plate away and ran next door Nathan had sighed, turning towards her. 'Just one of those things,' he said wearily. 'It took longer than I'd thought.'

A drunk in a playground, was what it boiled down to. He'd taken her to a place he used to go when he was a kid, the far side of Oakenham, he said. It had taken him for ever to find it and when they got there it was a lonelier spot than he'd remembered.

'Lonely?' she said, wondering at that. Lonelier than here?

Nathan shrugged. 'Overgrown. Tucked away behind houses.' He'd looked thoughtful. 'Not the kind of place they send their kids these days.' He sighed. 'Empty. That's what I thought, anyway, but he was lying behind a tree, he was more or less comatose. You couldn't see him straight away.' He knitted his brow, staring into the grass. 'I didn't see him at all. It was Emme that found him.' He pushed his empty plate back and looked away. 'He'd pissed himself.'

Emme had run back in blithely halfway through. 'Did you tell her? Mummy, he said Daddy was his friend only he didn't know his right name and he was crying. He had wet on his trousers, Mummy.' She made a face, glowering, put her fingers in her hair to spike it up. 'He had crazy hair, Mummy. He had a big beard, he was big like a giant.'

'He knew you?' She waited for Nathan to answer.

He had laughed, that dry dismissive sound. 'Drunks often think they know you,' he said. 'I persuaded him to get lost in the end. It took a while, he couldn't walk straight.'

He leaned down, elbows on his knees, and Emme ran to him. She put a hand on each cheek and stared into his face. He looked back, expressionless. 'He smelled bad,' she said.

Fran quite quickly came to treat that whole evening as almost something she had dreamed. She consigned the smell and the hum, the bad man and the eerie light at the horizon, to things imagined or hallucinated, the uneasy

201

by-product of pregnancy and loneliness and hysteria. The car parked under the poplars had seemed the most banal element of the dream, and the easiest to forget.

Walking round the side of the Victorian schoolhouse, Fran saw the children working at low tables through the glass. The woman who'd talked to her about Martin, the farmer and his wife and shit in bags all over the house, Sue, was there. She was sitting outsize and hunched over a table next to a child frowning down at an exercise book. Classroom helper: the thought did something nasty to Fran's stomach.

Harry, Karen's son, was on the table next to the window and he saw Fran straight away, his face lifted, eager, he made as if to wave but then sat on his hands instead, hunkering down out of sight of the teacher. He watched her, though, until she was out of sight round the building.

She'd left Ben in the car, asleep in his seat. She hurried.

Mrs Rayner was waiting in the reception area, gaunt and tired-looking. It can't be great, thought Fran, looking anxiously around for Emme. Keeping school out here, nothing to see but a grain silo on the horizon, and the wind blowing horizontal from Siberia.

'Is she all right?'

'She's fine,' said the teacher, and sighed, removing her glasses and rubbing the bridge of her nose. 'Under the circumstances.'

And in that tiny moment Fran saw how it began: social

services, questions asked, reports filled out. Just doing her job.

'I'm sorry,' she said. 'She just wanted to pretend things were normal.' The woman softened, fractionally. 'I should have kept her at home,' Fran went on, obediently. 'I'll do that, until—'

'Just give her a few days,' said Mrs Rayner. 'She's with the school secretary.'

But at the door Fran hesitated. 'I'd like to . . .' she began. 'I was thinking. I'd like to get more involved. Here, I mean.' Rayner looked startled. 'Classroom helper, I mean,' said Fran quickly. 'Help with reading. Spelling, you know.'

The headmistress looked taken aback. 'But you won't be . . .' But whatever she had been going to say, she changed her mind. 'Thank you,' she said instead. 'Yes. We'll look into that.' And bent her head quickly back over her desk.

Ben was still asleep when they got back to the car and Emme climbed in beside him obediently, leaning down to kiss his small hand lying limp in his lap, murmuring something to him that Fran couldn't hear. She just shook her head when they got back to the house and Fran turned to look at her in the back seat. 'Mrs Rayner said you were talking about the bad man, Emme. Darling?'

'I just said that because I wanted to come home,' she said, her mouth stubborn. 'Can I watch Peppa Pig on the television, please?'

The house was silent. On the kitchen table was another one of Ali Compton's cards, propped against the salt cellar. Now that she was gone Fran missed her. She turned around and locked the kitchen door and bolted it.

Emme ran past her into the sitting room and she heard

a burst of chatter as the television came on. Fran set Ben just inside the hall in his car seat, asleep, and made a tray of Emme's favourite food. Boiled egg, toast soldiers, little tomatoes, a chocolate biscuit wrapped in foil. A pear cut up into pieces.

After ten minutes, though, Emme padded past Ben into the kitchen where Fran had filled the sink and asked to be put to bed. A corner of the foil turned back and a mouse-sized bite taken from it, the rest untouched on the low table in front of the television.

It wasn't even six, but it was dark outside. Fran read her three stories, and when she refused a fourth turned off the lamp and lay down next to her, looking at the light coming in from the corridor. 'It's all right, Emme,' she whispered, and Emme's head moved up and down, a small hand crept up and gathered her jumper in a fist, holding on. She lay still until the fist relaxed at last and Emme's breathing was even and regular, thinking of Ben alone in the kitchen. How long did she have?

They needed her: she had to make it all right. She had to make it safe. That was all she needed to remember.

Ben was still asleep but his face was crumpled, as if he was in pain. What would happen to them if she couldn't keep them safe? The grimace on Ben's face faded, his small belly relaxed back in the padded seat. Fran stood up, moving stiffly at first, sink, dresser, table, dishwasher, one foot behind the other. Carefully she closed the curtains behind the sink. The bags of shopping were still on the floor where she'd dumped them. She started by putting the food away then moved on to the washing up.

The stack of bills and letters sat on the side, waiting,

reproaching her but the waste bucket under the sink was beginning to smell, so she took it to the yard bins. When she came back inside there the pile still sat: she could just put them away, out of sight. She tugged at a drawer in the farmer's Formica-topped units, they were home-made, thirty, forty years old. Nathan wanted them kept: *They're practically antiques*, he'd said, looking at them with an emotion she couldn't share or understand. The drawer stuck: she pulled harder. She could hear Nathan in her ear, exasperated, *Don't*.

Out of the corner of her eye she checked, Ben in his car seat, still asleep, out of harm's way, and then she tugged again, both hands. A fingernail splintered and the drawer flew free, spraying stuff everywhere, unopened bills, cards, photographs on the floor and on top of Fran as she staggered back and sat, hard, on the linoleum. The drawer landed on her shin with a crack and in his padded nest Ben gave a violent start and opened his mouth to wail. She lay back a moment, holding her breath, ready to sob herself with the pain in her shin, ready to lie face down on the dirty floor – but there was no cry and when she looked Ben's mouth had closed again.

Righting herself, Fran got to her knees over the mess and began to gather it up. Standing then, with the pile crushed against her, she stopped. She had heard nothing, but she felt the cold on the backs of her legs and in that instant she realised that she hadn't driven the bolt home again coming in from the bins, she hadn't turned the key. She stopped, she froze. She couldn't move.

On top of the pile of papers in her arms an old photograph with curled corners stared back up at her, a faded image. Behind her the door closed. She couldn't turn around. She turned around.

'Fran?'

The voice shook. It was Rob. At last. She took a step toward him, she looked.

He was so pale his eyes looked like black holes, the raw-boned hands that emerged from the sleeves of his all-weather jacket were freezing, trembling. It took her a second to understand that he was the one that was terrified, not her.

Awkwardly she stepped towards him and put her arms around him. At first he stiffened and then she felt his head rest on her shoulder. 'It's all right,' she said.

Chapter Nineteen

They'd been together not more than a month when Nathan had introduced her to Rob, leading her through the etched glass door of a Victorian pub buried away out to the east. They'd passed windswept plazas of new-build apartment housing on the way, the glass and steel towers of the city visible over the river, but the pub had been passed over for development and forgotten, sitting humbly on a corner between thirties tenements.

And then there was Rob, squeezed into a velveteen corner with a pint in front of him, looking up, apologetic. Fran could remember the warmth she'd felt when Nathan said that, his hand in hers. It all felt so safe: the dusty down-at-heel gloom of the pub, the skinny best friend, not much more than a boy himself in his football shirt and anorak and oversized trainers. Poor Rob.

'Here she is,' Nathan said, and Rob hovered between standing and sitting, offering a hand. Nathan turned to the bar.

'I've heard all about you,' he said and she grimaced.

'Do I pass?' she whispered, apologetically. 'Sounds like you're the man I have to impress.' And Rob had blushed and bobbed his head and smiled, quick, shy, unexpected, a wide child's smile.

Nathan came back, his hands full of drinks, and setting them down said, 'What do you think of her then,' he said, 'my fiancée?' And she'd just grabbed the glass and taken a drink, because she didn't know if it had been a joke. Barely a month and he was calling her that.

She couldn't remember what they'd talked about: a build; some walking holiday Rob had been on. She remembered the look Nathan gave her though, a quick apologetic glance across Rob's shoulders, then another one, exhilarated, when he saw she was up for it, *yes*.

Rob had just made to stand up and buy a round when Nathan's phone had gone off and looking at it he had said to Fran, 'Got to take this, sorry, work.' Then to Rob, 'It's Julian.' Rob nodding, barely breaking his stride towards the bar.

Whatever the call had been about it hadn't taken long, because Rob hadn't even set his round back down on the table when Nathan reappeared.

'Everything all right?' Rob had said, leaning down to the table with his hands on the glasses, looking up. And Nathan had nodded just once, brisk, then turned to her. She'd seen it then, a filament glinting in the dusty air between them, friends, brothers. It had shown her a Nathan she could trust.

'Have you spoken to the police?' she said.

Rob was staring down at the stack of papers in her arms, then he was on his knees gathering the junk that had spilled from the drawer and putting it back in. Setting the pile down she put her hand on his shoulder and felt him take a deep shuddering breath, then he stood up, carefully set the drawer back on its runners and slid it in.

'They got hold of me this morning.' Rob leaned back against the closed drawer. 'I was driving, I told them I'd call them back but they said to just come in when I got here.' He put a hand to his head. 'Tomorrow, I guess.'

He'd always been skinny but he looked like he'd lost weight, his jeans hung off him.

'Who do they think did it?' he said, staring, haunted. 'I asked on the phone, but the man didn't really seem to want to tell me anything.'

'DS Gerard?' said Fran and he shrugged, helpless.

'Was that his name? He said something about burglary. A break-in gone wrong.' Rob looked around the room, confused, and she followed his gaze, registering how much order she'd restored. Rob looked back at her. 'I didn't like him. The man I talked to. He asked me about your marriage.' He looked into her face, she saw he was on the edge of tears, or worse. Pleading. 'Why would he ask about that?'

'I suppose they have to eliminate me as a suspect.' It came out rougher than she planned and she knelt to the car seat so as not to have him stare at her. Ben was shifting, arching his back as if uncomfortable, and gently she reached her hands in and under him, felt the damp under him and the nappy's weight, smelled the hot reek.

'Who is Julian Napier, Rob?' she said from where she knelt, not looking up. She reached for the wipes she kept in the pocket on the back of the car seat, groped for the clean nappy there. Ben's eyes were still closed but he drew his knees up, ready, his face clenched.

'Julian?' She heard him step back, wary. She focused on the task, down here in the dirt the sweetish smell in her nostrils: no matter what, this had to be done. Ben was her shield against the past, her future. *They* were, him and Emme. She opened the nappy, raised his legs quickly, wiped, pulled the dirty nappy out and slid the clean one under him. Saw something, in the nappy. Little scrap of blue, before she folded it on itself.

'He's a guy . . . Julian?' Stuttering. 'He's the guy Nathan works for. He gave Nathan his first job.'

Quick. On her knees still, she got it done: strip open the tabs, secure the nappy, off with the sodden babygro, vest underneath would have to stay, back and up holding Ben up under his arms, he raised his knees, face screwed up, his mouth opening. She turned him, sat, set him on her knee, pushed up the sweatshirt and he latched on. Then she looked from where she sat, suddenly calm, up into Rob's face.

'I want to help you,' he said, almost a sob in his voice. 'I want . . .' but he was at the door, as if he wanted to run out.

210

'So just a regular guy.'

'I don't know anything about Nathan's work,' said Rob, rubbing at his wrists, an anxious movement.

'Then who does?' she asked. 'You're the only one who knew Nathan, really knew him.' The dirty nappy still on the floor. 'It wasn't a burglary. It wasn't some random . . .' She felt something contract in her chest, fear. 'You're all I've got, don't you see? On my side.'

He began to shake his head, 'I don't know what . . .' he said, and she saw his raw, sore hands. 'I don't know what I can do.' Fran put out her free hand, from where she sat she could just touch his sleeve. He looked lost, he gazed at her as if she might save him.

'Nathan told me he was going to the pub twice a week,' she said, focusing on Ben's small hot head against her, the steady pull of his feeding. He kept the fear down, shrunk to a hard knot. Don't think about that. Keep talking. 'Only the landlady told the police she'd barely seen him since the week we arrived.' Rob just stared. 'Do you know where he was going, Rob?' Fran didn't wait for him to answer, she went on, talking and talking, like she'd been set free.

'You know something, don't you?' she said, and she saw him flinch. 'What was it, going through your head while you were walking back down from that mountain? What was Nathan into? All those conferences . . .' She was ranting. Of course he'd been to the conferences. They had all the freebies – the mugs and the nylon laptop covers – but she couldn't afford to stop now. 'Was it something criminal?' She found she needed to take a breath. 'Who did he come back here for? He was never happy here. Why did he come back?'

211

Stiffly upright, Rob set his hands by his side, against the drawer behind him. 'Criminal? Who . . .' and his eyes flickered, afraid. 'I don't know what you mean.'

Who was he afraid of? Nathan? Afraid of that darkening look in Nathan's eyes? Nathan was dead. She would have liked to get up, to stand and shake him, but there was Ben. She steadied her voice. 'There was another friend, he talked about it. A man who ran a scaffolding business; Nathan said he was going to track the guy down. What was he called? Jeb, Jez, something like that?' For a moment she thought he was going to faint, to slide sideways and crash to the floor, but she had hold of his sleeve, she wasn't going to let up. He said something, so quiet she hardly heard it.

'Bez,' he said, then again, louder. 'His name was Bez. Is Bez.'

'A friend of yours.' Barely perceptibly, he nodded.

'Nathan told you, didn't he,' said Rob, 'about the house.'

'What house?' Ben had stopped, but he wasn't asleep. He pulled away, she could feel his eyes on her, waiting, but she didn't look down, she tugged her sweatshirt to cover herself. She felt dirty, suddenly, sweat in her armpits, grey in the folds of her body.

'We were just kids,' said Rob and suddenly he seemed to be about to cry. 'We were going to live there for ever. Nathan hated it at home, he said. Me and him and . . . Bez. We thought it would last for ever but it only lasted a summer, in the end. Nathan went to London, it all broke up.' He was staring, his voice had become a monotone.

'The place you squatted,' said Fran. She could feel Ben's eyes intent on her and she allowed herself a quick glance down. 'What was it called again?'

212

'Black Barn,' he said, staring through her to somewhere far off. 'Do you think it was something to do with that?'

'Rob, are you all right? Are you . . . are you on something? You need to tell the police, you know that, you need to go and tell them everything, tomorrow.'

'The police.' Rob's eyes came into focus. 'Right.'

'Where's Bez now?' Her hand still on his sleeve and he pulled away in sudden fright.

'Don't go after Bez,' he said. 'Bez is bad news.' He focused with an effort.

'Are you on something, Rob?' she asked again, but he just shook his head.

'Bad news, always was, when it all broke up, when Nathan went . . .' He took a breath. 'He lost the scaffolding business a year or two ago, because of the drinking. Then it wasn't just drink. It was drugs. Serious drugs. He went AWOL, off the radar. No fixed abode.'

'Could he . . .'

Karen had said it, when you come back, the people you left behind don't always like it, but it stuck in her throat. The man in her bedroom: the heavy tread. *No, no, no.* 'You've got to tell the police about him.'

'No!,' said Rob, and his eyes were all over the place. 'No, you don't understand, he wouldn't – Bez would never . . .'

And from upstairs it came, a sudden shout, from Emme's room. Not a whimper but a loud, fierce noise, *NO*, as if there was someone in there with her, and Emme, brave Emme was facing him down, she was fighting. Fran was on her feet, Ben against her shoulder.

She had got to the bottom of the stairs when she felt

the icy air and turned, but Rob was gone and the door was swinging open behind him.

Fran made herself cross the room and close it – lock it, bolt it – top and bottom, before she went upstairs.

When she heard the police car and the voices below the window from where she lay, Fran's first thought was that harm had come to Rob. Somewhere in the black fields, driving along an unlit road. She was on Emme's bed, squeezed between them, Ben asleep and snuffling in her armpit. She must have been asleep herself because she was stiff and disorientated at the sounds outside.

Struggling up, she tried not to wake Ben. She crept down the corridor and laid him in his cot. She covered him. The house was locked, they'd ring the bell, they'd knock, they'd wake him. But she didn't hurry. While they were outside and the door was locked it was her house.

They were knocking, softly, as Fran came into the kitchen where the lights were still on, but she paused to kneel and retrieve the nappy from under the table, she pulled a plastic bag from the holder, flipped the bin and set it on top, under the lid. She looked at the clock as she reached up for the bolt. It was almost nine o'clock.

'Sorry to come so late,' said Gerard and for a second she had a flashback to an old life, a parallel world, Nick turning up on her doorstep looking pumped, ready to go, and his low dark car blinking in the street behind him. *Hey, Frankie, I knew you'd be pleased to see me.* Gerard didn't look sorry, like Nick he looked energised, alive, as if late nights agreed with him. Carswell was behind him, his narrow little face bobbing to see her over his boss's shoulder. There was no sign of Ali Compton.

'You'd better come in,' she said.

The first thing Fran did when they left was to cross back to the fliptop bin and open it. She took out the plastic bag holding Ben's dirty nappy. It was true, really, they hardly smelled bad when the baby was so small but she wouldn't have noticed it anyway.

'Did you see Rob?' she had asked and Gerard had frowned, impatient. 'Rob?'

'He was here. He said . . . the friend, Bez, their friend from years back—'

'That's not what we came about,' said Gerard and she heard a warning in his voice.

'Where's Ali?'

'Ali will be back tomorrow,' he said, patiently. 'If you want her.'

Fran stared a second – Of course I want her – then hurried on.

'Bez, he ran a scaffolding business, you should be able to find him from that? He started drinking, Rob said, so maybe he's got a record, a police record.' They looked back at her, Gerard impassive, just waiting for her to finish, and Carswell curious. It felt as if she'd been waiting so long to say her piece, to give them a shove, Fran wasn't going to stop now.

'They shared a squat in Oakenham, Black Barn it was called. Years back. Fifteen, twenty years? Something happened there.'

And then she came to a halt because she hadn't known that was what she was going to say, and because of the way they were looking at her.

215

'We've heard something,' said Gerard, and beside him Carswell was raised on the balls of his feet, bouncing with anticipation. 'About you.'

After they'd gone Fran had locked the door again behind them and then she'd sat on her haunches with her back set against it a moment, waiting for the sound of the police car's engine. Now she stood over the bin and she opened up the nappy carefully, delicately.

She'd seen the way Gerard had looked around her tidy kitchen, momentarily distracted by its cleanness, briefly approving, like Nathan.

They had been watching her. She could see it now, as if from high above, they thought she wasn't behaving as a bereaved woman should, never mind she had children, and what was she supposed to do, was she supposed to go to pieces so they could swoop, get inside her house and tear it all apart? They had been waiting for her to make a false move. Who jumps first? And now they'd jumped.

'You came here to make a fresh start with your husband.' That had been Carswell, earnest and wide-eyed but sly all the time, and uncertainly Fran had nodded.

'Yes.'

'You came here because you'd had an affair.' And that had been Gerard. Fran had stared at him, overwhelmingly aware that these men were not her friends, not even her allies. Who told you?

Was one night an affair?

A man climbing out of a taxi in the rain, walking up some stairs in front of her, letting her in to a dim untidy room. A man who went over to a drawer and got something out of a packet before she had even located the unmade

216

bed, the tiny sound in her ears as she had sat on an unmade bed and concentrated on thinking nothing, feeling nothing.

What did they think they knew?

The nappy lay open in the bin and she saw it, the tiny scrap of blue packaging that had been under her bed when she'd left Ben there and he'd rolled on to his belly. He must have reached for it, inquisitive, sharp-eyed. Would she have recognised it even without the telltale letters the *−ex* that was all that was left of the brand name? The man in her bed the night Nathan died had used a condom.

Inside her that tiny scrap of information seeded, it grew. And then she smelled it, then she felt it coming up inside her like acid: it had been in Ben's mouth, in her baby's mouth, passing through his small perfect system. She ran blindly into the hall and blundered through the toilet door, head down in the dark. They're gone, it's all right, they're gone, they can't hear. Or were they out there in the night, listening?

Fran had known what they were going to say next before Doug Gerard said it. A newsreel of boyfriends, husbands, wives, weeping for the cameras, blinking in flash-bulbs, flinching at questions. Next, they needed a lawyer.

'We need witnesses,' he spoke gently. 'We need your help.' She nodded, dumb. 'We'd like you to hold a press conference, tomorrow morning.'

'Mum?'

Ali called up the dark stairs to the room with light coming under the door. As she came in her mother looked up from the bed, sweet and serene, the bedside lamp on, book in her lap, the little TV flickering on her bedside

217

table. All that was wrong this time was she was wearing her coat, done up to the neck.

'You cold, Mum?' said Ali, gently, unbuttoning the coat for her as she sat on the bed, checking round the room at the same time, registering the air smelled clean, the sheets were dry. 'They came in this afternoon then?' She leaned her mother forward to pull the coat out from under her in the bed. She knew the carers had been because the bins had been put out and the kitchen table was clear.

'Who's that, dear?' said her mother, smiling, and Ali saw in the faded periwinkle eyes that she was recognised, at least, she wasn't her dead auntie June or the postman's wife. 'I've had a lovely day, I sat in the garden, I think I caught a bit of sun. We picked the raspberries.'

The fruit cages had been gone from the back garden since the last millennium and the sun hadn't been out all day. There were no raspberries.

It was hovering around zero out there, but felt colder with the wind. Straight from Siberia, that's what they said, across the Wash and the snow would be here by the weekend. Ali's heart sank, thinking of Mum when the snow came, she'd probably think she was ten years old and go out skating on the Fen. For a guilty moment it seemed such a peaceful thought, Mum lying down in the snow and going to sleep. It wouldn't work like that, sod's law, the ice would crack under her and she'd drown, slow and painful in the freezing ditch, that long confusing life shaken up again and passing before her terrified eyes.

She'd have to call Adrian, get him over to cover for her. She was his mother too, after all, though he visited so rarely she probably wouldn't know it any more. 'Mum,' she began, tentatively. Fran Hall was holding on, she was staying put for whatever reasons she had, the children, or stubbornness, defending her home against the likes of DS Doug Gerard, but she was scared of something worse than him. 'I was going to give Adrian a call. He's been asking when he can visit, and now I'm back at work . . .'

Mum's head tipped on one side, her eyes all dreamy. 'Little Adie,' she said, soft as butter. 'I'd like to see Adie,' and she began to shift on the pillows. 'Will he bring that girlfriend of his?'

Ali's heart sank, God only knew which girlfriend she had in mind, but almost certainly not hard-faced Natalie, mother of his twins and keeper of the show home they lived in, twenty miles away. 'I don't suppose so,' she said gently, patting the pillow, and the old head settled back down.

'Shame you never had any.' There were moments like this, when the fog cleared and she was sharp as a tack, so sharp she even knew what Ali was thinking.

'Yes, Mum, it is.' Kids, was what she meant. Mum hardly saw Adrian's: Natalie said it would freak them out, even though Mum wouldn't raise her voice or hurt a fly.

The day would come, soon enough, that Mum would be loaded into some ambulance and taken to a place she didn't know to spin out the last days and weeks, no more raspberry-picking, no more skating on the Fen.

'Just get off,' Gerard had said, his eyes narrow. 'We can manage fine without you. She's got your number and she made no bones about it, wanted us out of there.'

Fran Hall. Dumped out here, in the middle of nowhere. You could see it in her eyes, though, she wasn't going to give in. She was holding it together with the kids. For the kids. Gerard didn't seem to understand that; the way he saw it, it was what Ali was there for, to monitor the children's safety – so he could leave it out of the equation. He could decide Hall was a cold bitch, he could apply pressure even though, Christ knew, she was under enough of it already, and wait, with that giggling kid Carswell gazing at him like he was God, they could wait and see what happened. Was that good policing?

Ali, without applying any pressure at all, could see that Fran Hall was hiding something. That she was experiencing guilt. She could also see that the woman hadn't killed her husband, or had him killed. And that when it came to hiding stuff, there was plenty Gerard wasn't saying, either. That husband of hers, Nathan Hall, if that's who he really was, Ali might have been tempted to hit him over the head with a rock herself but then perhaps that was why she'd never been married. Policemen round her day in day out, enough to put you off for life.

Under the coat Mum was wearing a cotton summer dress and a pink cardie. Ali laid the coat on the chair, pulled the satin quilt up over them and leaned back on the pillow, her head next to her mother's.

'You get on back to your mother,' Gerard had said in the corridor at the station, dismissing her. 'Hall will be in touch if she wants our support and if she doesn't . . .' he spread his hands, smiling briefly, 'that's not our problem, is it?' A burst of deep laughter from behind him in the canteen.

Had Doug Gerard always been like this? He'd always been a hard-arse, but he'd turned sour when the last woman left him, Lara, a horsey girl, a big blonde. They liked his looks, they liked his stern way with them, like he knew what he was doing, but they didn't like the hours he worked or the bitterness he brought home with him, the contempt. Let them drown in their own vomit, let them overdose, let them freeze to death boozed up to the eyeballs. *Not our problem*, that was Gerard. Ali didn't know what was underneath any more; once upon a time she could have been bothered working out what made a copper tick. Not any more.

'Valentine's on Sunday, Ma,' she said, on the pillow. 'They say it's going to snow.'

Chapter Twenty

Thursday

It was so cold at eight that the windscreen was frosted hard and Fran had to clear it. She drove slowly, gripping the wheel tight with Ben in his car seat beside her gazing through the window, reflections of the grey outside in his eyes. A long, straight road in the lee of a windswept dyke seemed to go on for ever, then it turned sharply at ninety degrees and there was a truck thundering towards her. She hit the verge and hung on, grim, registering the thought that popped up, beyond her control: that would be easy, that would wipe it all out, sideswiped by a turnip truck into the black fen. Except for Emme.

An affair. She didn't understand – it seemed impossible that the police could have found out about the one-night stand. Fran didn't even know his name herself, she had erased him.

Jo: the only one who knew.

She'd left Emme with Karen, who had accepted her without comment but had closed the door on her before she'd had a chance to say thank you, or sorry, or to try to explain what kind of shit she was in, up to her neck. But she had to leave Emme because Ben wouldn't ask questions, Ben would forget all this – but Emme stored things away. You could see it in her clear, pale, inquisitive eyes, hungry for information, for answers.

Waiting for her in the reception area, Ali Compton looked like Fran felt: stunned, exhausted, with dark circles under her eyes. She looked like she had picked the same clothes she'd been wearing the day before off the floor, too. Jeans and a sweatshirt with a logo on it.

'Where are we going?' she said. 'Is there a . . . a special room? A conference room?' She felt a knot form under her ribs at the thought that she would be the person on the screen, the evening news, blinking in the bright lights behind a table. Four days ago, less than a week: Sunday evening, was there anything safer than a Sunday evening, bad telly, school in the morning? He had been alive.

'I'll show you.' Ali knelt to where Ben sat in the car seat, and gave him her finger to hold. He seized it, tried to get to it with his other hand. Ali looked up at her, anxious.

'I'm taking him,' she said, and she detached his finger gently, took hold of the baby seat's handle. 'That's all right, is it?'

Fran felt things go into slow motion. 'No,' she said, 'I . . . you can't . . .'

'Just while you're in there,' said Ali, patiently, and patted her arm. 'Don't panic,' she said quietly. 'I'll be right there when you're done. I'll be right outside the door with him.'

The conference room was hot and crowded, rows of seats and twenty, maybe thirty people, a buzz of chatter that died as she was led in. Journalists; old hands, a day's work for them. There were only half a dozen women

223

among them, all younger than the men, all looking rough under the glare of striplighting. At the back Fran saw a camera, a man's face bobbing out from behind it to get a look at her, then it was gone again. She could feel the silent presence of DS Gerard at her back as they walked in, corralling her. There were three microphones, Gerard, a police PR man, and her between them.

The PR man addressed the journalists, giving a warning, this access was conditional on them respecting her privacy, staying away from the house. Fran hadn't even thought about that, journalists doorstepping her; she was grateful for the nods she saw in the audience. Then Gerard was on his feet outlining the case. He was precise, clear, his voice was strong. Fran registered that a number of the women focused on him, gazing. One in the front row seemed to have a particularly unwavering stare. A good-looking policeman, he'd have his opportunities.

'We are actively seeking information on Nathan Hall's whereabouts between eight and ten o'clock on the evening of February the seventh,' he finished, sitting down, and then it was Fran's turn. She put out a hand and touched the microphone.

Doug Gerard had told her she didn't have to stand up: as the walls seemed to close in she couldn't have stood up if she wanted to.

The door at the back of the room opened and as if down a long lens she glimpsed Carswell's narrow foxy face as he slipped inside.

Had they come here because she'd had an affair? She'd agreed to it because of that night. Yes. But Nathan hadn't known about that night. He couldn't have known.

'My husband Nathan Hall was a good man,' she began. 'I don't know who would have wanted to harm him.' She barely recognised her own voice, it sounded so light and thin.

Her children had lost their father, she said to the room of faces, Emme who was in her first year at the local school, Ben who was only three months old. She didn't even know what she was saying: the faces were a blur, the women's were sharper, brighter, she saw lipstick, shiny hair. A head bobbed over a notebook and a flash went off. She felt numb, removed, behind a glass wall. Just keep talking. 'He was a good man.'

At the table, flanked by the two policemen, Fran raised her eyes to the crowded room. 'We made a family together.'

She thought she'd been sure of that, since the first time: he wanted the children. He had said something to give her pause only once, a long way further down the line. About condoms, a terse comment along the lines of, he'd never been able to get along with them, they panicked him. But he had wanted a baby too, surely? By then she must have been three, four months gone, and it couldn't have been just because he didn't like wearing a condom? They were a family.

But the truth ticked away as she scanned the strangers in the grey room. A blonde woman with black roots, a man with dandruff on suit shoulders, another in a grubby cagoule, hollow-cheeked under his hood. It settled like mud. A scrap of condom on her bedroom floor, that her husband would never have used. A man had come into her bed and fucked her. A shutter came down. Fran felt herself stare and stare to keep it down. Could they see? The faces stared back, some averted their eyes.

What was love? Wanting to protect someone. Had she loved Nathan? She couldn't think about the way his skin felt when she put her cheek against his back in the bed now, or she would break down, in front of all of them. She couldn't see his face: she tried and tried.

Ed Carswell was watching her from across the room. In the ante-room no one had said anything more about her having an affair, not even a meaningful look. Gerard had just lobbed that in, it seemed to her, and now they were sitting back and waiting, they were watching for her reaction. They hadn't told her she was a suspect, but they were watching her. Was that what this press conference was about?

Or was she losing it, imagining things? Nathan had used that word, *paranoid*, when she said she thought the women in the playground stared at her.

Last night, on the floor of the downstairs toilet after they'd gone, she had sat against the wall in the dark, her own eyes squeezed shut to block it out, that tiny little scrap of packaging and all it meant, a line that ran unwavering from a one-night stand and a man unwrapping a condom on his unmade bed to here and now, the bright lights and all these people staring. And she had held herself so still, she could feel the hair rising on her scalp, she could feel her flesh crawl, but if she made one movement where would it end? She would start to tear at herself, wherever he had been, her back, between her thighs.

If they knew she'd ripped the sheets off the bed and stuffed them in the washing machine. Destroyed evidence. Fran felt sweat bead on her forehead under the lights.

'So if anyone out there knows anything, anything at all,'

226

she said, her lips numb, her voice dull and emotionless, 'about my husband's death, could they, could they . . .' and Fran turned to Gerard, and he was standing up, reading out the number of the helpline.

She'd come, there in the underwater dark as she dreamed of a man on a beach. How could she explain to them that was why she'd swept the sheets into a ball on the bed, she had lain her face on them and breathed in the smell of it, mysterious and pungent, she had put her arms around the sheets and hugged them against her. Had she known, deep down, somehow, had she known it wasn't Nathan? Had she been thinking so hard of someone else that she had brought him to her bed, and then in a panic wanted to remove all trace? All they would see was, she had destroyed the evidence.

I didn't know, Fran wanted to say, eyes down at the table. I wasn't thinking straight. Just say nothing, she told herself. Don't even explain to them that what they were calling an affair had been a one-night stand. That she had hated every minute of it.

Of course, she thought, there *were* no stains, were there? That was what the condom had been for. He had been careful not to leave any evidence. And now Gerard was inviting questions from the audience and there was movement among them, a settling of bums on seats, someone leaned forward.

'Is it true you found your husband's body yourself?' The man in the cagoule, his head taller than the others'. A murmur went around the room.

'Yes,' Fran said faintly and she understood, they wanted a story. Open season.

'Mrs Hall.' The woman in the front row was getting to her feet now with her hand raised. 'Might your husband's death have had anything to do with his work, is that a possibility? What was your husband's business, Mrs Hall?'

A good-looking, hard-edged woman, her eyes moved from Fran to Gerard and back again. Fran said, helpless, 'My husband was in the building trade.' She felt the panic rise then, knowing that they could ask anything, anything at all, and she would have to answer, but she pushed on blindly. 'I don't know what reason anyone could have had to hurt him, I—'

And then miraculously Gerard was standing again with both hands out, saying something, and it was all over, people were getting to their feet, turning to chat to each other as if this was all normal. Fran stayed seated, frozen as they moved to and fro, not raising her eyes when there was a burst of laughter. When she did finally get up there was no sign of the man in the cagoule or the woman who'd asked about Nathan's work.

There was a separate exit for her to leave through, while the press filed out on the other side of the room. Ali Compton was right outside the door with Ben, just like she'd promised.

Ali had watched it on a monitor, walking up and down with the baby on her shoulder, groaning inwardly. '*Christ*,' she even hissed and Derek had looked at her in surprise; she'd shaken her head impatiently.

Fran Hall looked scared to death. She also looked like she was hiding something. 'Talk to me,' muttered Ali into the baby's little warm neck.

228

Doug Gerard had been like a dog with two dicks all morning, full of it. Craddock had been in a video conference from eight a.m. and had had Gerard upstairs for a private briefing the minute he walked through the door.

On the monitor Fran was white as a sheet, she looked like she might actually keel over: this was what Gerard had wanted. People to look up at the screen and say, *Who's that, then? What's she done?* Then, *I've seen her somewhere.*

They'd done a job on her, all right. Laurel and Hardy. The last thing she was going to do was talk to them.

Ali was at the door when Fran came through it. Fran grabbed the baby like she was drowning.

'You eating properly?' asked Ali. 'Honest to God, Fran. Mrs Hall. You can't take care of those kids if you aren't taking care of yourself.' Fran Hall stared back at her, her eyes all pupils, staring, and Ali tried again. 'Won't you think about getting out of that house at least?' she said, lowering her voice. 'The temporary places, they're not all bad. Some of them are nice. You need looking after. You need some space.'

Fran Hall was shaking her head. 'I'm fine. Nerves. All those people.' She seemed to have trouble getting the words out. 'It's my home. You don't understand. Our home. He's not taking it away from me.'

'He?' But Fran Hall was tugging the car seat out of her hand.

'I'm coming back with you, at least,' said Ali.

'No,' said Fran Hall, sharp, and Ali let the car seat go. 'No.'

And then she was walking away and Gerard was there, at Ali's shoulder. 'Giving you trouble, is she? Losing your touch, DC Compton.'

Of course they knew, what was she thinking of? Of course someone would have seen her talking to him at the party, someone else would have known who he was, he might have told — and she saw the connections spread like fire.

And how did it jump the void, get to the police? Now they must know, then, at the magazine, that Nathan was dead. The police must have been there. And Jo hadn't taken her call. What had the police said to her?

At the last minute Fran stamped on the brake and behind her Ben wailed in protest: a red light. She just hadn't seen it.

A stream of traffic passed in front of her on Oakenham's grimy ring road, beyond it a scattering of squat Victorian cottages and then the horizon. She engaged gear and they left the town behind them.

Unless someone around here had been spreading rumours. Villages were like that, weren't they, you only had to exchange a word with a man in the street and it was adultery.

The landscape emptied, the big glaring sky flooded the windscreen. Ben was asleep again. She turned into the lane on the edge of the village and pulled up outside Karen's bungalow.

Bundled in her padded winter coat and jeans, Emme was in Karen's back garden — Fran could see her through the wide sliding glass doors. They were in the living room, a wide low room crowded with furniture, knick-knacks ranged on the mantelpiece and on shelves in two alcoves either side of a coal-effect fire, very tidy. Very warm.

There had been photographs hung all down the dim narrow corridor that led to the sun room on the back of the house. Studio portraits, school shots, Harry, Karen, grandparents at the back. Two girls with neatly brushed hair, side by side.

'She wanted to go out there,' said Karen. 'I told her it was too cold.'

Emme was intent on something, running to and fro from the frosted flower bed to a big glazed pot on the patio, depositing, returning.

'You all right?' said Karen, and hearing a note of rough apology Fran turned and nodded. She saw the TV remote on the coffee table.

'You saw it, then?' she said. 'The press conference.'

Karen sighed. 'I didn't mean to get narky with you. It's horrible, all this, him dead and coppers in and out of the house.'

Fran was so close to the window her face almost touched it. The sky was low and dark, she looked for snow but nothing was falling yet.

'I'd be like you,' said Karen to her back. 'Not doing what they want you to do, crying for the cameras.' She frowned. 'I'd be, it's my house, I'm not moving. I'd be, come and get me. Just try it.'

Fran turned quickly and caught Karen's defiant look. 'Funny,' she said. 'That's it. That's what . . . it feels like. I don't think they understand that though. The police.'

'That'll be because they're thick as planks, the lot of them,' said Karen gently, and she laid a hand on Fran's shoulder.

'They're funny with me,' Fran said, on the edge of tears at the gesture. 'I don't know why.'

Karen made a small snorting sound. 'They're men first,

231

police officers after. They're men, you're a skirt. Have they tried anything on?'

Fran thought of Carswell saying *Nice legs*, but she shook her head.

'Huh,' said Karen, sceptical. 'Well, you tell me if they do. You tell someone if they do.'

'I think,' said Fran slowly, 'it's something to do with the time of death. With me being so sure it was later because . . . I thought I heard him come in.' She could tell Karen. That's who she could tell. But there was something about the hard, beady look in Karen's eye that made her falter. 'He was dead by then. I thought he came in around midnight, but he couldn't have.'

Karen held her gaze a long moment.

'They think I did it.' It came out, just like that, but Karen didn't seem surprised: she just waited, alert.

'They think I'm not frightened.' Outside, Emme was crouching on the grass beside the pond, looking at something beyond it, although all Fran could see was the hedge. Her head bobbed, looking back at the house, then she stood up, and carefully began to pick her way around the pond.

'I am frightened, though,' said Fran, watching.

Karen studied her, arms folded across her front.

'He was still there when I found Nathan. When I came back inside, when I was on the phone to the emergency services, he was out there. He threw a stone at the window.' And despite the heat she felt cold, as she said it.

'Did you know him?' said Karen, and Fran stared.

'Know him? You mean did I recognise him? I didn't see his face.'

'Look,' said Karen, arms still folded, 'I just want to help. You understand?'

'I didn't know him,' said Fran, and she felt panic. 'I didn't have anything to do with this, Karen.' She sat, her head in her hands. 'That's why they did the press conference, isn't it? They think everyone will know. They want people to phone in and say things about me, not about Nathan.'

'Could be.' Karen sat down next to Fran on the sofa. It was some kind of dark patterned velvet, hard to keep clean, Fran found herself thinking, staring down between her hands, but it *was* clean, like everything in this house, like nothing in hers. Warily Karen put an arm around her shoulders and she felt a quick warm pressure, then it was gone.

'You want to be careful. Tough doesn't sort everything. I should know.'

'I'm not even tough,' said Fran. 'I just . . . don't know what else to do.' She removed her face from her hands quickly, remembering Emme, but she wasn't looking. 'Someone left a box of chocolates in my kitchen,' she said slowly, staring straight ahead.

'Chocolates.' Karen sat back with an abrupt, surprised laugh. 'Well, who's complaining? Valentine's coming up.' Her voice was wry, on the edge of bitter. 'Maybe he . . . maybe your husband—'

'They weren't there before,' said Fran quickly, because in that moment she was sure. 'They weren't there when he left for the pub. And the police are saying . . . they think he never even came back inside the house. He was . . . killed before he got home.' Karen didn't seem to hear how quickly she stopped talking, then.

The gilt-edged box. Years since Nathan had bought them for her. 'The kind of chocolates a bloke would give you to impress you,' she said. 'Or if he was in the doghouse. If he had something to make up for.'

Like sex you hadn't asked for. And suddenly she felt it again, the prickle of her skin, the urge to scrape and scratch at herself and she had to shift forwards on the sofa in case she had to make a break for the door. Outside, Emme was standing at the hedge with her back to them, almost set inside it, like a small statue.

'So where do *you* think they came from?' asked Karen, frowning, fierce. 'The chocs. He weren't . . . your Nathan. Had he been messing around? Playing away?' She was gearing up for outrage.

Fran almost laughed, she felt it turn into a sob. She swallowed. 'No,' she said. 'I told you, the box wasn't there when he left for the pub.' She looked down into her hands. 'And Nathan wasn't that kind of man.' Almost whispering.

'They're all the same kind of man, love. One way or another.'

But the sofa shifted suddenly and then Karen was on her feet. 'Hold up,' she said, because Emme was running towards them, she was stumbling in her haste. Her face was blank and white.

Chapter Twenty-One

'Just take it slowly,' Ali Compton was saying. It was already almost dark beyond the bedroom window and Fran was rocking in the twilight, side to side, the phone clamped under one ear and both arms around Ben.

He had finally stopped, abruptly, with a last shuddering gasp as if a battery had expired. It had been more than crying: for hours after they came back inside the dark cold house he had shrieked and writhed and if she hadn't seen something like it before in Emme as a baby, colic they'd called it which hadn't seemed sufficient explanation, it would have looked like demonic possession. Emme had fled through the door and upstairs to her room with her hands over her ears.

'She said what, exactly?' Ali Compton's voice was soft but alert. There was a hum of conversation behind her. Men's voices.

'She said she saw the bad man,' said Fran. 'She said she saw him through the hedge at Karen's house.'

All she had said at the time, white-faced as she tumbled through the big glazed windows, was that she wanted to go home now. 'Home now, Mummy, please.' Looking fearfully at Karen. And leaning down to get Emme's bag from beside a polished table, confronted with another row of those family pictures at eye level, suddenly Fran needed to get out too.

When she went up after Emme, back in the house, something was against the door on the inside when she tried to open it.

'Please, sweetheart,' she said, pushing harder, and the door gave an inch, so she could see Emme's jeans through the crack, her small body crouched against it. 'Tell me what it is, Emme,' she said, keeping her voice low. 'Tell me what frightened you.'

It wasn't fair on them. She had to get them out. She didn't know where to go.

Downstairs where she'd left him strapped into his seat Ben's crying had had something mechanical about it, regular as a metronome, unrelenting. She set her ear to the door. 'Emme?'

Silence. Then, 'Did you lock all the doors, Mummy?' Emme's voice was strained, high. 'Did he follow us? He was outside, Mummy. The bad man was outside.'

'What did she say he – this bad man – was doing?' Ali Compton's voice was gentle. 'Did she describe him?' What she'd said, straight away, was *Let me come over* and Fran had almost weakened and given in, at the thought of another woman padding peaceful through the corridors, keeping watch. 'We'll be all right,' she had said.

She needed to be able to listen, was the only way she could explain it. Listen at the doors, listen to the house,

236

listen for someone waiting under the barn's high roof, in the fields, in the yard, outside the door, without the police in the way. If she could only eliminate all extraneous noise she'd hear him coming.

You're losing it, said another voice in her head, dry, sceptical. The voice sounded like Nathan's. *Christ*, he'd said after finding her one night tearful over the bathtub, Emme writhing in her arms all slippery, *don't tell me you're losing it. Post-natal's all I need.*

In the dark bedroom Fran swayed with the sleeping Ben in her arms, unable to stop. She had tried to offer him the breast but he'd reared back, hysterical. She made herself breathe. Stop it. Stop it. She had to think clearly, if they were going to survive this.

'She said he was sitting on the ground,' she told Ali Compton. 'On the side of the road.' It had taken half an hour of coaxing to get that much out of Emme: she'd had to bring Ben up and pace with him, talking over his howls. 'I think . . .' She hesitated. 'She and Nathan saw a man in a playground, a long time ago, she called him the bad man. I think it's the same man. I think . . . I think Nathan may have known him.'

One of the fluorescent tubes in the kitchen had blown; it had gone as they came through the door from Karen's. The pop and sudden alteration in the light as it blew was what had sent Emme fleeing upstairs but Fran had forgotten until she walked back into the room. The kitchen looked starker, its proportions somehow lopsided in the thinner, greyer light, one wall in shadow.

A big man like a giant, with crazy hair. He had wet on his trousers.

237

She crossed to the side, to the drawer that Rob had painstakingly refilled with his big raw hands, his shaking hands . . . and slowly she opened it.

The photograph was there on the top. The three young men in trousers pulled up too high, shirts too big. Rob on the left, half out of the frame, his face blurred by some quick movement but in a funny way that was how she knew it was him, that dodging motion. Nathan was on the other side sitting up on the fence with his knees apart and hands holding on, poised as if he was about to spring off.

He was skinnier, very skinny, but still she recognised him immediately, the dark arch of his eyebrows, the angle of his jaw, his mouth. Fran had never thought about a man's looks too much, it was something else that caught you usually – a combination of cleverness and intensity and charm, to do with how much he wanted *you* – but with Nathan you couldn't ignore the looks. It occurred to her now that he knew it, too. The looks had taken him a long way. Was that what Jo had against him? For the first time Fran wondered about that speed-dating evening where Jo said she'd found him. It hadn't worked, that was what Jo had said, meaning they hadn't fancied each other. Or he hadn't fancied her? But she'd ended up asking him for dinner anyway because how could you not? Looking like that.

In the faded colours of the photograph the three figures shifted as she looked at them, between boys and men. In the middle was the one she didn't know: in the middle was Bez.

He leaned back, lordly, the tallest of them, an elbow

hooked behind him over the top of the fence, a shirt open at the neck, a great bush of red-gold hair. She could even see the tiny sharp jut of his Adam's apple above the collar. He was lazy, at ease, as if he could reach out and take anything he wanted. One of his hands was lifted to shade his eyes, and half his face was hidden.

Behind her on the table her phone blipped, receiving a message.

Carefully, Fran settled the drawer's contents and closed it again but the photograph was still out, propped on the side.

DS Gerard had given her a card too, with his number on. She stood still, looking around the room, and her eye fell on the wall-mounted telephone, where she'd wedged it.

'You have to communicate with all of us, though,' Ali Compton had said before she hung up, something formal and weary in her voice. 'Like it or not, Doug Gerard is in charge of the investigation. And he's a good detective. He's on your side.'

She dialled, looking at the list Nathan had pinned to the wall as it rang. His handwriting. *Doctor, Dad, Nathan, School, Dentist, Rob.* Rob.

On her side? It didn't feel like it. 'I'll see you tomorrow,' Ali Compton had said at last, patient, tired. 'I wish you'd let me come. I wish you'd talk to me.' Then when she hadn't said anything, a sigh. 'Lock the doors. Put the panic button where you can get to it.'

She was ready to hang up when he answered.

Tell Gerard everything, her wildest suspicions, her fears. She should tell him about the bad man, that the bad man was Bez, that he'd met up with Nathan in a playground months ago and Nathan hadn't wanted to tell her. She should say, I think my husband had a secret life, that has something to do with the big-bellied man in construction called Julian and that started all those years ago, in that squat with those boys, she should say, and while you're at it, what about the man who sold us this house? The creepy farmer whose wife left him and no one seems to care where she went.

She should say, the man who killed my husband came into my bed and fucked me, he put his mark on me and he is watching me, he is stalking me, he is leaving chocolates for me in my own kitchen. Someone wants me, and he is going to come back for me.

'Yes?'

Doug Gerard's voice was rough and gravelly, something loose about it, something intimate. She looked at the clock: it was eight o'clock. It sounded like he was in the pub and a couple of pints in; for a second she felt like a disgruntled wife or a jealous girlfriend, and with a quick tiny flash of anger from nowhere she thought, Fuck you.

'It's Fran Hall,' she said, stiff. 'I just wanted to let you know. We won't be here tomorrow.'

And only then, the phone in her hand, did she scroll down and read the message. She knew the number by heart but her phone didn't. I've got to see you, it said. Her lips moved.

She moved her thumb across the screen to the little box in the corner that said *Delete*.

Chapter Twenty-Two

Friday

The dawn was still a line at the horizon when they turned south. In the back seat Ben and Emme were asleep.

Fran had watched the road from the tall window of the spare room for a long five minutes concealed in the dark, before hurrying Emme out, Ben in the baby seat.

If someone had stopped her. Who are you running away from?

From the police, the men coming into her kitchen without knocking, sitting her in front of all those strangers with their cameras and their questions. Who are you scared of? Of Ali Compton, looking at her, kind Ali Compton, worried Ali Compton saying, *Talk to me.* If Fran opened her mouth to talk about *that*, though, what would come out?

But most of all she was running away from him. Scared of him. Because he hadn't stayed outside, he hadn't just thrown stones at her window, he hadn't just watched, from between the poplars in the dark. He'd come inside. Inside her house. Into her bedroom with the change clinking in his pockets. Inside her.

And he'd be back, she knew that now beyond a doubt, looking down on her terror from high overhead. A territorial thing: he thought she was his, now.

If the police had known where she was going, and were following her, they would wonder why Fran took the route she did, left on the main road and not right to the motorway, doubling back to Oakenham and skirting it on the ring road. The odd light was coming on in the small dim houses, people stirring, but Rob's was dark. His car wasn't on the drive. She rang the doorbell, but there was no answer. She rang it again; peering through the letter box she saw a drift of mail on the mat in the dark. Before she flipped the letter box shut with a clatter she caught a stale whiff, of things going off, unemptied bins.

Fighting the traffic she found her way into London: side streets, a ramp, a car park and a ticket barrier, down and then, in the warm subterranean concrete gloom she came to a halt, handbrake on, ignition off. *Here.* Gently she set her cheek to rest on the steering wheel, arms up either side, and breathed out.

A blessed muffled quiet lasted less than a minute and then from the back Emme said. 'Are we escaped, Mummy?' Then, 'I want a wee.'

She didn't know what she'd have done if Ken on the magazine's reception hadn't recognised her. In the foyer she had felt as out of place as a traveller selling heather with Ben on her hip and Emme wiping ketchup on her sweatshirt. Ken had lifted the phone and asked for Jo.

And then they were outside and in the garden square that lay two streets across, Jo's hand firm on her elbow, propelling her through the iron gates, and Emme

242

half-running to keep up. 'Jesus, Fran.' Jo sat abruptly on a bench, making space for her. Emme walked to the edge of the grass and stood there solemnly, watching a pigeon attacking a crisp packet. 'Jesus. What the hell? What happened?'

'I . . . he . . . I just . . .' And Fran didn't know even how to start, it choked her. 'I don't know what happened. I just found him . . .' and then it was coming up inside her, unstoppable, she blurted it out. 'You didn't call,' she said, and she could hear her voice shaking. 'You knew. You knew. But you didn't call me?'

Jo blinked, flushed, then said, terse, 'Sorry. I'm sorry. I should have sent a message, I should have . . .' She stopped, wincing: she'd never been great at backing down, over anything. She looked tense, shadows under her eyes as if she hadn't been sleeping.

'I needed you,' said Fran. 'I needed *someone*. And you think this is somehow my fault, that I got myself into this? Or is it *his* fault, is it Nathan's fault he's dead?' She jerked her head up and stared, furious, into the sky where an airliner was banking and tracking off to the west, then back down. 'I got pregnant. I wanted the baby, I did what he asked. If it was a mistake, it was a mistake, all right, it was a mess – but this? Does it make this my fault?'

And then as Jo stared, abruptly Fran ran out of anger. 'Did you read it online?' Fran said. 'Or did the police . . .' She faltered, thinking of Ken and the heads turning in the lobby, recovered herself. 'Did they turn up here? Who did they talk to?' She flicked an eye to the climbing frame where Emme was perched, solemnly, with her back to them, very still.

243

Leaning back against the low back of the old wooden bench, Jo pulled her hands out of her pockets and shoved them under her arms, leaning forward. 'They called.'

'You told them I'd had an affair,' said Fran, blunt.

Jo set her jaw. 'Have you had an affair?' Her voice was cold.

'What did you say to them?' Fran was quiet.

Jo flushed, furious. 'I said we had lost touch, mainly because I didn't like him, I didn't like the way he treated you. There was something . . . They asked me if I knew him as Alan or Nathan Hall. I mean, don't you think that was weird?'

'No, people do that.' She breathed out. 'You didn't tell them.'

'No,' said Jo. 'Did you?' Not giving an inch.

'I didn't . . .' Fran shook her head, 'I didn't want them to know. I didn't want it to have happened.'

Jo sat down again beside her, hard, her shoulders hunched in the coat. 'I did wonder,' she said, 'if you'd done it. I kind of . . .' She sighed.

'You wished I had?' said Fran bitterly. 'What, a blow for female empowerment? Bit late for that, once I'd had his kids. Why did you hate him so much? Was it that you . . .' She hesitated, a fraction too long, and Jo pounced.

'You thought I wanted him? Him, the babies, the big farmhouse and all the rest of it? No way. No. Fucking. Way.' So why? But before Fran could ask it Jo pulled her hands out from under her arms and she saw a ring. Jo held the hand out, defiant.

'The same guy? The . . . builder?'

'You remembered,' said Jo, frowning. 'He's a nice man.

244

It's not marriage I objected to.' And she leaned forwards, elbows on her knees, earnest. She looked down at Ben in Fran's arms, then up into her face. 'It wasn't the deal, it was *him*. It was Nathan, or Alan, or whoever the fuck he is. Was.'

'All right,' Fran said urgently. 'It was *him*. But what about him?'

'I need a coffee,' said Jo, standing. 'Christ, I need a drink. There's a stall over the other side. Remember that?'

Fran stood up, working Ben into the sling as he slept. She did remember. Jo looked weary: she looked almost soft. 'Him. How many times did I wish I'd never laid eyes on him, let alone invited him over that night? I thought he'd take your mind off Nick, is all.' She shook her head. 'He really did a number on you, though, didn't he? Pulled out all the stops. They say they can spot vulnerability from a hundred yards, they can see it from behind, in the way you walk. Guys like that. They find the weak spot and they go straight there. It's why he didn't bother with me.' She let out a short laugh. 'No weak spots.'

'Jo,' said Fran, hearing a far-off bell sound in her head, an alarm. 'He's the one that's dead, remember. You're talking like he was a psychopath.'

'He was a fucking dinosaur. Shutting you up out there. Carine said he'd told you you didn't need a new computer. Wouldn't let you use the car.'

'Carine?' She felt the wind knocked out of her, a kind of joy that she hadn't disappeared after all, all that time she'd thought she was on her own. 'You talked about us?'

But Jo didn't seem to hear. 'He was never your type,' she said, frowning into the distance as if trying to understand

245

something. 'That's what I don't get. You always liked the full-on boys, the ones who liked to show you off, to see you having fun.'

'Nick was, he was . . .' She stopped.

'At least Nick fancied you,' said Jo, blunt.

A silence. The little wheeled stall was in full view and Emme waiting for them there, staring from them to a row of drink cans, but they slowed, stopped.

'Nick was crazy about you,' Jo went on. 'He'd have done anything for you. The way he used to look at you.'

If she closed her eyes and let it, it would all come back. Those long nights sitting at the back of a dark club, men coming up and sitting next to her, people who knew Nick. 'He wanted to marry you,' said Jo.

Nick coming in late at night, euphoric over something. The money. The flat he bought, neon light sculptures, sound decks. A ring.

'You don't know everything about Nick,' Fran said, quiet.

'So tell me.' They were at the little trolley and Jo was buying them coffees, a carton of juice for Emme, who clutched it and ran off again, towards a neglected climbing frame where more pigeons were scratching.

Jo crumpled the tiny paper cup and dropped it into an overflowing bin. She brought out a packet of cigarettes and shook one out, reached for a lighter. She took a long drag. 'What about you, Franny?' she said, blowing out the smoke. It drifted and curled up between the London trees. 'You think I don't listen? If I don't know anything about Nick, it's because you never told me.'

Fran stared. When she'd walked out on Nick it was like she'd stepped out of the rubble of an explosion, deafened.

She couldn't have turned round and looked to see what had happened, she might just crumble into dust. But the world had changed, since then. She'd found out that worse things happen. Much worse.

She held Jo's direct gaze, returned it.

Another night, a different club, edgy, classy, brick-walled, industrial fittings and in the middle of it, the old Fran. Frankie, he always called her. Their last night. Hours before, he had been propped on the bed, watching her get ready. 'I might invest in it,' he said, casually. 'I've seen them queue round the block till three in the morning, to get in. The VIP area's always packed out.'

'It was some deal he was doing,' she told Jo, who pushed her hands deeper into the pockets of her coat. 'Nick. Buying into a new club, or that was what he said it was. He was doing a lot of drugs.' Jo nodded, without comment. 'You knew?'

Jo shrugged, uncomfortable. 'That's his world,' she said. 'They all do drugs, don't they?' She reached for a cigarette and lit it, blowing out a blue plume of smoke into the cold air.

'It was his world, then,' said Fran and Jo narrowed her eyes in the smoke, sceptical. 'Believe it or not, I didn't know, or I turned a blind eye. I was naive, not that that's an excuse. I was stupid.' She frowned. 'Anyway. That night, that last night. There was another guy, the man who wanted to go into partnership with him. Him and his wife, or whatever, at the bar.' She stopped, weary.

At the club she'd begun to dance; Nick would be over in ten minutes, half an hour, he always joined her in the end. The club was crowded but he was on her radar: he

247

was standing at the bar with a couple and watching her. The other man was stocky and older, there was a blonde woman with him and her hair shone gold under the light behind the bar.

Then something had changed, Nick frowning, Nick laughing, incredulous. The smaller man nodded in her direction and the blonde left, threading through the dance floor to Fran, she said something and Fran leaned down to hear. 'It's business,' she was saying. When Fran had looked up, frowning, the two men had gone from the bar.

'What?' said Jo, impatient. 'Partnership? And?'

'I was part of the deal. The other guy wanted to sleep with me. Do you know what? Now I think, sometimes, might it even have been just a joke, and I went off on one.' She meditated, taken back there a second, a time so remote it might have happened to someone else. She shrugged. 'No,' she said at last, 'it wasn't a joke. And Nick . . . well. Let's just say he didn't react to the request the way I'd have liked him to.'

'You mean, he didn't deck the guy,' said Jo, and when Fran smiled then it felt like she hadn't smiled in months.

'No,' she said drily. 'He asked me if I'd consider it.'

The cigarette had burned down to a stub between Jo's fingers; she frowned down at it.

'Your turn,' said Fran, and Jo looked up, wary. 'You tell me, because there's something, isn't there?' Jo hugged herself in the cold, her face closed. 'Something you're not telling me. About Nathan.'

Jo was staring over her shoulder and Fran turned to check that Emme wasn't within earshot, turning in a circle, the pigeons, the empty climbing frame, a gang of students moving off arm in arm, there was a man head down on his bench.

'Where Emme?' she said. 'Where's Emme?'

Jo was turning, looking, her face was white and drawn – and then from around a low clump of trees she came, like a bullet, head down and barrelling into Fran's midriff. *Mummy Mummy Mummy* heard Fran, the words hot and muffled against her, and she felt Emme's arms flung around her, holding on tight.

Emme tipped her head back and Fran looked down at her, saw her eyes still wide and searching her face. 'I thought I'd lost you, Mummy,' she said. 'I thought you were lost.'

'Tell me,' she said to Jo, as the relief flooded her, she could deal with it. Whatever it was.

Chapter Twenty-Three

It was dark again already, as they drove north.

It felt to Fran now that these days had gone on for ever, that there'd never been a summer except in her imagination. That this might be the future, these cold dark brief days when no sooner had the sun inched its way above the tree tops than it started the slide back to the horizon. Off to the west a fine crack of lemon-coloured light lay between huge dark banks of cloud, and on the radio they were issuing weather warnings.

In the back Emme lay asleep in the detritus of a take-away meal, too worn out from cold and terror to take pleasure in the lights and novelty and plastic freebies of a drive-in fast-food joint. It had allowed Fran to change Ben's nappy and feed him but even as she pulled in to the bright booth she had realised that Emme would be thinking not that she was getting a treat, but that her daddy would never have allowed this.

Jo had turned to them at the big revolving doors. 'Listen,' she'd said urgently then. 'The flat's tiny, I don't know about schools and stuff but . . .' and she'd caught her breath, as pale as if the blood had been drained out of her, 'stay with me. Don't go back there.'

And then her arms had been around Fran and holding on tight with Ben pressed between them, not caring where they were, who might be staring.

'It's all right,' said Fran into Jo's hair, smelling the cigarette smoke and perfume mixed then pulling back, gently detaching herself. 'I've got to go back.'

'No, No, you don't, you—'

'If I don't go back,' said Fran, and it wasn't until the words were out that she knew they were true, 'if I don't go back they won't get him. If I don't go back he'll always be out there.' Jo frowned furiously and Fran stepped closer. 'You're still here. I know I've got you if I need you. That's a lot. That's a lot.'

Jo had stood there, frowning at the words, and Fran knew she was trying not to show what she was feeling. 'I should have told the police,' she said. 'I was just so . . . gobsmacked, it went out of my head, I mean, murder? Murder? Tell them, I'll talk to them again, tell that police-woman you said was on the case.' Ali Compton: Fran had opened her mouth to tell Jo about the other two, Gerard and Carswell, but hadn't even been able to get started on that.

Jo was still talking. 'Because if it's what . . . if it's what I thought, then don't you see . . . it's over. It's done. It wasn't about you, it was about Nathan.'

What Jo had seen.

They were off the motorway now, the light had gone from the sky and the road ahead was empty. Their headlights illuminated telegraph poles, one after the other, and the frosted grass on the verge. Fran risked a glance back over her shoulder and there they were, asleep. 'Shh,' she found herself whispering, because this was it, all very well saying to Jo, it's OK, we'll be OK. This was real. They were back.

In the square with the traffic roaring round them and Emme wrapped around her and her heart still pounding with the panic, Jo had told her.

'I saw him,' she said and in unison they turned to walk back. 'I saw Nathan one night when you'd told me he was away on some conference or other. I saw him, late at night.'

'Where?' They stopped, at the gate out of the square. Emme leaned for a stick and began to run it along the railings: two steps then turning to make sure they were still there, another two steps on and another look back.

'Tell me again. Exactly what the police said about . . . how they found him.'

Haltingly, her voice low so Emme wouldn't hear, Fran told her. When she got to the bit about territory and men peeing outside, Jo nodded, briskly, to stop her. 'His clothing was disturbed.' She frowned down at her hands. She let out an angry breath. 'It was a part of the Heath that's . . . well known, let's say. I was coming back from a party.'

'Well known?' said Fran slowly. Jo was still staring down, jaw clenched.

'The traffic – it's slow there, a bit where you have to give way, plus roadworks, there was a long queue, and we were hardly moving, you'd think they'd sort it out but maybe they like it that way. The men . . . like an audience.'

She looked up again, into Fran's face. 'You know what dogging is, right? Not just gay guys, there's hetero versions too but this particular location, it's pretty much exclusively a gay guys' place, and I just turned my head, I was mostly looking straight ahead because I was tired, and it's not my thing, voyeurism, but I guess I was curious, or something caught my eye. Anyway.'

'You saw Nathan,' said Fran, and in the space at the back of her brain where things, all sorts of things these last days, weeks, months, had been rubbing painfully against each other, suddenly, smoothly they slotted into place, as neat as a puzzle cube. 'You're telling me Nathan was gay.'

'The funny thing,' said Jo in a monotone, as if she was talking to herself, 'was he wasn't trying to hide from anyone. From me. Just as I turned my head he turned his and I swear he looked straight at me and he didn't look frightened, he didn't turn away or panic, he just looked right back at me . . .' Her voice dropped, faltered.

'Nathan was gay,' Fran repeated and belatedly she heard it in Jo's voice. Nathan had looked at her, and she'd been frightened.

'He wasn't . . . they weren't actually . . .' Fierce Jo, fearless Jo, unable to get the words out.

'They weren't having sex,' said Fran, testing the words to see if they hurt: they didn't. Not much. 'But he was gay. It . . . well. It explains . . . some things.'

Does it? Does it? Yes and no.

'Don't you think . . .' Jo hesitated. 'The squat they lived in all together. Him going back there where he grew up looking for old friends—'

But Fran stepped back, calling to Emme at the railings,

253

she moved so sharply Ben was jolted, his face screwed up briefly, then smoothed again as she pressed him against her. Below her she could see Jo's face beginning to close. She thinks I'm in denial, she thought, there's no point . . .

'Yes,' she said. 'You could be right, you could well be right, it explains a lot of things, how he was with me, yes, yes . . .' Now she was overdoing it, though she registered bewilderment in Jo's eyes. 'It explains a lot of things.'

On the radio they were saying snow had fallen in the Highlands, there had been power cuts. Two bodies found in a snowdrift under a bridge, a crash on black ice. Gritting lorries.

It explained a lot of things, but it didn't explain everything. Back in the lobby of the magazine's building and Ken behind his desk keeping his head down while they whispered, Emme staring up in silence, Jo had looked worn out, her winter skin pale and powdery above the sharp collar.

'I know I should have told you,' she said, defeated. 'I didn't know . . . it wasn't concrete, you know? I didn't want to sound like one of those women, goes around reporting every little thing, trying to break things up because she wants her best friend back.'

'And then you were pregnant.' Jo turned to look out through the revolving doors to the grey world, a taxi pulling up. 'I could see how happy you were.'

Before she drifted off in the back seat, Emme had said, piping, 'Who was that lady, Mummy?'

'My best friend,' said Fran, even if the words weren't quite what Emme would understand by them, something a bit more worn and battered.

They were on the long straight road that ended at Cold Fen, banked up on one side against the watercourse. They were nearly home, the darkness thick around them. A lay-by was signposted and Fran pulled over into the lee of the dyke and turned off the ignition.

Jo thought Nathan had been gay. Not impossible, not a crime either, nor the end of the world. True, it had filled her with shame that was almost a kind of despair to begin with, but she had had years, by now, to get used to the fact that Nathan wasn't really hers. That look, his face turning blank, opaque, that would make her desperate. To please him. To get him back.

'You were *how* old?' she'd said, the first time he'd told her about the squat. 'Seventeen? And your parents didn't come and bring you home?'

She'd almost seen his face smoothing, deflecting as he returned to reading the newspaper at the kitchen table in London, with the little stack of property details by his hand, the top one the fine three-hundred-year-old house with its double front oblique to the road, looking out towards the line of poplars. Long windows with panelled shutters, the steep red pitch of the roof, the pretty neglected yard, a handsome house built for a prosperous farmer, sitting above a drained fen and still there as the landscape emptied around it. Too good to be true.

'Nearly eighteen,' Nathan had murmured, as if losing interest. 'That many years ago it was common to leave home at eighteen. University of life – and I was only a couple of miles away, they knew where we were.' And he had peered down at the newspaper and Fran's idea of what it had been like that distant summer had been settled: two

255

long warm months bleached to sepia, sunburned boys sleeping on dusty floors, swimming in the flooded quarry.

The photograph wouldn't have told her a different story either, not really, except for what she now knew, except when she thought about where they were now, those three boys. Nathan cold in the ditch with his head down and his blood, his shirt heavy with it. Rob, gaunt and frightened, staring at the photograph on the top of the pile in her arms. It came to her now that he'd looked at it as if it would bite him. And Bez, drugged out somewhere, lying in piss-soaked clothes in a children's playground.

The engine ticked and cooled, Emme stirred and grumbled behind her and was asleep again. She picked up the mobile and dialled Jo's number. It only rang twice before Jo picked up, breathless. 'Are you OK? Look, I'm sorry I . . . I shouldn't . . .'

'I'm nearly home.' Fran leaned back in the car's dark interior. She could hear a tap running, the clatter of pans. 'Are you eating?' she said, in sudden retreat. 'Are you cooking? I can call another time . . .'

'No,' said Jo firmly, and there was a muffled sound, then she was back, and a door closed. 'It . . . we're not eating for a bit anyway.' And she sighed. 'I'm sorry,' she said again. 'I shouldn't have just blurted it out like that. I should have said something years ago or not at all.'

'No,' said Fran, staying level and calm. 'I'm glad you told me. You could even be right.' Jo was silent: what happens, Fran wondered, when I tell her? If. *I was . . . it was . . . there was a man in my bed.* She cleared her throat, but it wouldn't come out. 'It's just that it seems . . . too easy. My husband doesn't fancy me, so he must be gay?'

There was a silence, that lasted long enough for her to hear something outside, a steady wind, a soft pattering in trees somewhere far off.

'So why did he marry me? This isn't the nineteen fifties. We know why I did it, I wanted the baby, I assumed if he wanted it too marriage was what came next. Stupid maybe, lazy maybe, cowardly, but why him? Why did he come after me and marry me, why did we have two kids?' Jo didn't say anything, so she thrashed on. 'Why did he want to move back out to the sticks with me, if he had an awful time here, if it was what fucked him up?'

Her voice dropped, almost inaudible. 'Do you think Nathan knew, Jo? Did you tell him, about that guy? The one-night . . . the—'

'No,' hissed Jo, 'of course I didn't tell him, what do you take me for?'

'Did you know his name?' whispered Fran. 'The . . . the guy. His name, where he works, that stuff.' She felt a flush up her neck, and she gabbled, 'But when this happened. Do you know what I thought? Just for a second. He's come after me. The guy.'

'That loser?' Jo scoffed. 'No. He . . .'

The hair rose on Fran's scalp, her skin crawled with shame, thinking of the long staircase and the man's back, she dreaded being even told his name and tried to escape, to forestall. 'No, don't, I don't want to know anything. Don't tell me his name.'

'He's been working on the other side of the world for almost a year,' said Jo. The relief that flooded Fran's system was only momentary, because Jo was pushing still. 'So you never found out why, what it was all about?

257

Why Nathan was so keen on going back to the sticks? Excited, you said.'

'No,' Fran whispered. 'I mean . . . it didn't come to anything, no big jobs materialised, it turns out his office was . . .' and she trailed off under a sudden sense of shame. 'Not much more than a . . . a shed.' A box on a light industrial estate.

Where had that excitement come from? What had it been about? What had he come back here for?

There was a silence, then Jo cleared her throat. 'I saw your press conference,' she said, hesitant. 'It's up on some crime website.'

'It is?' Fran felt cold.

And then, on cue, Jo said, 'What did happen that night, Fran? Because you're still not telling me it all, are you?' Beyond the windscreen in the dark something whirled and hung as fine as dust, it barely speckled the glass. 'You looked so frightened.'

'Oh, Jo,' she said. 'I wish . . . I wish . . . I wish you were here.' And quickly, before she lost it, 'I'll call you.' And she hung up.

When she looked down at the screen, she saw it as if from high overhead, a tiny blue rectangle of light in all the wide flat darkness. *Three messages*, it said. *Missed call*. Doug Gerard.

Chapter Twenty-Four

He was there when she hurried back out to lock the car, standing beside a battered Range Rover with no glass in the back windscreen, his cap in his hands. She felt her heart race until she recognised him. Emme cleaning her teeth upstairs, half asleep. Ben in his car seat on her bed.

There had been a terse answerphone message from Doug Gerard. 'You haven't been answering your phone. You'll be . . .' and there was a heavy pause. 'You'll be glad to hear we've had an excellent response to the press conference. We'd like a word. It might be best . . .' Another pause, then, with finality, 'If you were to come back into the station tomorrow morning at nine thirty.'

It had been the cap in his hands that had identified Fred Dearborn. 'What is it?' Fran said, weary to the point of despair, adrenalin beginning to battle it. They were alone inside. The back door unlocked.

'The wife sent me,' he said, and from his reluctance she believed him. 'Make sure you was all right.'

'I'm all right,' said Fran dully. She pressed the locking device on her key and the car's lights pulsed, the locks setting with a clunk. 'I don't need casseroles, Mr Dearborn. It's as much as I can do to get a bit of toast down, and the kids . . . I mean, thank you.'

'Don't matter,' the farmer said, gruff. 'I never meant to . . .' and he stepped back from her, reaching down for his car door.

Fran put a hand to her forehead – it wasn't as if she had help to spare at the moment, never mind friends.

'I'm sorry,' she said. 'It's very kind of your wife. Look . . . the baby's . . . I can't . . .' She gave up. 'Why don't you come in a minute?' She heard his footsteps behind her in the gravel. Mental, she thought, what made her think she had any instinct for who was safe? No wonder they all thought she was crazy, or guilty. Fuck the lot of them. He ducked his head to get under the lintel.

'Milk two sugars,' Dearborn said obediently when she asked and she spooned it in, stirred, handing it to him then went to the foot of the stairs to listen, but there was no sound. She came back and folded her arms across her body, watching him peer at the tea. He had bushy greying eyebrows that moved as he sipped, gingerly.

'Did you ever find anywhere for your pigs?' she asked, abrupt, and he raised his big head in surprise.

'Matter of fact I did,' he said. 'Twenty-acre field other side of Oakenham. Funny enough it's old Martin's, could've knocked me down with a feather when he come up to me—'

260

'John Martin? The . . . the man who lived here?' She shook her head stubbornly. 'No,' she said. 'He's gone. He said he was going to the seaside.' Agitated, she crossed to the sink, sweeping the dirty breakfast things into it, turning on the tap. Suddenly the room looked a shambles, she saw spilled milk, a ring where a mug had stood. She picked up a cloth.

'Not so's you'd notice,' said Dearborn watching her ruminatively. 'I see him at an agricultural auction up to Chatteris a month ago, he were just looking, he said, but it en't the seaside, is it? Not Chatteris.' He shook his head slowly, wondering. 'Funny one and no mistake. Twenty year he's refused to talk to me. Must have been getting shot of this place. Two year on the market and no one wanted it, not even his wife, she upped and gone, packed her bags one night and he turned into a whassit, *recluse*.' He pronounced the word as if it was foreign. 'Newspaper up at the windows. Estate agents had to send someone in to clean the place up in the end, make it look normal. Not that it was much better when she was around. Not that kind of female, she weren't.' And he came to a halt, as if surprised at the length of his own speech.

'Where did she go?' Fran asked, the cloth in her hands, because it had snagged somewhere, *packed her bags one night*. The missing wife. 'Ahh, I dunno,' said Dearborn, setting down his cup, not unkind. 'Back to the pikeys, no doubt, back where she come from, when she found out there weren't no money in it.' He spoke without animus. 'She did talk about the seaside to my missus, once, Yarmouth it was. Mebbe he was planning on going after her.' He laughed, puzzled.

261

'No one ever saw her again?' Fran heard herself, quick and breathless, and slowly he shook his head again.

'Just gone,' he said. 'But . . .' He frowned. 'You don't want to . . . she weren't your sort. You know where he found her? Internet. Went into the library and used them computers, chatroom, next thing you know she's getting out an Oakenham taxi in high-heeled shoes, three suitcases in the back.'

He cleared his throat. 'I better be off,' he said, rubbing at a watch on his wrist: it felt like two in the morning but she could see that it wasn't much after nine. 'Leave you to it, with them kids. Mine's grown now but . . . well. Dunno how she'd'a managed on 'er own, need eyes in the back of yer head, kiddies.'

'Are you saying . . . she was like a mail-order sort of . . .' It caught in her throat.

'One word for it,' he said shortly, uneasy. His hand was on the door, his head already lowered for the cap. 'They was married, I believe. But it weren't for love, not on her side.'

'I *would* like a dog,' she said abruptly and he stopped, turning in surprise.

'Right then,' he said, 'I'll look out for one. Mebbe a collie? Bit lively.' His face clouded. '*She* had a collie cross,' he said.

'She?'

'Soft on that dog, Martin's woman. Jilly-Ann.' Finally retrieving her name. 'Never took it with 'er, though. Tret it like it were her very own baby but never took it when she went.' And he was ducking through the door. 'Couldn't make sense of that. He had it put down.' He tipped his hat.

'I'll let you know. Get a puppy for you. Golden retriever's a gentle dog.'

Upstairs Emme lay asleep and fully clothed on the bed. By the time Fran had undressed her and settled her back under the covers she could hear Ben stirring in the car seat, protesting against confinement and a nappy that had soaked through to the seat's lining. She changed him and lay beside him on her bed, because she didn't want to be alone.

Not alone and thinking about a woman who climbed out of a taxi in front of her house in high-heeled shoes, a woman who disappeared one night and never came back. Jilly-Ann Martin. Where had she gone? Was she here somewhere, still, was there evidence of her? As she lay in the dark with Ben's soft regular breath in her ear she saw again, or dreamed, DS Doug Gerard bending over a frosted furrow. He straightened up with his policeman's pen held out, a pair of knotted tights, American tan, dangling from it and that expression as he turned his face towards her of amusement, or something like it. And in that half waking, half imagining state the figure on the field's edge was John Martin, standing among the poplars, the keys to a house that had once been his, jingling in his pocket.

Chapter Twenty-Five

Saturday

On the back doorstep Karen held the flowers out to her stiffly, Harry in her other hand in the cold yard.

She'd come to sit with Emme, so Fran could go to the police station.

'It's no problem,' Karen had said gently when Fran rang her, and down the line Fran could hear the hush in her tidy bungalow. 'I can stay as long as you like. Harry's got football this afternoon and she can come and watch.' A normal Saturday afternoon, kids on the sidelines in the frost. She had agreed, overwhelmed with gratitude.

Now Fran stared down at the cellophaned bunch, confused. 'They were on the step,' said Karen, peering past her into the kitchen. 'All right if we come in?'

Roses. Cheap, already limp. Emme darted over and took them.

They were waiting for her outside the police station, a reception committee, and the first thing she did was to thrust the dripping bunch into Gerard's hands. 'I want them analysed,' she said, red-faced, stiff, and taken by surprise he laughed. 'I mean it,' she said. 'And that box of chocolates.

264

Someone's doing this.' Impassive, he handed the wet cellophane to Carswell.

Ali Compton was the first one to step forward, taking hold of the baby seat, flashing a look at Gerard. 'You don't need to worry about this meeting, Fran,' she said, 'just keeping you up to date.' She had shadows under her eyes.

Surrendering Ben, she unslung a bag from her shoulder, she'd packed it before they left. A change of clothes, rattle, nappies.

'I can be in there with you too again, if you like,' said Ali, taking the bag in her spare hand. 'I just thought you might like . . . the concentration. The headspace, you know.'

She looked so weighed down now, like the plastic horse that flings stuff off if you pile on one thing too many. Fran realised that must be how she looked. Buckaroo.

'No need to worry, like Ali says.' Gerard's hand was on her shoulder and she stiffened. Coming from him, it didn't sound like reassurance. 'We just need to go over a few things.' He flicked a quick look at Ali, but not so quick she didn't see the hostility in it.

It was raw and cold and the wind blew steadily between the cars. Carswell had the collar on a too-thin jacket turned up to his ears, his shoulders hunched, his face peaked and cold.

'Maybe we should get on with it,' she said, stepping out from under Gerard's hand.

The room wasn't what she'd expected, not the one they'd been in before. Two steps inside and she stopped, looking, the men coming to a halt behind her. It was painted cream, with a floral border at waist height, a coffee table with tissues, some low, padded seating. Maybe this time they wanted to soften her up.

She'd woken early, from a dream where everything was bathed in a golden light and she'd been listening to a man in a shower, she could see his outline through a glass door, she knew who he was but the name wouldn't come to her. The light she woke to had been thin and grey, and the room had been cold. When she went downstairs the boiler had showed a red light.

'A couple of things, then,' said Gerard, one arm up on the back of the low seating, at ease. Carswell sat with his knees apart and his elbows on them, still jiggling, like a schoolboy footballer. His notebook was on the table. She set her mobile down beside it.

She'd knelt to explain to Emme, gazing into her face. 'I've got to go and talk to the . . . policemen. About Daddy's accident.'

'I don't want to go to Karen's house,' she said.

'Karen is going to bring Harry over,' she said quickly. 'I know it's not much fun to stay inside but . . .' She stopped, remembering Emme's Saturdays with Nathan. 'And we'll talk about what happens next week. About school.'

'I'll be OK, Mummy,' she said, pale. 'Daddy never came with me to school, did he?'

Fran had knelt beside her. 'It's all right if it hurts, Emme. It's all right to want to be at home with me and Ben.'

Emme shook her head stiffly. 'He won't come back, will he?' she said, frowning.

'Who?' said Fran, her breath constricted.

'Daddy won't come back.' Emme's small face was pinched

266

and serious. 'He was mean to you sometimes,' she said, and Fran sat back, shaking her head.

'No, he—' she began, but Emme stared into her face as if it was a blinking contest.

'He was,' she said, her lips pressed firmly together. 'You never had a go in the car, it was always Daddy.' And she tugged. 'I want to go now, Mummy.'

Karen had had the number of a plumber on her phone. Perhaps something about Fran's frown as she entered it on hers prompted her to say, 'You need me to have him too? The little one.' With a crooked smile. 'Wouldn't mind.'

'No,' she'd said, 'it's OK. Save you for emergencies.' Then it came out, in a rush, her back to the door so Harry and Emme wouldn't hear, playing in the sitting room. 'First it was chocolates, then flowers.' She held the rest of it in, all the fear, the moments of darting panic.

Karen shrugged. 'It'll be one of them from the playground,' she said. 'Sue, you ask me. Drop 'em round on the excuse for a nosy, like I said.' She sniffed. 'I'll ask her if you want. Snotty cow.'

On the way to the interview room they'd stopped beside a glazed partition down the corridor and Ali Compton had said, heaving Ben to one side, 'I'll be in there.' A big room full of desks, half empty, three or four officers in uniform beside a water cooler at the far side. Fran caught her own reflection in the wide glazed panel: she didn't properly recognise herself at first.

'If he gets noisy I'll be in the canteen,' said Compton to Gerard, who just shrugged.

'Before we get started,' said Gerard, with a frown, 'did you say your computer – laptop, right? – had gone in

267

for repair? You husband took it in, you said. I assumed you meant that guy in the little unit by the railway station?'

'That's the place,' said Fran. 'Nathan had used him before.' A man with long hair either side of a bald patch, and colourful shirts, operating out of a portakabin.

'That's right, he did know your husband,' said Gerard. 'I showed him the picture and he said he'd sold him a second-hand keyboard a while back.' She wondered where this was going. 'Only, he said he hadn't been in with any laptop. He was quite definite about it.'

'Really?' said Fran, thinking that Jo and Carine had been right, saying he'd confiscated her laptop. No intention of giving it back. He wanted her isolated.

'I don't know what you . . . what that means. Is there somewhere else he might have taken it?' Only then did it occur to her, with a prickle of apprehension, that Gerard might think it was her that had been lying. The laptop in a crusher somewhere.

'That's possible.' Gerard hesitated, tapping his teeth with his pen. Eyeing her legs in the jeans hanging too low now. She pushed her body back into the sofa.

'Why, if I might ask, didn't you just take the computer in yourself? Or at least pick it up?'

'I . . . I don't know.' It sounded pathetic, if you didn't know Nathan, the arch of his eyebrow, as if she was being stupid, that little snort under his breath, the sigh. 'I could have. Nathan just . . . he was doing me a favour. He said he'd take care of it.' Gerard's face was impassive.

'I hope you find it. I can't afford another one, not now.' Carswell murmured something under his breath. 'You said you had a good response to the press conference,' said Fran. 'It's been four days.'

'Ah well,' said Gerard, as if he hadn't heard. 'No doubt there's an explanation.' Sighed. 'Well. We've found out a number of things. First: we know where your husband was, the night he died. Where he went.'

'You do?'

'Did he own a briefcase, one of those nylon things? With some brand name on it?'

He wasn't answering her. 'Briefcases. Yes,' she said. 'A couple at least. He used to get them when he went away on conferences.' She thought she heard a sound from Carswell, but when she turned sharply he was just staring down between his knees at the carpet.

'Where did he go?' she said and Gerard flipped a hand up.

'All in due course,' he said. 'A hard drive,' he said, 'is about this big,' and he held his hands up, six inches apart. 'We're talking about a briefcase that could take one of those?'

'Yes,' she said. 'Easily.'

'The thing is,' said Gerard, 'the only prints on your husband's computer are his, as far as we can see.' He cleared his throat. 'You didn't see your husband leave, you didn't see what he was wearing, or carrying.'

'No,' she said, her voice cracking. If she could go back. If she could change that.

If she could change that, what? And then the thought of having Nathan back made her blink, made her sit up straight. What would she ask him? It made her feel afraid.

But Gerard was leaning to one side, extracting something

from a folder. 'Before I forget,' he said, 'we found this, among his things.' She took it. Nathan's handwriting. *A will is deposited with* . . . The name of a solicitor's firm, the address. She had thought, up to this point, that she didn't know any solicitors, if she needed one, say. Now she knew one. Karen, it occurred to her, might know a better one.

'Have you talked to the solicitor?' she asked. 'Do you know what's in the will?'

Gerard looked up. 'I've had a word, yes. She's assuming she'll hear from you.'

He was extracting something else from his folder. As he held it out to her she registered an inch of clean shirt cuff, broad, square hands. Capable: was that what he was? Strong. 'This is the death certificate. You'll need that too. Though probate . . . in cases like this. Murder, I mean. It's not straightforward.'

Numb, she nodded, staring down at the brown envelope. Was this a strategy? But the faces turned towards her just said, *This is our job. We're helping.*

'And the kids,' said Carswell earnestly. His suit jacket was shiny at the elbows. 'You got any back-up there? I mean, emergency, say we need to . . . call you in, like? Relatives? Because—'

'No relatives,' said Fran quickly. 'Mine are all dead, his are—'

'There's the sister—' Carswell was eager but Gerard cut him off.

'We can talk about that later,' he said and he leaned forward, looking into her face. He looked kind, suddenly, he looked soft, he looked as if he was worried about her. Her hands shook as she slid the papers into her bag.

270

'There's a couple of things we're finding . . . problematic,' said Gerard. 'The response to the press conference has highlighted them. Your husband's work is one: the office out there on the Sandpiper estate. Where he spent the evening of his death is another – and why he told you he was in the local pub when in fact he was here, in town.'

'He was here? In Oakenham?'

'The fact that there was practically nothing in that office.' Gerard's voice soft and sympathetic but not answering her question, spreading his hands as if at a loss. 'The other business people with units on the estate,' and Carswell shifted in his seat, Gerard went on quickly, 'those we've been able to talk to, say that he'd come in now and again, just for a visit. Wandering around. That he'd come in the evenings sometimes and stand out the front smoking. Watching them come and go.'

'Smoking?' Fran shook her head. 'He didn't . . .' but she supposed she had smelt it on him. Now and again, she'd thought, the pub. Except people didn't smoke in pubs any more.

'Are you saying . . .' She felt hunched on the low seating, the rough textile upholstery struck her as something out of an old people's home, or a funeral service, it was horrible. She made herself speak calmly. 'Are you saying he was . . . I don't know. Depressed? One of those men who's lost his job but he leaves the house every morning with his suit and his briefcase?' Gerard grimaced, but he said nothing. 'That he pretended he was going to the pub but he didn't?'

'Oh, there was a pub that he did go to,' Carswell said, cheerful, and Gerard shot him a warning look.

'He was obviously concealing quite a lot from you, by

271

the sound of it,' he said, gentle. 'You don't need to feel ashamed about that. Plenty of men do it.'

'"Ashamed"?'

'Did he have affairs, too? Was yours an open relationship?' She stared at him, but his voice was still gentle, still concerned. His eyes almost seemed full of pain, on her behalf.

'I wasn't having an affair,' she said, her voice rising. 'I haven't ever had an affair.' Beside Gerard, Carswell jiggled, rubbing his palms together. 'Why do you keep saying that? I...' *Confess, confess*, a little drumbeat in her head. 'Something happened at an office party, years ago. As far as I know Nathan never knew about it, I never saw the man again.'

High in the corner of the room the little eye of the camera gleamed down at her and she looked at the carpet, guilty.

'I did think . . .' Fran swallowed. 'It was crazy, because how would he even know how to find me, I . . .' I covered my tracks, she thought, but that made her sound guilty too. 'I wondered, just, you know, crazy thinking, if it was that guy, if he'd come after me, if he'd – Nathan – I mean, you hear about men stalking women,' and she flushed. 'Not that I'm all that, but you know,' and it was as though her tongue was thick in her mouth, she wished for Ali Compton. 'That's not what it's about, is it? Stalking?' The two men were looking at her patiently, without understanding.

She swallowed. 'Anyway, I saw a friend in London yesterday and she said he'd gone to work abroad, months back, almost a year ago. The guy from the office party.'

'You went to London looking for him?' Gerard leaned back, regarding her.

She froze, in the presence of enemies. 'I wanted to be

sure it wasn't him. That was one reason I went. I wanted to be sure . . . I didn't know anything about him,' she said, faltering. 'Not until yesterday.'

'OK.' Gerard nodded, reasonable, leaning forward. 'Your husband, though? Affairs.'

Answer the question. She made herself breathe, order her thoughts. 'No,' she said, only what Jo had said drummed in her head, Nathan exchanging cigarettes with a man on the Heath, under the eye of passing cars. She realised she was conflating what they had told her with Jo's story, cigarettes and sex. 'At least, I never would have thought so. Not that I ever suspected, or saw evidence – but he was away a lot. Conferences.' She looked into the police-man's broad, impassive face. 'Where was he spending those evenings?' she asked, quietly.

Carswell and Gerard exchanged glances. 'There's a pub,' said Gerard. 'The Angel in the Fields, in a backstreet by the river.' He sighed. 'They call it the Angel.'

'Them in the know,' said Carswell.

'In the know?'

'Drag nights Fridays, but otherwise you wouldn't really know, to look at it,' said Gerard, earnest, open-minded, a man who'd been on gender awareness courses. 'I mean it's possible that you might not know, it looks like a cosy little place, old-fashioned almost. Of course, there are the zumba classes, the salsa night, the drag night.' A pause. 'The lock-ins.'

'Sounds livelier than the Queen's,' said Fran, but it sounded hollow, unfunny.

Gerard went on as if she hadn't spoken. 'One visit, maybe by mistake, that's one thing, but it looks like your husband was a regular.'

'It's a gay pub,' said Fran, and she saw their eyebrows raised, in unison.

'You're not surprised by that,' said Gerard. Beside him Carswell had taken up his notebook again.

'My friend, Jo, the woman I went to see yesterday. She said she saw Nathan at a place . . . a place where . . . a gay meeting place. On the Heath.' She could say it, she found, without any feeling at all. 'She thought he was gay.' Carswell's writing was laborious, his nails grubby.

'That's Hampstead Heath,' she said, and something glinted in the look he gave her, before he bent back over the notebook.

'And do you think he could have been gay?' asked Gerard.

'Of course, you've spoken to her, haven't you?' she said, keeping her voice level. 'Jo Sinclair. She told you about the . . . what you keep calling the affair.'

'Miss Sinclair. Yes, I spoke to Miss Sinclair. She didn't tell us anything about your . . . anything of that nature. In fact, I did wonder if she was withholding information from us.'

'Perhaps she thought it wasn't relevant. Perhaps she thought it was my business. Private.'

'That's the trouble with violent death. Privacy goes out the window when people are murdered.' She said nothing. 'She didn't like him much, though, did she?' said Gerard mildly. 'Your husband.'

Fran just shook her head, mutinous. 'We – she and I – were very close before I . . . got married. He . . . maybe she thought he took me away from her. I don't know. No, she didn't like him.'

Non-committal, Gerard nodded, but he nudged Carswell back to his notebook. He'd been staring.

'So how *did* you know? About me.'

'We didn't know about that incident.' His implication was clear – there had been others. Someone had told him about others.

'Office party, was it?' said Carswell, his head bobbing up and she saw it again, that gleam on him, an instinct for cruelty. 'We didn't know nothing about that.' Impish, he ducked back to his notebook.

They hadn't known at all. 'So what . . .' She faltered. 'What did you mean, then? When you asked me if I'd been . . . seeing someone else?'

'Since you got here.' Gerard's voice was light. 'We were talking about you seeing someone since you got here. Meeting someone for coffee, little chats on park benches. Innocent, maybe?'

'I'm not having an affair,' she said. 'Are you talking about friends? What have friends got to do with this?' She sat tight, shoving her hands under her thighs to conceal the tremble. 'If he was gay,' she said. They looked back at her, their faces bland and helpful, and she went on. 'Are you saying he might have picked someone up in the pub? Someone—'

'Someone violent?' offered Gerard helpfully. 'The "management"' – he spoke with heavy irony – 'say not. Not that night, anyway.'

She made herself persist. 'But sometimes?' Did it fit with a man coming into her room, equipped with a condom? She had to tell them: *Confess, confess.* But she'd done nothing wrong and she couldn't, anyway. She'd stripped the bed, she'd destroyed the evidence.

At that moment she felt the weird insistent tingle that meant Ben was due a feed. She pulled her jacket round herself. 'My bedroom, you dusted for prints in there, too, didn't you?'

'We did,' said Gerard, 'I was going to get to that, yes.' Smiling. 'Not much, nothing on the light switch—'

'He didn't turn the light on,' said Fran quickly.

He turned to examine her and nodded slowly, 'So you're coming round,' he said lightly, 'to thinking you weren't asleep, you weren't dreaming, then?'

'Yes,' she said, submissive although his implication was clear. 'Yes.' Was this how coerced confessions happened? She felt like she'd been here before, as though her life with Nathan had all been leading to this point.

Gerard was talking. 'There were some small prints that would be your daughter's, though we're not keen on finger-printing her, for obvious reasons.' Perhaps he wanted to be thanked for that. Fran said nothing. 'Plenty of your husband's prints,' he went on, 'as we'd expect. All over the place, wardrobe, drawers, lamp.' She thought of Nathan's hands, inquisitive, Nathan holding open her wardrobe doors and looking at the dress she'd never worn.

Doug Gerard's smile was mild, enquiring. 'Though the bedside table, now. Your side, I mean. The little drawer there?'

She sat up, forward. 'My side?'

'That's it,' said Gerard encouragingly. 'Only a partial, which is frustrating. And doesn't match anything we've got in the database, as far as we can tell, though with a partial it's not straightforward . . . Oh,' he leaned forward, 'and there was a Valentine's card in that drawer,' and she gasped,

276

she couldn't help herself. 'There's traces on that, but the surface isn't good for a print, that heavy paper, the best we could do maybe is harvest a bit of DNA. I was meaning to ask though, had you bought that for your husband? It was in your drawer, after all.'

'No, I, no,' she said, shaking her head. 'I thought it was from Nathan, I found it and I thought . . .' She stopped.

And Gerard looked at Carswell, conspiratorial, then back at her. 'Sorry,' he said blandly, 'just wanted to clear that one up. Funny, is all. That you had it in your bedside drawer.' He smiled.

He thought she was keeping it there, a message from her lover, the man who'd been in her bed. And as her next thought arrived, I do need a solicitor, she saw Gerard's broad, thick-veined hand, come out slowly, unerringly to pick up her phone from the table between them.

He glanced up at the camera's eye, inviting its complicity, then back at her. 'Mind if I have a look?'

I mind. I mind. She felt her heart pounding. She thought of lie detector tests. She said nothing.

She'd walked into the kitchen after a long sunny afternoon in the town with Ben, and Nathan had been there at the kitchen table, reading the newspaper, Emme playing out in the field. He'd sat there watching as she unpacked the shopping, and there her phone had been. Sitting on top of her cluttered handbag on the table, among the bags spilling sliced bread and bananas.

He hadn't even asked, as she turned from the cupboard she just saw him lean across the table and pick it out of the bag.

Fran had stopped where she was, a multipack of tinned tomatoes in her arms, and stared. He looked up at her and smiled. 'Mine's out of battery,' he said.

Nathan could have come with her to Oakenham that day, he wasn't in the office but he said instead, 'I'll pick Emme up. You go in, take the car, make a day of it.'

Consciously or unconsciously she took the same route each time since that first time, when she'd sat by the bridge. Since she'd looked up and shaded her eyes to see who it was standing there. She whispered down to Ben in the buggy, willing him to fall asleep. They turned a wide bend on the towpath and the bench was there, waiting in the sunshine.

She'd stopped in the lay-by on the edge of the town, coming home, and taken out her phone, typed it quickly, two or three words, and pressed send. It didn't mean anything, she told herself, though her whole body hummed with the sensation. It was just the sunshine and the unexpected freedom, she told herself. She looked down at the screen and the words on it, it's innocent, she told herself, but something whispered back to her, what would Nathan say?

Delete. She deleted.

'Just got to look this thing up quickly,' said Nathan at the kitchen table, frowning down at the tiny screen. 'Can't be bothered to wait for the computer to start up again,' and she hovered. 'You don't mind?' When he said that, she had to turn away so he couldn't see her face.

278

Why would she mind? Old emails, photographs, messages, nothing she wouldn't let him see. What's mine is yours. 'Sure,' she said and she made herself go on with the unpacking. When she did come back to the table, sat down and reached for her tea she glanced, just quickly, and saw that he wasn't on the internet at all, he was looking at her photographs. Nathan could see that she was looking, though, because he held the screen up to show her: a seagull she'd seen flying into the wind over the river that morning. He had smiled, and handed it back to her.

Walking past the chair where his jacket hung an hour or so later, though, Fran had felt the weight of his mobile bump against her and she had stopped. She had listened until she heard his voice and then she had gone to the door to make sure where he was, outside, in the field, in the lee of the barn, calling for Emme, before going back and removing the phone. It came to life in her hand and she saw that it had eighty per cent charge. She put it back in his pocket.

After that, if not every afternoon before Nathan got home from work then regularly, at least, she got into the habit of sifting through her phone, examining its history and its settings. She saw that there was a setting called privacy, though she didn't trust it. She began to delete things, just as a matter of course.

Chapter Twenty-Six

Crossing the quiet residential street where she'd found the solicitor's office, a plain terraced house with vinyl windows and double-glazing just like the others except for the discreet sign on the door, Fran thought if anyone lifted a net curtain they'd be able to tell what had happened just by the way she walked back to the car.

The will? Karen had said on the phone, then there'd been a lull as her hand went over the receiver. *Sure, take all the time you need.* A wary note in her voice. *We'll go for a walk after football maybe. Get them some chips.*

Jerky, stiff-legged, with Ben bouncing startled on one hip, Fran hardly knew what to do with the information the solicitor had given her. He was dead, after all, how could you be angry with a dead man? Perhaps that was what he'd relied on. She was more than angry: she was on the brink of murderous rage.

She climbed into the car.

The solicitor had agreed to see her, even though it was a Saturday: Fran should have guessed, maybe, from that, from the guilty haste in her voice. The police, she said, had already called.

A woman of about sixty in a neat pale suit, she might have been someone's aunt at a wedding. Her hair looked as though it had once been red but now it just looked dusty.

'I'm sorry,' she had said, spreading her hands, and she had, genuinely, seemed sorry. In fact she had looked almost scared. The will had been made not long after Ben had been born; that made sense, Fran supposed.

'Why wouldn't he have told me he was making a will?'

The woman pretended to study the few pages in front of her. The will had been drawn up perhaps a week after Fran had gone in to Oakenham in the car with Ben, he'd have been six weeks old, perhaps. A week after Nathan had plucked her phone right out of her bag and started to look through it. As if he knew.

When DS Gerard had done the same thing, she'd been almost primed, she knew this situation. As with Nathan, she'd sat tight. Quiet as a mouse, give nothing away. She felt as though she had no more than a splinter of leverage left, and if she didn't take care she'd lose that.

'Sorry,' Gerard had said to her as he set the phone back in front of her in the room at the police station, 'just . . . you know. Covering all the bases.' And, frowning, 'You don't keep it locked?' She just shook her head. She should have told him, no. There was no right way to behave, once you were a suspect.

She'd left the phone where Gerard had set it back down

281

on the table between them and had waited one beat then another, before reaching for her bag and pulling out the photograph, holding it so they couldn't see it. She noticed that they both changed as she did that, they went still.

'A couple of things,' Fran said to the policemen, and she felt a little pulse of an almost forgotten sensation: she could make them listen, now.

'First,' and she carefully kept the photograph away from them, against her chest, 'what about John Martin? The man who sold us the house. The man whose wife disappeared only because . . . Well, the man who told me called her a pikey,' and she paused then, glancing up at the camera. 'Not my word, by the way. I don't even know what you mean by that word. Itinerant, traveller, whatever.' Carswell's eyes were wide, and she went on. 'Anyway, no one asked why she'd gone off in the middle of the night and left her dog behind.' She took a breath. They eyed her, Carswell almost panting like a dog himself.

'John Martin,' said Gerard, eyeing her levelly. 'Yes, we've heard that story, as a matter of fact. The wife who tried to get money out of him, a good twenty years younger than him, tried and failed, I know who John Martin is. Sorry, what is your theory?'

Had Dearborn told them? 'I don't have a theory,' she said. 'That's your job. But he told me he was moving to the seaside, and he hasn't gone anywhere.'

Gerard nodded. 'All right,' he said. 'Well, I'm sure we can find him. And his wife, for that matter.' He turned his head just a little, to include Carswell. 'I think you'd know if John Martin climbed into bed with you, don't you Ed? You could always smell him a mile off, the chickens on him.'

Suddenly Fran felt so sick she almost started to her feet. With an effort she stayed put.

'And what's that you've got there?' said Gerard, leaning forward, his voice gentle again as if he'd never said it, the crude thing.

Hours earlier, Emme had stared down at it when Fran had showed it to her in their warm kitchen, Karen at the sink drying up for all the world as if she was part of the family. 'Can I have it?' she asked, lifting her face up to look from the photograph to her mother. 'It's my daddy.' Her lower lip held firm. Fran saw the effort it took.

'I need to show it to someone else first,' Fran had said carefully at the kitchen table and then Emme had looked back down, examining the faces. 'That's Daddy, and that's Rob,' she said. And she leaned closer, her finger went out and traced the man at the centre. 'And that's the bad man,' she said, and her voice went high, higher.

'Emme . . .' she'd begun, catching Karen watching from the sink, but Emme had drawn herself up, stiffly, her hair in its tight ponytail swinging, her little white collar neat.

'It's all right, Mummy,' she said, still holding on to the picture. 'Harry's waiting. It's our game, he's going to be angry if I'm late.' But she looked at the photograph again, frowning.

'What is it, Emme? What can you see?'

Emme had frowned and blinked, then shaken her head so her ponytail swung. Her lip pulled back in, she had pushed the photograph back across the table at Fran, glancing sideways up at Karen. 'Nothing, Mummy. Nothing. I can't see anything. Except I wondered, if they're all there, I wondered who was taking the picture. That's all.' Her grey eyes lingered on it, she watched as, carefully, Fran slid it into her bag. *My daddy*.

Bastard. And now she sat behind the solicitor's stupid leather-topped desk, that looked so out of place in the cramped, bay-windowed front room stacked with box files in an ordinary semi and called him that, out loud. *Bastard*.

'The fact is,' said the solicitor, 'a will is a private matter, very often, even for parents, even for happily married couples.' She looked nervous. 'Of course it's advisable to be open, to work these things out together, to avoid exactly this kind of . . . kind of . . .'

'Injustice?' said Fran, and she felt herself begin to shake. 'I don't want his money. I never wanted his money.'

You should never, was the thought that had sprung into her head, the same thought that came back to her now as the solicitor spoke, you should never have given up work. Never. That's why you're here in this room listening to this shit. She looked back and saw, as though down a long lens, those weeks and months and years when inch by inch she'd let it go: Jo asking her to fly to Italy and interview a pasta producer; Carine calling up in excitement and saying, there's a spot on health and beauty, you could do it part time. Nathan's face when she said it. *Pasta. Lipsticks.* Not sneering exactly, but patiently uncomprehending. *And what about train fares? Childcare?*

'I'm sorry,' said the solicitor again. 'We do like to persuade clients to amplify their intentions in an addendum to the will, if there's . . . a situation like this. Setting out their reasons.'

'What reason,' Fran had said, very, very calmly, because if she lost it now, with Ben on her knee and a

284

representative of the legal system eyeing her across the desk, she thought it quite possible that she would never again have control, in any area of her life, 'what reason could he have had? I mean . . .' She drew breath in a big gulp. 'I don't want his money. I don't want his fucking money, I was the one gave up my job for the children, I could have fought, I could have gone back . . .' The woman was shaking her head, a warning look. 'But Emme? Emme?'

'I don't know why,' said the woman with her faded sandy hair. 'It's . . .' She spread her hands again. 'I've given up wondering what goes on in people's heads, where wills are concerned. I'm just a solicitor. You might have a case for challenging it, obviously I am the executor, I can't possibly . . . but . . .' She shuffled the papers. 'As I say, there's provision for you and your daughter while the children are dependent, and the house is paid off in the event of his death.'

'But then it all goes to Ben.' She and the solicitor looked at Ben then, in the crook of her arm. His dark eyes were on her, not leaving her face. She made herself smile down at him, he looked back, uncertain. 'So he left nothing to me, nothing to Emme.' The woman shifted in her seat and nodded.

It came out of Fran in a rush, she had no wish to stop it. 'The bastard,' she said. 'The bastard.'

Sitting behind the wheel of her car Fran listened to the engine. She couldn't drive with all this inside her, she had to wait, she had to let it percolate. She squeezed her eyes shut and thought of Nathan's face, open, smiling, choosing her. You're the one. It had all seemed so right:

285

baby, marriage. She had seen what she was feeling mirrored in him. The loving husband.

But he never loved us, she thought. He was mirroring, all right, he was watching to see what I wanted to see, it was fake. As flat and empty as glass. As she understood that she knew exactly why he'd done it: to show them he felt nothing. To show them he could move and manipulate them, set them against each other. Ben might get the money – and there was plenty of it, according to the solicitor, significantly more than Fran would have expected, there were several accounts, all in the name of Alan Nathan Hall – but no one who properly loved a child could set him against his mother and sister. Ben – and she turned back to check on him, he was frowning down at his own fingers – was as much of a pawn as she and Emme were. Nathan didn't feel anything for them, and he wanted them to know that. They had been his to use, and now he was dead he was still using them.

It meant something. She'd find out what. She engaged the gears and pulled out, smoothly, into the quiet suburban street.

'I want Ben back,' she said to Gerard, still holding on to the photograph. 'I'd like Ali in here, too.'

For the five minutes it took Carswell to track them down in the police station and bring them in to the room, Gerard had sat there in silence, perfectly still. It seemed to Fran a strategy designed to show her who was boss, and to insult her. She used his stillness to look at him, accumulating evidence: he wore aftershave; he ironed his own shirt. Either he wasn't interested in food, or he went to

286

the gym, or both. He wasn't married, he didn't have a girlfriend, he didn't like women.

She couldn't prove any of it, but that didn't make it inaccurate.

Ben was asleep in his car seat. Ali held it carefully in her arms so as not to disturb him, setting it down in the corner. She gave the men a quick look.

'Good as gold,' she said in a whisper, turning to Fran. 'He's lovely. Everything all right?'

'Fine,' said Fran, and Ali sat beside her.

Fran held out the picture; Gerard made no attempt to take it. 'This is Nathan and two of his friends. This photograph was taken some time during the summer when they squatted in a house here in Oakenham, I told you about it. His friends are Rob and Bez. There may have been others at this house. They were there for no more than a few months, the summer of 1995. Twenty years ago.'

'Yes,' said Gerard. 'Rob. Mr Webster. I was going to ask—'

'It's Bez I want you to find,' she interrupted. 'Where is he? My daughter calls him the bad man, isn't that reason enough? She says she saw him in the village, she thought she saw him outside Karen's house. Rob said he'd got into drugs, he'd been living rough. He's obviously unstable. Haven't you even thought it's worth looking for him?' She drew a breath. 'Have you talked to Rob again?'

Gerard exhaled. 'I'd like details of where your daughter saw this man, of course. I believe his name's Martin Beston.'

She stared. 'You know who he is?'

'We are working very hard to find your husband's killer,

287

Fran,' said Gerard, patiently. 'I wish I could make you believe that we are taking you seriously.' She began shaking her head. 'And as for Rob—'

'We got news on Mr Webster,' said Ed Carswell, and the way he said it, eager, excited, made her turn towards him. But Gerard held up a hand and Carswell stopped.

'First of all,' Gerard said, formally, his tone quite different since Ali's appearance, 'we need to ensure your safety and that of your children, Fran. We need to make sure you feel secure. You keep telling us you know there's someone out there, but you refuse to move.' Head on one side. 'Why is that?' Even Ali was frowning – Fran couldn't tell any more if she agreed with him.

'Now, I'm sure you understand, we're working flat out on this. We don't have the manpower to have someone outside the house, twenty-four seven. Why won't you just let us make those arrangements we discussed right at the start? Why won't you let us look after you and your children?' He sounded earnest, he sounded puzzled. He sounded caring.

And then Fran caught a flash of something, from Ali Compton, a spark of anger directed at Gerard that told her Ali didn't trust him, either.

'I'm not leaving my house,' Fran said, on the strength of that look. 'What would that do to the children? This is our home. I want him found. As long as I'm here, Nathan's killer's not going anywhere. You know that as well as I do.' But Gerard began to shake his head, *If we believed*, but she pushed on. 'And who's to say I'd be any safer somewhere else?'

Gerard regarded her. 'Well, there may be another solution, as of tomorrow.'

288

'What?' she said.

'Your sister-in-law,' said Ali, and for a moment Fran hadn't the faintest idea who she meant.

'Miranda Hall?' Gerard said. 'She called us, asked us to pass on the message. She's on her way back from . . . wherever it is she's working. Singapore?'

'Seoul,' said Fran, stunned.

'She's eager to help. Stopping over in Dubai or somewhere, she couldn't get a direct flight.'

Fran put her hands to her head, trying to take it in. 'She's coming here.'

'Should be tomorrow some time, weather permitting. So.'

He looked down at the photograph, that was now lying on the table. 'Ed,' he said, 'scan that in for us, will you?' As an afterthought he turned to Fran. 'If that's OK with you, Fran?'

'What about Rob?' said Fran, stubborn, at the sight of Carswell's narrow shoulders. 'So you have talked to him again? What does he say about Bez?'

It was Ali who spoke, though, resting a hand on her shoulder. 'Fran,' she said, 'we're worried about your husband's friend Rob. Mr Webster.'

'I'm right in thinking, they never lost touch?' said Gerard. 'Rob and your husband?'

She shook her head. 'Rob was his best man. What's happened to Rob?'

The door opened and Carswell stood there looking at them, a kid playing pass the parcel, impatient for his turn, and in that moment the whole thing felt like a game played over her head, between the men. Rob and Nathan and

289

Carswell and Gerard, more men further out, Julian, the farmers, the property developer at the wedding lunch whose name she couldn't even remember, throwing a ball from one to the other and no matter how hard she tried she couldn't get it.

'His neighbours haven't seen him in forty-eight hours, maybe more,' said Gerard. There was a pause. 'You were seen there, yesterday morning.' He watched her for a reaction. She just stared back.

'We gained access to his house but found nothing,' Gerard said.

She remembered the mail on the mat. Forty-eight hours would take them back to around the time Rob had turned up in her kitchen, scared to death.

'We got his car,' said Carswell, bouncing on his heels in the doorway, the photo in his hand, unable to keep quiet.

'His car?' Fran turned to Ali, in dread.

'We found it in the woods,' said Ali, putting a hand over hers. 'Up the other side of the airbase?' Fran put a hand up to her mouth, suddenly stiff with fright, trying to place it, seeing only the tufted dykes and low willows, wind-blown. What else was up there? Something.

'Someone . . . did he . . . did someone . . .'

'Car seems clean but, you know,' said Gerard, watching her. 'If it was staged, let's say, we'd expect more mess. We're carrying out tests. You'd be surprised what we can pick up.' Pointed.

'Staged?' Belatedly she registered the look he'd given her.

He shrugged. 'Made to look like . . . Violent, let's say. It's been known. Blood all over, rips in the upholstery. That

290

kind of thing. In fact a clean car like that tends to sound a few more alarm bells.'

'He's . . . he's that kind of man,' said Fran, and in her head she could see him, climbing on his bike, meticulous with his Velcro straps, climbing into that car, with its air freshener dangling and maps stacked in the side pocket and then looking at Ali's pale face, she cracked. 'Someone's hurt him,' she said.

Carswell made a face, uneasy. 'Well, now,' he said, but Fran didn't let him go on.

'He said he didn't know anything about Nathan's work,' she said, slowly. 'But he meant the opposite. He knew who Julian was, he knew what happened after that summer they spent in the squat, with Bez. He knew what Nathan was up to, when he was supposed to be working.'

She looked from Gerard to Carswell and back but their faces were impassive. 'Someone's hurt him,' she said.

'Maybe best to be prepared,' said Ali Compton.

'He was frightened, when he came to see me.' They were staring at her. 'You don't understand, Rob's . . . he's . . . without Nathan, he's vulnerable. He was frightened of someone.'

Chapter Twenty-Seven

Unappetising, thought Ali Compton, didn't even begin to cover what was on offer in the canteen, even if the previous hour and a half hadn't already left a horrible taste in her mouth. But behind her Ed Carswell was bumping up against her, impatient. She turned on him and he blinked, leering. She turned back and at random took a ham roll in cling-film from the cabinet.

He nuzzled against her neck from behind. 'The sexual tension, boss,' he said, holding eye contact with Gerard. 'Don't know what to do with myself.' She shouldered him out of the way roughly, feeling the sweat rise. At the till Mary-Anne in her polyester mob cap watched her tug her shirt back into place.

They corralled her into a table in the corner by a window overlooking the car park. Carswell had the all-day breakfast, beans overflowing the plate; Gerard plonked down his egg salad and immediately began to fork it stolidly into his mouth without interest. She tried to imagine him shacked up with a wife and kids and getting fat, but couldn't. Carswell was different, Ed Carswell was a slave to his hormones, and that's what landed you in a family situation, like it or not. Maybe he'd grow out of it – she wouldn't bet on it. Twenty years of beer, fags and shagging, then drop dead of a heart attack.

'Got her some nice lingerie for tomorrow,' Ed said, nudging against her with his skinny elbow. He pronounced it with an exaggerated foreign accent, not necessarily French.

'Let me guess,' said Ali, pushing away her plate and reaching for the cooling coffee. The coffee didn't taste of anything much but you drank tea till you were drowning in it, in this job. 'Red, is it?'

'Black,' he said, looking offended. 'She's sophisticated. Older woman.' He tilted his head to one side. 'Not as old as you, of course, no offence.'

She laughed, one eye on DS Gerard, who had finished and was sitting back, staring through the glass. 'None taken,' she said, and Carswell scowled.

Gerard spoke, abruptly. 'I need to be sure you're staying within the remit. 'Family liaison isn't about going behind the backs of the investigative team and dishing out information at random to a victim's family.' And he smiled, that broad, shit-eating grin that charmed them when he turned it on, but didn't fool her.

'I'm a police officer, same as you, sir. I know how an investigation works.' Gerard gave a snort that wound her up just enough.

'But you don't seem to be listening to her,' she said, gritting her teeth. 'I mean, I'm sure you have your reasons for keeping your focus so narrow, but would it hurt to explore a few more—'

'Which of her theories,' said Gerard, his voice all quiet and dangerous, 'would you like me to follow up? The phantom husband who got into bed then got up again to get himself murdered? This mystery man standing in the field who seems very happy to keep his distance, just the odd box of chocolates to let her know he still loves her?' To Carswell, 'You put those flowers in for analysis?' ever so casual. 'And I hope nothing untoward has happened to that box of chocolates, by the way, Ed, I wouldn't want anyone to have eaten the evidence.' Carswell snickered, uncertain.

'Chocolates?' Surely he wouldn't have. Arsehole.

Gerard leaned back, looking up at the ceiling. 'You want us to dig up the floor of that chicken barn looking for the body of John Martin's wife? Get Beston out from under his stone? I'll find him, don't worry, but from what I hear he can hardly stand up, never mind kill a man as fit as Nathan Hall. Or perhaps you'd like me to track down the whore whose knickers we found in the field while I'm at it?'

Yes, thought Ali. Of course I fucking would.

'Tights, wasn't it?' she said. 'Not knickers.' And took a breath. 'With respect,' she said, 'I think putting all your eggs in one basket is a risky strategy, not to mention at odds with the evidence.'

'*With respect*, Detective Constable Compton, you know fuck all about the evidence. About the other agencies we're having to deal with over this. And for good reason, the way you're cosying up to her.'

'It's my job, to keep her informed.' She leaned forward. 'Who are these other agencies?'

'I'm not at liberty to say at this juncture.'

'Bullshit,' she said, under her breath.

'DC Compton,' he said, his voice dangerously low, 'what was that? It wouldn't take much more of that for me to take you off this case.' Carswell was goggling at them over his massacre of a breakfast plate. 'We're hanging on to this investigation by the skin of our teeth and if I lose it . . . If we lose it because you fancy a bit of a feminist crusade . . .'

He stopped, she could see him resetting.

He sat back. 'She doesn't want you,' said Gerard, smiling again. 'I'd wash your hands of it if I were you, not like you haven't got commitments elsewhere.' She kept her face still.

'Last time I looked at the conditions of my employment,' she said quietly, 'I stay on the job as long as the investigation runs, unless you find evidence of misconduct, of which there is none. And you wouldn't want to be scurrying around looking for another FLO at this stage, would you, DS Gerard?'

'All I'm saying,' said Gerard, reasonable, 'is remember who's paying you. Kick back a bit. I can move you off this any time I want, and you know it.'

'What do you think was on the hard drive?' she said, tough. 'Are you saying she took that too? From what I heard, there's evidence he had it with him.'

'Could have been anything in that briefcase.' Gerard sat back, watching her. 'She could have destroyed the hard drive and his phone while she was at it. We don't know what he found out about her.'

'A one-night stand?' She scoffed. 'You don't need a hard drive to store that piece of information.'

'More than that,' said Gerard, and his smile spread. 'You know it is. Not just that she's been seen with a man, either. It's who he is.'

'Family liaison should be for missing kids, and that's it,' said Carswell, drumming his skinny fingers on the table top, a slop of ketchup on the side of the plate between his hands. Spouting Gerard again: she ignored him. She was thinking, hard. Other agencies, like who? Another agency that could have this case off them, who could get Craddock to take a Skype conference at crack of dawn.

'See that book she had in her sitting room?' said Carswell, sitting up straight, eager. 'Very fifty shades, I don't think.'

Gerard clicked his tongue. 'Porn for the middle classes,' he said with a sour laugh. 'They should see what we see. And it was her kitchen knife. Woman's weapon of choice.'

Ali stared at him. 'You think she could do that to her husband, I mean, physically?' She gave up, her hands flat on the melamine table top. 'He had his guts hanging out, from what I hear.'

'Who's saying she was on her own?' he said, calm and cold. 'There's men all over her, this one.'

Ali recoiled, because his hand was so close she felt the brush of the hairs on his knuckle. His little finger extended and tapped hers, softly.

'I want her under police protection,' she said, trying to ignore the flush that spread uncomfortably under her blouse. She didn't move her hand – let him move his. 'I want her out of there, whether she likes it or not. You're playing her; you know that the more you offer her some grotty safe house, the harder she's going to dig her heels in. She's a victim until you have charges to press. But it suits you to have her out there, doesn't it, for all the world to see, in the middle of nowhere next to a stinking chicken barn. If she did it, alone or with whatever man you've got pegged for her, she'll crack, is that the theory? If someone else did it, he's going to come after her, her and her kids, but that doesn't matter to you, does it?' She came to a halt, out of breath, the anger still pumping, she leaned towards him. 'Because you've got her dangling.'

And you love it, she thought as he just kept smiling, it's where you want women, full stop.

'Gonna nail her,' said Carswell, gleeful, but Gerard didn't turn his head, he didn't speak.

Men all over this one. Who had Fran Hall been seeing? A new boyfriend? Where would she meet one, not the type to go on Tinder, was she? Internet: no computer either. New boyfriend, old boyfriend, business contact, mate. She needed to talk to Sadie Watts.

'She's vulnerable, and it's our duty to protect her and her kids,' she said, unable to shut up. She had no power, and they both knew it, but that wasn't going to stop her. Gerard sat perfectly still and she could feel him checking her out, examining her unwashed hair, her roots, her knackered skin. She stared him down.

'She's a bitch,' said Gerard and Ali looked for witnesses but all she could see were backs turned to her, lined up along the service counter.

'She's a bitch,' he said again, leaning forward, turning his face to look into hers, 'And she's lying.'

★   ★   ★

297

Beyond the pub the river slid by, dark green and slow, weed streaming in it like hair. She sat in the cramped car park under a dripping tree, Ben asleep in the back. Four months, two, he'd be sitting up, he'd be crawling, he'd be asking questions. *Did you kill my daddy?*

Close to, the Angel in the Fields did still look like an ordinary pub, a little bit shabby, maybe, the low roof mossy, the crates of alcopop empties uncollected. The sandwich board chalked up with specials: you'd have to walk around it to see *Sunday Night Drag Race, Valentine's Special*, and a pair of pouting red lips drawn on.

The car cooled quickly and she closed her eyes, thinking of the woods where they'd found Rob's car. Thinking of Rob, his big raw hands, Nathan's oldest friend. Was it grief that had sent him up there, into the dark? Or had someone lured him there? She put both hands on the steering wheel and tried to think. All she could think of was his voice when she'd called to tell him, when he'd picked up the phone up there on that mountain and said Nathan's name, cheery, expectant, and she'd had to tell him, Nathan was dead. The silence. Like he knew.

Would Nathan have told Rob about the will? She opened her eyes again and took out her mobile, held it in both hands. She wrote a message, five words, sent it, deleted it.

The woods, the airbase, that was where they'd found Rob's car. This wasn't her territory, this was theirs. Rob and Nathan and Bez – and whoever had taken that photograph of them, at Black Barn.

The airfield, ringed with fencing. The trees. Then she sat up, she knew what else there was up there, beyond the woods. The flooded quarry where they'd used to swim.

The picture that sprang up in her head thrummed, urgent. The expanse of black water, the spidery willows clumped on the dykes. The car's temperature gauge said minus two: you would die in that water, wouldn't you? In minutes. Even someone fit and healthy. Rob ran marathons; she grasped at straws. Not Rob.

Behind her Ben stirred and wearily she climbed out and got in the back with him. She sat and began to feed him, cocooned in his wadded suit. A man in a tatty ski jacket with a shaven head came out of the back door of the pub and lit up a cigarette, standing with his back to her and staring at the water.

A message buzzed. Bringing one hand free from around Ben she looked down, read it, answered with a thumb, **All right, all right.** Moved the thumb to *delete conversation.*

It occurred to Fran, numbly, that she wouldn't be alone for much longer; she had a sister-in-law who was coming to help. Her sister-in-law, Miranda, who would about now be boarding a plane, she'd be landing in Dubai in a smart suit and heels, desert heat and luxury hotels.

All she knew about Miranda was a photograph in a frame of the two of them, she and Nathan side by side in a swingboat, a serious chubby girl with a straight black fringe. And the message on Nathan's phone, the day they got married. As she remembered that a tiny pulse set up. There were things Miranda would be able to tell her. Their childhood, their parents, that summer, him and Rob and Bez, and then nothing, then cutting ties, leaving it all behind till now. Just like Miranda had done herself.

Ben detached himself, straining backwards and turning his head away, already saying no. The man in the ski jacket had gone back inside. Fran climbed out of the car with Ben at her shoulder, and followed him.

The ceilings were low and it was fusty and dim but Fran registered that they weren't open, the place was empty and the tables in disorder. As her eyes adjusted she saw a garland of tinsel over the bar, a big red heart of padded and frilled velvet hanging askew against a black curtain behind a podium. Still in his ski jacket the man she'd seen smoking was halfway up a stepladder on the other end of the heart in the far corner. He eyed her but said nothing, his mouth full of tacks. He turned back and finished what he was doing and then stepped off the ladder.

'Can't bring a kid in here,' he said, frowning, but not hostile. He wore a black shirt under the jacket, he was skinny, clean-shaven, about Carswell's age but nothing like Carswell.

'You're not open for customers though, are you?' she pleaded, shifting Ben to one side. He strained to reach for some tinsel and the man sighed.

'What then?' he said, turning to go behind the bar. She followed, standing there. Ben tugged at a beer cloth and she tried to pull it out of his hand.

'Let him,' said the barman. 'What's his name?' He took off his jacket, hung it up and held out a hand to Ben. 'I'm Eric,' he said. 'Shake, mate.'

'I'm here about my husband,' she said and Eric paused mid-handshake. 'Oh, yeah,' he said. 'One of those. Haven't seen him, haven't shagged him, seen nothing, done nothing, don't know nothing.'

'He's dead. He died.'

Eric looked down, extracted his hand from Ben's, leaned

down and began to lift steaming glasses from a dishwasher behind the counter. 'Right,' he said flatly. 'It was Al, was it?' He reached for a cloth.

'I called him Nathan.'

'But the one . . . the one the coppers came about?' A twisted sad little smile, as slowly he began polishing a glass. 'Nice-looking pair. I think they liked it here.' He reached up and hung the glass from its rack, leaned down for another.

'So he was a regular? They were telling the truth.'

'For once,' said Eric, regarding Ben. 'Christ. What a fuck-up.' He hung the next glass, then started on another.

'The police said you wouldn't tell them about his . . . partners. What he got up to.'

'And you want to know? What he got up to?'

She frowned. 'I've got no choice,' she said, flatly.

He nodded. 'Listen, love. It's not as unusual as you think, it's all sorts, you see all sorts. Some of them too scared to come out, some of them say they love their wives, some of them are in it for the kink. Their secret life. It's a big world out there, live and let live, is what I say.'

'He's dead, though.'

And Eric's smile twisted again, kinder this time. 'What do you want to know?' he said, with a sigh. She got out the photograph and laid it on the table; he peered down. 'That's a while ago, isn't it?' he said, but he put a finger to Nathan's face. 'Can still see it, though. Looked after himself.' And the finger moved along, to Bez, he frowned. 'Where is that?' he said, leaning closer.

'They squatted at a place. Their last summer after school finished. Nineteen ninety-five, something like that.'

301

Eric was hunched over the picture. 'Summer of love,' he said. 'That sort of deal, was it?' He looked up. 'I'd have been not much bigger than him then.' He nodded to Ben then looked back at the photograph. 'A lot of E in the system, those days.' He sounded wistful. 'All-nighters, shiny happy people. Stuff got nastier, didn't it? Getting out of your head got hardcore. Ketamine an' that.' He straightened. 'Looks like Black Barn, out that way.'

'Where is that?' she said, breathless. Eric squinted back down at the photograph, his head tilted. 'Out Chatteris way, this side of the reservoir?' The oily dark surface of the water swam in front of her eyes in the gloom. 'There were stories about what went on there, kids and that, they closed it down. Something happened, someone died. Ten a penny, OD deaths round here, you want to spend a night in Casualty now and again.'

'Drugs? Did the police ask you about it, when they came about my husband?'

He snorted. 'They just wanted to know who he was shagging.' He looked back at the picture almost tenderly, as if it told him something about himself.

'Did he come in here with either of them?'

The barman ran a hand over his shaven head, puffed out his cheeks. 'Jeez, I dunno if I'd even have recognised Al from that photo.' He shook his head. 'Not sure, is the answer.'

'Did Nathan . . . did Al come in here with anyone in particular?' Fran said quietly, and he shrugged, uneasy.

'No, he always came in alone. As for who he talked to, who he left with, well . . .' His shoulders were eloquent. 'Gets busy. Gets a bit full-on.' He frowned. 'And he always

302

sat in the snug,' he nodded towards another room, where the corner of a booth was just visible, 'you know. A bit more private. There's one booth just behind a pillar, Al liked that best. Maybe because you couldn't see what he was up to.' He gave her a sheepish look. 'Sorry.' He looked back down at the photograph.

'Sort of familiar, that one.' His finger was back on Bez in the photograph, the lean shoulders, the head thrown back. 'Something about him.'

'He's called Bez,' and Eric said, 'Never. Fuck.' He began to shake his head. 'Warning to stay off the booze if ever there was one.'

'You know him?'

'I seen Thorney talking to him, once or twice. He's down the war memorial sometimes with the other boozers, not lately though, come to think of it.' He pushed the photograph back towards her and she stowed it quickly as Ben reached out a pudgy hand to grab. 'Never came in here, he'd be a four-pack of Kestrel and a Thunderbird chaser, no money for pub prices.'

'Who's Thorney? Did the police talk to him?'

'Ray Thornton. Older guy. Collects glasses, cleans the toilets. Yeah, they talked to him, being as he's the only one sees what they're up to in the glory hole. Man of few words though, especially where the police are concerned. And he's a drinker.'

She shivered suddenly – it was cold in the gloomy low-ceilinged room, and Eric said, 'It cheers up of an evening, you wouldn't believe. Put the heating on and everything. Tomorrow night it'll be like Vegas in here.'

'Tomorrow?'

'Long as the snow holds off,' he said dubiously, leaning to peer towards the window, where the outside world showed grey. A shadow passed it, the crunch of tyres as the beer truck moved off. 'Valentine's, Ray's back on then, if you want to talk to him. Catch him before he's pissed though. I'll put in a word, if you like.'

'Get my showgirl outfit ready, shall I?' she said. Eric cracked a proper smile at last, and the gloom retreated, just fractionally.

'Maybe leave the kid behind for that one,' he said, and the smile was gone as quickly as it had come. 'Lose our licence that way.'

And then abruptly he turned his back, opened a door in the back of the bar and she glimpsed a rectangle of striplit kitchen, a row of catering jars on top of a fridge.

'Ray'll be in at three thirty,' he said over his shoulder, 'He's old enough to remember the summer of love, first time around.' But before she could even say thanks, Eric was through the door and it was closing behind him.

Outside, she scanned the grey car park but it was empty as she walked across the gravel with Ben clamped tightly to her. The sky was low and white with cloud and the air freezing and clammy, the chill crept up on her even between the pub door and the car, seeping under her coat, up inside the cuffs of her sleeves. There was moisture inside the car windows, and she could see her breath as she strapped Ben in.

Keys. She sat there with them in her hand, turned to check on Ben but he seemed stunned by the cold, strapped in his padding, his eyes black and round. Fran heard the car pull in alongside them, on the passenger side, and still she sat there with the keys in her hand, she didn't turn to look.

The other car's engine turned off and she leaned her head back against the seat. The door opened and he was inside.

She closed her eyes and there was his smell, of what she didn't know but she'd know it in the dark, the ghost of sweat, washed cotton and shaving foam, with it she recalled the texture of the skin below his chin, the roughness against her cheek. The breadth of his hand. When she opened her eyes again there was his shoulder as he looked back between the seats at Ben. He turned back and when he smiled she saw the lines beside his eyes, the lines that hadn't been there in the old days.

'Needs a dad, now, doesn't he?' he said, quietly, turning back to look at her, his eyes narrowing as he did, and he lifted a hand to her face, she felt the warmth of it as he rested it against her cheek. Quickly she brought her own hand up to stop him.

'He's another man's kid,' she said. 'Would you want that? Would you, Nick?'

Chapter Twenty-Eight

He hadn't spoken to Fran the first time: he'd just stood on the bridge and watched her there, pregnant in the sunshine, with Emme in the buggy beside her. She'd lifted her hands to shade her eyes, so that she could be sure of what she was seeing, though she already knew. She knew Nick's haircut, she knew his jacket, the angle of his shoulders, and recognising it all Fran had felt her body propelled upright and towards him on the bench, her belly momentarily forgotten until she shifted forwards over it. Then she stopped, catching her breath, warning the baby against the sudden movement, *careful*.

Nick was leaning on the bridge's parapet but as she moved forwards he lifted his hand in a half-wave, awkward, nervous, shy as she'd never seen him. And then he had turned and walked off, jerky and anxious, and she was almost on her feet to call out and stop him, or run after him. But she hadn't called after him. She hadn't run. She had only wanted to.

It was a week later that he sent her the first message. I miss you. She'd deleted his contact but she hadn't blocked his number: a shrink would probably say that was a dead giveaway. And when the number came up she knew it straight away.

She left it ten days before she answered. How did you find me?

Of course, it hadn't been like that, or so he said. And besides, he could have found her easily enough if he'd wanted to – she wasn't hiding, was she?

He had stroked her belly, the week before Ben was born. He'd set his cheek against it. It seemed to her by then that Nathan was actually averting his eyes from her, never mind feeling her belly, but still she stepped away from Nick abruptly when he touched her.

'We're friends, aren't we?' he had said when she recoiled, and he seemed genuinely hurt, his eyes dark.

'I don't know if Nathan would see it like that,' she'd said. 'I can't see you, Nick.'

The snow was beginning as she drove back with Ben behind her in his seat, although Fran didn't notice it at first, it was so fine, like dust in the greying afternoon. She parked along the side of the house. Slowly she put a hand up to the button that locked all the doors

The car that had pulled up next to her in the car park of the Angel had been dark and big and solid but nothing special; no more top-end Range Rover with tinted windows, no more chauffeur-driven Italian job with doors that opened the wrong way and leather seats.

'I'm done with all that,' he had said to her the first time they sat down together, a month after she saw him on the bridge. Five weeks, not that she was counting, not that she found herself on her weekly visits to Oakenham hunting out something decent to wear, circling back always to the bench by the river. They were in a coffee shop down a lane behind a church, a big dark tree shading the window. Nick took her there, he already knew it.

'It was . . . that wasn't me, Frankie.' He ducked his head as he said it, ashamed – which she supposed was to his credit. 'I'm a businessman now, pure and simple. I've had enough of the rest of it.' Averting his eyes. 'One way or another I'd be dead by now if I hadn't got out.'

He told her he'd been there more than a year. 'Cheap storage, cheap property. And there's a market for clubs out here in the middle of nowhere like you wouldn't believe. I've got a chain of them, up as far as Hull. End-of-date beer, off-season guest DJs, it might not be glamorous, but it's a foolproof formula. It's hard work.'

She stopped him when he started telling her where he was living – it seemed dangerous. The next step would be him asking her if she'd like to see it. 'So I came out here before you did,' he said abruptly, and looked mystified, on the edge of wonderment at the miracle that had brought them back together.

He had looked tired, he had looked as if he'd spent two years tracking up and down from the Wash to Lincoln to Wisbech, sorting out premises and security, back to an office in a warehouse on the edge of town where he stored his speaker stacks and decks and props and whatever else.

'I was out of my depth,' he had said back then when she'd first seen him again, in the coffee shop in Oakenham he'd led her to.

Helpless, when she turned on him as he'd put his cheek against her belly to whisper the words, and she'd shoved her chair back and said, 'You do remember, don't you? Why I left you?' The girl in the coffee shop had turned at the loud sound of the chair against the floor and given them a look.

Ben was wide awake in the back of the car: something beyond the window fascinated him, perhaps the tiny particles of snow, barely visible, just a glitter in the low light.

Someone had seen them, someone had told. The girl in the coffee shop. Of course. Long before the press conference, Nathan's death, someone would have whispered, saw that Londoner. Saw her with a man. And it seemed to her in that moment of revelation that Nathan had known it all too, Nathan who watched her, who knew her. Nathan knew Nick was here, before she did.

But that was stupid. How would he know? And why would he have let her go, urged her to go, if he had?

'What do I have to do,' Nick had said to her, 'to show you? I love you. There's only ever been you.'

The snow was beginning to dust the hedges; she had passed a gritting lorry miles back on the Oakenham ring road, but nothing since.

Known what, anyway? What did they all think they knew? Because she hadn't slept with Nick. And that was what an affair was, wasn't it? Loving someone, wanting to touch him, remembering the smell of his sheets in the morning and the sound of his humming in the shower – that wasn't an affair.

And was it rape, if you didn't know it at the time?

With Ben asleep behind them in his seat Nick had gone very quiet when she told him: the first person she had told. The person who wouldn't judge.

'Did you enjoy it?' Nick's voice had been so low she barely heard it and then, as if he'd felt what she felt, all her limbs going rigid at the question, he went on quickly, as if he hadn't said it at all, 'I suppose the question is, were you in a position to give your consent?'

And he had looked down at his hands, as if at a loss. The ice they tiptoed across was thin, it cracked under them.

'He must have just killed Nathan,' she said then, in a voice odd and bright and clear in the enclosed space of the car. 'Murder trumps rape, doesn't it? I mean. Why should I scream and shout because a man screwed me while I was half asleep, when Nathan got murdered? That shouldn't make me feel guilty, should it? That shouldn't make me feel ashamed, should it?' Her voice was getting higher and thinner, and she stopped, dead.

For a second as she glanced sideways at him, saw his hands, the fabric of his coat, the ghost of stubble on his chin in her head, she was scrabbling to get out, to get away from him. A man, a man, a man, he touched me, a man.

'You didn't tell them, then,' he said. 'You didn't tell the police, about the sex.'

'You don't know,' she said then, numb with horror. 'You don't know what it's been like.'

From where she was parked now Fran could see the lit

windows of the school beyond the gates, and the dark shapes in the playground. She thought of the big solid shape of Nick's car beside her tinny battered one; she thought of him sitting in the passenger seat next to her, warm and familiar; and then she thought of the cold unlit house waiting for them, she remembered that the boiler was on the blink. She would only need to say a word or two, to put out her hand, and she wouldn't be alone. She felt drained, hollow.

'Hey!'

The voice, rough and close and the rap of knuckles loud against the window, made her heart race. She started forward and then she saw it was Karen, and she had Emme with her.

In the end Ali resorted to waiting outside for Sadie to come off shift. There wasn't a desk for an FLO in the incident room and there'd been no sign of her anyway. She'd stood for a bit looking at Gerard's scrawl on the whiteboard, arrows and rubbings out and names. Teamwork, was what it was supposed to be about.

Ali looked at her phone: almost five. She'd told Mum she'd be there by half past, at the latest – had written it on a post-it by the clock. Christ knew what chaos would ensue if she was late, having written it down. Adrian had promised, reluctantly and with the trophy wife bleating in the background, that he'd be there tomorrow evening. Would stay over.

Martin Beston wasn't top of the list of names, nor was Rob Webster. Gerard had breezed past her on his way up there, to the reservoir. 'I'll keep you posted, DC Compton,' he said. 'Ed's stopping here, if you need to . . . go over anything.' A smirk from Ed Carswell.

'Where's DC Watts?' she asked, and the men shrugged at each other.

'You send her out for sweeties again?' said Gerard.

Gerard might have been picking his spots at the other end of the country when rumours were going around about Black Barn that summer, but Ali had grown up five miles away from the place, and even though she'd been off doing her training when it was closed down, it would have been her first port of call in this investigation. So how come Nick Jason was top of Gerard's list?

Half an hour's googling on her phone in the car park had told Ali that Nick Jason owned Club Sound Logistics, the warehouse on the Sandpiper estate opposite Nathan's empty office, so Gerard knew that much, and hadn't bothered informing Ali.

Nathan had been watching Jason, not the other way around. But as an idea began to form, the sliding doors opened and there she was.

'Sadie,' she said. 'DC Watts.' A shifty look: Ali knew what this was about. It was about different ways of handling Doug Gerard, and getting on, and who knew? Sadie's was probably cleverer. Head down, mouth shut, ears open. 'I get it,' Ali said, wearily. 'I get it. I won't tell him you've said a thing. But let's suppose he's wrong about that woman taking a knife to her husband – I'm all she and her kids have got. So tell me. About Nick Jason, and what Nathan Hall was up to.'

Sadie Watts set her mouth in a line.

'All right, Sadie, how about I tell you what I think?'

* * *

312

Fran was on the ladder under the trapdoor to the attic when it came back to her in a rush, it raised a prickle on the back of her neck.

Nick had mentioned it almost as an afterthought, diffident, cautious.

'I saw him, you know,' he said, and he'd looked down at his hands, relaxed in his lap. 'Of course, I didn't know it was him, I didn't know it was Nathan, your Nathan. Alan Nathan Hall, according to the paper.' He looked up then. 'I saw him where I keep my stuff. The warehouse. The Sandpiper.'

It had been Karen that had put it out of her mind, leaning down at the window to take charge, all brisk and refusing to take no for an answer. 'Out you get,' she said. Plumber's on his way. Got him on speed-dial, as a matter of fact, he's got a bit of a soft spot for me. Snow coming? You can't just leave it.'

And that had been the next couple of hours taken care of, the blessing of not having to think, just for a bit. There had been tea to be made and the plumber in her kitchen within a half-hour, a big bashful man eyeing Karen with wonder as she sat at the table with her plump, soft, manicured hands round a mug.

It was Karen who'd sent her up to the attic, too, although indirectly. She would probably have been horrified, thought Fran, to think of her halfway up a stepladder on her own. But it had been Karen who'd cocked an ear at the sound, as they stood together on the landing outside Emme's room, the faint spidery scuttle of something.

Fran and Karen had been on the landing together outside the bedroom, the house had been beginning to warm up at last and the plumber sent on his way, flushed with pleasure at a job well done and Karen's approval. Emme was playing on the bedroom floor with Harry, together they were building another elaborate fortress, dividing the labour. Emme was bossing Harry into a corner, his small head bent over as he banged with a wooden hammer. It had been in the sudden silence when the banging stopped that they heard it, just for a second, a scratchy echo over their heads that stopped as though it knew they were listening.

'Rats?' Karen's upturned face had been grim and pale. 'You want to put something down,' she said, pushing the door into the bedroom open wider. 'Come along, Harry. Time to get home.'

'I've got some stuff,' said Fran, 'for the rats.' Remembering Nathan coming back with the plain cardboard box of lurid green pellets trying to think where he'd put it.

It came as a shock to her that Nick had even known who Nathan was. She had told him nothing, in the months then years after she left him, not about Nathan, about getting pregnant, not about getting married. She hadn't answered his messages, she hadn't made arrangements to retrieve the toothbrush, the books, the old, soft, much-washed T-shirt under his pillow nor the pairs of heels and clean knickers she'd left in his wardrobe – she just turned her back on all of it.

Fran supposed he had asked around: someone would have told him Nathan's name.

'The Sandpiper?' she said, bewildered. 'But that's where he had his office.'

Nick had raised his head then, looking through the

windscreen at something she couldn't see. 'Small world,' he had said, eventually, but when he turned his head to her his eyes were dark, thoughtful.

'I looked for him,' he said abruptly. 'I tried to find him online, when Carine told me his name.'

'You did?' And apprehension stirred. She hadn't let herself wonder what Nick was thinking or doing, those long-ago months. She'd just dumped the roses when they came, and then one day they'd stopped coming. 'And what?'

'Not much,' he said shortly. 'Look, I'm not proud of it. But I had nothing. You wouldn't talk to me. I found some website for his firm, is all. Pretty basic stuff. I didn't know what you could see in him. I wanted to see his face, but there was nothing. A few other Nathan Halls, in New Zealand, one in France.'

'Carine was talking to you?' Carine had always liked Nick, Fran could remember the quick flash of excitement when she'd heard they weren't a couple any more.

Nick laughed miserably. 'For a bit. She got bored pretty quick, when all I wanted to know about was you.' He looked tired: for a second she wanted to put an arm round him except then he turned his head just a fraction and she saw, he was waiting for that, for her to soften, and she wasn't sure it was in the past, at all. Nick turned back to the windscreen.

'No pictures of him,' he mused. 'On all the internet, hardly a trace of him at all, in fact. It was frustrating, and it was odd, I thought. Maybe because I wasn't looking for Alan Nathan Hall. But still. Not Facebook, not LinkedIn, nothing personal or professional. Odd.'

She didn't do Facebook but Carine did, the girls from

315

school who'd come along to the wedding did, it had been in their conversation while they took selfies outside the registry office on the busy road. Had the property developer taken photos? Julian hadn't. Even as she wondered it came back to her, his hand up quickly to shield his face. 'No press,' he'd said, joking, and Carine had put her camera down indulgently. They'd thought he was sheepish about his big beer gut, the red face, too old for that sort of thing.

But in Oakenham, in Cold Fen, out here they remembered Nathan, they didn't need Google, they didn't need to search the internet for images. Had he understood that, how long memories were out here? Nathan hadn't recognised Dearborn, but Dearborn had known who he was.

On the back doorstep in the icy dark with Harry pressing himself fearfully into the shaggy fur on her coat, Karen had said, 'I couldn't stand it, knowing they were up there. Rats. You get 'em sorted.' There had been something in Karen's face she'd only glimpsed before, something drawn and ruthless. Was that country people?

It was only after she'd gone, she'd thought, she should have asked Karen about Black Barn, because Karen had been here her whole life, because her dad had been a police officer. Instead, she had just sat there between Karen and the plumber, wanting the peace not to stop, the cups of tea and the other quiet voices in her house.

And now on the ladder with the box of poison in one hand and the other pressing tentatively at the trapdoor, she had remembered that it had been Karen who'd first pointed it out to her. That you could move away from your childhood home and think that all those faces belonged in the past, almost like you'd made them up – she'd thought that way about Nick, until she'd seen him on the bridge, until she learned that he hadn't forgotten her, not for one minute.

Cemented shut with spider-dust and damp, the trapdoor resisted. Fran pushed harder and she felt the ladder wobble.

If she fell.

Emme was asleep in bed; she had taken a little while. Sitting beside her Fran had said, thinking it was something to look forward to, 'Your auntie's coming tomorrow, Daddy's sister.'

But Emme had sat bolt upright and said, her eyes wide and black in the dark, 'My auntie's not dead, she's not dead too?'

Fran had had to hold her arms gently. 'It's all right, just because one person dies, it doesn't mean . . . We're safe, Emme.'

She had lain back down then, murmuring, 'No, it's just Harry's auntie.'

'What?' whispered Fran, but Emme turned on the pillow, burrowing, already asleep.

Ben was in his cot, fed, not sleeping but gazing at a magic lantern someone had given them; as she set her foot on the ladder she'd heard a soft gurgle from him.

If she fell. The panic button on the side in the kitchen. Gingerly, Fran bent and set the box of pellets down on the top of the stepladder. She knew the sensible thing would be to do it tomorrow, do it by daylight, with someone else here, but instead she straightened, one hand free now to steady herself as with the other she gave the trap a shove, upwards, as hard as she could. It gave. At the same time the ladder tipped under her and she grabbed, got her fingers under the trapdoor and got a purchase on the frame it sat in. The ladder settled back on its feet.

Gingerly, she pushed the trapdoor right back and put the box down inside, on something soft. Just leave it there, she thought, but she knew that wasn't what she was going to do. Why else had she tracked down the torch, checked it had batteries, stashed it securely in the waistband of her jeans? If it's up there, I want to see it. She felt a fine gritty dust dislodged by the opening of the trap settle on her face and she clamped her mouth closed against it, up and hauled herself in over the ledge.

The steep-pitched roof space rose above her, towering in the dark. She smelled ancient timber and the things that lived in and on it out of the light, the air filled with spores. She sat on the edge and fished for the torch although the square of light shed up through the trapdoor illuminated the angled beams immediately above it and showed her that the soft she'd felt was wadding put down as insulation. She slid the trap back a little way, reducing the light to a triangle, and stepped back. Turned on the torch.

'So you saw him on the Sandpiper,' she had said to Nick. 'What was he doing?'

Nick had looked at her, long and thoughtful. 'Did you love him?' he asked. She saw his eyes look to where her coat was open and she knew what he wanted even before his hand moved inside her coat and he made a sound in his throat, a groan. 'Did he do what I did for you?'

She looked at him a moment and said nothing. She closed her eyes just a second to feel the warmth and weight of his hand, then it was gone, she heard Nick sigh. She opened her eyes.

'He looked like he was waiting for someone,' he said, and his hand was out of sight, his voice was cool and remote. 'Smoking a cigarette, walking round the back of my warehouse. He stopped when he saw me, and trod out the cigarette, looking at me all the time, like some kind of hard man.'

'Did he know who you were?' she asked quietly and as his eyes widened in surprise she saw a trace of the old Nick, quick on his feet, looking for possibilities.

'I don't know, I hadn't thought of that.' And they'd looked at each other, weighing it up.

In the attic the torch shone on something stacked, four, five yards away from her in the gloom.

On her knees she crawled over the wadding towards it. She felt sharp fibres from the insulation material catch in her skin, the air thick with choking particles, but she kept crawling until she was there. A box. Some stuffed carrier bags – she shone the torch and saw fabric, a fastening, a strap. A couple of plastic bags from chain stores, one was made of card with ribbon ties, a lingerie shop. She propped the torch between her knees and pulled at random: cheap slippery black fabric, then something transparent, crackling with static, scratchy lace.

She took up the torch and peered down into the box. A stack of magazines, old porn mags to judge from the top one, she saw spread knees, white stockings and a woman's hand under the lettering. She reached down into the box beside the stack to where something was tangled, a nylon wig that slid under her fingers and then buckles, leather, a harness of some kind. As she lifted it a small spray of paper was dislodged in her face, like a shower of playing

319

cards, and for a moment she was disorientated. She couldn't tell what she was holding but then she raised the strapped apparatus and saw what was attached to it, and a sudden sweat broke under her armpits.

Her face burning in the dark, she shoved the thing back inside the box and went into reverse, scrambling backwards to the trapdoor where she stopped, her feet through the hole. She breathed, she fought the urge to scratch at herself where the sweat and dust had caked on her skin, to pull off her clothes where the spores had settled. It's not illegal, she repeated in her head, it's not criminal, it's not – but it was. Wrong. What was wrong was that it was still there, it had been left behind.

Something had caught in her sweater: one of the cards released when she lifted the black leather harness. She lifted it out carefully: not a playing card but a business card, of a kind. She turned it over.

Below her the yellow light shone, she could see the worn landing carpet. Ben must have gone to sleep because it was so quiet she could hear the minuscule creak of the lantern turning in his room. She leaned forwards, her hands on the lip of the trapdoor, she leaned to listen because she was sure she could even hear him breathing.

Some quirk of the acoustic, high up here under the badly insulated roof, meant that she could hear it. Down below, out there where her car was parked. Footsteps in the yard.

A sound, not quite human.

Chapter Twenty-Nine

Had she left the back door open after Karen? Stupid fucking moron. Stupid lazy feckless fucking idiot.

Did she even think for a moment about staying where she was? Of sliding the hatch closed and sitting in the dark? Not with the boxful of stale underwear and rubber, with the ladder on the landing pointing to where she was hiding, and the children asleep in their rooms? No. Was the sound outside, or in?

There hadn't been more than a second before she moved. Lowering her hips through the gap towards the ladder it was as though Fran's senses had narrowed to a single focus, tracking through the house to where that sound was coming from, and her brain was in overdrive behind it. Could be anyone, the pig farmer back again, could be the police, but they'd knock, they'd ring, could be Karen, left something behind and letting herself back in. Karen, come to help her kill the rats.

No. Karen didn't breathe like that, she didn't blunder, like an animal. Fran knew who it was, she knew before she ran into the kitchen and saw that she hadn't left the door unlocked after all. He was there, though, he was right outside her door. She could hear him.

There was a split second when Fran thought, Stay inside, before she charged the door. She yanked at the bolt, she turned the key, her breath hoarse, she tugged it open and was outside. 'Come on then,' she yelled, into the darkness. And then he came out of the night and was on her, his hands were on her shoulders propelling her back inside, his breath was in her face, and he was in her kitchen. Bez.

He was so tall he seemed to fill the kitchen. His matted hair brushed the ceiling, and his eyes were bloodshot. The room smelled of earth, of river and sweat. Of booze: as they came through the door he staggered, steadied only when he came up against the sink and she saw his hands, lined with dirt, his fingernails were black. It was as if she knew him, had always known him, had seen him leaning against that war memorial or passed out in the shade, under a hedge by the river. He was part of Nathan; he was the part of Nathan she had never got to.

You'd smell him a mile off, she remembered hearing Gerard mutter to Carswell of John Martin, and involuntarily her hand came to her mouth at the thought of the box in the attic. Bez stumbled towards her at the gesture, his hands out, 'No,' he said, 'no, don't, no, I never meant, I never meant . . .'

She stood her ground, but it wasn't *his* smell that turned her stomach: if she closed her eyes she would only smell the outside, the standing water in the fields and the river,

322

weed and iron and earth. Fran didn't move and Bez came up close so she could see the red in the great bush of his beard, and the grime on his collar. The blue of his sore eyes, and to her surprise in that close moment she felt no charge come off him, no fear. He held his hands inches away from her and trembling as if he didn't dare touch her; as if he was the one in danger.

'I loved him,' he said, and the alcohol on his breath smelled almost pure.

She put up her hands to his, hovering, not touching. 'It's all right,' she said, bracing herself to stop the shaking before it began, feeling it rise from her knees. She was up against the counter, her backside pressed against it. It was there behind her, plugged in, charged, the panic button. This was what it was for.

He looked down at her hands and swayed, then when he looked back up she saw she could have been mistaken. What she had thought was innocence in the blue of his eyes could be something else, like the alcohol she smelled on his breath, a capacity for violence so pure it ran clear.

'He come back for me,' Bez said, his lips red and wet, too close to hers. His eyes brimming. 'I heard he was back, I see him, I waited for him there but he never come.'

And at her back, beyond the door into the house she heard something, footsteps on the stairs. Not Emme, no, *back to bed*. Back to bed, good girl. The footsteps stopped. Bez showed no sign of having heard but just that fraction of inattention had caught him, enraged him. He began to shake his head.

'What happened in that house?' she said, quietly. 'Black Barn. What happened there?'

323

'It were her fault,' he said. 'We never needed no fucking women,' and he leaned towards her, as though he might fall on her. 'Just us. The three of us, back together. What did he want you for?' he said, and then he was murderous, in the same moment when she heard Emme beyond the door, a tiny sound, a footstep taken uncertainly backwards on the stairs. Bez's hands went to his ears as if he heard it too and he swayed, his head jerked wildly to take in the shelves behind her, the jars, the cookbooks, the plates. 'He never wanted this, this shit, this shit . . .'

And then the door opened behind her and Emme was there, her mouth an o of terror, Silly girl, thought Fran, brave girl, and she reached out a hand to grab Emme's, holding it fast, and in the same moment brought the other down on the panic button, a quick jab and then withdrawn, before he saw.

It better have worked, she thought. Only one chance.

Bez staggered back from her and she pulled Emme close and took hold of her shoulders. She looked into her face. 'Go back up to bed, Emme,' she said, keeping her voice level, holding her gaze. 'We're just talking. It's OK.'

Emme stared back uncertainly, mesmerised, then suddenly she turned and flew, through the door, the sound of her quick feet on the stairs, her door banged. Fran turned back to Bez. He was swaying, on bound and swollen feet, she glimpsed a big gut under the layers of torn and dirty shirt. He took a step towards her and she saw the scale of him, the breadth of his shoulders.

'You killed Nathan,' she said quietly, setting both hands on the counter behind her to steady herself and talking quietly. He began to shake his shaggy head and a rumble began deep in his chest. 'Did you mean to do it?' she said. 'Was it a mistake?'

But it couldn't have been a mistake. Not the violence of it, the knife pulled down through Nathan's body. It was passion, it was hatred, it was love. If it had been a mistake he would have run away, he would have tried to hide, he wouldn't have waited, patient, he wouldn't have staked her out like a deer. The bad man.

She lifted her hands away from the counter and held them towards him, palms up. She could feel her heart race but all she needed was to keep him there, until they arrived.

'No,' he said, and his voice was sullen and dangerous. 'It was you. You did it.' He lifted his hands between hers and up, to her throat and his reddened eyes told her he was capable of it, he hated her. She reached for them, his forearms like hams, she could get a purchase and he was tightening his grip, she could feel a throb in her temple as the blood supply reduced. She dug in her nails.

'What are you talking about?' she said, her voice clotted with the pressure. 'Where did you wait for him? If you loved him . . . those are his kids upstairs. If you loved him . . .' How long did he take to die? She didn't know: her eyes felt as if they were being forced out of her head, she couldn't see.

And then suddenly the pressure was gone. She reeled as he lurched away, stumbling against the table, and she saw his cheeks streaked with tears, he didn't have it in him, after all. A glass tipped, rolled, smashed in front of her, already going after him she trod in it, she felt a stab and the quick hot gush of blood, instantly slippery underfoot.

She slid and grabbed, the door flew back, she felt the icy damp of the outside and he was gone.

She could heard the roar of the engine across the fields as she crouched in the blood and glass but by the time the car crunched up on the gravel it was too late. He was long gone. Too late. *For all you know, I'd have been dead.* They didn't seem to care.

It was DS Gerard, and he was on his own.

Chapter Thirty

Had she expected that they would come in pairs? When he had knocked at the back door she was still bleeding. She hobbled to the door at the stern sound of his voice. 'Mrs Hall? Fran? Are you all right?'

Doug Gerard stood there in the dark. Beyond him she could see a gleam of white on the shed roof, no more than a dusting. What snow there had been had stopped. He was wearing jeans, trainers, unshaven; he could have been anyone, a dad, a bloke watching the football in the pub, a dating profile. He saw the blood on her hands, on her foot and tutted.

'Just one of you?' she said, angry suddenly. 'He's long gone.'

'Who?'

'Bez.' He made that sound again, of impatience. 'He was here,' said Fran through gritted teeth. 'He was angry, he . . .' She put her hands up to her throat, feeling the tenderness.

He pushed in past her. 'May I?' he said, not waiting for an answer, and he was looking around, taking in the broken glass and the blood on the floor. She remembered what he'd said about staging a crime scene: she had no faith he would believe her.

'Just you?' she said again.

'Back-up'll be here in five,' he said, peremptory. 'I was nearest. Off-duty, came in my own car but . . . I like to get the use of the siren.' Unsmiling. 'So he's just gone, this minute?'

'Maybe ten minutes.' He stepped back out into the yard and she heard him talking. When he came back in his manner was more leisurely.

He eyed her: bare feet, blood on her jeans. The T-shirt she'd put on for bed, and no bra – could he see that? 'Sit down,' he said, brusque. When she stayed where she was he said, 'The foot.' Reluctantly she sat down. He tipped washing up out of the bowl and refilled it and set it on the floor beside her.

'We'll get him,' he said, lifting her foot into the water. 'We've got the infra-red, helicopters, if it comes to that . . .'

'Was that who you were talking to? Are they sending out a helicopter?'

He barely smiled. 'They don't come cheap, and it's not hard to track down a drunk. They move slow, they leave traces, and we know him of old, Mr Beston. He's got form.'

'But you hadn't got him.' His thumb was on her instep. 'What form has he got?'

'The usual,' said Gerard dismissively, his head bent over her foot in the water. 'Drunk and disorderly, causing a disturbance. Affray, but that was the once. A historic caution, but he was a kid.' He got up, looked under the sink, came

328

back with a clean j–cloth. 'No violence.' Carefully, he rolled the leg on her jeans. 'Did he say anything?'

'He said something about a woman, at Black Barn.' She turned at the thought, she strained to look across the table to the counter, trying to remember. 'About the three of them being back together.' Gerard's hands were on her foot, restraining her. 'Do you know about Black Barn? He said he loved Nathan.' She heard herself, emotionless. 'He said I killed him.'

He sat back on his haunches, regarding her. 'I didn't kill him, you know that.' She swayed a little in the chair.

'I don't know that I do,' he said, and suddenly his voice was so gentle, his hands on her foot were so warm. 'What do you think your husband was up to? Have you got any idea? Because he wasn't working as a builder, or site manager, or whatever, was he?' She just gazed. 'Where did you think the money was coming from, to pay the bills, to pay the mortgage?' She began to shake her head. 'Did you find out? Did you find out what he was using you for, is that why? Or was it your boyfriend?'

'Is that why what?' she said. Then, too late, 'I haven't got a boyfriend. Using me?'

Gerard stood up. 'Towel?' he asked and although she didn't answer, when her eyes moved there he opened the big cupboard, an old linen press Nathan hadn't wanted her to buy, too big, too permanent. There they were, her towels, stacked neat and clean, her old life. Gerard whistled soft admiration, teasing her, and took one down. He knelt again, and lifted her foot out of the water.

'There's Nick Jason,' he said. 'He's not your boyfriend? You've been seen together.'

329

'Ex,' said Fran, lifting her foot away from him but he reached for it, wrapped the towel around it. 'I didn't know he'd moved out here.'

'If you say so,' he said mildly, pressing the foot dry. 'Out here on your own, trying to manage it all, you're vulnerable, you're tired.' He held her ankle, his finger on the soft skin under the cuff of her jeans. 'Just let me help,' he said, and then he looked down again and she felt his mouth, his lips on her instep for just a soft second before his head was up and he was sitting back again, as if she'd imagined it.

'I don't know what you're talking about,' Fran said. Hearing the faintness in her voice she pulled the foot away from him. The cut was small but deep, dark blood welling up. 'I can do this,' she said, pushing the chair back, hobbling to the drawer where they kept plasters. With her back to him she could think straight: Black Barn, what happened there. What she'd found in the attic. There was something connecting them, a thread so fine it might mean nothing, it might only mean, this place. This flat, watery, abandoned land.

'There was something,' she said, grasping for control. 'Something I meant to tell you. Where you found Rob's car. The reservoir's out there, isn't it? They used to go there, him and Bez and Rob. From Black Barn. Have you dragged the reservoir?'

He frowned, put out. 'It's a couple of miles from where the car was found.' He spoke warily. 'And . . . divers, all that. It's a big operation, but yes. The search will be moving to the reservoir first thing tomorrow morning.'

She swallowed. 'He was scared, you see. Rob was. Someone died at Black Barn. In Oakenham. Nathan told me Oakenham was lovely, he said I should go there with the kids.' It didn't make sense. A place where something horrible had happened. A place where Nick saw her from a bridge. 'He was insistent. What do you mean about him using me?' Gerard was watching her, gauging her responses. 'Why were we here? I don't understand why he came back if only bad stuff happened here.'

'Maybe he brought you back here,' said Gerard, and he was at her shoulder, reaching past her to take the plaster from her hand. 'Maybe he thought there was something in Oakenham for you.' His head tilted, enquiring. 'Do you think, for example,' and his smile said he already knew the answer, 'do you think he knew you'd met up with your ex again?' He watched her for a reaction.

She stared, trying to grasp what he was saying. That the thing that had come into her head sitting there in Nick's car, her lunatic idea that somehow Nathan had known all along – that it wasn't just in her imagination? She wasn't crazy, not paranoid after all – only guilty, in Gerard's eyes.

'I don't know,' she faltered. 'I didn't . . . Nick and I weren't . . .' She thought she felt his hand brush her cheek and she flinched.

Focus. She'd already asked him about Martin's missing wife, she should tell him about the thing in the attic but she couldn't, he was too close, too big, he surrounded her. She pulled the plaster back from his hand. 'I can manage.'

'Yes, we were aware of what went down at Black Barn, that's all a long time ago now,' he said, his jaw set. 'Kids, that's all. Your husband doesn't sound like the kind of man to let a bit of teenage trauma throw him off track.'

She stared. 'What would you know,' she asked, with a

kind of creeping apprehension, 'about what kind of man my husband was?' She took a limping step away from him and sat heavily, the plaster in her hand, its wrapping already torn. She tried to peel it back but her fingers wouldn't work properly and he was beside her again.

'I don't want you here.' She couldn't look at him.

'I don't think you know what you want.'

Sunday

It was sleep like she hadn't had in years, in maybe a decade: warm, black, dreamless fathomless sleep, as if a blanket had been laid over her cage. *There.* One minute she was under, totally under, she was safe. She wasn't alone any more.

And then Ben wailed from the next room and it turned to light as suddenly as if the covers had been lifted off. Fran sat bolt upright. The alarm clock with its red numerals. She blinked. *Shit.* Eight thirty. Emme? Late, late.

Her foot hurt, the moment she put it down on the carpet beside the bed, and as she ran along the corridor it started bleeding again. There was blood on the carpet.

She got to Emme's door before she realised it was Sunday. Sunday. No school. She leaned back, feeling her heart pound. Ben's wail had started up again and she hobbled to him. She leaned into the cot and he raised his arms, his face creased.

He'd have to write a report, when he got back wherever he was going. He could say what he wanted, couldn't he, and what had he done, anyway, what could she accuse him of? His fingers under the cuff of her jeans. She'd heard a crackle from a police radio as he climbed into his car, he had murmured something into it and laughed. Had there ever even been any back-up?

332

She took Ben into bed with her to feed him. Emme's footsteps pattered soft along the corridor and her face peered in: wordless she climbed into the bed beside Fran.

There was Ali. She could talk to Ali. She held the phone to her mouth. Gerard had said something about that too, turning in the yard in the dark as he left, something about the girl who cried wolf. 'You want to wait, you want to wait till you've got the wolf by the balls, then you can call for help. Works better that way.'

Was Ali on her side? She'd seen the way she looked at Gerard, she knew his game. But they were colleagues. It was a closed system. Ben wriggled, struggled against her and for the tiniest flash of a second she understood those women who put everyone in the car and drove it into a reservoir. She squeezed her eyes shut at the thought that that was where Rob was, down under the black water somewhere with his tidy car parked in the woods.

Ben's suck slowed, he pulled back and gazed up at her.

Emme was quiet by her side. Quickly, she dialled: it went straight to answerphone.

Was he in bed, was he asleep? Did he have a woman, a girlfriend, or some kind of casual thing going on? She hung up. The tan tights in the field had held the DNA of a woman with convictions for soliciting. She tapped in a message. **4pm Angel?** She still hadn't put Nick's number in her address book, but she didn't need to. Send. Delete. But before she could set the phone down again it rang. Her heart pounding, she answered.

It was Karen.

'This bloody weather,' she launched, without preamble. 'Harry giving me grief because there's no bloody snow,

333

can you believe it?' She didn't wait for an answer. 'I tell him, it'll come soon enough, you'll be sick of it then, it's slush and dirt and wet socks.' Fran thought of the neatness and order in Karen's bungalow, the carpet in the dim hall where photographs hung. 'Last time a truck jackknifed on the ring road, five dead, people stuck in their cars twelve hours.' Karen stopped, drew breath. 'What? What's happened? Don't tell me they've collared someone, that pair of jokers? Wonders will never cease.'

'Hold on,' Fran said, laying the phone down carefully. 'Emme,' she said cautiously, 'would you go downstairs and see if you can find the . . .' she racked her brains. 'Your snowboots?' Emme gazed, trusting. 'They might be in that cupboard under the stairs.' Obedient, unquestioning – soon she'd start to question, Fran knew that – Emme slid off the bed and when Fran heard her careful footsteps on the stairs she picked up the phone again.

'I was going to say, let's get out for a walk,' said Karen, wary.

'It's not that . . .' Fran hesitated. 'Gerard was over last night. They know something but they won't tell me. They seem to think . . . there's this guy. Someone I knew a long time ago.'

'Coincidence and a half,' was all Karen said, drily, when Fran finished. There was a silence. 'How about I come over for that walk, then?' Karen said finally. 'Give the kids a run.'

They were out of the village toward Oakenham and had taken a path down by the bridge that turned into a towpath, Fran walking gingerly on her bandaged foot, the children running on ahead in long frosted grass, before Karen spoke.

'Did he follow you out here, then, or you follow him? This Nick.' The fen ran beside them, dead straight into the mist.

Coming to a halt Fran thrust her hands down into her pockets: she felt something there. 'He was already here. I didn't follow him. I would have crossed the road to avoid him for years after it ended.' She felt Karen's eyes on her. 'I don't understand,' she said, stubborn. 'I never talked about Nick. Nathan didn't know him from Adam.' And then it came back to her, she and Nathan walking past one of Nick's boarded up clubs and him asking her, did she miss the excitement.

'Doesn't mean he didn't want to know,' said Karen, brusque. 'Quiet type, your Nathan, was he, right? But liked things the way he liked them, right? I mean, I didn't need to meet him to know that, the way you are.'

Fran stared. 'What do you mean?'

'Stories my dad used to come out with, Mum used to tell him to shut up in front of us,' Karen went on. 'Nice quiet blokes that wouldn't say boo to a goose, get the wife followed and first the police know about it is when the suitcase the husband put the body in gets caught in a fen sluice, five years later.'

Something caught, snagged on Fran's train of thought, then. She took her hand out of her pocket and opened it for Karen to see. *Busty Blonde.* A woman in a blonde wig, with her boobs in both hands, thrust up and out. *Call Roxie*, and a number. She thought of the farmer with his stiff dyed hair and eyes going in different directions, knowing it was up there.

Up ahead the children were barely visible in the mist, running in circles in the long grass.

'I found this,' she said. 'When I went up into the attic

335

last night after the rats. I found, I found . . . underwear and all sorts. Leather.' Karen took the card, snorted, then she gave it back.

'So John Martin had to pay for it? Front page news. He wouldn't be the only miserable bastard round here.'

'They were married,' said Fran and Karen shrugged as if to say, *same difference.* Was that what marriage was? An exchange of goods and services. If only she knew what Nathan had wanted out of theirs: too late now.

'Everyone knew Jilly-Ann Martin – had history,' said Karen. 'It'll have been how he met her. John Martin's not much of a catch.'

'Why did she leave the stuff behind?' said Fran, stubbornly. 'And her dog. The pig farmer, Dearborn said he got her a dog, she loved the dog, Martin had it put down after she went.'

Karen sighed. 'Christ knows. Maybe she just wanted out, quick. Maybe she had a better offer.' She raised her head, questing. 'Harry? Harry?' A fierce bark. 'Wait, please.'

'You don't think he would have . . . done something to his wife then?' Fran said as the two small figures materialised at a fence ahead, and Karen shrugged.

'I'm saying, people move on. People like her. People like me, if you like. We don't all have somewhere safe to go back to.'

'That's me, too, come to that,' said Fran, thinking of her mum, pottering around each new bedsit, hanging stuff up, putting pans away. 'That house is all we've got. Me and Emme and Ben.'

Karen wasn't listening though, she was far away.

'Have you heard of Black Barn?' Fran said, quiet.

Karen's head turned, quick. 'That place?' she said, and she was pale, suddenly. 'You couldn't be a kid around here back then and not hear about it.' She sat forward. 'That was the place? Your Nathan, he was one of *them*?'

'One of who?' said Fran, but Karen just shook her head.

'Mum told us, don't go near 'em. Said she'd have the hide off us if she caught us there. Never mind me dad, Christ knows what he'd have done.' Along the fence a big shaggy horse, like a mythical beast out of the fog, had laid its nose on the wire. Holding back, they let the children go along towards it.

'And the police knew . . . what was going on there?'

Karen turned her head sideways and rested it there, looking at Fran. 'A while after . . . after they'd closed Black Barn down, some old mate of my dad's from the force, not a bad guy, wanted to make an honest woman of Mum but she would have none of it. Anyway, he got pissed and said, someone high up in a neighbouring force had been moved sideways pretty quick after Black Barn, moved right under the radar. For being involved. For being a regular visitor.'

'Are you talking about a senior policeman? What went on there, exactly?' Feeling her throat close.

'What kids get up to, I suppose,' said Karen, and her eyes slid away. 'Drinking, eating takeaway. Shagging whoever turned up.' She shook her head, staring through the windscreen. 'We imagined all sorts, didn't we?' Her voice sounded far off. 'Drugs.'

'Another one of them turned up last night, it's why Gerard came round. Nathan's friend Bez, the one I've never met. I was up in the attic after you left and when I came down he was at my kitchen door.'

'Oh yeah, pissed, was he?'

'You know him?'

'Everyone knows him. Everyone's tripped over him sleeping it off in a ditch at least once.' Karen looked around, as if he might be somewhere out there in the freezing fog, in the long grass crunching underfoot. 'One day he won't be sleeping it off but . . .' she shrugged, 'there'll be no one left who cares. That's drunks for you.'

'The police don't seem that interested.'

'Well, they're lazy sods, aren't they? He's not going to run very far, is he?' She set her mouth. 'Do you think he did it? My money'd be on this ex of yours over Martin Beston any day.'

And then like a sign from her pocket her phone pinged: a message. But it wasn't from Nick. Karen turned sharply. 'Who's that?' she said, and Fran frowned down at the message.

'My sister-in-law,' and Karen's eyes widened. 'Nathan's sister, Miranda,' said Fran. 'DS Gerard says she's on her way from the airport.'

'Better get home then,' said Karen, and she was lifting a padded arm to the children and Harry already head down to her summons, even before she shouted, 'Oi!' The horse shied a little at the sound, steam coming out of its nostrils. 'Don't want to slow you down.'

They marched the children ahead of them, Karen surprisingly quick on her feet for a big woman. It occurred to her that Karen was already suspicious of Miranda.

There was no one there when they got back to the house but Karen stopped abruptly.

'What is it?' Fran said, Ben sweaty against her front with

the speed of their pace and somehow jolted into sleep. Karen was standing there at the back of the car, a funny look on her face, and Fran came round her to see. Big words had been written in the fine crusted dusting of snow on the rear window. Where she'd seen YOU in the supermarket car park, now it was all there: BABY IT'S YOU.

Chapter Thirty-One

All she could think was, at least I've got a witness. I could tell Karen everything, all of it. She'd understand.

The snow had been falling through the mist in the yard, big soft flakes invisible against the white of the sky, they fell almost like the first leaves of autumn, one coming loose here and there and drifting aimless, harmless to the ground.

Karen followed her, through the kitchen where she set Ben down in his car seat, up the stairs, hardly breathing. She was barely aware of where Harry and Emme had got to, but she heard the television come on in the sitting room. Light-headed suddenly, she turned around only when she got to the bedroom, suddenly aware of the silence but Karen had followed her after all, there she was, standing in the bedroom door.

'Here,' Fran said, struggling with the drawer to show Karen the card where the words came from, and then abruptly it opened.

Karen folded her arms, a guarded expression on her face. 'It was there,' Fran told her. 'It was there.' And for a second, as the only explanation that came to her was that he'd been back for it, he'd been inside the house while she was out, God knew how, she felt the room turn black at the edges and she had to sit. As she focused on breathing she sensed Karen there, standing on the periphery of her vision, but for a second she couldn't be sure who the figure was. And then she saw a scattering of fine white powder and she remembered: Carswell and Gerard had been in here, dusting for prints. They had taken it.

Then she did look up, to tell her, and Karen said of course it was before turning into the corridor at the sound of a car pulling up outside. The slam of a door and two voices, one of them a woman's.

From the spare room window they saw her, paying a taxi driver, his head bobbing in receipt of a tip. A small, stocky woman, dark-haired with a black nylon suitcase on the grass beside her. The taxi driver said something, pointed up at the sky, then he was back in his cab and pulling away, and Miranda Hall, turning, looked up at the house.

Karen had already gone, and Fran could hear her heading downstairs. Alone at the window she waved to Miranda and pointed round the side of the house and saw her nod. Fran went after Karen.

'The police'll tell you,' she said, breathless, at the foot of the stairs, the dark hall behind her, the big panelled and beaded front door that hadn't opened all the time they'd lived here, trapping them in the dingy back quarters. 'The card was there. That's what it said. "Baby It's You".'

341

'Harry,' Karen called sharply from where she stood, her hand already on the back door. Ben was on the floor between them sitting wide-eyed in his car seat, alert to the presences in the room.

'Something's messing with your head,' said Karen, stiff. 'Something or someone.' Her hand was on the doorknob. '*Harry!*'

'I should have known it wasn't Nathan,' Fran said. Somehow Karen had to understand, she wasn't nuts. Karen was important. 'Five years and he never once got me a Valentine. Not that I cared,' she went on hurriedly, 'not that that sort of thing—'

'Yeah right,' Karen said, tough. 'Just don't let anyone mess with you. Not Doug Gerard, not whoever's writing shit on your car. Tell the police, get it down, get it all out there. Words is all it is. A ninety-nine pence card, in a drawer.' And then there was the sound of feet on the gravel and the door opened, and Nathan's sister was there.

'You must be Fran,' Miranda said, unerring, hauling her suitcase over the threshold and holding a hand out to her. She didn't look like Nathan, she was more solid, she gave out something steadier than the jumpy restless energy he'd had even when he was sitting down. She had the same fringe as in the old family photograph and Fran saw the picture in her head: Miranda on one end of the see-saw, chubby and fierce, wiry Nathan on the other, a malicious gleam in his eye as if about to jump off.

Behind them inside the house Emme and Harry had appeared in the dim corridor. Emme stared; Harry threaded his way between them to his mother, his little bullet head unerring. Miranda fixed on Emme. 'Emme,' she said. 'Is

342

that right?' Emme nodded slowly, her lower lip caught between her teeth.

'I'm out of here,' said Karen, ushering Harry ahead of her out of the door.

'This is Karen,' said Fran, quickly. 'She's been, she's been . . . I don't know what I could have done without her.' Miranda looked at Karen, cool, nodded.

'Gimme a call,' Karen told her, and she was gone, and Miranda was turning in the kitchen, scrutinising. She wore a suit, expensive, but crumpled with travel: she brought a different world into the room.

'Christ,' she said, stopping to look back out of the door and beyond the shed to the thin trees on the horizon, the low grey sky. 'It's good to be reminded why you left a place. The taxi driver said I'd been lucky to get here before the snow.' And as she peered out, a big stray flake drifted down in the grey yard. 'I'm not so sure.' And closing the door, although until then she'd shown no sign of registering his presence, unhesitatingly Miranda turned and knelt beside Ben, her small hands moving to unfasten him. 'And this must be Ben.' He gazed at her, wondering. Emme edged into the light, gazing.

'So Nathan did tell you things,' Fran said, letting her lift him. Miranda frowned, working out how to hold him as he writhed. 'The minimum. Threw me a bone now and again. He knew I'd cause trouble if he didn't,' and she sat, parking Ben on her knee.

'Oh, yes,' said Fran, remembering the phone message, after their wedding. 'I wish I'd known.'

Miranda was examining her, curious, over Ben's head. 'To be honest,' she said, 'until I knew there were kids

343

involved, I'd have stayed away from Nathan for the duration.' She compressed her lips. 'The policeman said they'd be along,' she said. 'Gerard, that his name?'

'Yes.' Next time Gerard walked into her kitchen, she'd have reinforcements. It was a good thought.

'They want to talk to me,' said Miranda, thoughtful, and Ben's head turned to look at her, hers to look at him and then she did look like Nathan, after all, that sharp clever look.

'You know Nathan better than anyone, I suppose. Knew him.'

Miranda made a dismissive sound. 'No one knows Nathan,' she said. 'And that's just how he likes it. Liked it.' Gently Fran took Ben from her, and Miranda put two hands to her head. 'Shit,' she said, in wonder. 'He's really dead, isn't he? It's really happened.'

The sound came from outside, and she knew it was them. Fran was getting to know the sound of the police car on her gravel. The first thing they'd see as they pulled up was, BABY IT'S YOU.

'Where's Ali?' she said, straight away, because it was just the two of them. At the sight of them Emme had disappeared back into the sitting room, quick and quiet as a cat. Gerard held Fran's eye, frank, open. 'Did you want her?' he said, earnest, fishing out a mobile. 'I'll give her a call if you like, was there something—'

'It's all right,' said Fran, stiffly. 'I wanted to know about Rob. What have you . . . have you found his . . . have you found anything yet?'

An exchange of glances. Gerard examined his hands a

minute then looked up. 'The divers started first thing this morning. We think we have, yes.' Hesitant, his eyes clear and honest. 'Something's trapped, it's taking a while to free it, but when we do . . .' He paused. 'Unfortunately there's no next of kin that we've been able to trace.' Again he looked down at his hands. 'Might you . . . I mean, if it comes to it . . .'

She shook her head in horror, thinking of his raw hands, his pale waterlogged flesh, *poor Rob, poor Rob*, thinking, Why are they asking me this? 'No,' she managed. 'I don't think . . . couldn't you ask someone at the hospital? A colleague?'

'Yes, of course, I do understand. And I can see . . . yes, I'll talk to Ali, I can see that she . . . that you might need her support.' Fran felt Miranda move restlessly, impatient in her seat. 'She's got a bit of a family crisis herself at the moment,' said Gerard, adopting a sympathetic face.

'Someone wrote something on my car,' she began, then Miranda was between them.

'Where would you like to talk to me?' she said, briskly. Unafraid.

Gerard pulled out a chair. 'May I?' he said, and he was looking at Miranda not Fran. He sat. 'We could just go over a few things here, if you like. As a preliminary.' A sharp nod to Carswell, who planted himself awkwardly across the table and got out his notebook. They both glanced at Fran, then away.

'I'll be next door,' she said, shifting Ben to her hip, 'Leave you to it.' Gerard barely turned his head back to acknowledge she'd spoken, so she said, 'You know where the kettle is, don't you?'

345

Emme was cross-legged in front of the television. Fran turned the sound down so she could hear and Emme just shifted closer to the screen. Fran sat with her back to the door and listened.

Their voices rose and fell, interrupted by chairs shifting, the kettle going on. They were talking about Black Barn.

Chapter Thirty-Two

'You heard it all, right?' said Miranda, when they'd gone.

They were in the sitting room and Emme was in the corner bent over a puzzle, apparently absorbed. Fran could see her sister-in-law eyeing the low ceilings, the big draughty grate. When she said nothing Miranda went on, conversationally, 'It's all right, I'd be the same. They struck me as a bit thick, those two. The police. Do you think it's a strategy?'

'Gerard's maybe,' said Fran, nervous, as if of a trap, but couldn't stop herself. 'Carswell's thick for real.'

Miranda sat down on the sofa and peered forward. The Helmut Newton book was there again, open on the coffee table. A naked woman with big breasts, Amazonian in high heels. Had they left it there? Fran couldn't remember: she didn't even know how they'd come to own it and now she couldn't slam it shut and put it back on the shelf without looking guilty.

But then Miranda closed it, swift and casual. Ben started at the clap of the heavy pages, and stared at Miranda in admiration. 'Never liked Helmut Newton,' she said. 'Old perv.' Fran laughed in surprise, a sharp sound, and Miranda turned to her. 'Why did you marry Nathan? Actually, that's what they asked, too. What I thought of you. I said I didn't know you at all.'

She wasn't going to tell Miranda why she'd married Nathan: the thought made her weary. She'd married him for the same reasons anyone ever got married, fuck it. It wasn't a crime. It had been a mistake. You had to assume you could make a life together. You had to believe you wanted the same things. Nathan had given her good reason, holding her hand at scans, stroking her hair in bed, talking about the countryside and how they were going to make a new life for their children. All lies.

'They asked you about Black Barn,' said Fran.

'He looks like Nathan,' said Miranda, frowning at Ben. 'So do you.'

'We were nothing like each other,' Miranda sighed, rubbed her eyes. 'He was such a beautiful kid, it was my favourite thing to do, look at pictures of my big brother as a baby. I worshipped him.'

'There was something about him,' said Fran, blinking.

'Oh yes, he could make you feel like you were the only person in the world. Make you believe anything. Charm, I suppose you'd call it, but it felt like being hypnotised. My dad's a cold bastard but at least you can see it, you can stay away. Nathan had the charm laid over the top. He used it to make people do what he wanted, whatever the hell that was, power, or something, and he just walked out of their lives when they weren't useful any more.'

'Like Bez?'

'Like all of us,' said Miranda, and her mouth turned down.

From behind the door Fran had heard her talk about Black Barn. She had opened the door a crack to hear more.

'I was the kid sister,' Miranda had said to Gerard in the kitchen. 'Six years between us, I was twelve, playing with dolls still. I tagged along once, he was furious. I didn't know anything about what went on there.'

'Your parents didn't discuss it? What he was getting up to at Black Barn?' That was Gerard, she heard urgency in his voice.

Miranda had scoffed. 'They were the sort to keep any discussion behind closed doors.' There had been a pause so long Fran had wondered if Carswell had got up and closed the door. 'Our parents should never have had kids,' Miranda had said eventually, without inflection. 'They were cold people. I think all they were worried about was Nathan bringing shame on us. They were happier when he disappeared completely, after.'

'Do you know where he went? After Black Barn?' Gerard spoke softly but the urgency was still there.

'I knew he went to London for an interview. That was all. It was Rob told me, his friend Rob.' A murmur. Gerard to Carswell, the scrape of a chair.

'Then he just went off the radar,' Miranda had gone on, her voice flat now. 'I didn't hear from him again for ten years, and suddenly five years ago he sent me an email. I was working in Germany then, I was at a bank in Frankfurt.

349

He sent me a link to his webpage, he told me he'd been at college, got some qualification, and now, just like that, he's some kind of builder. Gave me his mobile number, an address in north London.' A quick laugh. 'He hadn't changed that much, though. Told me he'd got married in a text, six months later.'

'And he didn't tell you what he'd been up to since he left home?' Gerard probed.

'No, I told you,' she said, urgent. 'I knew someone he'd met at Black Barn got him that interview, gave him a leg-up. Whatever it was, it took him off the radar, he never looked back.' Gerard had gone quiet then.

Now Fran stood up under the living room's low beams, and shoved the big book of photographs back into the shelves, high up. 'There were police involved at Black Barn,' she said. 'A senior policeman.'

Miranda looked up at her, as if she hadn't registered what she said. 'I never worried about him at Black Barn,' she said, forlorn, and for a second Fran saw the kid sister behind her eyes. 'I knew he'd survive.'

'Only he didn't. He didn't survive this time.'

Miranda stood up. 'I want to see the house, I want to know what's so special about this place. To bring Nathan back here.'

In the corner Fran saw Emme go still. 'I'm just going to show your auntie Miranda around a bit,' she said.

Miranda noticed the trapdoor into the attic straight away, stopping and looking up: the ladder was still leaning against the wall under it. 'It's got that smell,' she said, her mouth turning down, the back of her hand to her nostrils. 'Don't you smell it?' Fran tipped her head back. Old wood, the powdery scent of mould and something else. The air around those heaped possessions in the dark roof space, a creeping staleness. For a moment they stood under the trapdoor, both holding their breath – then they walked on. Into the spare room, where she'd found the figurine with its porn breasts, as if Miranda knew.

'The one time I went to Black Barn,' Miranda said, on the threshold, 'I didn't even go inside. I had the same feeling. I smelled the same smell, dirty sheets, old socks, dry rot, maybe, I don't know.' She walked on into the room, to the window, and stood there, her back to Fran.

'I clean my sheets,' said Fran, but her voice felt lighter than a whisper and Miranda didn't seem to hear.

'It was a place where bad things could happen,' she said. 'Were happening. I got to the door, I'd gone on my bike. It was all overgrown, a sweltering day, I remember the river too, the way it smells in the heat, all green and cold.'

'Green's not a smell,' said Fran.

Without looking round Miranda said in an undertone, 'Some things you need more than one sense for, you can taste them, you can feel them.' Her voice had risen a notch, breathless. 'I heard something in the house, some groaning sound, someone laughing, high-pitched, and I just ran. I tripped over my bike in the lane and I thought I would die if I had to stay there.' She drew her fingertips closer on the glass. 'It was just right for Nathan. Like this place, maybe. A place where Nathan could feel at home, king of the castle, and the rest of us don't even want to cross the threshold.' Beside her Fran nodded, unseen. 'It's men on their own,' Miranda continued, 'left to their own devices. That's the smell.' Then she turned. 'You've got a visitor.'

351

The car the policewoman pulled up in was battered and ancient. She didn't bother to lock it, she just stood at the kerb and looked up at them, at Miranda.

'That's Ali,' said Fran. She stepped into Ben's room to put him down and heard Miranda on the stairs, heading for the kitchen, or so she thought. But Fran was halfway down when she heard it, a loud grating and a shudder, and turning at the bottom she saw that Miranda, in her ignorance, had gone to the front door, and had somehow miraculously managed to get it open. Ali Compton was standing on the snow-dusted grass in front of the house, bewildered.

'I just,' Ali said, faltering as she looked around, 'I just . . .' She was wearing a battered weatherproof jacket and the same sweater as before only with a spatter stain across the bottom, as if someone had thrown food at her.

'Gerard said you had trouble at home,' said Fran, and Ali made an impatient noise and then was next to her, a hand on her elbow.

'I just needed to know you were OK,' she said. Miranda folded her arms across her body, weighing Ali up. 'You and the kids.'

'I . . .' Fran felt it come up in her throat, the thing she had been fighting so long to keep down. 'I need to . . .'

'We need to talk,' said Ali, and although neither of them looked at her, Miranda said, 'I'll put the kettle on, shall I?'

It had to be upstairs. Not just because it was where it had happened. Fran wanted to put doors between her and anyone who could overhear. Miranda and Emme; she didn't even want Ben to hear.

Ali closed the door behind them, looking around the

room in the low pale light falling through the long windows. Fran sat on the bed, feeling suddenly completely alone, no Nathan, no Emme, no Ben. There was something in Ali's face that made her avert her eyes.

'I found a load of stuff in the attic,' she said, mumbling. 'I found John Martin's wife's stuff up there, and he's still around. Where is she? Is she out there, is she in a ditch somewhere?' She looked up and Ali's eyes were wide. Fran swallowed. 'Is she under the concrete in that barn, and Nathan worked it out?'

'You think John Martin killed him?' Ali said, and her voice was flat.

'Gerard said the tights they found outside belonged to a woman with convictions for soliciting,' she said, pushing it away, the thing she really didn't want to say. John Martin's stiff hair, his sliding eyes.

'I know that,' said Ali quickly. 'DC Watts brought me up to date on her. The woman – she's called Gillian Archer.'

They'd told her that. Gillian. Jilly-Ann. This felt like the wrong conversation, somehow. They were each skirting something, not wanting to go there. 'What about Black Barn?' Fran said, faltering. 'Would John Martin have known about the place? Would she, his wife? Someone died there.'

'He might have done,' Ali said, grim-faced. 'Depends what kind of sex he was after. I remember that. I remember that girl. The one that died at Black Barn.' Fran raised her eyes to Ali, and she couldn't keep it in any longer.

'He came into my bed,' she said in a monotone, and Ali's face changed.

'Who?' she said sharply.

'The man who killed Nathan, the man who came into

353

my bed. I wasn't asleep. We . . . he came into my bed and we . . .'

'You *what*?'

Fran swallowed. 'We had . . . we had sex,' she said. 'And now he's out there. Leaving chocolates, flowers, Valentines. Writing stuff on my car. He's been in here.'

'He raped you.' Ali spoke the word calmly, levelly. Wordless, Fran nodded. 'I don't need to ask,' said Ali, 'why you didn't tell Doug Gerard,' and now her voice was flat and angry.

'I . . . I . . .' *Tell her.* 'I had washed the sheets,' she said, stiff. 'I don't know why, it was before I knew, before I started to wonder. There was something about the way they smelled, something about how it felt, and I didn't want . . . I didn't want them looking. At me, at my dirty sheets. Gerard and Carswell.'

Ali's shoulders dropped, and she sighed. 'Fran,' she said, sadly, 'Fran, Fran.' Shaking her head, then her head was still. 'There's something I need you to know. But I can't be the one that tells you.' Frowning fiercely.

Fran stared. 'About the man that . . . the man that was in my bed?' she said. 'Is it, was it John Martin?'

'It's about your husband.'

'About Nathan,' Fran repeated dully. 'Not that he was gay? I don't care if he was gay.'

'About his job,' said Ali, arms folded tight across herself now. Fran stared and Ali went on. 'Did you know your ex-boyfriend Nick Jason was allowing drugs to be dealt in his clubs? Did you know he was probably arranging drugs shipments himself, while you were his girlfriend?' A pause. 'Was Nick Jason a violent man?'

354

'Violent?' said Fran, shaking her head. 'No. No!' Though what did she know, about what he'd done, when she wasn't there? She hadn't thought he'd pimp her out to a business contact, either. 'What's Nick got to do with Nathan?' Fran said, and Ali just looked at her, intent, willing her to understand something.

Fran spoke slowly. 'Nathan went down to London for an interview nearly twenty years ago and just disappeared. What was he doing? Was he in prison?'

'I can't tell you that.' Ali held her gaze. 'I think you know I can't tell you.' A pause. 'Did you think it was just by chance Nathan took a unit on the same industrial estate as Nick's warehouse?'

Fran exhaled, shaky. 'Not any more. What had Nathan got into?'

When Ali still didn't answer she pushed, harder. 'Drugs? Was it sex? Was that what Black Barn was about?' Fran was feeling the cold in the room, the long draughty windows rattling in their frames, letting the outside in. 'Karen says the police knew about Black Barn and turned a blind eye. Miranda said a visitor to Black Barn was the one that got him the interview for his first job, the job that took him off the radar for ten years. What was that job?'

She could hear Ali's breath. 'Ali? What was that job?'

'You think about it,' said Ali, pulling her jacket around her in the cold room. 'I can't tell you. Think about why I might not be able to tell you.'

From downstairs there was a sudden clatter and Fran was on her feet, but Ali was on the stairs before her.

In the kitchen Miranda looked pale and tired; a mug lay in pieces on the floor.

355

Fran took Ali back to the front door, knowing it wouldn't open for her but she tugged anyway. It resisted, she gritted her teeth and hauled then suddenly it gave, in a swirling gust of icy air. Hunching in the outdoor jacket, Ali said, 'It's going to snow. Just do me a favour. You've got her now,' nodding towards the kitchen, 'and I've got your back. I have. Just lock the doors and stay put. Go nowhere, talk to no one.'

Fran opened her mouth but Ali just shook her head. 'Nowhere,' she repeated. 'No one.'

Chapter Thirty-Three

Miranda.

Ali couldn't tell her, but Miranda could. Softly, she closed the kitchen door behind them and knelt to gather up the pieces of the broken mug. She could feel Miranda watching her.

'So you didn't ask, even,' Fran said, straightening, dustpan in hand. 'When Nathan got back in touch. You didn't say, where have you been?'

'Not straight off,' Miranda said, terse. 'You must have known that much about Nathan. You poke him, he closes up. I had my ideas.'

'What ideas?' said Fran, determined. But before Miranda could answer, the phone rang, startlingly loud, on the wall.

It was Jo.

'Jo,' she said, feeling a sob of relief. 'Look, I'm sorry—'

'It's all right,' said Jo. 'Two things.' Brisk. 'First off. There's some work here if, when, you want it. Some maternity cover starting in two months' time, yes . . . I know, crazy, but . . . and two interviews further down the line, it's not much . . .'

Christ knows how she would sort it, childcare, where to live . . . 'Yes,' Fran said quickly. 'Yes, please, yes. Totally.' And waited, because she heard a hesitation in Jo's voice.

'It's Craig,' Jo said, abrupt, and Fran was thrown. 'Who?' Jo cleared her throat. 'Craig's the guy, the new guy. I told you about him. My . . . my fiancé,' and suddenly she sounded uncomfortable. Fran put a hand to the wall, staring at Nathan's handwriting, the list of useful names. Doctor. Dentist. Rob. Nathan's office number, his mobile number.

'I told you, he's in construction, didn't I? He's a builder.'

'Yes,' said Fran, turning, setting her back against the wall.

'Anyway. At the wedding, your wedding, that guy that was there. Practically Nathan's only guest, the guy.'

'Rob?' She turned back again, studying the numbers without really seeing them. She remembered Jo talking to Rob.

'No, not him,' said Jo, impatient again. 'The big bloke.' Fran's finger went to the numbers, down the list. Julian.

'Julian Napier,' she said. Rob eyeing him along the table, after the wedding. Rob's expression turning flat in the pub when Nathan took a call from Julian.

'Anyway, Craig says he's dodgy.'

'Dodgy how?'

Jo sighed, puzzling. 'The company, for a start. The only jobs they ever run, he says, are vanity projects, bits and pieces put his way where the client's abroad, or has money to burn.'

'So?' said Fran, almost impatient. It seemed like nothing.

Jo went on. 'Craig says someone must be propping him up, somewhere down the line, because he doesn't run the company professionally. Plus . . .' She hesitated. 'He's a serious Mason. You know, the rolled-up trouser leg, all that, connections here, there and everywhere, the network.'

'Masons,' said Fran, feeling her ignorance, the world outside black as a cellar and her blundering about in it. 'I don't know anything about Masons.' She heard Jo hold her breath. 'That's not all, is it?' she said, seizing on the hesitation.

'Look,' said Jo, exhaling, resigned. 'It could just be gossip. I don't like this kind of rumour, and I'm no investigative journalist, am I, but . . . well. Apparently Napier has got specific sexual tastes.' And then Fran heard a sound in the background, a clearing of the throat.

'Is Craig there?' she asked.

'Yes,' said Jo, her voice muffling for a second, a door closing, then she was back. 'Boys,' she said. 'Julian Napier likes boys. There were rumours he was . . . apprehended on the Heath having sex with a fourteen-year-old. Craig says more than rumour: someone who'd worked with Napier confirmed it.'

'Apprehended?'

'It never got to court, even though once that rumour went round there were plenty of others. The police never seemed to take them seriously, apparently.'

She turned then and saw that Miranda had got to her feet, pale and intent, as if there was something she wanted to say. Quickly Fran said, 'Thanks, Jo, look, that's . . . that's important. Really important.' Staring back at Miranda.

'Just take care,' said Jo, suddenly awkward, she never liked being thanked. 'I only want to know you're all right.' As she hung up Fran turned to Miranda.

'What is it?' she said.

'Julian Napier,' said Miranda. 'That name. I remember that name.'

Outside, someone was shouting.

On the desk Derek barely lifted his head as he buzzed her through. Invisible, she was, thought Ali, lifting a hand to thank him.

The carers' agency had finally responded to her threats and pleas, after forty minutes of holding, of being hung up on, of being put through to the wrong extension, as she sat there glued to the mobile in her car, parked up outside the station. It had taken her telling them she was a police officer for someone to say, (deep long-suffering sigh), 'We'll get someone over there.' A carer. 'Your mother's safety is our priority, Ms Compton.'

Derek called up the stairs after her, 'You won't find them up there, Ali, they're all off to Chatteris, or they were, to the morgue.' And as she got to the turn of the stairs, refusing to take the lift, too many beer bellies in this business as it is, 'They might've left Sadie behind to hold the fort.'

And there she was, earnestly bent over her computer in the corner of the cramped operations room. She looked up warily as she saw Ali. 'Ali,' she said. 'All right? How's Mrs Hall doing?'

Sadie hesitated. 'Sounds like we're going to have some news for her soon,' she said, then a shadow passed over her face as though she wasn't sure she'd done the right thing.

360

'Oh yes?' said Ali, stopping.

There were the photographs, pinned up. You could look at them on the computer, these days, but they all still liked the real thing, Ali included, when she was in one of these rooms. You could stand at this angle or that, you could touch them, get up close to the detail. Nathan Hall's white face under flash, the blood reading black. The shirt, ripped up to the aorta and saturated. A close-up on his trouser button, undone, an image almost arty, folds of fabric in the dark.

She put a hand up to the photograph. No sign of sexual assault, Gerard had said, almost disappointed. But something had gone on.

There were other photographs. Fran Hall, smiling outside a registry office in a pale dress, holding a baby. Ali wondered who had provided them with that. A shot of Rob Webster taken from his hospital ID. A fuzzy mugshot of Martin Beston, Bez, staring sullen at the camera, bleary with booze. She stepped closer. Nick Jason, a photograph taken in a club, a tall man leaning back against a bar in a dark suit with bottles behind him, something about the line of his shoulders in the expensive jacket. Impossible to tell if he was capable of almost disembowelling a man, in the dark in a muddy field. If you had money you didn't usually do that kind of thing yourself, but it didn't feel like a hit. A hit would have been a shotgun. Nick Jason was nice to look at: if she'd been Fran Hall, she'd have been tempted back there. Of course she would.

Gerard's suspects. There was no photograph on Gerard's whiteboard of the man who'd owned the Hall's farmhouse: John Martin, whose wife had been a prostitute. That chicken barn out the back with its uneven concrete floor, she'd smelled it every time she went through their yard, you'd have thought they'd have had it taken down by now. Was that what John Martin was hanging around for? To see what they found?

No reference to Black Barn, either, not here on the board, not to the girl who died, not to the rumours that had flown around, as to who was going there, and for what.

Beside the photographs was the whiteboard, Gerard's scrawl all over it. *FRAN HALL*, in capitals, then *INCONSISTENCIES*. Underlined three times. And an arrow winding across the board, to Nick Jason's name, at the head of another column, with dates, club openings.

'News?' she said, turning to Sadie, who fidgeted. 'Just . . . mind if I . . .' said Ali, indicating the door to Doug Gerard's office, and still flushed with anxiety Sadie bobbed her head. Sadie was engaged, deposit gone down on a new-build flat by the river, didn't want kids. Or so she said — that conversation was another thing that made Sadie flush and fidget. Ali pushed the door open.

Now it was too late, Ali knew she'd have had kids like a shot, given the opportunity. Even seeing the way they weighed on Fran Hall, the way she twisted and turned, trying to free herself. Lie down under the weight and fuck the job. But sometimes the opportunity isn't there. Sometimes the time's right and the man's wrong, or vice versa. Sometimes you have three miscarriages in a row and he can't hack the unhappiness. So the job it is. Someone's got to do it.

Gerard's room smelt stale and sweaty, the windows grimy. She went to the desk, and sat down. There was a photograph in a frame on a shelf, the girlfriend before last, if she wasn't mistaken, a film of dust on it. A calendar hung on the back of the door, photographs of muscle cars: once upon a time it'd have been a girly calendar, but they had to keep those somewhere else these days.

'Good news?' she called through to Sadie, leaning down, pulling open a drawer. No half bottle of whisky, no girly mags. A paper folder, though, scuffed at the edges, the label on the front curling off, the ink fading. Dates. A stamp. An investigating officer. Careful not to make a sound, she lifted it out and opened it. A photograph sat on the top: three lads, the middle one leaning back against a gate like he ruled the world. Ali turned it over. Handwriting faded to sepia, decades on and down in the corner the name of the photographer. Julian Napier.

Ali heard a chair move back next door, and she closed the folder, taking a cloth bag from her pocket, the one she used for Mum's shopping, now they made you pay for the plastic ones. Putting the folder inside and setting it on her knee.

Confidential, the folder said. *Black Barn, Oakenham, 1995.*

She was closing the drawer when Sadie appeared in the doorway, her face paling as she saw Ali in DS Gerard's chair.

'Just the . . . you heard about the body?' Sadie faltered. 'In the reservoir.'

Ali got to her feet, slinging the cloth bag across her shoulder and seeing Sadie follow the movement with her eyes. 'I heard,' she said. 'Where did you say they'd got to? Those two jokers?'

Chapter Thirty-Four

When she came round the side of the house the two women were spitting hostilities at each other over a buggy. The one with the child, Fran registered, was Sue from the playground. She was leaning aggressively forwards, her knuckles white on the pushchair's handles. The other woman – a chunky blonde standing in the open door of a silver convertible saloon, its wheel arches spattered with rust – Fran had never seen before.

They both turned towards Fran as she came into view. 'Ask *her*,' said Sue, yanking the buggy back so savagely the toddler inside it began to squall. 'Stupid bitch,' and she was off down the bumpy pavement, hunched over the pushchair. Fran didn't know which of them she was calling a stupid bitch. She took a step back but it was too late, the blonde had slammed the car door and was stamping past her in heels.

Strongly built, big in the shoulder, as she made straight for the back of the house the woman seemed to know exactly where she was going. Fran was behind her when she banged the door open and she saw Miranda's face, fear ambushing her as she stood helpless behind the kitchen table.

'The fuck,' said the blonde, rounding from Miranda to Fran, savage and contemptuous. 'Who the fuck are you two, then?' And when they gaped back at her, 'Is it true then? The old bastard's dead?' Her jaw thrust forward, in a tough, unlined face, though she must have been fifty if she was a day. She was wearing a camel polo neck and a tight skirt, small gold earrings; she might almost have been a businesswoman except there was something, just something about the way she held herself, her big chest thrusting, like a figurehead.

'Nathan?' said Miranda, staring, gobsmacked.

'He owes me money,' the woman said. 'He's got my shit.' Then, with a frowning double-take, 'Who the fuck is Nathan?'

'You'd better sit down,' said Fran, feeling nothing through the adrenalin, no fear, no panic.

Emme had taken one look at her and fled, up the stairs.

Fran went to the fridge and pulled out the bottle of white wine that had been open since the night Nathan died; since before he died, as a matter of fact. But before she'd set it on the table the back door opened again, and there stood Karen, pink with exertion as if she'd run there, with Harry in tow.

'Had to see it with my own eyes,' she said, pushing him in ahead of her. 'Before Sue got the whole village round to get a look. Where did you spring from, Jilly-Ann?' In two strides she was at the table. Harry took one look at the women ranged around the kitchen and ran before

365

anyone could call him back, on the stairs and knowing where to find Emme by now. Miranda, head down, was filling glasses, frowning in concentration, to the brim, and without a word she pushed one over to Karen. Fran watched her. *She knows.*

'What did you come back for?' said Karen. 'You don't look bad, as it goes.' Laughing her rasping laugh. 'Not dead, anyway.'

The blonde – Jilly-Ann, Gillian, whoever she was, she wasn't much like the picture on the card but were they ever, Fran knew that much – circled the glass Miranda had set in front of her with her ringed and manicured hand and glared. 'Me dead? You what?' she said. 'I'm still his legal wife, I'll have you know. Someone said he'd been found dead out in the field. If he's snuffed it this place is mine.'

Karen eyed her. 'He's not dead, Jilly-Ann. He sold the house.'

'You're John Martin's wife,' said Fran.

Jilly-Ann laughed, sour. 'For all the good it do me. He's sold up, eh?' She looked around the room, scornful.

'Why'd you leave, then, just like that?' said Karen, setting her glass back down. 'Must have been a cushy number, out here.'

Jilly-Ann snorted. 'You're kidding, aren't you? Always after me for sex, smelly old pervert. Tight with it, kept saying he'd look after me but never saw any of it, did I?' She lifted the glass to her lips and made a face. 'Not worth the candle. I'm set up nice now, quiet little street on the other side of town. Regulars.' The flicker of a smile. 'Police off my case, out there.'

She looked from face to face. 'How much you pay for this old shithole, then?' she said, drily, then let out a snort when Fran told her. 'Maybe worth getting after him after all,' she said, sidetracked into calculating. '*Mr* Martin.' Her head lifted and turned, like a predator's, and she stalked for the door.

Then she stopped, her hand on the doorknob. 'Who did die, then?' she said. No more than an afterthought.

'My brother,' said Miranda, sharp and clear, the first time she'd spoken and they all turned to her. 'My brother,' and nodding towards Fran, 'her husband.' *She knows.* Jilly-Ann pouted, indifferent, and, in that moment, turning for the door, she seemed only contemptuous of all three of them still trapped there while she could go free.

As they heard her car fire noisily in the street, at the table Karen let out a whistle of grudging admiration. 'She's kidding herself if she thinks she's going to get anything out of old Martin. The landlady of the Queen's found him washing in the Gents' last week. I wouldn't be surprised if he's sleeping rough, with your money in the bank. Sue said someone's been kipping in her shed, too. Found a leather jacket and some tins of beans.'

'Leather jacket?' said Fran, because that didn't sound like the farmer. Bez?

She must have looked pale because Karen filled the glass again but this time she pushed it towards Fran. 'Go on,' she said. 'Do you good.'

But Fran shook her head. 'I'm driving. There's somewhere I've got to be.'

He sent her the message as she was sitting at lights on the ring road contemplating an illuminated sign, **Severe weather warning**. The sky was grey as iron, but still nothing had

367

settled, the flakes materialising, ghostly, only to disappear as if she'd imagined them.

Running late. Got a plan, though.

Karen hadn't stayed long, and Fran hadn't tried to keep her. For these four, five days, when her life had threatened to fall apart Karen had been there, her safety net – and now Fran was watching her back away. But she needed to be alone with Miranda.

'That woman,' said Miranda. 'Your friend. What did you say her name was? I remember her. Or someone like her.' They were in the spare bedroom, making up the bed, each on one side.

'Karen? Her surname's Humphries.' But her mind wasn't on Karen.

Miranda had been waiting for the question, from the sigh she gave when Fran straightened on the other side of the bed and said, 'You knew what Nathan was up to, didn't you? At Black Barn. And after, when he went off the radar.'

'I'm not stupid,' said Miranda, shortly. 'Little sisters keep their eyes open and their mouths shut.' Then, 'The police think you did it. And you've got to ask yourself why. What they think you found out?'

In the spare room the light had been fading. The two of them had left the smooth, clean, made bed, pillows neat and plumped, and were standing at the window. The landscape turning white.

'My friend Jo thought he was gay,' Fran said. 'She saw him on the Heath, with a man.' She shook her head. 'I don't think he was anything.'

'People found him attractive,' said Miranda. 'I remember that. Men and women. But he wasn't interested in sex. He used it.' She paused. 'And he used people.' She leaned forwards over the table, her chin in her hands, frowning. 'He did badly in his exams. He hated that. He took off for Black Barn, he disappeared inside that house with the other two. And when he came back out again, he'd learned something. I don't know who taught him, but he'd learned he had a talent.'

Fran pulled into the car park of the Angel in the Fields. Pink lights had been strung over the dilapidated porch, in preparation for the Valentine's night. He still didn't have a name, in her mobile. Nick.

From the spare room window layers of purple cloud had sat on the horizon like a mountain range, a straight silver gleam of water where light escaped from somewhere in the thick sky to reflect in a ditch. The poplars had been invisible from where the women stood but trees feathered the dark land somewhere off to the left.

'You knew,' said Fran, and in that moment Miranda shivered, and backed away from the window.

'I'm not used to this,' she said. 'Out there it's either air-con or sweating in the streets. Day in, day out.'

She looked pale, suddenly, she moved towards the door and Fran followed. It was on the stairwell, in the gloom, that Miranda stopped and turned, the two of them enclosed in the dark, neither up nor down. A place to tell secrets.

'Yes, I knew. Once I got far enough away, to the other side of the world, it seemed almost like a dream, something I'd made up. He'd told our father. God knows why, to impress the old bastard, and Dad would drop hints. Once,

369

when I'd had enough of him going on about his golden boy and I said, he's nothing but a glorified builder, he said something about that being just window dressing. He said he was doing something much more important, but no one could know. Something for the police.'

In the warm enclosed space Fran leaned back against the wall, thinking of the old man's voice on the phone to her, and feeling her heart thunder. Miranda's face a pale oval below her.

'When were you sure?' she said, and Miranda shifted in the shadows.

'When you got married,' she said at last. 'Dad called me. He said I wasn't to think it was a real marriage. He said it was just part of Nathan's cover.'

And in the dark Fran saw Ali's face, heard her voice. *Think why*, she'd said. *Think why I can't tell you.* 'All that time?' she said, and it whirled around her, as if a tornado had struck and her life had been thrown up in the air around her. She gripped the banister. 'All that time. He was working undercover, for the police.'

'He didn't ever want an ordinary job, he didn't want an ordinary life, he didn't care about family, or children, he just wanted control. I suppose whoever recruited him at Black Barn saw that in him.' She almost whispered. 'That ability to suspend normal needs, to give over his whole life to a lie.'

Nathan walking through the door of Jo's front room and fixing on her, his target. Nathan watching her to see what she wanted, what would hook her. What was it? Was it having no father? Was it growing up in bedsits, packing up and moving on? Mum had loved her, for all the crap.

370

'You hear about them,' Fran said. 'The women they marry, kept in the dark while they're off, embedded, undercover, whatever they call it. All those conferences, all those elaborate props to show he'd been where he said he'd been, the mugs and totes . . .' She remembered the nylon briefcase then but it didn't slow her down. 'You think, how could anyone be that gullible? That thick?'

As for why.

'We don't know for sure,' said Miranda, uneasy. 'I'm sure he . . . he . . .'

'Loved me?' Fran tipped her head back, looking up into the house's tall roof space, the invisible whirling sky, willing the pieces to return to earth. My house. My family. Not his. 'You know what? I'm past that. I want to know what he was using me for.'

And now she got out of the car and walked to the clumped willows between the car park and the water. It was raw and humid and the water moved slowly, as though thickening in the cold. Nick, Nick, Nick.

Standing on the bank as the green water slid past, Fran got out the phone. It had to be done carefully, because Nick was smart, Nick was as smart as Nathan, and if she sent the wrong message back, too bright, too eager, he'd know. It was time for her to be the clever one, the user – she needed to know if Nick had been lying to her, too, if he was up to his neck in his old life still. If he had been the one had followed Nathan in the dark across the muddy field. *Baby It's You*. Nick thought she was his, all right. She heard the pub door behind her and she turned.

For Valentine's Eric was wearing a black T-shirt,

emblazoned with a heart dripping blood and skewered with a knife. His legs were skinnier than a child's in black jeans as he stood in the doorway. 'You're back,' he said, stepping aside to allow her in. 'Thorney's inside.'

The pub was serving but it was quiet; she could see a couple of men talking quietly on stools at the bar. Eric led her behind the bar to the kitchen door.

The room was brightly lit, low-ceilinged, with a shelf of catering jars of pickles and it smelled of old grease. There was a big range, a row of deep-fat fryers and a stainless steel sink where a small, hunched man in shirt-sleeves and an apron was doggedly scrubbing at a huge saucepan. Thinning grey hair around a bald spot, when he turned she saw pale watery eyes but he was clean-shaven, the shirt was ironed and the cuffs carefully rolled.

Sloping shouldered, holding the brimming half of cider Eric had poured him, Thorney walked ahead of her into the dim end of the bar. The old man set the drink down with care, but didn't touch it, easing himself stiffly on to a bar stool. 'I saw it in the paper,' he said, looking at the cider. 'I thought,' frowning, 'Al wasn't the sort to get himself done over. I mean, it happens.' He drew in his shoulders a little, defensive. He must have to watch himself, thought Fran with a pang, hard to get old, if you're gay round here. He must be seventy.

'I called him Nathan,' she said, as the last of the man she'd married slipped out of her grasp. 'What sort was he, then?'

The old man eyed her. 'You got kids,' he said, and she nodded. He reached for the glass then, and took a sip, and brightened.

'It's all right,' she told him. Not caring if they thought

she was in denial. 'I don't think he came here for sex. I want to know what else he was up to. I want to know who he met that last night. I want to know how he got himself killed.' Music had come on, behind the bar, a soul song, twenty, thirty years old, and in the dim room things mellowed, shifted. 'But first I want to know about Black Barn.'

Thorney took another drink and leaned back on the stool, and she caught a glimpse of a younger man, with the drink and the music. 'I don't know what Eric said, but I only went over to Black Barn the once.' He sighed. 'They had a stash of E from somewhere, the word was. I was too old for E even then but I went along with it, and I was curious, the place had a reputation, like all sorts were going on there. But they were just kids, I dunno, seventeen, eighteen, I'm not into kids, Christ.'

He reached for the drink again, agitated. 'Weird old place, black weatherboarding, they had no electric, I remember a bathtub full of dirty water, mattresses everywhere, music playing day and night, leaves growing in through the windows, green light. Green.' He mused. 'Maybe it looked like paradise. Somebody was giving them money, because they had booze, and drugs. There was a girl when I went, but then it was just lads.'

'The girl died,' she said, and Thorney nodded.

'Surprising it was only one,' he said. 'And some of them as good as. There was fallout.' He shifted, uneasy. 'There was the big lad.'

'Bez,' said Fran, and he nodded.

'That's him. Poor little fucking bastard, what he is now, you should have seen him then. Big soft lad, he was.

373

Beautiful.' And then his voice was sharper. 'You don't think he done it? Done Al?'

Miranda had asked the same thing after Karen left, leaning forward in the kitchen. About Bez. The leather jacket in Sue's shed had done it. 'Nathan had a leather jacket,' Miranda had said, remembering. 'That was him, that was Bez. They used to fight over the jacket, Bez wanted it but it was too short for him. I don't know where it went, but I never saw it after that summer. It didn't come home with him from Black Barn.' She had turned to Fran. 'Bez was soft as butter, I remember that much. Putty in Nathan's hands, do anything for him. You don't think . . .'

'No,' Fran said in the dim pub. 'I don't think it was him.'

Thorney leaned back against the wall, satisfied. She hadn't been able to say why she was so sure. There was a reason in there somewhere, something to do with that afternoon when she'd walked out to the barn, with Emme finding him face down in a kids' playground. 'Do you know where he is now?' she asked. 'Bez. Where's he living?' and Thorney looked at her, his old face tired, mild, forgiving.

'There were others,' he said. 'There were men going there for sex, for a hit, or just to drop out, people who wouldn't have liked it to be known, let's say. People who could hit you harder than that soft kid ever could, and make sure you stayed down.'

'Like . . . police?'

'You didn't hear it from me,' said Thorney, tipping his glass to see the level in it, half full now, carefully setting it back on the ledge. 'I don't know why he'd want to go back there, all considered. Sometimes, sometimes . . . no matter what the damage is, you go back to what you know.'

'Bez is at Black Barn?' But he didn't answer, he just leaned back to look around the pillar, at Eric behind the bar.

She waited, as long as she could. 'So who,' she said finally, 'did Nathan meet in here?'

He turned back then, studying her. 'Huh,' he said finally. 'He'd chat to whoever. But you know what I noticed? He never left with anyone, so you got it right, it weren't for that kind of action he came. More gay than straight, maybe, but not too interested either way. Interested in something else, you get to know them. It could be fetish, it could be power games.' Smiled. 'Or could be vice. You know, police.' A knowing look. 'They think we don't know them. See 'em a mile off.' She nodded. 'Anyway. Al just sat and waited. Some would chat, once or twice I saw him slip cash across. That happens, you don't ask who's being paid for what. But that last night – I'd seen them together before, him and the big man, didn't look the usual punter but one thing you learn is don't judge a book by its cover. They went back a way, you could tell, your husband and that one.'

An idea formed. 'You told the police about this big man?' she asked. Thorney nodded. 'And I told them about the briefcase.'

'Yes?' Fran leaned forward and he allowed himself another sip. 'The big bloke thought Al should give him the brief-case, one of them nylon things, not leather, but Al was shaking his head, I heard him say something like he was too close, it wasn't safe. Something about having a safe home for it. Had it with him when he left.'

'Old, young?' she said. 'The other man.'

'Old,' said Thorney, fastidious. 'Or getting there. Upper

375

crust. Plenty of them types like it rough and they got money to pay for a younger man.'

'He was called Julian,' she told him. 'I think he knew Nathan from Black Barn.'

Thorney shrugged, eyes sliding away. 'If you say so,' he said.

'Did they leave together?' Thorney shook his head. 'I told the police. He left the fat bloke ordering another pint. He left quick. Looking at his phone on the way out.'

She slid off the bar stool, and he looked at her in surprise. 'Got what you came for, then?' he said and she nodded, but her mind was moving on, ahead, and she was gone, off through the gloom and out into the cold, her thumb already scrolling down through the numbers. She must have known, somehow, because she'd copied the number across from where she'd seen it, there by the phone on the kitchen wall. Julian Napier.

New message. *Nick, Nick, Nick.*

Chapter Thirty-Five

A phone couldn't hold battery in this wilderness. Fran pictured it exhausting itself, seeking a signal across the wastes, dodging silos and windfarms. Twenty per cent should hold out: it was just Ben she was worried about. Would he wake and look up at Miranda's face and think, it's a stranger, after all?

She should never have left them.

Miranda had been insistent. 'We'll be fine,' she said. On the shelf were two feeding bottles, never used. Fran had taken them down, doubtful. 'Karen's given him formula, when she's had him.' Karen's gleaming kitchen, her steriliser.

'How hard can it be?' said Miranda, robustly. 'And I need to get to know him. My nephew.'

'I'll be an hour,' Fran had said. All she'd told Miranda was, she was going to the Angel in the Fields, to speak to the last man who'd seen Nathan. 'Maybe two, at the outside.

I've just got to do this. I can't trust the police to do it.'
Ali Compton had said, *Go nowhere. See no one.*

But Miranda had nodded. 'I wouldn't trust them to find their own backsides, if it was a woman giving them directions.'

And now it was snowing properly.

Julian's number had rung a long time. Perhaps he was at home, in the country, with a wife and dogs and a tennis court. Then he answered.

'Mrs Hall.' Julian's voice had been jovial, reassuring, sombre, but now she knew, she heard something else.

'You don't need to keep up the pretence,' she said, and he was in, smooth.

'It's grief,' he said. 'It's bereavement, Fran.'

She had cut in then, hard. 'I'm not grieving, because I know. I know what you were doing, you and him, I know you saw him the night he died.'

'Be careful, Fran,' the man said quietly. 'About what you think you know.'

'I know he had the hard drive of his computer. Where is it now? What was on it? He brought me here, to this . . . this horrible place.' Because as she said it Fran saw that was what it was, the house standing stiff and unloved on the wide plain, the panelling painted over, the high ceilings stained and cobwebbed. 'He was using me, to get to Nick, he knew he'd come out here. He targeted me, none of it was real, not to him. Marrying me, our children . . . we have children.' Her voice broke, but there was only stony silence, and she knew it was true. 'All the details of his . . . his . . . what would you call it? His operation? Is that what would be on that

378

computer? His undercover activities. What makes you think, what makes you think you have the right . . .' She stopped.

'If you think,' Julian's voice was steely now, and she registered that there was no background noise, nothing, as though he was in a soundproofed room, a secure line, she thought, of course, 'if you think that this display convinces me, if you're trying to threaten me by withholding that hard drive—'

'I don't have it,' she said, almost euphoric to think that she had wrong-footed him. 'I don't know what safe place he had in mind for it, but I don't know where it is.'

'I heard you,' Julian had said, then, his voice very cool, very precise. 'Why do you think you are being investigated? Why do you think those police officers are so certain it was you? You telephoned him while he was there with me, the night he died. A woman's voice.'

'I didn't,' she said, but Julian didn't seem to hear.

'A difficult conversation, by the look of his face when he returned. I'd never seen him look so pale. You called him.'

'It wasn't me,' she said, and Julian sighed.

'Can you really be so naive?' he said. 'We don't dedicate five years to pursuing a man for nothing, you know.' Then something gave him pause, it entertained him. 'Of course,' he said, 'there's always the possibility that Nick Jason had got wind of something himself and he was using *you* to find out about *our* operation, isn't there?' And hearing him almost entertained she heard her breathing rise, ragged.

'Can you really,' Julian said, hearing her on the brink,

379

'not have known what kind of man Nick Jason is? What kind of things he's done?' And then, with a click, he had hung up.

Pulling into a lay-by she got out her phone again. Through the windscreen the big flakes drifted soft and innocent and harmless, blurring the hedges. A car came by, the hiss of slush under its tyres.

She squinted at the phone's map one last time before closing it to save battery. **Ferry Lane**, Nick's message had said. Next left. Another car, this time with headlights on, and in a panic her mind whirred, just how late was it?

But her phone said 14.15. She'd been gone an hour and twenty minutes. She dialled home.

I'll be fine with them, Miranda had said with Ben on her arm, looking round the kitchen. Assessing the situation as Emme peered around the door at her new aunt, fascinated. *I'll be fine.*

It rang and in her head she saw the phone on the wall and the house, the dishes on the draining board, she almost hung up before she could imagine Ben's face, what if he was unhappy, what if he was howling— 'Hello?'

There was no background noise, she could detect nothing but cheerfulness in Miranda's voice, but then, how would she know? They were strangers. 'Is he all right?' she said, high-pitched with anxiety. 'Still asleep,' said Miranda, brisk. 'Your friend Karen came and got Emme, said something about Sunday school. How about you?'

Sunday school? Karen? But Fran didn't have time to wonder about Karen's hidden depths.

'Half an hour,' she said. 'I'm . . . I'm pretty much on my way back.' Don't tell her. Don't think about it. Nick,

380

Nick, Nick: *you'd never hurt me, would you, Nick?* She had to know, though.

A gritting lorry rumbled by, flecking the car. 'I don't want to get caught in this snow,' she said, and the tick of impatience set up, *Come on, come on.* 'Is everything OK? You haven't . . . nobody's come round?'

'Yes, no, everything's fine. It's just . . . well. It gives me the creeps, maybe, being back here. Half recognising people, from way back. Faces, voices.' A strained sound. 'We'll sit tight.'

She turned down Ferry Lane. It was narrow and over-grown, she glimpsed a churned field behind the bedraggled, snow-dusted hedge, a tumbledown prefab, a patch of trees, and the road ran out. A gate. Carefully she turned the car in the narrow space, handbrake on, lights off.

I think I've found what you're looking for, Nick's message said. And here she was.

She climbed out of the car and immediately the softly whirling snow found her, it was in her hair, it crept cold under her collar, it settled on her shoulders. She could see the shape of a dark building through the tangled thicket of overgrown trees ahead of her. There was no other car, but she could see a lopsided gate in the undergrowth, and she went towards it.

The snow muffled everything, there was no sound, it seemed, at all. She could smell the river. She pushed the gate open. 'Nick?' She listened, but there was still nothing.

What things he's done. I know some, she had wanted to say to Julian, I'm not innocent. She thought of the way Nick had looked down at Ben's small head, *He needs a father,* he'd said, but it was Emme's face she saw then. Emme

381

solemn, Emme scared, Emme sitting up with nightmares. You're not a father, Nick.

Someone killed Nathan. And then it was as though it all narrowed and she was looking down on that black land, flat and sodden, at his body head down in the winter grass, it bypassed her bedroom, a man climbing warm and heavy into the bed beside her, it left that behind, that was the distraction. A knife pulled up through a human body, leaving it to bleed out into the slime and ditch water, that was where she needed to look. *You wouldn't hurt me, Nick?*

She was at the front of the house. There was a splintered wooden veranda, a porch half collapsed under the weight of tangled leafless creeper where snow caught and clung, a door buckled with damp. Something gathered inside her, her heart ready to race as she put her hand to the door and pushed, and it gave.

The carers were in. Ali sat in the car with the folder in her lap. She couldn't go back inside and look at it. She had a different head on once she walked in through the back door and saw Mum's kitchen, the aluminium pans one inside the other, scratched from years of Brillo pads, the glass figures on the window sill behind the sink. She wouldn't be able to think straight for listening to what they were doing upstairs, were they being kind.

Something had stopped her in the kitchen, on the way back out to the car. Something Fran Hall had said, about flowers, and Valentines and chocolates. She'd gone to the cupboard where she'd put them, wondering as she reached for the door if Mum might have found them, put them

382

out for the bin men or eaten them all one after the other, but there it was, the plastic carrier bag. Receipt still in there, too.

It wasn't even four in the afternoon but it was dark and she had to turn on the light to see what she was looking at. A shop in Oakenham that sold knick-knacks, pink glass and mirrors and little pots for dressing tables but every February they got in fancy chocolates. Twenty-nine ninety-nine. Pricey. There was a phone number.

The cardboard folder sat on her knee. She dialled the number on the receipt and when it rang and rang she thought, Shit, it's Sunday, but then a dozy-sounding lad answered. Well, it was Valentine's, maybe they thought it was worth opening. 'Yes,' she repeated when he began to stutter, 'the police.' He hadn't been in on Saturday last, he said, for which she inwardly thanked providence, that had been Lindsay and should he get Lindsay to call? They'd hardly sold any of those chocolates, she'd remember. 'Yes, get Lindsay to call.'

She lifted the folder to the light, the cardboard was soft with age. Plus she hadn't wanted it in the house, in Mum's house.

There was a two-page report on the girl's death. Accidental overdose, heroin plus alcohol. Interviews with Martin Beston and Robert Webster; Webster the one who called an ambulance, Beston was found unconscious in another room, had his stomach pumped. No mention of Alan Nathan Hall. Psych reports, social services reports, on Beston and Webster, no more than perfunctory, just reading them made Ali feel something hard as a stone in her gut. No one cared where they'd gone next, whether they scrambled out like Rob Webster, or lay there battered and bleeding, like Martin Beston.

It's better now, she told herself. We do more for them now. But now was too late.

She turned the page, almost at the end, and there, barely even a footnote, was a photograph of the family of the dead girl, arriving at the inquest.

When the mobile rang, she assumed it would be him, Nick. She was standing in the cavernous hall, just beginning in the half-dark to make out the space. It stank. Not river water, not mould or damp, dead leaves in corners: it stank of human waste and rotten food.

It was Doug Gerard.

'I called the house,' he said, his voice cold. 'Where are you? Is Ali Compton there? Christ knows what she's playing at, chasing us round the country. There's been a development. More than one.'

'Is it Nick?' she said, and when she heard his hard laugh she regretted it.

'"Is it Nick?"' he mocked. 'We'll come to Nick Jason in due course.' The line jumped and cut out. She held the phone away from her and saw the tiny icon that told her how much battery she had left was nothing but a sliver of red. In the silence she heard something, through the arched window, the sound of a car in the lane behind the house.

Then Gerard's voice crackled back at her and she put it back to her ear. 'I'm at Black Barn,' she said, 'I'm meeting—' But he cut out again.

'What?' she said, covering her other ear with her hand. 'What?'

Fran held the phone away from her but the screen was black.

The door opened. 'Frankie,' said Nick, and for a second she saw, through the door behind him, how white it was in the outside world and then he closed it.

Chapter Thirty-Six

The look on his face as he came inside: fear and disgust. Why had he brought her here?

'Christ,' said Nick. 'That smell.' Then his arms were around her, and it was his smell in her nostrils, his familiar smell. It must have been him – her body would have known a stranger, she would have rolled over in the bed, she would have woken and screamed and stopped him.

(And what would have happened then? her logical mind asked her, and then would he have killed you, the stranger?)

'It's all right,' she said, and she felt him stiffen, wary. 'What?' he said and she shifted ground.

'Why did you ask me here?' she said. He stood back from her, holding her by the elbows.

'You wanted to find this place, right? I found it for you. I thought we could . . .' He faltered. 'I don't know. Look around, see if—'

'They were after you, Nick,' she said. 'Those suitcases

you bought me in Amsterdam. Were you bringing stuff into the country in them?'

He shook his head, uneasy. 'It was a one-off, I was never . . . I didn't deal, I didn't buy the stuff. I was out of my depth.'

'Liar,' she said, holding her ground. 'They don't put undercover surveillance on someone for five years – five years, of my life, five years, two children – they don't do that for nothing.'

He was pale, defeated. 'I was a fucking idiot. You know me, Frankie. I just wanted the clubs, I didn't know the drugs were going to . . . people were after me to let that happen. It got out of control.' She said nothing. 'Maybe they knew I would have done anything to get you back.' She held his gaze, seeing how lost he'd been, without her. Then he looked away.

'All right,' he mumbled. 'All right. I'm still in it. I'm still moving stuff, still selling. I'd stop in a second if you asked me, though. If you'd come back.' Pleading; begging.

'Did you kill Nathan, Nick?' But before she'd finished the question she knew the answer, faltering, grappling, it must have been him, only him, in her bed. But it hadn't been.

'You're crazy,' he said, his voice falling away. 'Kill a man? Knife him? I mean, you're kidding, right?' He put his face close to hers. 'Frankie, please.' She pulled away from him and pushed the door open, into the bedroom.

Not a bed, but more like the great nest of a filthy bird, occupying most of the floor, heaped and mounded layers, she saw tangled clothes, the ragged corner of a blanket. No one there: he was gone. She turned and there was

Nick, his back to her. He was looking at something that had been pinned to the wall. A newspaper cutting. Standing, she saw, *Star Student Found Dead*, and beside it was a photograph. Two girls in school uniform.

And it tumbled down around her, falling from the sky. Nathan's phone number in the list on her kitchen wall, where anyone could see it, where Karen could have seen it, noted it. Emme saying, *My auntie's not dead,* my *auntie's not dead.* Harry's auntie. Nathan walking away from Julian Napier to talk to a woman on his phone, the night he died.

That look in Karen's eyes.

She turned and ran, down the splintered wooden stairs in a big cold hallway where the light had once shone green, she ran for the door, and the wide dark outside.

Ali had got halfway to Chatteris when they bothered to send her a message, curt: See you at the station. On our way back.

The dual carriageway had been clear. For once they'd got the gritting lorries out, Christ knows they'd had enough warning. Reports were coming in of chaos on the smaller roads, a tanker in a ditch somewhere.

She called, and got Carswell. The monkey not the organ grinder. 'You wanna hear what's going down now,' he said, jittery and gleeful.

Ali cut him short. 'Where are you? I mean, exactly?'

She waited in the lay-by, just above where they would turn off to get back to the station. Gerard climbed out, as pumped as a gorilla at being given instructions on where to meet, and when, his angry breath clouding as he came for her across the gravel and litter and used condoms dusted with snow.

She'd left most of the folder in the passenger seat. Would Sadie Watts take the fall for her nicking it? She couldn't think about that. She had the photo with her, though. The dead girl's mother, half her hair plastered over her face and hardly able to walk straight, a bleary look of misery at the photographer. A younger woman beside her, face set in wooden fury: the sister. Ali stepped in front of Gerard.

'We're going to Black Barn,' he said. 'You want to come and hold Fran Hall's hand? Because that's where she is. With her boyfriend.'

Holding her ground, Ali lifted the picture up to his face. 'You recognise her?' she said. 'That's the sister of the girl that overdosed at Black Barn. Seen her anywhere before?'

He stepped back in a hurry but Carswell came in past him, eager, wiping his nose then reaching for the picture. '*Never*,' he breathed, up close. 'Yeah, boss, look at that. Whassername, isn't it? In her kitchen. That bossy cow, remember. That *bitch*.' Trying to please him.

'Karen Johns, as was,' said Ali. 'Karen Humphries these days, married, divorced, one kid who happens to be the best mate of Fran Hall's daughter Emme.'

She could see the tendons in Gerard's neck tighten as he took another threatening step.

'You think Nathan Hall knew Karen Johns had befriended his wife? Was offering to help with his kids? You think she'd forgotten the man she held responsible for her sister's death?' She shook her head. 'You're all the same,' she said. 'You're so busy trying to look the big man to the under-cover guys that you can't see what's under your own nose.'

389

Behind them, hopping from foot to foot, Carswell said, 'Tell her, boss. Tell her what we found up the reservoir.'

But Doug Gerard paid him no more attention than a fly. 'Where did you get that?' he said, and Ali knew if he could have killed her there and then he would have.

But in her hand the phone began to ring.

Chapter Thirty-Seven

She was in the ditch.

Nick had offered to drive her, he'd begged. 'You can't go out there on your own, not in this.' Then when she shook her head, stiff with revulsion, and shoved past him to the door he said, 'Just take it then. Take the car, it's got four-wheel drive, it'll—' she had snatched the key from him. It wasn't until she turned off the main road that she realised she hadn't given him her keys in exchange, he was stuck.

Fran pumped the accelerator but the wheels spun, the car began to rotate beyond her control. The rear end dropped and the whole thing slid backwards, down, and she was in the ditch. Gasping with panic she battered at the heavy door with her shoulder, at last it gave and she fell out, knee-deep in snow, soaked before she righted herself. She could see the poplars, perhaps half a mile ahead.

Under snow almost everything else had changed and

her bearings were skewed, the light was almost gone, the fields gleamed pale and endless, criss-crossed with black. On the horizon the red eyes of the big wind generators, a mobile mast, too late, too far to help her. And she began to run, towards the line of trees.

It was nothing like running. With every step she sank, the snow sucked at her, it drenched her. Within yards she couldn't feel her feet but under her clothes she sweated steadily. Don't stop. Don't fall. As she ran she scanned the vista, she tried to triangulate, but the line of the horizon see-sawed crazily with every dipping step. One more land-mark was what she needed: where, where? Snowflakes filled the air, they whirled, landed cold on her face.

This was the road. It almost stopped her in her tracks. *This was the road, this was where he* . . . Not he, she. It made no sense: she couldn't force sense out of it. The car parked under the poplars, the body in the ditch, those were her points of triangulation. Not Bez, because that afternoon, that warm, long-ago Saturday afternoon – when something had drawn her out to the barn, that humming in the night air and the car parked under the trees, watching her wander alone through the house – he had been lying face down, pissed into unconsciousness, in a kids' playground. Not Bez, because it had been Karen.

Fran was at the poplars. Panting, she turned and looked across the field. Had that been Karen's car, parked up in the warm afternoon? Had she sent Harry on a sleep-over so she could watch and wait? She could work out his routines and see that when light fell he would come out, expansive, proprietorial, lord of all he surveyed, to piss in a ditch. So that one day, when the time was right, she could come up to him in the dark and whisper in his ear, *I've waited twenty years for this*. The arrogance of him, coming back here. Fran held still, she focused. There was the dark formless shape of the barn and to one side, her house, in the dark. Their house. There was a light on in her bedroom, there was someone in the window, and as she saw it her heart rate accelerated, and she turned towards the lighted window and she ran.

'She's not here.'

On the mobile Doug Gerard sounded frightened, now, almost like he was asking for her help. 'We haven't got her.' The phone wedged under her chin, carefully Ali indicated, pulling in to the lay-by. She was four miles from Cold Fen, and the road was treacherous, a layer of slush under her worn tyres.

'It was Nick Jason she was meeting here,' Gerard said, panting, the line crackling with interference. Behind him Ali could hear Carswell's scouse whine, wheedling or accusing someone, you couldn't tell which. Doug Gerard made a noise in his throat. 'Jason said she'd gone back to her place,' he said, fighting to sound like he was in charge. 'She'd worked out who Karen Johns was and she went haring off after her in Jason's car, left him high and dry.'

Not exactly the work of a criminal mastermind, lending your car to a bird, but all the chances to have a go passed before Ali's eyes: there wasn't time.

'Is he telling the truth?'

Gerard's reply was muttered. 'I think so.' Of course he was. It wasn't Nick Jason who'd bought Fran Hall chocolates, it wasn't her husband, it wasn't John Martin, either. And it hadn't been Martin Beston.

It had been almost an afterthought, back there in the lay-by with Gerard clenching his fists as he came down on her, Ali staring down at the mobile, *number unknown*, before killing the call. Carswell piping up, perhaps trying to avert violence, the right instinct for once, and it had worked, give him his due. Gerard had stopped, straightened up. 'It wasn't him in the reservoir,' he said, and she had stared. 'Not Robert Webster, after all. It was Martin Beston.'

And the phone in her hand had begun to ring again.

It had been Lindsay, from the shop on Oakenham high street that sold pink glass and Valentine's crap. Yes, the girl had said, quite pleased with herself, she remembered the customer quite well, her cheerful certainty on the other end of the line in her safe little shop so at odds with the black lay-by and trucks hissing past through the slush and Carswell's white little ferret face looking properly scared, at last.

'Tall gentleman,' Ali repeated, and Lindsay babbled on.

'Slim,' she said. 'In an anorak, not the usual romantic type but you can never tell. Turned up on a mountain bike, would you believe, thirty pounds those chocolates cost.'

Ali had barely hung up before Gerard and Carswell had reached their own conclusions. 'She was meeting someone at Black Barn,' Gerard said, yanking at the car door. 'Come on. Black Barn? Got to be him, hasn't it?'

Shame you didn't think of it earlier, Ali didn't say, but all the time her own instincts taking her somewhere else. Those kids, that house. Family liaison. 'I'm going to her place,' she said, and they'd roared off, barely correcting a skid on the road surface like an ice rink now. One-track, one-note, one-way: Doug Gerard and Ed Carswell not capable of executing a U-turn if their lives depended on it. And now they were stuck out in Black Barn and she was still four miles from Cold Fen. She checked her mirrors, indicated.

Got to be him, hasn't it?

Chapter Thirty-Eight

Along the top of frozen ruts where the snow lay lighter Fran ran, dodging. The ditch appeared but by then she had worked out where she could cross it and she turned, gauging her angle and unhesitating because there wasn't time for it. All this time she had thought the threat was outside, watching her, and all the time it was inside. Karen holding Emme's hand, standing at Fran's sink. Karen taking her chance, how many months ago, to run her eye down the numbers on the wall by the phone and take Nathan's. The last one to talk to him.

The house moved into line, behind the barn; she could see through the barn to its oblique elevation, a bedroom window as she went on running. It blocked her view and she was there on the barn's edge, a girder beside her and the empty space looming. And then she stopped: then she found she couldn't move.

It didn't fit, though. Karen had been in her kitchen . . .

but in her bedroom? Flowers, chocolates, a Valentine's card. She hadn't imagined those things. A man's hand on her from behind, in the bed. A man pushing himself inside her. Had that been in her head? She hadn't imagined the condom.

There was something there. She stood very still, she held her breath and she heard it before she saw anything, something ragged, stifled. Then she looked, she turned her head very slowly. Something insubstantial hung in the dusty darkness, it dangled, drifting, she couldn't make it out, and then she could. A length of empty rope, a box below it, on its side and as she tried to understand it he stepped out beside her, a ghost, brought up from underwater. 'You,' she said. 'Rob.' He was all angles and shadows, no flesh on him, his skin raw. He gazed at her, his eyes in the gaunt face huge and liquid.

'We meant to do it together,' he told her.

'Who?' she whispered. 'Do what?' But she knew: the reservoir swam behind her eyes, the dark water, and a body trapped in the depths.

'Me and Bez,' he said, gasping. 'He came out there last night, late. I'd told him where I'd be if he wanted me and I waited for him there.'

'The police were searching the woods,' she said, numbly, and he just looked at her blank.

'Were they?' he said, lost. 'I saw no one.' He was shivering, and she thought of a leather jacket, left behind in someone's shed. 'I couldn't go home,' he said, as if reading her mind. 'I watched him go in the water, he was so tired, he said someone gave him a lift half the way then he'd walked. He was pissed and he just lay back, he put his arms out and let himself go down. But then I couldn't do it. I had to come back for you.' A sound came out of him, low down, and he swayed as if it had hurt him.

'It was you,' she said, and her hands went out, almost without her volition, to hold him. 'You killed Nathan.' His head went down towards her, as if to nuzzle, she could smell his skin, a tainted chemical smell. She held firm, keeping him where he was.

'He had said he'd go with me, to Wales.' His voice eddied, welled, a child about to cry. 'Way back he promised and then he blew me out, last minute. That's when I told him, the reason I wanted him to come was I had information. I told him Nick Jason knew all about it, I told him you knew too, you were planning to take it to the newspapers, the two of you. I told him he'd better find a safe place for his hard drive.'

'Nick didn't know,' she whispered.

He stroked her hair. 'He wouldn't give it to Napier, I knew that,' he said.

And a hardness crept in. 'Nathan would never let Napier think he'd screwed up. So I told him,' and his voice lowered, confidential, 'I won't go to Wales, we'll meet in Oakenham instead. Just give it to me, I've got a place for it. He trusted me, you see. Because I was always there, waiting to be told, he thought I was his, I would always be his.'

'His hard drive,' she said and her heart jumped, she had to see it. What he had said about her. 'His mobile.'

He stilled, focused. 'I kept them for you,' he said and in a jerky imitation of his old self, his shy, methodical self, he turned, searched, patted low down in the darkness. 'There.' Something was mounded at the foot of the nearest girder, where he must have been waiting. His mountain-biker's backpack and the bike itself resting against it, lying on its side. And then he was so close she could almost feel the stubble on his chin, the tears on his cheeks.

'I was at the Angel, that night,' he said, his breath on her neck. 'I was waiting outside, I followed him to where I told him to meet me, I watched. I'm good at watching.' She gasped, a sob of terror, and swallowed it. 'I can wait as long as you like,' he said, his lips moving against the soft place under her ear.

'I can't, Rob, I can't . . .' but he didn't seem to hear.

He pulled away, looking down at her. His cheekbones sharp, the eyes just wells of shadow. 'He came out, he was on his phone. I heard him talking to a woman. "You bitch," he said. Walking up and down in the car park.'

'Karen,' she said.

'She was making him angry,' Rob muttered into her neck. 'I knew it wasn't you. You never got angry, no matter what he did.' And he held her tighter, tighter, till it hurt. 'You're like me. He looked for people like us.'

There was a name for people like Nathan. She'd read somewhere, a psychopath knows you from behind, the way you walk. He can see your weakness, your need. She tried not to struggle, to save her strength.

'What did he do to you?' she said. 'What did they do, him and Napier? At Black Barn?' Rob's head went up and his eyes looked into hers, they seemed filmed over, opaque and dead. 'Nathan?' he said, wondering. 'At Black Barn he said, just let them do what they want to you. He said, take the money. Take the dope. He said, it doesn't mean anything.' His head swung away, she saw his eyes roaming, empty, across the dark flat land. The sound broke from him again. 'I tried. Worse for Bez, because he loved Nathan, and I hated him, I was just waiting . . . waiting . . .' The words seemed to choke him, he gasped for air. 'I tried. I sat there at the table with them, him and Napier, when you got married. I tried. To pretend it didn't mean anything.' He couldn't even say it: sex. She thought, unwillingly, of sex with Nathan, of his fastidious movements, his disdain.

'It was you I needed,' he said, and his hands were on her cheeks.

'You were in my bed,' Fran said. She could see his face wet in the distant gleam from the house, and hoped he couldn't hear the uncontrollable thing that climbed up inside her. She wondered if they would come. If they would be in time. Somewhere she found her voice. 'You can't do that,' she said, loud, wanting them to hear. All of them. 'You raped me.' He flinched.

He pulled his head back, to avoid her eye, *No, I . . . no, I . . .* but she held him there. 'He had you, you see?' he said. 'Do you see?' What she saw were his eyes on her in that Italian restaurant after the wedding, as Nathan's hand clapped him on the shoulder. Stiffly, she nodded. 'I wanted you.' Now his voice was different, not lost, sad Rob but an angry child, an angry boy who would do what he wanted. Would take what he wanted, and smash it.

'He told me, "We're nearly there." He'd nearly nailed you both. "She's fucking him again. She's just like all the rest."' Rob's voice was choked with something, rage or misery. 'Nick Jason. Your drug-dealer boyfriend.' But when he spoke again it was flat. 'You were so kind. You were so gentle. I saw the way you looked at Nathan, more and

400

more, trying to understand why he'd married you. I could have told you why.'

'He married me to get to Nick,' she said dully. 'Five years, on the offchance.'

'You were part of it,' said Rob. 'You were a gamble, a side-bet. They were conducting a big undercover operation to get to – to him, that had nothing to do with you. You were Nathan's little private game.' His voice was thin, reedy with misery. He couldn't even bring himself to say Nick's name.

'It's not true,' she said. 'What he said about me and Nick Jason. It's not true,' but Rob didn't seem to hear. 'What was he going to do next,' she said, insistent, 'if I had been sleeping with Nick?'

'He was going to have his fun,' said Rob, turning his head slightly, not to look into her face. 'He said, she'll feel so guilty, I know her inside out, she'll torture herself. I'll wait till she's ready to top herself then I'll show her how she can make it better. She can get information on Nick Jason for me.' Then Rob turned back and his face was so close to hers again she could feel the brush of stubble. 'He owned us. If he wanted to nail us to the floor there would be nothing we could do about it, we could twist and turn but we'd only hurt ourselves. Me and you. I couldn't let him.' In the dark she put her hands on his shoulders. 'He called you a stupid cow,' he said, his voice wondering, rising to anger again.

'I met him at his office, on the Sandpiper. I took his hard drive. I said goodbye. Then I drove back here, to wait.' He turned his head to the line of poplars. 'I didn't know what for, not then. He didn't come back and didn't come

401

back and then I couldn't stop myself. I went to your kitchen door and it was open, I came inside, in your house.' A long ragged breath escaped him. 'I had to be so quiet. I just wanted to be in there, in the house with you. I wouldn't have come up, I wouldn't have touched you. And then I saw the knife.' She thought of it, in her jar among the spatulas and wooden spoons, innocent things. 'And I took it. I didn't even know what . . .' he sobbed. 'Then I heard the car and I ran out, I hid here in the barn.' His breath came in gulps. 'I didn't know if I'd do it. I didn't know if I'd have the guts.'

'It wasn't the first time you'd waited out there,' she said, quiet, and he nodded.

'Every time I came to watch, he'd do it. I sometimes wondered if he knew I was there, if he was pissing on his land just to show me. One day, I would say to myself. One day.' And his voice wandered, frightened.

She thought of him standing there, a terrified kid with a condom in his pocket and Nathan, bold as brass, invincible. And then the kid had a knife in his hand. Now Rob was talking, his voice going lower and lower. 'And then after. After. After. I just wanted to be . . . I needed to be close to you. I thought that would make it all right. I wanted to know, what it was like. To be in your bed. With you. To be touching you.'

The words broke from her, desperate. 'It's all right, Rob.' Hopeless. 'It's all right.'

'No,' he said and his voice was raw, dangerous. 'It isn't.' And he pulled away from her and ran, deeper into the barn, to where the rope hung. He was too quick for her: the darkness drew him in and raised him up over her head

402

but she lunged, she caught him. The box overturned, she felt a jerk and thought, no, but then something slithered, came undone and he went slack in her arms, they lay entwined on the filthy floor with the stink of the chicken barn on them.

When they came she was still holding him. He lay in her arms like something dead, something run over and left by the side of the road, but he was alive, and she held on. Ali Compton held her from behind and she said it too, 'It's all right, Fran.'

All she could do was shake her head.

Afterword

Several months later

The big kitchen was full of light. It had a wide bay window where Ali was standing, looking at the grey-green sea, wave-tops whipped up in the wind. A row of mugs hung along the dresser and Fran was at the table behind a computer: the back of the screen facing Ali was plastered with smiley stickers.

Somewhere down there Karen and Miranda were sitting on the beach with three children, throwing chips into the air for the seagulls. You couldn't just see the sea, you could smell it, salty and clean. Ali wondered what it would be like to live here. If Mum would like it. She turned back into the room. 'Nice place,' she said.

There'd been another kitchen, a room full of crap and chaos when Ali had burst in out of the darkness, bringing mud and snow with her and had seen Karen and Miranda on either side of the table. They'd both looked at her, and all three of them had known, in that instant, that Fran was in trouble.

It had been from the window of her bedroom that they'd seen it, though they didn't know at that stage what it was. Movement in the blackness, the plane of a face catching the light.

And without waiting to be sure Ali had been so fast on the steep stairwell and out of there it was like being back on the track, hundred-metre sprint.

Gerard and Carswell had turned up an hour later, with Nick Jason shivering in the back seat of the vehicle. Gerard's face telling her everything she needed to know: blank, shit-scared and knackered. She might have felt sorry for him if he'd been a whole entire human being, instead of just the arsehole.

Now Fran looked up at Ali from what she was writing, thoughtful. 'Yeah,' she said, absently, 'it's another world, isn't it?' She still had nightmares, Ali knew that. But when she looked like this, she wondered if she'd even have recognised Fran Hall as the same woman.

'So what's she say?' Ali asked, coming back to the table. The email Fran had just opened was from the woman who'd been sitting in the front row of the press conference, glaring at Gerard. An ambitious local journalist who had nonetheless left it a respectful three days after the trial – at which Rob had pleaded guilty to Nathan's murder – before asking Fran for her story.

'She says,' and Fran leaned back in the chair, pushing the computer away, 'she says, she'll take it on, even if the police refuse to release the hard drive of Nathan's computer. Rob's said he'll talk to her.' Her face pale. 'Karen's going to talk to her too.'

Karen Humphries, Johns as was. She'd admitted she'd called Nathan Hall the night he died. Tough as old boots, Karen Johns. 'Why wouldn't I?' she'd said, more than once since. 'Once I was sure it was him, once I got his number off your kitchen wall. He told me to fuck off. He was so sure he could keep me quiet. If he hadn't died I'd have had him.'

Now Fran wasn't crowing, not even smiling, she was too focused, thought Ali, she was going to make it work. 'Miranda's not going anywhere either, so Emme and Ben know they've got a family, even if they never really had a dad.'

And then there was the sound of footsteps on the stairs and a key in the lock and before Ali could even turn her head Fran was out of her seat, she was running, she was flying across the big bright room. They came through the door all talking at once and bringing fresh air with them, but Fran was meeting them low down, she was kneeling to her daughter and Ali saw the girl's arms, little Emme's arms, snaking around her mother's back to hold her, tight.

'You're home,' said Fran, muffled at first then clearer as she raised her head from Emme's. 'You're home.'

Christobel Kent was born in London and educated at Cambridge. She has lived variously in Essex, London and Italy. Her childhood included several years spent on a Thames sailing barge in Maldon, Essex with her father, stepmother, three siblings and four step-siblings. She now lives in both Cambridge and Florence with her husband and five children.